Dear Reader,

We women have always understood the feminine power
of just changing your mind. A major shift in direction
lifts your spirits and somehow makes anything possible.
So our theme in Harlequin Duets this month is women
on a mission, makeovers, girl power!

In *Great Genes!*, our creative but klutzy heroine takes
charge by designing her own baby by finding a hero
who has all the qualities she lacks. Then Nell Phillips
of *Make Me Over* transforms herself into a killer
babe—only to fall for the man who teaches her how.
(Harlequin Duets #13)

Margo Haskell definitely doesn't want to marry a
cowboy in *Sex and the Single Cowpoke,* but once
she turns herself into a Texan, the idea of making the
cowboy a permanent part of her life begins to feel
right. Then Dru Logan, a woman for whom career
definitely comes first, finds herself under the influence
of a love potion in *Lovestruck*—and loving it!
(Harlequin Duets #14)

Lift up your spirits with Duets!

Malle Vallik

Malle Vallik
Senior Editor

Great Genes!

"I want to father this baby in the usual way."

"You want to what?" Cleo gasped.

"I want to do it the ordinary way." Bryce's calm, assured smile had returned.

"You mean you want us to..." She moved an index finger rapidly back and forth between the two of them.

"Yes."

"But we can't do *that*. *That* carries all sorts of emotional connotations! *That* wasn't part of the deal."

"It is now," he said implacably.

Cleo couldn't find a flicker of emotion other than stubbornness in his gorgeous blue eyes. He meant what he said. If she wanted him to father her baby she would have to...

And if she did, he would know she hadn't kept her end of the deal. He would know she *wanted* to make love with him, wanted him to love her....

For more, turn to page 9

Make Me Over

"Your underwear needs some work."

Mac pulled out his pad and jotted something down, as if he was at a crime scene. "I couldn't help but see it," he explained. "You popped a button."

Nell looked down. Sure enough her blouse was gaping open; she grabbed the edges together. "Do you have a safety pin?"

Mac chortled. "Not on me, Deputy. I've got a gun though, if that'll help. You can shoot anybody who tries to look." Then he lowered his voice. "The main target is in sight, Slim, and the timing is perfect."

"The main what...?"

"That guy you had your eye on—he's coming this way. Toss your head." Mac tossed his. "Get your hair falling around your shoulders in that sexy, tousled look."

"*Hello!* I have short hair. If it falls around my shoulders it'll be because it's falling out. Besides, I'm not ready for this."

Learning to be a sex kitten was a lot harder than she'd thought. Especially with Mac giving the lessons!

For more, turn to page 197

HARLEQUIN DUETS

ISBN 0-373-44079-0

GREAT GENES!
Copyright © 1999 by Barbara Daly

MAKE ME OVER
Copyright © 1999 by Lynn V. Miller

This edition published by arrangement with Harlequin Books S.A.

® and TM are trademarks of the publisher. Trademarks indicated with ® are registered in the United States Patent and Trademark Office, the Canadian Trade Marks Office and in other countries.

Visit us at www.romance.net

Printed in U.S.A.

BARBARA DALY

Great Genes!

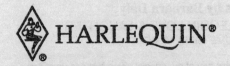

HARLEQUIN®

TORONTO • NEW YORK • LONDON
AMSTERDAM • PARIS • SYDNEY • HAMBURG
STOCKHOLM • ATHENS • TOKYO • MILAN • MADRID
PRAGUE • WARSAW • BUDAPEST • AUCKLAND

Dear Reader,

While my True Love and I dined out one evening, we had a serious discussion about my writing career. "You're supposed to write about things you know," I worried, gesturing with my knife, "about people you know and understand."

"Write a book about a klutz," said the TL, scraping butter off the lapel of his dark blue suit.

And so Cleo Rose came to be. Many of her trips, slips and pratfalls are purely autobiographical, but would that I had inner grace and sheer determination that make her the unique person she is. As for Bryce Hampton—well, is there anything more fun than watching a stuffed shirt come completely unstarched when a warm and winsome woman falls into his arms demanding the use of his great genes?

I've had a great time with Bryce and Cleo, her friends and her crazy family. I hope you'll come to love them as much as I do.

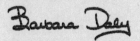

Books by Barbara Daly
HARLEQUIN LOVE & LAUGHTER
60—HOME IMPROVEMENT

For John, the best and most supportive son any mother could have and one of the six nicest people I've ever known, whose superb eye-hand coordination remains a complete mystery to me.

1

EVERYBODY SAID the Metropolitan Museum on Sunday afternoon was a terrific place to pick up men. Not that Cleo intended to pick up a man; she just needed a reasonably large selection of them to look over because no ordinary man would do. He had to be perfect, and she had to find him immediately.

The man in the tan summer suit standing back from a Rembrandt portrait, arms folded across an attractively broad chest, looked promising. She'd stalked him from the Egyptian gallery to the American wing, up the back stairs to the second floor and into nineteenth-century European paintings, and was prepared to see him through the Early Impressionists if necessary because if he had a fatal flaw, she'd yet to detect it.

His dark honey hair was wonderfully thick and shiny with the glow of good health. Her own hair was nearly black, so a blonde would add an intriguing element of chance to the outcome. His features were neat and regular, a little strong, perhaps, but they added to the impression he gave of being a person of character. One light brown eyebrow arched up at the moment, reacting to the painting.

No, not merely reacting, *analyzing*. Fresh new hope bubbled up in the arid desert of Cleo's heart.

She'd gotten close enough while he frowned at a Winslow Homer to see that his pale, sunshot eyelashes were very long and curled up at the ends. Her eyelashes were considered long, too, but they were as straight as her hair and were constantly crumpling against her glasses. She was after a softer look. His was a softer look.

His ears were elegant, and in spite of his blondness, what she could see of his skin was tanned to a delicious-looking caramel.

She was tall, but he was a lot taller, had to be in the six-two, six-three range. He carried his height well and was on the slim side, which Cleo, who had to keep a close eye on her weight, saw as a definite plus. In other words, he was much more attractive, much better built than Rufus, or Stefan, or any of the men she'd loved and lost.

But handsomeness wasn't her top priority. Good motor control was close to the top; during the time she'd followed him he hadn't dropped anything, slid on the waxed floors or bashed his elbow through a Monet water lily, but that one characteristic would bear further observation.

Number one on her list of essential attributes—well, to know if he met that all-important criterion she'd have to talk to him. It was time to take the plunge.

Her gaze still raking him from top to toe, giving herself one last chance to change her mind, she crossed the room on winged feet, failed to notice the bench in the center of the room, slammed her shins into it, fell flat across it and somersaulted when her hands hit the floor. Since he had rushed forward to her aid, she rolled up directly in front of him.

"Are you okay?" he said, reaching out to steady her.

His eyes were wide with alarm and they were indigo-blue. Blue or black like hers—either would fit nicely into her design. Peering at his eyeballs through her black-framed glasses, she couldn't detect the giveaway glare of contact lenses. And his hands were large and warm, the touch of his fingers firm but not rough. With a sigh she forced herself to concentrate on some aspect of him more objective than the way his hands felt.

Teeth. She wouldn't know how healthy they were until

she got him to smile, which probably wouldn't happen any time soon, but they'd made such significant strides in dentistry recently she supposed the teeth weren't crucial.

Her silence seemed to have increased his alarm. "Miss," he said. "I asked if you were all right. Did you hit your head?"

"No, no, I'm fine," said Cleo, brushing down her long flowered skirt.

"That's a relief. I was starting to think you'd..."

He was losing interest, about to slip away on a gentlemanly note of concern, so Cleo interrupted him in mid-sentence. "But I would like a word with you," she said briskly. "It's important."

He drew back. The question, combined with her close scrutiny of his eyeballs, clearly was making him uneasy, but still his response was polite. "Do you need help?" he said gravely.

Great voice! Medium to deep, hint of a soft Southern accent, nice melodic undertones. She bet he could sing. Not that she was looking for a professional musician. Quite the opposite! "Desperately," she said.

"What's the problem?"

"It's more of a project than a problem," Cleo said. "May I buy you a cup of coffee?" Over coffee they'd exchange business cards, and then she'd know for sure.

His mouth, a wide, full mouth she'd like to wring a smile out of, tightened. "Afraid not," he said, obviously disapproving of her invitation, "but have a nice afternoon. And watch your step."

"I meant we could have coffee right here in the museum," she said quickly. "Goodness, I wouldn't dream of going anywhere with a man I just met."

"I'm glad to hear that," he said. "You'll live longer that way." He gave her a look that assessed her life expectancy at well below the national norm. "Goodbye."

"Wait," she said, and put a hand on his arm. His gaze

shot toward the security guard hovering in the doorway. "I'm sorry to be so pushy," she apologized, "but really, I'm not dangerous."

He stared at her for a long moment. "You don't look dangerous," he admitted, "just—" he stared for another moment "—unbalanced." And with a long, strong-looking stride, he escaped to an adjoining gallery.

Cleo caught up with him in front of a van Gogh. "I'm not unbalanced, either," she insisted, "not mentally, anyway. Look into my eyes and tell me I'm crazy." She looked up; he looked down at her for a breathtaking moment.

"You're crazy," he said flatly. "Please, miss, whatever game you're playing or scavenger hunt you're trying to win, leave me alone or I'll have to call a guard."

"It would be a first," Cleo said thoughtfully.

"Beg pardon?"

"It would probably be the first time a man had summoned a guard because a woman was harassing him."

"High time," her prospect muttered.

She didn't know what clued her in to the right tactic to use next. Maybe it was the Southern accent. "It would make a scene," she said.

She could almost see the words *make a scene* explode into capital letters in neon colors inside his head. "How," he snapped, "can we avoid making a scene?"

She gave him a conciliatory smile. She was moving forward at last. "All I want," she said, "is to talk to you for a few minutes, right here in the museum in front of hundreds of people. There's a restaurant on the..."

"I know where it is."

"You do? Wonderful, because I usually get lost trying to find it. Come there with me and let me ask you a few simple questions," Cleo coaxed him.

"Let's cut this short," he said. "I think children's pajamas should be inflammable, that bikers should observe automobile rules and that inner-city green spaces should be preserved, whatever the cost. I plan my charitable contributions at the beginning of each fiscal year, and I will not discuss politics, religion or my sex life with you. I hope that answers your questions.''

''I share your feelings,'' Cleo said earnestly, ''including your reticence about...certain matters. I promise I don't have a seven-page questionnaire in my handbag, and for heaven's sake, I don't want money! I'm offering to buy you—'' she glanced at her watch ''—lunch, actually. It's one o'clock and I'm starving.'' She paused, gazing at him. ''Aren't you the least little bit curious?''

He gazed back. Lord, those eyes! And the way his lashes fanned out when he blinked, which he had done several times in the past few minutes.

''I'm curious,'' he admitted. He sighed. ''Okay, we'll have lunch and you can ask your questions. But I'm warning you, if you ask me to carry a package for you on my return flight, the answer is no.''

She gave him a sparkling smile. ''Walk this way,'' she said, and looking back at him, crashed directly into a family of small people. While she covered them with cries of distress and apology, he righted the elderly grandmother, retrieved the grandfather's glasses, reassured the more youthful couple and reorganized the baby in its stroller. With the family safely positioned in front of a Gauguin, he turned a glower on Cleo. ''I'll lead,'' he said succinctly.

''Reservation for Cleo Rose,'' she told the maître d' a few, incident-free minutes later.

''Yes, Miss Rose. Come with me, please.''

''You made a reservation?'' He seemed bothered that she'd planned ahead.

''Just in case,'' she whispered.

''What's this about?'' he said as soon as he was seated.

''My name is Cleo Rose,'' she repeated, handing him a business card. Her watch snagged on the preset wineglass, sending it over the edge of the table. He caught the glass on its way to the floor, accepted her card with his other hand and shoved it beneath his bread plate without looking at it. He didn't hand her his business card, either, but, of course, his hands were full.

"I was wrong earlier," he hissed, brandishing the wineglass in her direction. "You *are* dangerous."

A waiter appeared at his elbow. "May I suggest one of the many excellent vintages from our cellar, sir, to enjoy with your lunch?"

"Not on your life," he said. "And my mind boggles at the thought of what this woman might do under the influence." Glaring at her, he handed both wineglasses to the startled waiter and ordered a sandwich and a cappuccino. She did the same thing, although she was so excited about finding him she could easily have devoured a three-course lunch. If he'd only stop scowling, he would be as appealing as any man she'd ever met.

"Now. Get to those questions before you maim somebody."

"Happy to," said Cleo. He'd mentioned a return trip. "What brings you to New York?" *Start easy, get harder.*

"Business."

Still no card. "Where do you usually, ah, do business?"

"Atlanta, where it's safe for a single man to go to a museum in broad daylight."

She smiled. She'd checked for a wedding ring first thing, but it was good to have confirmation. "I thought you had a Southern accent," she said, nodding her head. "Do your parents live in Atlanta, too?"

"Yes."

"Do you have brothers and sisters?" This question was an important one.

"One sister."

"A girl and a boy." She smiled, satisfied. "Does your sister have children?"

He frowned. "Yes."

He could save time by volunteering a fact or two. "Girls? Boys?"

"One of each. But let's leave my sister out of this, if you don't mind."

No family tendency toward boys. That was a relief. "How long will you be in town?" she asked, working on the calendar in her head.

He folded his arms across his chest again. "I'm not answering any more questions until you tell me what I'm being interviewed for."

"I understand how you feel," she reassured him. "Just one more question."

His jaw tightened. It was a very strong jaw, and she felt it locking her out as effectively as a bolt across a door. "Just one," he said.

"What business are you in?" she said humbly.

He sighed deeply. "I guess it can't hurt to tell you. I'm a research chemist."

"A scientist," she breathed. "Then you *are* a left-brain person."

He raised one eyebrow. "I guess so. But my right brain's not exactly empty."

"I'm sure it's not," she said hastily. "I'm the one with a problem. My left brain is a vacuum. I've often wondered if that's why I'm so clumsy." She hesitated, choosing her words carefully. "I'm heavier on the right than the left. So when you described me as 'unbalanced' you weren't entirely wrong."

He was starting to look more puzzled than angry. With obvious reluctance he fished her elegant black-on-cream card out from under his bread plate. "Cleo's Clothes. You design clothes?" he said. "Like Donna Karan?"

"Not like Donna Karan," she said, distracted by an unworthy stab of professional jealousy. "But I do design clothes."

"I don't model," he said, his jaw tightening.

"What a coincidence. I don't design men's clothes. I do custom clothes for women in a little shop in the West Village. When I say little, I mean tiny," Cleo clarified, "but I have room for..." She halted. She didn't want to get ahead of herself.

"Anyway," she said, "since I've got all these creative, right-brain genes, you can imagine how it pleases me to hear that you're the left-brain sort. You can probably figure things out, like how to hook up a computer and program a VCR."

"What do you want?" he said in an impatient whisper, slamming his hand down on the spotless white tablecloth. "Half my brain?"

"In a manner of speaking," said Cleo. "I want you to be the father of my baby."

"You...want me...to..." His gorgeous indigo eyes widened, his mouth opened slightly, although not enough for a dental-health check, and he stared at her in stunned silence.

"Goodbye," he said suddenly, and stood up. He tossed a twenty-dollar bill on the table. "That leaves me cab fare. I hope you have a credit card."

"You can't leave now," she said. "Here's the waiter with our sandwiches. I bet he's wondering why you just threw a twenty-dollar bill at me," she added for good measure.

Her reluctant guest snatched up the bill and pocketed it, sank back into his chair and gazed at Cleo in silence until the waiter had finished serving.

"I knew you were crazy," he muttered. "I knew you were stalking me. I told myself, 'You have nothing to worry about. You're a grown man, you're tough, you work out, do tae kwon do...'"

"You do?" Cleo marveled. "That takes a lot of coordination, doesn't it? Do you do other athletic things?"

"Yes," he said, casting a desperate glance around the

restaurant, as though looking for help. "I play tennis. I swim. I fence."

"You fence? Really?" She was delighted.

With reassuringly large, straight white teeth, he took a significant bite of his sandwich, chewed and swallowed. The familiarity of this action appeared to have a calming effect. Leaning forward, he rested his elbows on the table and fixed her with the sympathetic gaze of a minister about to counsel a parishioner.

"Look," he said, "I know life can be hard in this town. People get lonely. And when they get lonely, they…"

"I'm not lonely," said Cleo. "I have tons of friends. But I do want to have a baby, and this is the perfect time to have one."

Put another way, it was the perfect time not to not have one. In the year 2000 she would celebrate her thirty-fifth birthday without a marriage prospect in sight—and a lifetime of rejections already under her belt.

He interrupted her thoughts by smiling gently. "The perfect time to have a baby—" he glanced at her card "—Cleo, is when you are happily married, gainfully employed, fully insured, have a home of your own and a head start on the child's college fund."

"Scratch married," said Cleo, "but I'm okay on the rest." She reflected happily that a man like this one could greatly increase her chances of having the sort of child she longed for—one who sold lemonade on the street corner, saved her profits and always won a blue ribbon in the science fair. Her heart thudded. Maybe a child of his would be able to play soccer without injuring her teammates! "I can offer her other advantages, too. She can come to work with me. As I was about to say earlier, there's room in the shop for a cradle at first and a playpen later, and my apartment's on the floor above it. She will be hand reared."

He dropped the counselor pose. "You keep saying 'she.'"

"I want a baby girl."

In his otherwise expressionless face, a tic pulsed gently at the corner of his eye. "Is there some reason only a girl will do?"

"I just think it's easier for a single mother to bring up a girl, don't you?"

"I don't know. I've never analyzed the single-mother question."

Neither had she, but then, she'd never analyzed anything. "It certainly would be easier for me. I'm an only child, I don't know anything about boys' games or clothes or emotional needs, and I want to do this right." She paused. "I want to do it perfectly," she amended herself. "It's possible in this day and age, by timing everything right, to plan the sex of the child. Or so I'm told."

"Yes, that's something I..." He halted. "Anyway, you've decided to have a baby without going through any of the usual channels. Are you thinking of in vitro fertilization or, um..."

"Well, of course in vitro fertilization," said Cleo. What a question! "Did you think I was asking you to...to, um?" Her voice rose. "Did you think for one minute I was asking you to...?"

"Shh," he hissed violently. "Of course not. Well, maybe. I mean, why else are we having this bizarre conversation? All you have to do is go to a sperm bank. Qualified professionals will help you pick out a donor."

"I'm not taking any chances with my little girl," Cleo snapped. "I want to see the donor on the hoof!"

"And that's me? I'm the donor in this fantasy of yours? Sorry. No way."

"What do you have to lose, except a few...you know?" she asked him. "Once you've donated, you're in the clear. I want to raise her myself, support her myself. You'll never hear from us again."

His voice was an angry whisper. "When I father a child,

I intend to take full responsibility for her. Or him. I wouldn't let a child of mine be reared God knows how, supported by a dingbat who cruises museums, who probably has no money sense."

"Money's not a problem," Cleo began.

"The answer is no," he interrupted. "I will have nothing to do with this project of yours. Goodbye, Cleo Rose. I wish you luck, but not with me."

"Won't you think it over?" Cleo protested. This was turning into a disaster. Worse, a waste of time. She didn't even have his name yet!

"No. And I'm paying. I don't want to owe you anything." He summoned the waiter, whipped out a credit card and laid it on the table.

Cleo polished off her sandwich, a construction of mozzarella, meats and roasted peppers on warm foccacia. The cheese was melted and drippy, and the combination was wonderful. So was her view of his card, and the silence while she ate and he glowered made it easier to concentrate.

There were certain advantages to her random intelligence, one being the ability to read about as well upside down as right side up. His name was Bryce Hampton. His expiration date was comfortably off in the future, and his number was... *Three-one-two-five,* she chanted silently, *eight-oh-oh-six, threeonetwofiveeightohohsix,* or was it six-oh-oh-eight?

Damn her memory for numbers! Bryce Hampton silently fumed; the waiter approached. *Five-five-nine-five, two-three-four-five. Threeonetwofive—what?*

It was too late. Bryce slapped the card on the folder that discreetly held the check. His hands were long, the backs lightly furred with crisp blond hair, the palms broad, the fingers tapered. She was momentarily distracted by the memory of the way they'd felt on her skin when he grabbed her. She couldn't let him get away, not if he was as suitable as he seemed to be. Maybe he wasn't. She'd try one more time to find something wrong with his otherwise perfect genes.

Thinking hard, she glanced down at her bosom, noting with displeasure the way her little-bit-too-full breasts challenged the fabric of the flowered dress, showing cleavage even though the dress had a modestly rounded neckline. And her mother was positively voluptuous! She didn't want to saddle her baby with an unmanageable bosom. If Bryce Hampton's mother was equally well endowed, losing him as a prospect wouldn't be so painful.

"Could I ask one more question?" she asked timidly.

The waiter was coming back across the room with the folder. "Is there any way to stop you?" Bryce growled.

"Does your mother have a large bust?" she asked him.

He leaped up from his chair. "Does my mother…?"

The waiter handed him the folder. "Thank you, sir."

He snatched up his card, scratched in a tip, scrawled a signature and slammed the folder on the table. "The next thing you'll ask me," he trumpeted, "is how big my father's…" The clarion call trailed off, he looked around the room and seemed to see every pair of eyes turned upon him, the gentleman from Atlanta. "Dear God," he said, and strode out of the restaurant.

Thoughtfully Cleo opened the folder. He had forgotten to take his copy of the credit-card bill. It was interesting that he'd left it there for her, interesting, significant, perhaps, and extremely fortunate. No way could she commit that credit-card number to memory. Her brain could barely hang on to his name. Now she had both bits of information—in writing.

She reached down for her handbag, put the receipt inside, then rose to leave. A warning sigh rose from the diners near her table, and someone said, "Wait, miss…"

Cleo spun away from the table, and looked down—too late—to see the point of the tablecloth gripped between dress and handbag. Helplessly she watched as the entire table setting for two crashed to the floor.

ONLY IN NEW YORK. Bryce sank into the back seat of a taxi, covered his face with his hands, mumbled ''Marriott Grand Marquis'' through his fingers—and realized he was smiling. He could dine out on this story for the next five years.

''She somersaulted over a bench, came up right in my face and said, 'I want you to be the father of my baby.''' The guys at the lab would die laughing.

Francine wouldn't laugh. Nor would his sister, his parents or Aunt Moira. They were already in a state over the idea that he might move to New York.

The chief executive officer of Whitehall Pharmaceuticals wouldn't laugh, either. Whitehall, the New Jersey-based company most interested in buying *his* baby, Nopro, was notorious for a conservatism in personnel rules and regulations that would have been right at home in a nineteenth-century banking firm.

He'd swear the guys to secrecy.

Maybe he wouldn't tell the guys, either. Did he want them laughing at...?

He began to fish around in his pockets. Of course he hadn't picked up her card. Good Lord, there it was after all, even though he truly did not want this reminder of Cleo Rose with her shaggy hair, her lively dark eyes and eyelashes so long and spiky they bent behind the lenses of her glasses or her promisingly rounded figure in that long cream-colored dress with flowers all over it.

Why had he pocketed the card? As if he ever wanted to see her again! What he wanted was to put this insane incident and its perpetrator behind him as soon as possible. Still, as he thought about it, he didn't like the idea of the guys at the lab laughing at her. He'd keep the story to himself.

But what a story. Behind his hands, Bryce chuckled. A

ditsy dress designer decided to design herself a baby, and who did she choose for her sperm donor? Bryce Hampton, known to the pharmaceutical-research world as "Mr. Birth Control."

2

NUMBER 7 PERRY STREET WAS a narrow townhouse in Manhattan's West Village. The first floor housed two shops, Cleo's miniature atelier and a milliner selling her own handmade hats. Above the shops were four full-floor apartments, and behind the building, a walled patio paved with old pink bricks, its borders alight with blossoming vines and flowers in summer. It had been the patio, the images it had evoked of long, lovely summer evenings with a devoted husband and many happy children, that had sold Cleo on the place. For now, it was here that the tenants of Number 7 gathered on pleasant weekend evenings.

That particular late summer Sunday they were all out: Delilah Burke, once a professional—the world's oldest profession—woman turned milliner, who occupied the floor above Cleo's apartment; fourth-floor tenants Sandi and Deke Millhouse, a most proper couple who were house hunting in the suburbs, with their baby and their dog; and Macon Trent, all-star computer jock who had the technological capability to rule the world from his fifth-floor aerie.

All so different, Cleo thought as the Millhouse Portuguese water dog bounded over to greet her, yet they had become her second family, with Delilah as the mother, baby-sitter and shoulder to cry on, Sandi and Deke as the conservative daughter and son-in-law, Cleo as the eccentric spinster aunt and Macon as the bachelor uncle.

"How much did the museum agree to settle for?" Sandi asked her anxiously.

Cleo captured a lounge chair and settled into it with a glass of wine and a recent issue of *Parenting* magazine. "They said not to worry about it."

"Sure," said Delilah. Her carmine lips curved into a mischievous smile. "They looked up your contribution record."

"I'm sure they were just being nice," Cleo said, "and they're probably insured for breakage." She picked up the magazine and put it down again. The sun shone soft and golden through the branches of a tall old plane tree, dappled by the gnarled wisteria vines that climbed a neighboring wall. Soft golden light, like the light that touched Bryce Hampton's hair.

"Macon," she mused, "if I knew a man's name and his Visa number, how could I find out everything else about him?"

"You found your sperm donor," Delilah breathed, looking up from the hat she was crocheting in purple-and-white stripes. "We're going to have another baby in the house." Her bottle-red curls quivered, her piercingly blue contact lenses misted over and her lifted face relifted with excitement.

"Don't answer her, Macon!" Sandi said. Her silky blond hair swung forward over her slim shoulders as she reached out to the stroller and ran her hand through her son's silvery curls. "We mustn't encourage her."

"You're going to get yourself in trouble, Cleo," Deke warned her.

"That's the idea," Cleo said, hearing Delilah giggle.

"You know what I meant," he said. "You've been going to all sorts of unsafe places looking for this hypothetical perfect man, going out alone at night to..."

"Baseball games," Sandi breathed, "seminars on financial planning, medical-equipment trade shows, political rallies, the opera."

"The opera's dangerous?" Cleo said.

"The heroine always dies," Deke said. He leaned toward her. "Cleo, this town is full of men whose intentions aren't the best. You're leaving yourself wide open to the lechers, the crazies."

"Don't be silly," Cleo said. "I don't approach lechers and crazies. You know the kind of man I'm looking for." She sighed deeply. "Somebody like Rufus, or Stefan, but better. More...understanding. More...accepting. More..."

"More able to deal with your mother's *Memoirs of a Begonia?* Wasn't that what scared Stefan off?" Delilah said bluntly.

"Yes. I know her books are a bit *unusual,*" said Cleo. "In fact, I realize that my *mother* is a bit unusual, but..."

"Rufus should have been smart enough to realize that the rooster wasn't really talking to him," Sandi said loyally. "Your grandfather was only playing a joke on him. He overreacted."

"Maybe not," said Deke. "Hard to know how you'd react if you were wandering through a garden in suburban Connecticut and met a rooster, much less a rooster who accused you of seducing the daughter of the house."

"Grampa's quite an effective ventriloquist," Cleo admitted. "His act with his trained chickens has been very successful. What got to Rufus," she mourned, "was when he realized he was talking back to the rooster, defending his intentions toward me." She sighed. "Rufus was my last hope."

"He lacked a sense of humor," Sandi insisted. "It was a good thing you found out before it was too late."

Cleo decided not to explain that a sense of humor was pretty far down on her list of requirements. Her family gene pool had plenty of *that* sense. Ordinary, everyday *common* sense was what she was looking for. "The man I met today," she said, returning to the issue at hand, "is everything Rufus was and more. He's Southern. A perfect gentleman."

"Have you read William Faulkner's books about those Southern gentlemen?" Sandi said.

"And a scientist." Cleo said the word with reverence.

"So was Frankenstein, damn it," Deke yelled. "Excuse me," he said to the world at large.

"Couldn't be easier," Macon said suddenly.

They all turned to stare at him. Macon had apparently focused too intently on Cleo's original question to hear the rest of the conversation. He stared back. "What Cleo said," he said, seemingly affronted that the rest of them couldn't stick to the topic. "Couldn't be easier to find out about a person from his name and credit-card number. Semi-illegal, of course, but as long as you don't sign his name to anything we won't get into trouble."

"Don't do it, Cleo," Sandi begged her. "Deke's brother is coming in from Chicago next Friday. He's good-looking—" she paused to glance admiringly at her own male-model-handsome man "—smart and so nice, too. You'll adore each other. He's here every month or so. A couple of years of courtship, then a long engagement..."

"I don't have that kind of time," Cleo explained.

"You do so. You're being very silly about turning thirty-five, and about the century turning. Superstitious, even," Sandi lectured her. "I've met women who had babies when they were nearly fifty. There's no reason for you to be in such a hurry."

In her mind's eye, Cleo saw the next fifteen years slip past in a haze of silk chiffon, in the hum of her sewing machine. Juxtaposed against this picture was an image of a little girl, tall for her age, blond and blue eyed, the movements of her long, tapered hands deft as she manipulated the contents of her miniature chemistry set.

Ignoring Sandi's advice, she turned to Macon. "Do you have a few spare minutes in the next couple of days?" she asked him.

"I've got a few spare minutes now," said Macon.

"Atta girl. Go for it," Delilah said.

Sandi and Deke grasped each other's hands, gazed into each other's eyes and shook their heads sadly.

An hour later Cleo said, "Are you sure this article is about my Bryce Hampton? It's in the *Wall Street Journal.* Doesn't that mean he's awfully important?"

"*Who's Who* already told us he was smart. Why shouldn't he be important?" Macon read from the screen,

> "Bryce Hampton, of Hampton Pharmaceutical Research, Atlanta, Georgia, is in the New York-New Jersey area seeking a buyer for his new discovery, the drug Nopro. Hampton alleges that the results of thousands of trials show that Nopro, if taken once a month by male rats, offers one hundred percent protection against pregnancy in female rats."

"I knew he was somebody special," Cleo breathed. "Just think! No more rats!"

Macon looked up, shifting a surprisingly rich brown lock of hair out of his eyes. "Cleo. This is not about rats." He read on.

> "Hampton says Nopro is ready for testing on a larger scale than his company can handle. 'The implications for human population control are astounding,' he told members of the local Association of Pharmaceutical Companies last Thursday in Manhattan. 'Nopro has shown itself to have virtually no side effects.'"

Cleo clutched his arm. "Human population control! Men are going to take this pill? Macon! You don't think he could be taking Nopro himself!"

Macon frowned at the screen. "The article said it's *ready* for testing on humans. So I don't imagine he's taking it. Yet. Uh-oh, he says here,

'My faith in the safety and effectiveness of this drug is such that I would gladly volunteer my services to the first test group.'"

"Ohh," Cleo wailed. "I've got to get to him before he becomes a Nopro test case! Come on, Macon, help out here. How am I going to meet up with him again?"

"I got you the lab address and phone number in Atlanta," said Macon. "Why don't you call him?"

"Because he would hang up," Cleo said, "and anyway, what would I say to him?" She thought it over. She hadn't made him understand how important it was that he, not someone chosen at random, be her sperm donor. Once she told this pragmatic, analytical scientist about her family, he'd be more sympathetic to her cause. But first she had to get him sitting down quietly, listening. How was she going to corner him, and fast?

"At the end of the article," said Macon, "it says,

'Hampton will speak on the topic of Nopro Monday evening at a special meeting of Feminists United, to be held in Shimmel Auditorium on the New York University campus at 8:00 p.m. The public is invited to attend.'"

"Tomorrow night?" said Cleo. Her mind whirled. "Macon, you're a genius!"

"That's what everybody says," Macon said glumly. "I wish somebody would tell me I'm cute."

He was more attractive than your stereotyped computer nerd. She'd tell him so, soon, but it wasn't her top priority now. "Sometime within the next week," said Cleo, "is the perfect time for me to conceive a baby girl!" As she threw him a kiss and let his door slam shut, she heard his Everything I Ever Needed To Know I Learned From *Star Trek* poster crash from the wall to the floor.

"THANKS, VESTAL. You saved my life." Cleo leaped from the back of the Chinese-food-delivery bike manned by her neighborhood friend and frequent rescuer from starvation, Vestal Makepeace.

"For the last of the big tippers, nothing I wouldn't do."

Money couldn't buy happiness, but it certainly could smooth the way on occasion. She was late from a difficult fitting—a woman who bulged in all the wrong places wanted a sleeveless, skintight black Lycra "basic" to wear with beaded jackets—and hitching a ride with Vestal had gotten her to the sidewalk in front of NYU's Tisch Hall, where Shimmel Auditorium was located, at 7:57.

For Cleo, this was punctual. She hadn't looked at her face and hair since eight this morning, and was all too aware that the pizza, her seamstress's lunch choice, had vindictively shot its layer of tomato sauce all over her sleeveless black top and slim-cut black pants, but she had made it to Bryce's speech on time, and she had gotten off most of the sauce, at least the reddest and lumpiest parts of it.

Just in front of Vestal's bike, a limousine driver was opening the door for a man who leaped nimbly out onto the sidewalk. After throwing a last kiss and wave of farewell to Vestal, Cleo turned to find herself confronting the face that had haunted her dreams last night. Bryce's blond hair was brushed and shining, his dark blue suit hung perfectly from his broad shoulders and the astounded, open-mouthed look he sent in her direction reinforced her middle-of-the-night decision that a man didn't have to laugh to reveal the condition of his molars. His were gleamingly white all the way back to his uvula.

"Ah," he said. He didn't actually link arms with the driver, but Cleo gained the impression that he wished he could.

"Bryce," she said, stepping toward him, "I'm Cleo

Rose. Remember me? I hope we have a chance to talk after your…''

"Close ranks, Joe," said Bryce. The driver moved protectively between him and Cleo's forward rush.

He wasn't a particularly articulate man, but she had plenty of articulate genes to pass along to the baby. She pursued him. "I need to explain my motives," she said, clumping along beside him in her fashionably high platform sandals, "so you'll understand why I'm so determined to find a left-brain type to father…"

"Help!" Bryce croaked. An NYU security guard moved swiftly toward him. He actually did link arms with Bryce. Carried along on this wave of pure muscle, her quarry vanished inside the building.

Cleo sighed. Opportunity had knocked, but she'd been too rattled to take proper advantage of it. She made her way downstairs to the auditorium, where she saw Bryce shaking hands with a pair of women who occupied the dais. He smoothed his hair, unnecessarily straightened his suit jacket, shot his cuffs. He sat down but his expression as he confronted the packed auditorium was wary.

Cleo searched for a seat, at last finding one in the center of a row close to the dais. Tiny screams punctuated her path down the row as she stepped on feet and as her enormous handbag thumped against knees and noses. When she was seated at last, her gaze sought out the hunted indigo eyes of Bryce Hampton, caught and held them for a breathless second before his jaw tightened and he pulled out his notes.

CLEO ROSE WAS the craziest thing that had ever happened to him.

Correction—she was the only crazy thing that had ever happened to him.

The realization startled him. Thirty-five years old and he'd never had a wild, reality-bending experience?

Briefly he scanned over his life. Middle-class parents whose closest brush with marital discord was the rare clipped exchange over lint on his father's socks. Mainly A's in grade school. Two weeks with each set of devoted grandparents in the summers, then camp, where he learned the manly skills and made lifelong friends of boys just like him.

Mainly A's in middle school and high school, taken at a prestigious all-male academy. More manly skills, graduating to gentlemanly. More lifelong friends.

The whole gentlemanly pack of them—except Boxer, whose trust fund, if divided by his IQ, would actually increase in value—went on to prestigious colleges, where they all made good grades and segued effortlessly into status jobs or graduate school. Now they saw each other—and Boxer, who was happily living on that trust fund—at Rotary meetings, at the country club, at reunions.

He also saw Francine. No need to itemize the events in Francine's life. "Copy" his life and "Paste" it into a "New Document," "Replace" the masculine nouns and pronouns with feminine ones, "Edit" the grades a bit and through the magic of computer technology you had Francine's biography. "Save," "Print," and it was ready for the *Atlanta Constitution*'s obituary file. Or Francine's wedding announcement.

He'd had a great life, but it made a hell of a dull story.

What if the story took a weird twist? What if, when he least expected it, the hero had a chance to do something so bizarre, so out of character...

"...and now our speaker, Bryce Hampton."

Jerked back from the brink of the sucking bog he had been close to stepping into, Bryce clutched his notes and went to the podium. His life wasn't dull; it roiled with the excitement of scientific discovery! And Francine wasn't dull; she was...safe, understandable, someone he felt comfortable with. Not like that woman sitting there in the audience. She made him…twitch. He could never concentrate on his work with her around.

HE WAS ARTICULATE ENOUGH when it came to Nopro. Listening admiringly to Bryce's speech, Cleo was struck by its logical organization, its audience-targeted language, its undercurrent of humor, but also by its passion. Bryce Hampton knew his product inside out and cared deeply about it.

Well, she cared about this unborn baby girl as passionately as he cared about Nopro! He wouldn't give up until he saw Nopro on the market, and she wouldn't give up until she held her scientifically designed baby in her arms.

"And about time, sisters," cried the president of Feminists United when Bryce had modestly sat down in the midst of a standing ovation.

"We want Nopro!" the audience shouted back.

Tiny screams marked Cleo's exit from the row.

"Nopro and condoms for really safe sex at last!"

As unobtrusively as possible, Cleo sidled to the rear of the auditorium, slipped out the big double doors, found a smaller door from which Bryce would almost certainly leave the podium and patiently waited.

In her mind's eye she saw him walking out alone. In reality, he burst through the door surrounded by a flood of chattering, questioning womanhood. Courageously Cleo waded to the center of the flood. "Bryce," she said, "do you have a minute to…"

"Mr. Hampton," shrieked a much louder voice, "what are Nopro's side effects?"

Casting a startled gaze toward Cleo, Bryce informed his questioner that to date, no side effects seemed to be plaguing the male rats in his laboratory. In fact, they seemed unusually carefree. There was a burst of raucous laughter.

"Bryce," Cleo tried again, "I really must talk to you about…"

"Mr. Hampton," shrilled another woman. "I'm with the *Village Voice*. Can you be more specific about…"

Slowly but inexorably, Bryce was moving closer and closer to the stairway and his final escape. Cleo made a daring move. "Give us Nopro!" she yelled.

It temporarily silenced the group. Bryce took a step backward. A pair of NYPD officers stepped forward from their stations outside the auditorium doors. Cleo wondered why they'd been so close at hand. Were they expecting a riot?

"Give the men Nopro," the Feminists United president amended.

"March against sexism in the Food and Drug Administration," Cleo trumpeted.

Bryce's fans took up the charge. "March," they cried, forming a line and charging up the stairs. "March! Nopro, Nopro, Nopro!"

Having organized the march, Cleo slipped back to Bryce. He stood staring at her in the relative quiet of a broad hallway through which the less curious, less militant of his audience flowed from the auditorium. "Now," she said, giving him a smile she hoped would reassure, charm and enchant him, "we can talk. I feel that if you truly understood how carefully I've thought out this matter of the baby, how important it is that the father be…"

Instead of reassured, charmed and enchanted, he seemed alarmed, annoyed and defensive. He nodded toward a spot over her shoulder. She jumped when a hand clamped down, politely but firmly, on each of her elbows. Cleo spun to the right, then to the left. She was surrounded by the NYPD officers.

"I'm Officer Callendar, ma'am," said the middle-aged policeman who held her left arm. "And this here's Officer Bennett. We gotta remove you from the premises."

"For heaven's sake, why?" Cleo protested.

"Harassment," Officer Callendar said sadly. "This gentleman says you been harassing him."

"It's true that I've been trying to talk to him," Cleo said. "But Officer—" through her black-rimmed glasses she checked his badge "—Callendar, to describe my attempt to iron out our differences of opinion as harassment, well, that's just too… I mean, look at him. Does he look harassed?"

She glanced at Bryce. He'd folded his arms across his chest. "I gave you fair warning," he reminded her. "But this time I'm willing to make a scene."

"I guess he's harassed enough to press charges," said Callendar. "We don't have a lot of precedent for this kind of case, a lady harassing a gentleman. Just kinda feeling our way along. But men need protection, too."

They certainly do! Cleo thought, then realized the officer wasn't talking about condoms or even about the future miracle drug Nopro. Her mind was churning; she couldn't let this happen. Being arrested would be extremely inconvenient. She needed to get pregnant this week. She wouldn't want to get pregnant in jail!

"Officer," she said meekly, "I confess. I was harassing Mr. Hampton."

Bryce's eyelashes shot up to his eyebrows.

"All I want from him—" her chin trembled "—is a little help with the baby."

"Hold on," said Bryce. "You are deliberately misrepresenting your…"

Callendar and Bennett stared at her. "Say what?" Officer Bennett said.

"I can handle most of it by myself, but there are things I just can't—" her voice broke in a sob "—just can't take care of all by myself! I am totally dependent on his contribution to this baby."

In the near distance she could hear a rhythmic chant: "Nopro, Nopro, Nopro!" The militant group had circled Washington Square Park at power-walk pace and was returning to Tisch Hall.

"Oh, my God," Bryce muttered. "Officer Callendar, I am not..."

The marchers burst through the doors above and streamed down the stairs to the lower concourse.

"Just another deadbeat dad," Callendar said disgustedly.

His voice projected so beautifully he should have gone into show business. The group of women ceased chanting and fell into stunned silence.

"I am not a deadbeat dad!" Bryce barked. "I'm not even a..."

"Scum!" Bennett countered.

"Lyin', no-good..." Callendar seconded.

"Toad!" said a voice from the group of women who, just minutes ago, had surrounded Bryce adoringly. Cleo observed with interest that the speaker was the Feminists United president, and that Bryce had given up protesting for wincing. "You're telling me you got on that stage and gave us a talk about male responsibility while all the time you..." Words failed her, probably for the first time in her life.

"Sounds like you're the one oughta press charges," Callendar said to Cleo.

"No!" Cleo said. "No," she said more gently, "I wouldn't do that to him. I understand how he feels. The baby is my idea, my responsibility for life. All I need is—" she got her voice to quavering very nicely "—a little help."

"With the rent money," Callendar snapped.

"The grocery bill," Bennett snarled.

Cleo waved a forgiving hand. "That would be too much to ask. I just need..."

"Say no more, ma'am," said Officer Callendar. "We'll talk to the gentleman." He turned a menacing gaze on Bryce.

"Tear his liver out with my bare hands is what I'll do!" Bennett declared.

"Right on!" snarled the women, advancing on Bryce.

"Please don't hurt him!" Cleo said, regretting that she'd gotten everyone so stirred up. "What I want—" for a moment she listened to silence as it pulsed through the crowd "—is a few minutes alone with him."

She looked at Bryce and her confidence faltered. Banned from the conversational loop, he'd apparently used the time to assemble his impressive logical resources. She had a feeling that this man was virtually unblackmailable.

His arms were folded across his chest again, and he looked as impenetrable as the Great Wall. "Forget it," he said, confirming her worst fears. "I'll take jail."

"Okay, buddy, let's go. Come along peacefully."

"Or maybe not." Bryce paused, gazing at Cleo with a thoughtful expression. "Actually…" he said, and paused again.

Her heart beat hard with anticipation. He sounded as though he were considering having a talk with her. What could have changed his mind?

His voice was suddenly gentle. "Actually I'd much rather go back to my hotel than to jail. Would a few minutes in my car be enough?"

Relief buckled her knees. "Oh, yes," she breathed. "Quite enough."

"Are you sure? A few minutes in the car will satisfy you?"

Although his tone had sharpened a little, Cleo supposed he couldn't help being suspicious of her. After she'd talked to him, he'd understand. "Positive," she said.

"Officers," he said, "would you see this lady to my car? I need to say my goodbyes and whatnot." He gestured vaguely toward the Feminists United president and her faithful followers.

After settling Cleo into the back seat of the limousine, the officers seemed to feel that the current crisis was over. Through the tinted window, she watched them strolling toward, presumably, the next crisis. Ignoring her, Joe the driver took calls on the car phone and fiddled with the temperature controls.

Time passed. Cleo examined her fingernails. A manicure wouldn't be out of the question. She could start filing now.

"Joe," she said timidly, "Mr. Hampton said he'd be going back to his hotel."

Silence.

"Which hotel is he staying in?"

"I'm not at liberty to say."

"Oh," Cleo said, embarrassed that he'd think she was trying to pump him for information. "I was only wondering if he was in Midtown or Soho, whether I could ride all the way to the hotel with him and then take a taxi back, or maybe…"

Silence. The Feminists United president passed by the car, the *Village Voice* reporter at her side. Cleo finished rounding off her nails, then freshened her breath with a spray from her handbag. As long as she was burrowing in the bag, she burrowed until she located a notepad, on which she began to sketch a blouse to coordinate with her client Miranda's going-away suit.

Her attention drifted. She took off her glasses and leaned back, watching the active life of Fourth Street by night. On the next corner, a tall, broad-shouldered man stood in the street, desperately trying to flag down a taxi. Poor guy must be a tourist, or he'd know he could do better by going another block to Broadway. Maybe she should walk up to the corner and suggest that he…

She opened the car door, got out and put her glasses back on, started toward the man on the corner, then froze, staring at him. His blond hair gleamed in the light of a streetlamp, and his dark blue suit hung perfectly on his broad shoulders.

"Bryce," she screamed, "come back here!" just as a taxi screeched to a halt in front of the man. For a moment all she could do was gaze helplessly after him, and then she swung into action. "No fair," she yelled, racing toward the taxi. "You promised me."

Her toe hit an uneven brick in the sidewalk. She flew forward, leaving the platform sandals behind, and landed on the backpack of an innocent student, taking them both to the pavement. As she rolled him over to assess the damage, she heard a familiar voice rise above the hubbub on the street.

"...a few minutes in my car," Bryce boomed, "and you had a few minutes in my car. So long, Cleo, it's been fun."

THE STUDENT WAS hardly injured at all, just a little shaken up. He wished her luck with the man she'd been chasing.

So she wouldn't be getting pregnant this week after all. Utterly despondent, Cleo kicked the sandals into an inviting spot beside a trash can for someone less awkward to adopt. Belatedly remembering the limousine and driver, she turned back to the car, intending to dismiss Joe for the night, but Joe was already gone. He'd been an accomplice, darn him. Barefoot, she skulked into brick-paved Bobkin Lane and drooped her way toward Third Street.

It was time to give up the whole baby project. She couldn't attract a husband; she couldn't even attract a sperm donor! Bryce Hampton would have been the perfect father for her baby girl. If she hadn't been sure of it before, she was now. In the past few minutes, he'd even proved to have a sense of humor.

...a few minutes in my car... Are you sure? A few minutes in the car will satisfy you? Just look how fast his mind had worked, how quickly he'd found a way out of his dilemma—her or jail. He hadn't said a word about being in the car with her; she'd only assumed it. In spite of herself, Cleo smiled.

In the near distance she heard a familiar whir and series of squeaks. "Your carriage awaits, milady," Vestal said, pulling up in front of her. "Hop on."

3

"LOVE THIS SUIT," Miranda said. "It's like a storybook 'traveling costume' for the new bride." She breathed a romantic sigh.

"And it looks beautiful on you," Cleo said dully, turning up a hem on the sleeve. Miranda was a bit stouter than was currently fashionable—to be perfectly honest, with a thirty-pound weight loss she still wouldn't be currently fashionable—and Cleo had designed a suit that led the eye toward her exquisite complexion and away from her thunder thighs. She was very proud of her effort, but nothing could lift her out of the depression she'd sunk into after letting Bryce Hampton's perfect genes escape.

"I hope you don't mind," Miranda bubbled, "but my fiancé's coming by to take a look at it." She giggled. "I had no idea Kevin was interested in clothes. Yipes!"

"Sorry," Cleo murmured, swiftly extricating the pin point from Miranda's wrist. "Oh, good, I didn't hit the artery. Did you say his name was Kevin?" She clamped a tissue down on the single dot of blood. Of course, the world was full of Kevins.

"Kevin Thorpe," Miranda said with another bridal sigh.

Cleo paused with a pin in one hand. "Kevin Thorpe. Ah. Tell me about him. What does he do?" There had to be lots of Kevin Thorpes, too. Couldn't be the same Kevin Thorpe. Life had already dealt her enough blows.

"Kevin's an astrophysicist."

Cleo lurched suddenly backward, catching herself in time

to keep from falling, but not soon enough to prevent an entire box of pins from raining down on the floor.

At least none of them rained on Miranda's sunshine. "Poor baby," she said sadly, "it's taken him such a long time to finish his degree. He'd actually located a whole new solar system. He was going to base his dissertation on it. It was going to make him famous, and then some dingbat he was dating decided to adjust the focus on the telescope and he lost it altogether. It's taken him another five years to… Cleo, are you all right?"

"I have an idea," Cleo whispered hoarsely, snatching up another tissue to mop her suddenly sweaty hands. "Kevin doesn't need to come here. We'll send the suit to Kevin! You can take it home with you."

Hearing the shop door open, Cleo tried to turtle her entire head into the neckline of her black tunic, but it was too late.

The thin, stoop-shouldered man who'd entered the shop halted, staring at her. Unintelligible, foamy sounds emerged from his mouth before he finally pulled himself together and yelled, "Run, Miranda, darling, run for your life!"

"Oh, Kev, don't be silly," Miranda said, sounding surprised. "This is Cleo Rose, the designer."

"I know who she is," Kevin Thorpe growled. "I just didn't know she was making your going-away suit." His sallow complexion paled even further. "My God, Miranda, she's loose in here with pins and needles and scissors. Quick, my sweetest, we must get away while you're still unharmed!"

Miranda folded beefy arms across a fully blooming bosom. "What's going on here?" she said suspiciously. "Do you two know each other?"

Kevin pointed a shaking finger at Cleo. "This is the woman!" he declared. "This is the woman who ruined my life, who brought my career to a screeching halt."

"You lost Kevin's solar system?" Miranda whinnied.

"How nice to see you again, Kevin," Cleo said warmly. "I have the most wonderful idea! This suit, this *beautiful* and *becoming* suit, is on the house! My wedding gift to both of you." She smiled sweetly, quaking within.

Kevin, who seemed ready to lift Miranda bodily and carry her from the shop in his bony arms, halted. "Well," he said.

Miranda seemed uncertain. She examined the pinprick on her wrist, glanced at Cleo and seemed to see her life passing before her. "Thank you, Cleo," she said, "and because you've been so generous, I'll have a tailor hem the suit, and I'll just buy a little silk shell to go with it." Distractedly waving a plump hand, she whisked Kevin from the shop, the raw edge of her skirt slapping against her bulging calves.

Cleo pressed her forehead into the cool surface of a mirrored wall. Kevin, Rufus, Stefan—she and her family, with their klutziness and their eccentricities, had driven away every marriage prospect she'd had. Suddenly she straightened and firmed up her chin. Marriage might be out of the question, but having a baby wasn't. And that baby *would* have Bryce Hampton's wonderful, normal, scientific genes!

She'd track him down if it killed her! All she needed was a little more help from Macon. Just as the thought went through her head, the phone rang. "You made headlines last night," Macon said. "Come upstairs and read all about it."

"WHAT A STORY," Macon said, his eyes glued to the computer screen, where he had downloaded the *Village Voice*.

"Don't you ever long for the feel of newsprint in your hands?" Cleo said waspishly. She plopped herself down in Macon's only other chair.

"Nope," Macon said. "Turns your fingers black. Has to be recycled."

Cleo gave up on her plan to add texture to Macon's life.

"What does the story say about me?" she said, prepared for the worst. His call had brought her on the run, and she'd forgotten her glasses.

"'An unidentified woman was apprehended last night as she attempted to...'"

"Unidentified?" said Cleo. "How strange. Bryce identified me at once."

"Maybe he asked the reporter not to use your name."

"Don't be absurd. The whole idea was to humiliate me." A vision flashed through her mind of herself sitting in the limousine, alone. "Still—he may have been the only person there who knew my name. Do you think he actually protected me from public disgrace in the *Voice?*" She looked hopefully at Macon.

"I can go with that. And it seems to make you feel better."

"It does," Cleo said. "Not only better, but optimistic."

"Optimistic is not good," Macon said. "You've got to stop chasing this guy before you get into serious trouble."

Cleo sat back for a moment. She thought about Bryce Hampton. She thought about the nice thing he had *perhaps* done for her by *maybe* not telling the reporter who she was. She thought about his gentlemanly manner, imagined what his Southern upbringing must have been like and suddenly knew what was wrong with her steamroller approach.

"What I need, Macon," she said at last, "is a proper introduction. I have to find somebody I know who knows him, or someplace he goes where I can go. Some connection. And I have to do it fast," she moaned. "I'm getting older every second, and any day now he's apt to become...become..."

"Infertile?" Macon suggested.

"I knew *impotent* wasn't the word I wanted," Cleo said. "So get on with it, Macon. Find that connection!"

"Not going to give up, are you?" said Macon. He sighed deeply. "Well, let's look him up on the Internet again."

This took a while. "You could try to join the American Pharmaceutical Association," Macon said at last.

"I think you have to sell drugs to belong," Cleo said. "Keep going."

"Here's a possibility," said Macon, snapping his fingers triumphantly. "You could join the Peachtree Country Club in Atlanta."

"Wouldn't they think it was sort of crazy, me wanting to join a country club a thousand miles away?"

"This whole thing is crazy," Macon said without the slightest hint of disapproval in his tone. "It would fit right in."

"But it takes time to join a country club. They're exclusive, they vote on you, they have waiting lists." Cleo wrinkled her nose. "I wish I could think of something that grew more naturally out of the circumstances, something that would look accidental. What he's doing right now is talking to pharmaceutical companies, giving speeches at their organizational meetings. Who do I know who works in pharmaceuticals? Nobody. Maybe I could get to know somebody."

She fell silent. Her lips parted. She felt herself zinging with creative energy.

"What, Cleo?" Macon said nervously. "The last time you had that look on your face you went off to a Feminists United meeting and almost got arrested."

"That was a shot in the dark," Cleo said, breathless with excitement. "This is a sure thing." She explained her new plan.

"Here we get onto the fringes of semi-illegal," said Macon.

"Don't waste time arguing with me!" said Cleo. "Time is my enemy!"

"You're asking me to get into confidential personnel files. I could get into big trouble. I'm not going to do it."

"Then show me how to do it," Cleo demanded.

"Don't touch that mouse!" Macon yelled, flinging his body across his keyboard.

"Calm down, for heaven's sake! First I have to go downstairs for my glasses."

"Watch that cord!"

Cleo's foot caught the computer cable and jerked it out of the wall. Retaliating, the cord wrapped itself around her ankles like a lasso and flung her to the floor. From her prone position, she saw the screen go black.

It was a shame to have slowed things down, but the threat of permanent damage to his state-of-the-art computer brought Macon right around. In a very short time she had a printed mailing list consisting of the names and home addresses of every female, whether employee or spouse, connected with the major pharmaceutical companies located in northern New Jersey. A week later she had sent each of them an attention-getting advertising card from Cleo's Clothes, offering a discount for orders placed in the month of September.

It had been an extremely expensive promotion. She hoped it proved to be a good investment. While she waited for it to pay off, she worked hard. Evenings and weekends she went shopping, but she didn't find a single man who fit.

"OUCH," JULIA HARDY SHRIEKED.

"Oh, Julia, those scissors just got away from me!"

"It's all right," Julia said, sighing a bit. "I'm getting used to it."

"We'd better see if they broke the skin," Cleo insisted. "We don't want you bleeding all over your new dress."

"I never thought of that." Julia whipped the skirt of the dress up nearly to her waistline. "I want to wear this dress Monday night."

"A mere scratch," Cleo said as she examined Julia's calf. "I will try to be more careful." Carefully she snipped off the last of the loose threads, lined up a row of pins in her mouth, knelt on the floor and began pinning up the hem.

Julia stood on a raised dais to be fitted into the slim column of heavy silk that matched her salon-blond hair. Her reflection repeated itself a number of times in the mirrored walls. White silk taffeta curtains shielded the interior view of the shop from the quiet West Village street. Behind the curtains, a mannequin in a bay window displayed a single elegant ensemble—a stone-colored sheer wool pantsuit accessorized with a peacock-feather hat by Delilah. A card on the floor of the display read Cleo's Clothes, By Appointment Only, with a telephone number.

Cleo dressed in black for work. Today she wore a long skirt and skinny silk sweater. Her face was freshly scrubbed and free of makeup, her fingernails short and lacquered with clear polish.

"I think just diamonds, don't you?" Julia asked. "This dress doesn't need accessories."

"Uh-huh," Cleo agreed through a replenished mouthful of pins. "Ere er oo ohing Unday?" she inquired. "Um ace escial?"

"To one of Herb's drug deals," Julia said, giggling. "I love to make jokes about his business, especially at parties where we don't know many people," she confided. "I wait until we're surrounded by stuffy social types, then I say, 'My husband, Herb, sells drugs.' Makes him crazy." She sighed again. "He's pretty stuffy himself."

"E-e-inh?"

"Oh, my, yes. And he applies his personal values to the whole company. You'd think Whitehall Pharmaceuticals was a fundamentalist seminary instead of a scientific enterprise. He looks for family men, won't tolerate any sort of hanky-panky in the office or outside it—he invites spouses to the office Christmas party, for heaven's sake!"

"Hmm."

"On the other hand," Julia said, "it's nice to know he's

not keeping a mistress somewhere, or a second family." She paused a moment to admire her reflection. "This party ought to be more interesting than most, though. It's a benefit dinner Herb's company is underwriting for Parents on Purpose."

"I know the organization," Cleo said. "It's a family-planning group." She fanned a new bunch of pins between her lips.

"It should be quite an event. The Plaza's such a beautiful old hotel. There's a speaker, of course. There's always a speaker," she added in a tone that indicated she'd prefer a dance band. "But this time it's Bryce Hampton. Ow! Cleo! For God's sake!"

At the sound of his name, Cleo had blown the row of pins out of her mouth to keep from swallowing them. "Oh, my gosh, Julia, I am sorry," she said, picking them out from between Julia's perfectly pedicured toes. "But when you mentioned Bryce Hampton, well, I am just dying to meet that man. I'm fascinated by his research!"

"I wouldn't say I'm fascinated," Julia said in a pin-pained voice, "but I do think it's about time men had a pill to take. And besides being a politically correct brilliant scientist, the man is gorgeous!"

"I know," Cleo murmured. "Julia, is there any way I could hear this speech? May I buy a ticket for the benefit? I could contact the Plaza and offer to wait tables, or fill in for the rest-room attendant."

"Don't be silly!" Julia exclaimed, her pricked feet forgotten. "Herb's bought six tables. There must be an empty seat at one of them. I'll check with him."

In the time it took Cleo to think the word *When?* Julia darted toward her handbag and extracted a cellular phone. Seconds later she was querying her devoted Herb.

She looked down at Cleo, who was fine-tuning her hem. "Herb says no problem," she assured Cleo. "His person will fax you all the information and a ticket will be waiting for you at the door. Don't tell a soul," she warned Cleo, "but it wouldn't surprise me if Herb's company bought the rights to Nopro. If he does, he'll start testing on humans right away."

As Cleo drove a pin straight through the hem into her ankle, Julia screamed.

"WHEN ARE WE GOING to talk about 'it'?" Francine said.

"It" was getting married, Francine's favorite topic. "Francine," Bryce intoned, "you know how I feel about 'it.' I want to be settled first, my future assured. The road to Nopro has been a long and difficult one."

"Long, anyway," sulked Francine. "You're thirty-five years old, Bryce. We've been dating for three years! I was a mere child when you escorted me to that first Spring Fling." Her pretty pink pout trembled; her baby-blond curls quivered. "Now I'm almost twenty-six! An old maid! People are talking!"

His senses dulled by the heavy, scented air of Francine's mother's garden in late September, his tailbone numbed by long contact with a wrought-iron garden chair, Bryce tried to remember how and why he and Francine had been declared destined for one another. Was it a deal their mothers had cut? Or their fathers? He couldn't recall having been involved in the transaction, but then his mind had been firmly fixed on his research.

His mind still was firmly fixed; other parts of him were merely firm, insistent, keeping him awake at nights. Francine insisted she would wear white honorably when she wed. This had serious implications for their relationship. Eliminated everything but chaste kissing, in fact. What really worried him was that Francine usually had to remind him to give her that occasional chaste kiss. The chaste kiss did not seem to relate to his frustrated libido. Was something wrong with him?

Of course not. When he and Francine were married,

when the holding-back rule had been rescinded, she and his libido would come to an understanding. He respected her wish to wait; it made him feel gentlemanly to honor it. She was the right person for him to marry; everyone expected them to marry. Any doubts he was having had to be a result of the tension he'd been under since the moment he sensed the importance of the drug he'd developed.

This portion of his life would soon be over. He was negotiating with several pharmaceutical companies. Secretly he hoped to find a buyer for Nopro who would ask him to join the company as part of the deal, assigning him the job of seeing Nopro through the testing phase, the Food and Drug Administration bureaucratic phase, the marketing phase.

Nopro was *his* baby. He wanted to watch it grow up.

Now, what had made him put it that way, and not for the first time: *his* baby? He must have been thinking about Cleo Rose and *her* baby.

He should not be thinking about Cleo Rose. He should be thinking of his and Francine's future.

The CEO of Whitehall Pharmaceuticals, Herb Hardy, had subtly suggested that Bryce himself on the payroll would be crucial to any contract he'd be interested in signing. He had less subtly suggested that he'd be happier if Bryce were a closer fit to the Whitehall personnel profile—a stable family man—and had seemed reassured that Bryce had plans to become just that.

But going with Whitehall meant moving to New Jersey, or living in New York and commuting. Francine got hysterical every time he mentioned the possibility of leaving Atlanta. If he settled her into one of the pleasant suburban neighborhoods near Whitehall's headquarters in New Jersey, pretty soon she'd hardly know she wasn't in Atlanta anymore.

Of course, neither would he. An unexpected ping of dissatisfaction made Cleo Rose flash into his mind again, like a gnat that simply would not leave the picnic. That could be an interesting way to live, an apartment in Greenwich Village, an area teeming with life in infinite variety...until you got mugged, or attacked by a crazy woman who wanted you to father her child.

"What are you smiling at?" Francine said. "This isn't funny."

Francine didn't find anything very funny. If she did, he could tell her about Cleo Rose and her determination to see her "donor on the hoof."

"As soon as I have Nopro's future assured," he promised Francine, "we'll talk about 'it.' This trip to New York may settle everything."

"It'd better," Francine said.

"DARLING, YOU LOOK FANTASTIC," Julia Hardy said, eyeing Cleo in the scarlet dress of her own design. "I hardly recognized you without your glasses."

"They didn't go with the dress," Cleo sighed. "I had to wear contact lenses. I hate contact lenses. They make my eyeballs itch." Delilah had insisted on curling the shaggy ends of her hair for the occasion, too; now they swirled in waves around her head. "You were right," she said, shifting the focus to Julia's dripping diamond earrings, enormous diamond pin, flashing blue-white diamond rings and lineup of narrow diamond pave bracelets. "All your dress needed was the subtle touch of a few...hundred carats of diamonds."

Julia laughed. "Come and meet Herb," she coaxed Cleo.

Cleo followed as Julia twinkled her way across a glittering reception room of the Plaza Hotel, where dinner attendees sipped champagne and nibbled on fresh shrimp and smoked salmon canapés. Herb Hardy, the source of Julia's diamonds, was a handsome gray-haired man who looked considerably older than Julia—although Julia's expert facelift might account for the age difference. He gave Cleo a courtly bow. "Great dress," he said. "So's Julia's. She says you're interested in Parents on Purpose."

"I am deeply interested in family planning," Cleo said earnestly.

"We'll have to get you involved," Herb said.

"I am already personally involved," Cleo said. "Has the speaker arrived?"

"Bryce Hampton? Not yet. Julia said you wanted to meet him." An assessing gaze replaced his friendly expression. "She says you're interested in his research."

"Deeply," Cleo said. Her investment had paid off more handsomely than she could have dreamed of. Once she was formally introduced to Bryce by the CEO of a pharmaceutical company who was more than casually interested in Nopro, he would surely reconsider the prospect of handing over his genes to her baby.

"Julia insisted on seating you together at our table," said Herb. He studied her intently. "So you can discuss his research."

Joy, oh joy. Bryce wouldn't dare escape from that table. She was finally getting her chance, and this time she wasn't going to blow it. "That was kind of you," she said politely, wondering why he kept emphasizing research.

Herb seemed to relax a little. "Julia thinks highly of you," he said. "I admit I was a little concerned about your interest in Hampton. I'd feel pretty silly if I put him next to a flirtatious sort of woman when he's planning to marry a young woman from Atlanta. But you do seem to be a person of fine character." The social Herb came back full force. "I'll get you a drink, Cleo. What's your pleasure?"

"I'll have one of these," Cleo muttered, whisking a glass of champagne off a tray passing by. She didn't know why the news that Bryce was getting married had dealt such a painful blow to her midsection. All she had in mind was a business deal. It wouldn't hurt anyone, wouldn't impact

Bryce's plans to marry. Surely his fiancée could spare one little batch of his...

But what if she didn't see it that way?

How could she have dreamed this simple project would be so fraught with frustrating twists and turns? Now she had deliberately misled Herb Hardy, the man who would unwittingly make her dream possible, a man who did appear to be as stuffy as Julia had described him and who would be appalled if he knew what she had in mind. Not that she intended to come on to Bryce, but she didn't intend to focus on his research, either.

Maybe she'd better prepare herself with a few questions about Nopro. Excusing herself, she tossed back the champagne, traded the empty glass for a full one and wandered through the gathering crowd, thinking hard. *Should one take Nopro with food or without? Were your research rats fairly prolific prior to taking the pill? Do you think they resent the loss of their reproductive powers? Has Nopro diminished their—* Cleo paused in her thought process, looking for a ladylike word *—their virility? How is it affecting the female rats?*

"Cleo Rose? Is that you?" a woman called out.

"Why, Jane," said Cleo. "How nice to see you." Jane Bentley was another of her new clients, one of her "pharm" women.

"I hardly recognized you in red," Jane said. "I wish my new dress had been ready in time for this party," she sulked. "I had to wear this old thing."

"You only came in a week ago," Cleo reminded her gently. "And the dress you have on is lovely." *Except for the color, the fit and the neckline.*

She banished this unworthy thought. She liked to think she didn't so much design dresses as design women. The purpose of the dress was to make the woman look beautiful. While the long, straight, pale dress was perfect for Julia, the dress she had conceived for Jane was black, and it made good use of diagonal lines and a frill here and there to hide Jane's occasional bulges. The magenta silk Jane wore tonight simply outlined them.

Across the room she saw tall, silver-haired Celeste in her "Cleo," a sternly cut gray satin pantsuit. In an unaccustomed rush of practicality, it occurred to Cleo that it wouldn't be a good idea for the three new clients to get together and compare notes. Wouldn't they think it was quite a coincidence that they were all pharmaceutical-company connected, and that all three had received the same promotional card?

"If you'll excuse me," she murmured to Jane, who was already rattling on to someone about the dress she could have been wearing if only she'd found time to call Cleo sooner.

Cleo retreated to the back of the crowd, snagged a third champagne and caught sight of Herb Hardy in a corner engaged in an apparently serious telephone conversation. He finished the conversation, stepped over to Julia and whispered in her ear. Julia searched the crowd, found Cleo and hurried toward her.

"I have terrible news," Julia whispered.

He's not coming. After I turned poor, honorable Macon into a hacker, after I spent all that money, after I wangled an invitation to this party, he's not coming.

"The company plane had to put down at an airport in Virginia for a small repair," Julia moaned. "Bryce won't make it for cocktails or dinner. We can only hope he gets here in time to give his speech. If he doesn't, I guess Herb will have to make up something, and Herb, bless his heart, is a terrible speaker."

"I'm sure Mr. Hampton will get here in time to make his speech," Cleo assured her. *He has to!* Her eyeballs itched madly.

But the minutes dragged on, and Bryce did not appear. The party eventually streamed up the stairs to the ballroom, where crystal chandeliers sent rainbows across the snowy table coverings and tall centerpieces of exotic flowers perfumed the air. Cleo sat at the Hardys' table directly to the left of the podium, fidgeting with anxiety over the empty chair to her right. Herb twirled a fork through his fingers; Julia did a routine with her bracelets, spinning them as if she could magically produce a speaker by lining up the diamonds correctly. The dance band competed with their hysterical chatter while the dinner marched through the appetizer, main course, salad and dessert. When coffee was served, Cleo felt that all was lost.

Disappointment was eating away at her as rapidly as she was eating away at a chocolate tulip filled with hazelnut mousse. This would not be her only chance to see him, she assured herself. He would come to the area again and again until he found a home for Nopro. But she wanted to see him now!

The thought came at her so intensely it shocked her. She didn't want to *see* him; she wanted to have a simple business discussion with him. She only needed enough time to make him understand how simple it was. Herb's concern with the success of his charity benefit seemed trivial compared with her urgent need to talk Bryce into fathering her baby girl. She felt deep sympathy for Herb, though, when he took a position behind the podium.

He greeted and thanked the audience. He introduced his committee, the POP staff and board members, state legislators, a senator, a congressman, the mayor's representative, the governor's representative and Julia. Ignoring an audible rumble of dissatisfaction from the audience, he introduced a film promoting Parents on Purpose. The film ended, and when he seemed about to tell a joke, the rumble of dissatisfaction grew mutinous.

"Ladies and gentlemen," he said, "I know you didn't come here to listen to me. You came to hear Bryce Hampton, whose discovery, Nopro, is making waves in the pharmaceutical industry. Well…''

"Here I am."

The voice came from the back of the room. A surge of heat rose to Cleo's face and her heart beat painfully fast. The audience turned as one to see a tall blond man, elegant and assured in his well-tailored tuxedo, make a skillful path through the tables to join Herb at the podium. Herb looked as though he'd like to hug Bryce.

"Skip the flowery introduction, Herb," Bryce said with a flashing smile. "If I'd wanted to hear what a terrific guy I am, I'd have gotten here on time. You'd think," he addressed the audience, "that in this age of advanced technology, it would be easier to fix the windshield wiper on a jet."

The dissatisfied murmurs swelled into a wave of laughter. Looking as though he'd been delivered from a den of lions, Herb sat down. Cleo could only stare.

The impact of seeing Bryce again left her breathless. Had his hair always been that thick and shining, his eyes that blue, his broad-chested, narrow-hipped body that full of energy? Her heart fluttered irregularly, her fingers and toes grew cold as heat rushed to the center of her body. More than her eyeballs itched, grew moist. What was going on here?

Julia turned to share her relief with Cleo. Her amber eyes widened, then narrowed knowingly. She smiled. Julia knew.

But what was it, Cleo thought desperately, that Julia knew? And could she trust Julia not to tell Herb whatever it was that she knew?

"Ten years ago," said Bryce, his eyes sweeping the audience, "I was a mature, twenty-five-year-old adult. At least, that's what I thought I was," he said to another rustle of laughter. "Now I know I was a twenty-five-year-old kid with a random set of interesting ideas."

As he said the last words, he saw her. The dark blue eyes widened, the pale, curling lashes flew up to tangle with his eyebrows. His head tilted to one side. The abrupt change from fluid to halting delivery made the audience shift restlessly. "...which included genetic planning." His gaze returned to Cleo's face, then drifted down the bodice of her dress. "But more importantly for society, included the embryo of a plan to put birth control in the hands of the males of the species. After all—" he seemed to tear his eyes away from her, and suddenly he was back into his speech "—the women already had enough to do."

AT LEAST HIS MOUTH WAS moving again. If he kept a death grip on the podium and didn't let his eyes wander to that front table, he'd be okay. Dear God, what was happening to him?

He was surprised, that was all. A man of his temperament didn't like surprises. He was surprised to see Cleo at this event. And he was surprised by her appearance. Two surprises at once—enough to rattle the strongest man.

She was stunning in red. Her hair was more glamorous than gamine, and without her black glasses, her impossibly long lashes shot shadows down her face. The fact that his position at the podium gave him a view straight down her cleavage was a blow below the belt. Not so much a blow as a surge. He clung tighter to the podium. She had beautiful breasts, perfectly rounded and full, and that red dress cupped them the way he'd like to cup them.

"Not to get too technical, the way Nopro works is... May we run the film clip? Sorry, folks, this isn't going to be a stag movie."

Laughter. He must be doing all right. At least he could turn away to watch the film with the audience. But not too far away. No way was he going to let go of that podium. After his speech he would escape to his room before Cleo Rose had a chance to...

But no, he couldn't escape. There was an after-dinner reception still to get through. People would want to talk to him, to ask questions. The event was underwritten by Whitehall Pharmaceuticals, who seemed ready to make him an offer, and was attended by executives from other pharmaceutical companies who might make competing offers.

He allowed himself one more glance in Cleo's direction. She was sitting with Herb Hardy himself. This time there was no way out.

4

"LET'S WAIT until the crowd around him thins a bit," Julia said.

"I should mingle," Herb murmured.

"You will stay where you are, Herb," Julia said firmly, "until we have introduced Bryce and Cleo. You are the carrot."

"The what?"

"The, ah…" To Cleo's relief, Julia seemed to realize she'd shifted into dangerous territory. "The catalyst," she said firmly, "to bring Bryce and Cleo together in a discussion of certain serious concerns Cleo has about Nopro."

"Serious concerns?" Herb said, frowning.

"Deadly," said Cleo.

"If it's anything I should know about…" said Herb.

"Deadly serious *personal* concerns," Cleo said. *Like making sure he doesn't test the stuff on himself until I'm through with him.*

"Okay," Herb agreed, apparently convinced. He grabbed Julia and Cleo by the hand and marched them forward into battle. The crowd around Bryce melted away, and Cleo found herself gazing dizzily into his eyes.

"Wonderful speech, my boy," she barely heard Herb saying. "I was never so glad to see anybody in my life. I want you to meet a friend of Julia's. Cleo Rose, Bryce Hampton."

Bryce looked a little dizzy, too. "Cleo," he repeated, holding out his hand. "Nice to see you."

"Cleo is very interested in your research," Julia chimed in. "Aren't you, Cleo?"

"Ah. Yes," Cleo said, embracing reality once again. "I am particularly interested in the early work you mentioned in your speech, in the field of genetic planning." She emphasized the words, swimming deeply in the indigo lakes of Bryce Hampton's eyes. "I hope you return to it after you get Nopro on the market."

Julia's eyes darted between them. "I have a suggestion," she said. "Bryce must be exhausted, and you two sound as though you have a lot to talk about. Let's find you someplace quiet and private." She snapped her fingers. "The Plaza gave us a complimentary suite for changing clothes and staying the night if we wanted. You can talk there."

Bryce recoiled as though Julia had punched him in the stomach. Cleo began to feel a little sorry for him; he must feel so helpless just now.

"Julia," Herb said, "do you think that's wise?" He gave his wife a meaningful glance.

"Yes," Julia said, taking Herb's arm.

"How kind of you," Cleo said. "I promise not to keep you up late, Mr. Hampton."

"Cleo? Is that you? I hardly recognized you with your hair curled."

Cleo groaned. It was her new client Celeste of the gray satin suit.

"Do you know each other?" Julia said.

"Cleo designed this suit," Celeste whispered. "Isn't it gorgeous?"

"Yes," Julia said, looking contemplatively at Cleo. "She designed my dress."

Bryce came out of his zombied state. His gaze traveled from Celeste to Julia to Cleo. By the time it got to Cleo, it was rather sharp.

"You both look marvelous," Jane Bentley said, attacking from behind Cleo. "And so would I, if I hadn't been so busy getting the children back to school."

"My goodness," Julia said. "Isn't it the most amazing coincidence? We've been seeing each other for years at drug parties." She gave Herb a wicked glance. "Now it seems that each of us found Cleo quite independently."

Bryce made the rounds again, including Jane this time, and ended by lifting an eyebrow at Cleo. She lifted an eyebrow back.

"I didn't find her. She found me," Celeste said. "She sent me a card."

"Me, too!" Julia and Jane said in tandem.

Now everyone turned to look at Cleo. "It was a very successful advertising campaign," she said brightly. "In fact, I'm extending it through the month of October." She glanced at her watch. "Mr. Hampton, it's almost eleven. I have so many questions, and I know how tired you must be, so we'd better be running along."

Bryce's jaw hardened. "Herb and I haven't had a chance to talk yet," he said stubbornly.

"Right," Herb said, sending suspicious face signals at Cleo. He suddenly bent over double from the impact of Julia's fat-free elbow in his ribs. "We'll have time to visit tomorrow," he said, recovering. "We're expecting you at headquarters at about eleven, I believe."

"So you and Cleo can talk now," Julia said. "In fact, I'll walk you to the room. Be back in a minute, Herb."

Short of screaming "Save me, save me!" Cleo didn't see that Bryce had the slightest hope of getting away from her this time.

"I'LL GRANT YOU THIS," said Bryce, running his hand over his jaw. "You're smart."

They were alone in the sitting room of a small, silky, velvety, flowery hotel suite. Room service had brought brandy and a plate of pastries. As Bryce poured brandy into two snifters, Cleo's eyes opened wide. "Smart? That's a new one."

He stared back at her. "Nobody ever told you you were smart?" he said. He was dumbfounded by the news. The woman was a genius at getting his attention.

"No," said Cleo, "just creative." She gave him a pointed look. "Or crazy."

He winced, remembering he'd used that precise word to describe her. "What about pretty?"

He'd surprised her again. "Cute. Fetching. Gamine, maybe. Not pretty."

"But you are pretty," he said, turning his head to one side to examine her. Her dark hair and her red dress made a sharp-edged design against the pale velvet of the chair she sat in. "In any objective sense, you are a very pretty woman."

"It's because I'm not wearing my glasses," Cleo explained. "Would you mind if I took out my contact lenses?"

"Be my guest," Bryce murmured. He watched Cleo extract a small case from her evening bag, open it, drop it and pick it up, quite unconsciously giving him a full view of her lush, ripe breasts. Next she positioned her left eye over the case to drop in a lens, and landed it right on target. She positioned her right eye, and dropped the second lens on the Aubusson carpet. Her evening bag slid off her lap, scattering her black-framed glasses, lipstick, cash, comb and a gold compact as she dropped to her knees in a blind search for a tiny lens in an overwhelming floral pattern.

"Don't move," said Bryce, stifling a groan and trying not to stare at her bosom. "I see it. It's under your foot." He bent to pick it up, brushing her ankle as he retrieved it, feeling fine bones beneath wispy stockings. He started to hand the lens to her, but decided it might save time to drop it into the case himself.

"There," Cleo said, sitting back on her heels, then rising gracefully to return to her chair. "I feel much better now."

He'd been so diverted by her juggling act that he just now noticed the way she'd turned away his compliment, as though it had made her uncomfortable. Didn't she know how utterly smashing she was in that red dress? Had she designed it herself? It fit her just right, hugged those tempting breasts, ducked in at a waist nearly as small as Scarlett O'Hara's and outlined the curve of her hips. Her arms were slim, smooth and ivory-white, and her thigh, long, strokable and black-veiled, peeked out through the slit that ran halfway up the side of the dress. His mouth watered; she was like a perfectly presented entrée at a fine restaurant, and he was suddenly starving.

"What I was leading up to," he said, taking firm control of his wayward mind, "was that I don't understand why a smart, pretty woman has let such a crazy mission take over her life."

"Put differently," said Cleo, "a crazy klutz decides to have a baby before she's too old to make that choice. So she finds a handsome, coordinated, intelligent and apparently sane man to father that baby, no strings attached. I guess that was rather smart of me, now that I think of it. What's your problem with the idea?"

"Everything," Bryce blurted out. What did she mean, *apparently sane?* "It's not conventional, it's not the sort of thing I can relate to."

"I've already told you, you don't have to relate to it. You just have to give me a few sperm. It's not a big deal."

Her bluntness shocked him. When she didn't react to his reproving expression, he realized she hadn't put her glasses back on and he was probably nothing more than a fuzzy shape in her line of vision. "Fathering a baby is a big deal!" he protested. "Why do you think I've devoted my life to making it a matter of choice for men as well as women?"

"Well, well, well," Cleo said admiringly. "That's the first intelligent thing you've said on this particular topic. Are you afraid someone will find out that a single woman is having your baby?"

"Yes!" he said. "Of course I am. It wouldn't look at all good to Whitehall's personnel department. I'm not even sure they allow their married employees to have babies because of what it implies!" He was worried about how it would look to Herb Hardy, but somewhere deep down inside him there was a more intense fear, and he couldn't quite put his finger on what he was afraid of.

"Are you going to work at Whitehall?" Cleo breathed. She seemed truly interested, even excited for him.

"I shouldn't have mentioned it," he said. "It's not firm yet."

"I won't tell a soul," Cleo promised. She hesitated. "Just as I won't tell a soul that you are the father of my baby, well, nobody except family, and they'd never tell Herb. That takes care of discretion. What else worries you?"

"The baby." Yes, that must be what was bothering him down deep. He was concerned about the baby. "I want to know what's going to happen to it."

"What's the matter? Are you afraid I'll drop her?"

"I wasn't," Bryce muttered, "until you mentioned it."

"Your fears are unfounded. I'll use one of those baby carriers. I've already told you she'll be hand reared in the shop with me, one floor away from her own home, and I've been shopping for flat shoes with high-traction rubber soles."

"Okay, okay," said Bryce. "Look, Cleo, I'm very tired, it's been a very long day and the last thing I expected was you at the end of it." He paused, thinking that he wasn't feeling as tired as he should be feeling. "How do you think you're going to convince me to dilute your genes with mine?"

Cleo smiled. "I want to tell you about my family. After you know about them, you'll understand why you're crucial to my cause."

"Oh, come on. Everybody's got some—unusual family members."

"Do you?" She suddenly looked worried.

He thought about it. "No."

"I didn't think so," said Cleo, visibly relaxing. "While I have nothing but unusual family members, even though I'm very fond of them."

"You insist on telling me about them."

"Yes. I think it will make my point."

He sighed, giving in to the inevitable. "Okay, go ahead. I'll try to act shocked." He leaned back in his chair and put his feet up on a footstool he'd been eyeing since they arrived.

"First my parents, Sonia and Thornton."

He opened one eye. "You call them by their first names?"

"Yes. They didn't want the barrier of parenthood to come between our absolute frankness with each other."

"What will the baby call you?"

"Mommy at first, graduating to Mom," said Cleo. "In this day and age, bringing up a child is so difficult I think you need all the barriers you can raise."

Bryce nodded. He couldn't argue with that. "Go on."

"Sonia likes flowers," Cleo said. "She named me Cleome—that's an annual," she explained, "with a tall, thorny stalk and blossoms that look like Kooshes."

He could ask her what a Koosh was, but he could save time by looking up cleomes in a gardening book. He'd assumed her name was short for Cleopatra. "My mother enjoys gardening, too," he said comfortably. "See, there's nothing so unusual about that."

"I said Sonia liked flowers. I didn't say she gardened," said Cleo, frowning. "Although she does spend a great deal of time outside with her rhododendrons and peonies and roses and whatnot. She interviews them.''

Bryce opened both eyes. "Interviews them?" Hearing his voice crack a little, he reached for his brandy snifter.

"Yes. Many of the species go back a long way, so Sonia interviews them about their history and writes stories about them."

Bryce put both feet flat on the floor. "Her...flowers... talk...back?" He emptied the snifter down his throat.

"I've never heard any of them say anything," Cleo said, "but she claims they do. Frankly, I think she does research when nobody's watching and writes the stories as though they were interviews, but I don't have the nerve to ask her."

"What does your father do?" Bryce snapped.

"Thornton paints."

"Houses?" Nothing wrong with steady work as a house-painter.

"Nuts."

"What?"

"Nuts. Nutshells, actually. It takes a lot of skill, as you can imagine. His open pistachio shells were featured in an art magazine. He paints them as though they were whales' mouths with Jonah in them, or spooky coffins with vampires emerging, or eggshells with chicks popping out, things like that. It's beautiful work," Cleo sighed, "but dangerous. I had a boyfriend once who inhaled the solar system Thornton had painted as a present for him."

With what wisdom he had left, Bryce decided to let that one go by. "How did he learn this amazing skill?"

"His mother taught him."

"Of course."

"She paints paisley designs on eggs."

"Naturally." Could he possibly be getting drunk? "And Thornton's father?"

"He raises chickens."

"A farmer," Bryce cried. "An honest, God-fearing…"

"None of the above," Cleo said. "He raises them because they're easier to train as baby chicks."

"Train?" His voice faltered.

"For the movies, television, commercials. First he trained a rooster to open his mouth and squawk on command—that one got a part in a movie about a talking chicken."

Cleo paused, looking reflective. "But not until it had frightened the wits out of another of my men friends. Next he taught one to ride on a dog's back with little reins in her beak. He gives Grandmother Rose the eggs for her art projects."

"How efficient," Bryce said tiredly. "What about your aunts and uncles?"

"Oh, Bryce, you don't really want to hear about Aunt Ellie and Aunt Adelaide or my cousins."

"Yes, I do," he said stubbornly, pouring more brandy.

"There's no need," Cleo assured him. "We're all eccentric in one way or another. On both sides of the family. It started a few generations ago when Great-Great-Grandfather Rose lost his head and married a ditsy redheaded showgirl named Roxy. Since then the right-brain offspring have tended to choose equally right-brain people to marry. Surely you can see why I'm so determined not to do the same thing! I've *got* to add some *left brain* to this gene pool."

Bryce's head swam from trying to trace the generations. "What makes you think I'm willing to have my genes stranded in your lunatic body?"

"That's the beauty of my idea! You don't have to worry about the result. I do, and I know you will only improve the strain."

"She's not a strain! She's a baby! Oh, God, what am I saying?"

"You're adjusting," Cleo said, giving him a bright smile. "You're adjusting to the idea of helping me have a baby."

"Am not!"

"You're thinking about it. I can tell."

Bryce clenched his teeth together. "If I were thinking about it, which I'm not, it would prove I'm not sane, either! You'd have to look for a new donor."

"Don't be so dramatic," Cleo scolded him. "You're making a decision to do something out of the ordinary for the first time in your life. That's not crazy."

Suddenly clearheaded, he could only stare at her. This woman with a random device for a brain had honed in on the truth. What she was asking him to do was unusual, different, and the Bryce Hamptons of the world had to think long and hard before doing something different.

"Are we still on the same subject?" said Cleo, gazing at him as intently as if she could actually see him.

"Yes. I'm thinking." *I'm thinking you're beautiful, one of the sexiest women I've ever run across. I'm thinking I don't know why some man hasn't already latched on to you and given you five babies—and hung around to watch them grow up. I'm thinking... I'm thinking some really weird thoughts.*

"More brandy?" he asked briskly.

"No, thanks." When she sighed, her breasts rose, swelled and retreated back into the red dress. "I can do so much damage sober, it would be irresponsible of me to get drunk."

Bryce smiled.

"Would you mind terribly if I put my glasses on?" Cleo said nervously. "I want to watch you thinking."

"Yes," said Bryce, and throwing caution to the winds, he leaned over and kissed her.

Her mouth fluttered under his like the wings of a frightened bird, then, with a small sigh, accepted his caress.

Lightly he explored her lips, holding back an intense need to take her in his arms and crush her to him. Her mouth tasted sweet from chocolate and champagne, brandy and cream. He took her more deeply, and when he felt her kissing him back, he put his arms around her, his hands sliding up the rich silk of her dress to her slim shoulder blades. She didn't protest; she snuggled a little closer to him, and his heart pounded. He closed his eyes, licked his tongue into the corners of her mouth and felt her quiver. His arms tightened, his hands slid to the small of her back. This wasn't at all like kissing Francine. It was like...

His eyes flew open. He'd forgotten all about Francine!

"I don't know why I'm doing this," he murmured against her mouth, not quite willing to let her go.

She drew away. "Neither do I," she said in a voice so flat he thought he must have imagined her response to him. "Kissing was not part of the deal."

"No, of course not," he muttered, hearing the giveaway hoarseness of his voice, feeling the giveaway hardness in his groin.

"No harm done," Cleo said briskly, and before he could stop her, she put on her glasses. Something made her eyes shine rather than sparkle as she scanned his face. She had to see how flushed he was, how his lips were swollen with quick-rising desire. She had to know he wanted her.

Her smile slowly faded. "I'd better go," she said.

"I guess so," he said.

"Have you decided?" She looked up at him hopefully.

"I'm still thinking."

"How long will you be thinking?"

"I don't know. Several days. I'll call you. I have to go back to Atlanta tomorrow night, but I think there, too." He frowned. What a dumb thing to say. "I mean, I'll think over your proposal. Proposition. Plan," he finally said, lighting upon a word that didn't have all those other connotations.

He had to have a frank and painful discussion with Francine, that's what he had to do, before he lost his head like Great-Great-Grandfather Rose and did much, much more than kiss Cleo.

She opened the door. There was a dreaminess in her movements that prompted him to say, "Can you get home all right?"

She sent him a flashing smile. The hot sparkle was back in her eyes. "Are you kidding? I've been getting home alone for twenty years."

He managed a laugh. "Sorry, just reacting to my early training."

"It was good training," Cleo said approvingly. "So. Is there anything else you need to know to, well, speed up your thinking?"

"In a few days I'll know what additional data I need," he said.

"And then you'll call me."

"I'll call you," he said gently. "Good night, Cleo." He couldn't help himself. He kissed her again, longer this time, more lingeringly, unable to break away until he felt her slip out of his arms. Her fingers trembled as she gave him a slight wave, then vanished down the hallway.

When she was gone, he flung off his clothes, his mind still spinning. Without even brushing his teeth, he slid naked between the cool sheets and lay there for a moment, staring at the ceiling. He had to admit it; her argument made sense. Her present gene pool was a dismal one and she was smart enough to want to improve on it. He couldn't argue with that. It was almost scientific. Was he actually thinking about being a sperm donor?

She'd bewitched him. He couldn't be thinking about being a sperm donor. He was Bryce Hampton, who was thinking about marrying Francine and having children with her. So he couldn't possibly be thinking about being a sperm donor, and yet he seemed to be thinking about being her sperm donor.

He heard a sound, a sound that might have been a plastic key plunging into a lock, and another sound, which might have been the suite door opening, and finally voices, which were definitely voices. He froze; he recognized those voices, and they were coming closer, and closer.

"Nice of the hotel to do this for us. How did they know we'd be so exhausted? Yes, darling, I brought everything we'd need, just in case." A sleek blond head and a glitter of diamonds came through the bedroom doorway. "Bryce?" said Julia Hardy when she spotted him.

"Bryce is here?" said Herb Hardy.

Clutching the covers up to his chin, Bryce stared at Julia, then gazed wildly around the room. His clothes lay flung across a chair in disarray, with his white oxford cloth boxer shorts right on top. What were the Hardys doing here? Where were his bags? Where were his blue-and-white-striped robe, his slippers?

The chain of events of the evening came back to him in a cold, logical rush. This wasn't his room!

"Oh, Bryce, I am so sorry," Julia said, skittering back into the living room and calling to him through the wall. "We saw Cleo leave."

"My mistake," Bryce hastened to call back. "I was so tired I forgot I hadn't checked in yet, thought this was my room. Gosh, I'm really embarrassed."

The dead silence from the living room did not decrease his embarrassment in the least. "Don't think a thing of it," Julia said at last. Bryce found it ominous that Herb remained silent. "We'll run back downstairs, have a nightcap."

"No, no, just give me a minute," Bryce said. "I'll call housekeeping, get the sheets changed." He paused in mid-leap out of bed. "Herb," he said tentatively, "would you mind closing the bedroom door?"

The expression on Herb's face as he reached one hand out for the doorknob was, to say the least, censorious.

He heard them leave. Muttering expletives he'd learned in prep school and hadn't used since college, he dressed himself completely, went down to the desk, registered, requested housekeeping service in the suite he'd borrowed, vowed to write a satisfied-customer letter to go into the file of the desk clerk who received his garbled explanation with a straight face and at last found himself and his luggage in his own room, his own bed, with his own troubled thoughts.

No doubt about it. He'd lost his reason. He was actually thinking of having a baby with Cleo Rose. Francine was not going to find this very funny at all.

CLEO FOUGHT DOWN THE TEARS in her eyes as she whizzed toward the Village in a taxi. Bryce Hampton was the kind of man she'd always wished she'd fall in love with, marry—and then have babies. But it would never happen. He'd kissed her because she *did* look more approachable without her glasses and this *was* a flattering dress, and because he was keyed up with the tension of being late and had had two snifters of brandy, not because he could ever fall in love with her.

He was going to marry a girl from Atlanta, someone normal and conventional, just like him. They would probably get married as soon as the future of Nopro was settled. That's the way Bryce would do things: in order.

There was not a shred of hope she could ever have a relationship with him. Even if there were, there wasn't time to find out.

5

"BRYCE, MY BOY," Herb Hardy said, but the words lacked warmth.

"Good morning, Herb," Bryce said. He smiled and shook hands, starting the conversation as though it were an ordinary, everyday one. Then he dived headlong into the crux of the matter. "Before we talk about Nopro, I must apologize for the confusion last night. It wasn't what it seemed. Cleo Rose is..."

"A lovely young woman," Herb said thoughtfully. "Julia's quite impressed with her, and I always listen to Julia."

"I'm sure she is," Bryce said, quickly pivoting away from *insane*, the adjective he'd been planning to use in place of *lovely*. "I hardly know her."

"Julia convinced me that was the case," said Herb, "that you hardly know her, I mean. She said your story about forgetting you weren't in your own room was too strange to be fiction. And when we passed Cleo in the lobby she didn't seem to be in disarray. In fact, Julia said she was rather more put together than usual."

He got up from the huge handsome desk in his huge handsome office and paced for a moment, pausing to stare out the huge window at the handsome grounds. "Whitehall Pharmaceuticals is a company with strong family values," he said slowly. "We discourage even the *appearance* of behavior that would undermine these values. *Appearing* to have leaped into bed with a woman you'd just met..."

"I'd met her a couple of times before," Bryce said unwisely.

Herb turned on him. "You told me you were planning to marry a woman from Atlanta!" he thundered.

"Yes, sir, that's what I told you and that's what I intend to do," Bryce said, but he felt a nagging doubt start to simmer in the pit of his stomach. Was it what he intended to do? Marry Francine?

"Then you can't be leaping or otherwise levitating yourself into bed with another woman!" Herb said, appearing thoroughly shocked.

Bryce remembered his fine Southern heritage and drew himself up in a very straight line. "I did not go to bed with Cleo Rose," he said sternly, "and I resent your implication that Ms. Rose is the sort of person who would go to bed with me on such short acquaintance."

"Well," Herb said, suddenly admiring. "That's the sort of attitude I like to see in a future Whitehall man."

"Thank you," Bryce said, still angry.

"So here's my offer," Herb said. "Sell us the rights to Nopro, and come here as director of the Nopro project." He slapped a thick document on the desk. "Interested?"

Several hours later, in the back of the limousine provided by Whitehall, Bryce chewed a thumb knuckle and brooded. He was confused—that's what he was.

He intended to marry Francine. Of course he did. So why did he have this peculiar, urgent desire to kiss Cleo?

Cleo didn't even want him to kiss her. She just wanted him to father her baby. Was there any reason he couldn't do both?

Marry Francine and father Cleo's baby, that is, not kiss Cleo and father her...

Bryce growled.

"Sir?" said the driver.

"I want to go to Manhattan," said Bryce. "There's time before the flight. Take me to..." He pulled the card from his pocket. It was smudged and shredded at the edges from having lived in one coat pocket or the other since the day he met Cleo. "...Number 7 Perry Street. It's in the West Village."

"Now you tell me." Muttering to himself, the driver dodged taxis, trucks and a couple of Harleys to swing the long car onto the George Washington Bridge. There he ribboned his way among the bumper-to-bumper traffic until, at last, he guided the car off the bridge onto the Henry Hudson Parkway.

"Is this about normal for traffic this time of day?" Bryce asked. He whispered hoarsely from the center of the back seat, where he'd ended up as the result of shrinking away from impending collisions on both sides.

"Nope. Light," the driver said chattily. He swung around a curve, slipping over into the next lane, where a startled driver braked and honked. Neatly positioned in the right lane, he made a left turn and roared toward a red light, which turned green before he had to brake, made the next several lights on yellow and shimmied onto Seventh Avenue.

Was this what it would be like to commute between Manhattan and New Jersey? But of course he and Francine would probably live in a New Jersey suburb close to the Whitehall lab. He wouldn't have to commute. "Watch the road!"

"You said Perry Street?"

"Number 7."

"We're here," he announced at last, and Bryce rolled from the car on jellied knees.

He took a deep breath, steadied himself and fixed his eyes on the townhouse across the street. Three arching trees in the space between sidewalk and street shaded its red brick and freshly painted white trim, its tall front door of polished wood and the bay windows that jutted out on either side.

There were enough passersby in the quiet West Village neighborhood that he wouldn't attract attention, so he moved closer. The late-afternoon air had a pleasant, October chilliness, and a few bright leaves skittered down the sidewalk in a sudden rush of wind. He stared into the bay window to his left. Against white curtains, a mannequin displayed a classic dark brown suit with a red paisley shawl thrown over one shoulder. A velvety brown hat slouched on her head. Close to her brown-shod feet he saw the card: Cleo's Clothes, By Appointment Only.

Until last night he had assumed Cleo designed white patent miniskirts, gold lamé evening wear and tight black dresses to wear with feather boas in electric hues. He'd seen plenty of windows like those while he shopped for suitable "sorry I went to New York" gifts for his mother and Francine. Instead, Cleo designed clothes for grown-up women. His mother could wear that suit.

Last night he'd put two and two together, which he'd always been able to do very rapidly, and figured out that Cleo had sent that advertising card of hers to women who might provide a connection to him. About the time he was ready to get really ticked off about it, he had been struck by the genius of her idea, just as he'd been struck by the brilliant way she'd turned the tables on him at the Feminists United meeting. She might not be able to stand on her feet without falling down, but she sure could think on them.

CLEO SHOT ANOTHER brief glance through the curtains at Bryce as he window-shopped, then snatched up the phone. "Delilah," she whispered, feeling breathless, "he's here."

"The man? Mr. X Chromosome?"

"Yes. Looking in my window."

"So invite him in."

"Cleo," came a querulous voice from the fitting dais, "I'm on a tight schedule today."

"I have a client," Cleo explained. "I can't." With Bryce

in the shop, no telling what she could do to the woman while she rearranged her darts. She cautiously peered through the white taffeta curtains at her display window. Bryce no longer gazed inside. "Never mind," she said, "he's gone."

Bryce wandered to the other bay window. Hats. He glimpsed a black one just like the brown one on the mannequin, went up the steps and found himself in a long, narrow entryway. He faced the brass door of a tiny elevator at the end of the hall; doors to his left and right read Cleo's Clothes and Hats By Delilah. He gave Cleo's door a wishful glance. He wanted to tell her about the job offer, but how could she understand how important it was to him? He turned toward the opposite door.

"He's not gone, honey," hissed Delilah. "He's coming in here!"

"He's checking us out!" Cleo hissed back.

"Cle-oh!" said the client.

"And I," said Delilah, "will check him out."

"Report back," Cleo said crisply. "I want to know everything." She slammed down the phone. "Now, Andrea, I was working toward a softer look over the bosom. What we have now are Maidenform bra points."

Bryce went into the shop. "I'd like a hat like that black one in the window," he told the blond woman who quickly ended a phone call to greet him.

"What size?" she asked him, forking it off the mannequin in the window. She had huge blue eyes that twinkled with life and mischief, and appeared younger than her past-middle-age face.

"I don't know," said Bryce. "My mother's hair is so…" He swept a broad arc around his own head.

"Teased?" said the woman, twirling the hat on one long, dark red fingernail.

"Out to here," said Bryce. "Then frozen in place."

She laughed. "Actually, this particular hat has a soft

elastic inner band," she said. "It should adapt to any head. If it doesn't work, bring it back."

"Thanks," said Bryce. "Then for Francine..."

"Francine is your sister?" Her smile was wide and interested, her mouth the same dark red as her nails.

"Um, no."

"Then who the hell is she?"

Bryce jumped at the snap in her voice. "Ah, she's, ah..."

"I'm sorry," the blonde said, and actually blushed. "I don't know what came over me. A hot flash, maybe."

Bryce blushed, too. The women he knew didn't discuss hot flashes with total strangers, certainly not with customers.

"I meant to ask," the woman went on, "what sort of hat you'd like for this...this Francine."

Taken aback by her mood swings, Bryce couldn't remember what Francine's clothes looked like. He darted a glance around the shop. Hats everywhere, sitting on bald heads with sightless eyes. "Do you have anything pink?" he blurted out.

"Not in October." Another swing to frosty.

"Something feminine, then, something for a small blonde."

The woman—Delilah herself?—produced a Robin Hood hat in forest green, complete with feather. "I don't think so," said Bryce. "She has eyes like yours," he added to be helpful.

Just now those eyes were distinctly unfriendly. "I have an idea," the woman said. "A casual little winter model." From beneath a counter she produced a hairy fluff of baby-blue. "Angora," she explained. "Just the thing for a snowball fight."

It did look like Francine, however improbable it seemed that he and Francine would ever have a snowball fight. "I'll take it," he said, and produced a credit card. "Nice place you have here," he commented as she rang up an alarming total. He gazed up at the high ceilings and down the long windows. "What's above the shops?"

"Apartments," said the woman. "They're nice, too. I live here."

"Safe neighborhood?"

"Safest in New York."

"Is there a hospital nearby?"

"St. Vincent's just around the corner."

"Schools?"

"Why, yes." Her voice unexpectedly warmed. "Would you like to speak to Cleo in the shop next door? The apartments are all rented now, but we have a young couple we expect to move to the country any day."

"No, don't bother her," said Bryce. "I was just curious."

"Hope your girlfriend likes her hat," said almost-certainly-Delilah, handing him two distinctive black-and-white hatboxes lashed together with black ribbon.

"Hmm," Bryce temporized, and strode quickly to the limousine, swinging the hatboxes. Doing research always made him feel better. He'd seen firsthand where Cleo planned to bring up this baby of hers—theirs—and so far it seemed suitable. He'd have to see the apartment itself to be sure it wasn't full of fifties furniture with sharp edges.

What was happening to his mind? He wasn't going along with her plan for a scientifically designed baby. No way!

"MY REPORT IS GOING to depress you," said Delilah, bustling in on the heels of Andrea Morgan's exit. "Are you sure you want to hear it?"

"Hit me," said Cleo. "I want to know everything."

"He bought her a hat."

"Who?"

"Francine."

"The girl he's going to marry?"

Delilah sighed. "Yes. She's a small blonde."

"Why am I not surprised?" Cleo said. "Of course she would be small and blond, and beautiful, I imagine." She took a deep breath. "But this has nothing to do with me. I'm not asking him to do anything that would interfere with his relationship with—" she could hardly say the name "—Francine."

Why was her heart throbbing so painfully? Because his kiss had not been the kiss of a man who was planning to marry another woman.

She took another deep breath. "This is a business transaction I'm proposing to him. She doesn't need to know. I'm not trying to steal him from her. She'll never miss the one thing I want from him." She waved a dismissive hand, noticing that her fingertips were icy.

Delilah's mind was on millinery. "I sold him that sick blue angora cap I knitted, you know, the one I made bigger when you told me the baby would be a girl."

"How sweet," said Cleo, managing a mischievous smile. "Were there booties to match?" Now she wished she hadn't asked Delilah to report. "Did he describe her in glowing terms? Did he drool?"

"No drooling," said Delilah, "and he bought his mother a hat first."

"How gallant," said Cleo.

"He did seem very mannerly," said Delilah.

Cleo didn't like the look Delilah was giving her. "Good," she said. "I wouldn't want the father to be anything but."

"On the bright side," said Delilah, "he asked some interesting questions."

At least Bryce was involved enough to be asking questions about her baby's environment. When Delilah finished her report, Cleo's gloom had lifted. A little.

IN ATLANTA, BRYCE LIVED in a newly built townhouse, one of several dozen identical townhouses on a choice piece of rolling property landscaped with fledgling trees. The location had appealed to him because it was conveniently close to the lab and refreshingly far from the "old Atlanta" inner-city neighborhood where his parents had always lived. It had been decorated in tasteful masculine fashion by an interior designer his mother had dredged up and with whom he had had no contact except to write a whopping check or two. It was clean and neat, thanks to a housekeeping service with whom his contact was also limited to monthly checks.

He usually experienced a feeling of comfort when he came home, knowing that nothing about it would have changed. Tonight its sterile perfection depressed him. He didn't want to call Francine when he was depressed; he'd do it tomorrow.

A casserole waited for him in the refrigerator; it bore the stamp of his parents' cook, in that whatever it was made of was swimming in creamy sauce and topped with about a pound of buttered bread crumbs. He put it in the microwave and watched it go around and around. When bread crumbs started shooting like little rockets into the interior of the oven, he decided it was probably done.

He sat down at the breakfast bar and ate the whole thing, and still couldn't figure out what was in it except creamy sauce. Creamy sauce made him think of kissing Cleo.

What in the world had made him decide he couldn't go on living another minute without kissing her, in spite of Francine, in spite of the devious methods Cleo had employed to conscript him into her crazy "project"? She hadn't even tried to be seductive, and yet she was incredibly seductive in that red dress, her breasts lurking just below the neckline, occasionally peeping out to...

Feeling uncomfortable on the bar stool, he began to pace the kitchen. These were not the thoughts a man who was soon to be married should be having, especially when he was having them about someone other than the person he was soon to marry.

It wasn't even the red dress, not entirely. She had amused and touched him when she dropped everything; scrambling around on the floor, she'd looked more like a kid playing dress-up than like the elegant woman she'd been just seconds before. It had made him want to put his arms around her and say, "That's okay. Everybody drops stuff."

But it was her mouth he had had to touch, her generous, sweetly scented lips. And she had let him, and he had liked it. He felt the kiss all over again, felt the soft interior of her mouth, felt his tongue move against soft velvet, felt the urge to hold her, felt the ache in his groin.

This was ridiculous. He'd been without sex too long, that was all. Once he and Francine were married he wouldn't have these thoughts.

Whoa! After they were married he'd better have them— about Francine!

Hot and restless, he slept in fitful, dream-bombarded spurts, waking for long spells of fretful soul-searching. At five in the morning he couldn't stand it anymore. Giving up, he made coffee, armed himself with a ponderous book and settled back into bed to wait for sunrise.

The bottom line, he decided two ponderous pages later, was that he might father Cleo's child—if he could be sure she'd be brought up in a sensible environment. To know that, he had to know more about Cleo. There lay his problem.

To find out more about Cleo, he would have to spend time with her. Before he could in good conscience spend time with her, he had to consult Francine about this bizarre thing he was thinking of doing. It would be good to have an unbiased feminine perspective on the issue, and Francine was coming from the same place he was coming from— not merely Atlanta, but a whole way of life, a conservative, middle-class outlook.

Yes, Francine's opinion would be helpful. Besides, he had to be honest with her. He couldn't do something like this—if he did it—behind her back. He wouldn't, of course, mention his crazy need to kiss Cleo. Francine could hardly be unbiased on that subject. That was something he would just have to get over.

One step at a time—that was how to handle his dilemma. Having decided that the first step was to consult Francine, he felt as good as he'd felt on the day he narrowed down his dissertation topic. He did forty sit-ups and thirty push-ups, then fell sound asleep with the white porcelain mug of coffee balanced on his stomach.

As EARLY AS HE THOUGHT he dared, he called Francine. "Francine, I have something important to discuss with you."

"Oh, Bryce!"

The thrill of anticipation in her voice alerted Bryce to the need to be candid. "Not 'it' exactly," Bryce said. "Something else."

Her exasperated sigh nearly broke his eardrum. He had a plan for the conversation. First he would give her her present. Then he would tell her about the offer from White-hall. And last, he would ask her what she thought about his being Cleo's sperm donor.

"What a cute hat," she said to him early that evening after he'd wrapped up things at the lab. Francine still lived at home, and they were once again in her mother's garden, her favorite spot for intimacy Francine style. When they weren't in her mother's garden, they went to cocktail parties, or dinners, or black-tie blowouts, but Francine had ruled that nothing important should be discussed on those occasions. People might see them talking, and wonder what they were talking about, and speculate, and "that's where gossip comes from, honey."

"The woman who sold me the hat said it was to wear

for snowball fights," Bryce said. That was as good an opening as any other.

"I sure hope it snows, then," Francine said. She snuggled into her pink cashmere sweater, the temperature having plummeted to seventy-five degrees.

Bryce cleared his throat. "I have a very good offer for Nopro," he said.

"Good," Francine said, clapping her hands. "So that's settled?"

"I hope so," Bryce temporized. "The offer's from Whitehall. They want me to come to work for them, head up the lab where Nopro will be tested."

"You can use your lab right here, can't you?" Francine said serenely.

"No. My lab's not large enough for full-scale development. That's why I needed to sell Nopro to a large pharmaceutical company like Whitehall. It has laboratories that are large enough. I would work in one of them." He didn't see how he could make the situation any clearer than that.

"Where?" A thunderstorm bumped against the serenity.

"New Jersey."

"New Jersey! You can't move to New Jersey." Her eyes filled with tears.

"This contract is what I wanted, Francine," Bryce said gently, "and *I* wouldn't be moving to New Jersey, *we* would."

A medley of expressions crossed her face, but Francine's face was no mystery to Bryce. Optimism—he'd implied he was ready for "it." Uncertainty—she didn't want "it" just anywhere. Stubbornness—she could damn well have "it" anywhere she wanted.

"You have to say no, Bryce, that's all there is to it," she said firmly. "I am not moving to New Jersey. I've worked my way up in the symphony association and the Junior League and I am not throwing away all my hard work by moving to New Jersey! My life is here, always has been, always will be.''

''You haven't seen New Jersey. And lots of people live in Manhattan or Connecticut and work in New Jersey. We wouldn't necessarily…''

''Manhattan!'' Wide open, her mouth was a pink oval. ''You'd ask me to move to a dangerous place like that?''

An image of Cleo's wide, generous mouth flashed through Bryce's subconscious, then nudged its way to the very front of his consciousness. He wished it would go away. It wasn't fair to Francine.

''It's not that dangerous,'' he said. ''Nothing has ever happened to me there. Well, just one thing.'' He wasn't absolutely sure this was the right time to bring up Cleo, but his voice box seemed to be working independently from his brain. Or maybe Cleo was just in a hurry to get it out in the open.

''What happened to you?'' She had the good grace to look concerned.

''A, um, a woman picked me out to be the father of her child.''

Stunned—that's what he'd call her new expression. Stunned into a brief, electric silence. ''A woman,'' she babbled at last. ''Picked you out,'' she said after hyperventilating for a moment, ''to be…'' She was back in control of herself. ''Where? At one of those singles bars? What were you doing at a singles bar?'' She stood up and put her hands on her hips.

''No, the Metropolitan Museum,'' said Bryce. ''All she wants is a sperm donor. She's not asking me to have anything to do with the baby after it's conceived. She has this crazy idea that she can design a baby girl who's not as right brain as she is, and she chose me. I was interested in knowing what you thought about…''

''She…chose…you?''

While he explained the unusual situation, quite cogently,

he thought, Francine's creamy pink skin turned scarlet. Her mouth screwed itself up into a snarl, and her eyes flashed viciously. She was virtually unrecognizable. Bryce was concerned that her mouth might not ever be able to resume its normal shape.

"You're actually thinking about it?" Her voice was building up volume, too.

"Well…" *Be honest!* However amazing, he did seem to be thinking about it—a lot. "Yes. Her family history presents a compelling case. I thought you might have an opinion on whether I should…"

A scream of fury pierced the air. "You have gone completely insane," Francine raged. "You need a psychiatrist! I knew this would happen," she wailed. "Can't you see why I don't want to leave Atlanta? You make a dozen trips up north and come home with all these crazy left-wing liberal feminist ideas! Your mama would have a fit! As for that woman…" The snarl reappeared. Francine grabbed the blue angora hat, jammed it down on his head and held it by its edges, spitting anger into his face. "You tell her she can't have any of your sperm! Those sperm are mine! Every last one of them! Do you hear me, Bryce Hampton?"

"So what you're saying," Bryce said, "is that you don't think it's a good idea."

For a second she stared at him, then screamed, "Daddy!" and ran into the house.

Bryce was left alone in the garden, wearing a blue angora cap. He gazed after her. A delicious feeling of freedom began to rise up in him, but he squelched it, feeling guilty. He'd been honest, but he hadn't been fair, not at all. How could Francine have an unbiased opinion on such a personal topic?

All hell would soon break loose. Thoughtfully he rose,

placed the blue cap on a cherubic garden statue and went through a side gate to his car.

HE RECEIVED a tearstained note the following day:

> Dear Bryce,
>
> I convinced Daddy not to kill you by telling him how very sick you are. I insist that you seek psychiatric help before we make any plans for our future. In the meantime, I intend to explore other options. There are plenty of fish in the sea—sane ones! Boxer was simply thrilled when I asked him to take me to the Harvest Ball next weekend—which you didn't invite me to!—so don't you dare show up! I'll tell everyone you're out of town—if you're smart you will have committed yourself to an institution by then anyway! And don't mention this to anybody! I can't bear the thought of the gossip!
>
> Sincerely, Francine.

Of course he wouldn't. He didn't want to hurt Francine. But he did feel that he had the right to choose whether to be a sperm donor or not, and he saw no reason why he couldn't make a simple contribution to Cleo's dream with no strings attached.

While Francine cooled down, which she would, he'd continue to gather data on Cleo as a prospective mother and then make his own informed decision.

The decision about going with Whitehall was his to make as well. He was beginning to wonder if Francine could fit into his life after all. What an odd thought to be having after dating the woman exclusively for three long years. Francine must have changed.

Or was he the one who had changed?

6

"I CAN'T DECIDE until I've met your parents," Bryce said.

At the sound of his voice, Cleo's heart had taken a brief vacation. It had barely started beating regularly again when he delivered this bombshell. She switched the phone to her other ear, hoping it might make a difference in what she'd just heard. "Meet my parents? You don't want to do that, Bryce."

"Yes, I do." His voice sounded very firm. "In fact, I insist."

"But why? It's not as though you'll have to spend any time with them. I mean, there's no need to take one's sperm donor home to meet the folks, is there? Isn't it enough that you know what they're like?" Since Sonia and Thornton had managed to frighten off each marriage prospect she'd brought home, she supposed their skill might extend to frightening off a sperm donor.

"Do you see them regularly?"

"Yes," Cleo said. "We're very close."

"Aha!" said Bryce.

"Aha? I'm not following."

"That means you'll be taking the baby to see them. Maybe even leaving the baby with them while you take a business trip. What you've told me about them—it's enough to worry any responsible father. Donor. I insist on seeing for myself. I want to be sure the baby will be safe in their home."

"I'm going to name her Anne," said Cleo.

"That's fine, but what does it have to do with the conversation?"

"If you're determined to take a personal interest in her life-style and the experiences of her impressionable years," Cleo explained, "you might prefer to call her 'Anne' instead of 'the baby.' Do you think Anne is a normal enough name, a conservative enough choice?" she asked, because she'd thought about it carefully.

"Anne is a very safe name," said Bryce. "Back to your parents. Do they live somewhere close?"

"In Connecticut," Cleo admitted reluctantly. His sense of responsibility was beginning to wear on her. All she needed was a single sperm, and the man was nickel-and-diming her to death!

"I'm coming to New York this weekend, so I want to treat them to breakfast, lunch or dinner, whatever is easier for them. I could pick them up, actually, and bring them into the city. Give me a chance to see how and where they live."

"I'll ask them," said Cleo, sick with dread.

"I'll call you back tonight," said Bryce.

As she had feared, Sonia and Thornton were thrilled at the prospect of meeting Bryce and would accept nothing less than having him as their houseguest.

"They want us to spend Saturday night with them," she reported to Bryce when he called that evening. "I told them I was sure you didn't have time."

She paused, listening to the death knell tolling for her plan. "You do? You'd love to?"

She hung up with a deep, deep sigh.

"CLEO, I WANT YOU to make me another dress."

"It would be a pleasure, Julia," Cleo said. "Let's set up an appointment for you." The phone clutched to one ear, she grabbed for her appointment book.

"You and Bryce hit it off so well!" Julia marveled while

Cleo tried to remember what month it was and finally got herself into November.

"Thanks for giving us a place to talk," Cleo said politely.

"Surely you did a little more than just talk," Julia teased her. "Herb tells me Bryce is engaged to a girl in Atlanta, but I saw the way you two looked at each other. And then— when we found Bryce in our bed, well!"

Cleo dropped her pencil. "How's next Thursday for you, Julia?" she said, crawling around in the lint, the threads and abandoned pins in search of it. In their bed? What was going on here?

"I'm not letting you off that easily," Julia said. "Tell all!"

"There's nothing to tell. Really," said Cleo. In search of the pencil, she'd stabbed herself on a long-lost seam ripper. "I don't know what you mean about Bryce being in your bed," she said, dabbing at the wound. "I left him in black-tie."

"Don't worry, darling, I assured Herb that Bryce was telling the truth about the circumstances." Julia paused. "But you know and I know that you and Bryce weren't meeting for the first time."

"Julia," Cleo said firmly, "Bryce and I aren't a romantic item. Our interest in each other is…is…purely business," she finished, grabbing the pencil triumphantly and coming up straight under the sharp edge of the cutting table.

"Oh?" Julia said. "What sort of business?"

With both hands holding her aching head, Cleo whirled her brain around in the opposite direction, hoping something would fall accidentally into place. "A dress," she said. "A dress for…for his bride-to-be. Blue," she said, "blue…angora. A blue angora dress. That's what he wants to give her for, um, Christmas! To go with her hat," she added wildly.

"What hat? Oh, never mind," Julia said with a long-suffering sigh. "I don't believe you, Cleo, not for a minute. Which is the real reason I called."

"You don't want a new dress?" said Cleo.

"Of course I do, but we'll get to that later. I called to warn you about Herb and his blasted Whitehall policies."

"Julia, the Whitehall policies have nothing to do with me."

"But they have a great deal to do with Bryce."

"You mean they've made a deal?" Cleo breathed. "Signed a contract? Nopro's about to be tested and..."

"And Bryce is coming with Whitehall to head up the project. Didn't he tell you?"

"Why should he?" Cleo said stiffly. "We barely know each other." Tears stung her eyes. She wished he had told her; it was obvious that his dream had been realized with this offer. She was thrilled for him, of course. But if he really meant it about being part of the first test group, she had to hurry, hurry, hurry.

"Sure," said Julia. "All I want to say is this—I think you and Bryce have a thing for each other, and if you have a thing for each other, he certainly shouldn't be marrying the girl from Atlanta. On the other hand, Herb is expecting him to marry the girl from Atlanta..."

"Francine," Cleo interjected glumly.

"Francine," Julia echoed, "and Herb doesn't approve of philandering. So whatever you do, do it carefully. Give Herb a chance to absorb the changes slowly."

"There aren't going to be any changes," Cleo argued, even while her mind drifted away to the memory of Bryce's mouth against hers. "As for this matter of Bryce being in your bed..." It was bugging her; she couldn't get it off her mind. "Julia, you don't think klutziness is *infectious*, do you? It's inherited, but you don't *catch* it from..."

"Cleo, you do have such an imagination!" said Julia. "I've got to run, darling. If you decide to confide in any-one," she went on, sticking to the topic she couldn't get off her mind, "you can trust me. I adore Herb, but he is such a prude sometimes! Okay, see you Thursday. I want something gorgeous and red to wear to Christmas parties, something like the dress you wore to the benefit." She paused. "Cleo?"

"Yes, Julia?"

"Wouldn't you have to knit an angora dress?"

"WE CAN STILL BACK OUT," said Cleo.

Behind the wheel of his rented car, Bryce had been admiring Cleo in her slim black trousers and tweedy-looking black-and-white sweater. Her hair was back to shaggy and her glasses crumpled her lashes as always, but she looked both chic and appealing. Bryce was uncomfortably aware of something else about Cleo that bode ill for the weekend. From the moment she flung open the car door and slid sensuously inside, he realized he found her utterly desirable.

He squelched the thought. Desire was not part of the weekend plan. "We are not backing out," he said firmly. "It would be rude."

"They'd never notice," said Cleo. "But if you're worried about it, we could claim intestinal flu, or a root canal, or tell them one of your rats back at the lab got pregnant."

Bryce held up a restraining hand. "Honesty is the best policy."

"It's also true that a stitch in time saves nine," said Cleo, "but it doesn't mean we have to stop in the middle of the West Side Highway and sew up a ball gown."

"Stop worrying," Bryce said. What he'd like to do was to stop the car in the middle of the West Side Highway and pull Cleo's deliciously rounded bottom into his lap. "The weekend will be fine."

"Fine as in 'fine weather' or fine as in 'everything will be fine'?"

"The latter. Probably the former, too."

To figure out which was the latter and which was the former, Cleo had to count on her fingers. "I wish I could be so optimistic," she said when she was sure he meant that everything would be fine.

"What are you worried about?" Bryce said patiently, at last recalling the things he was worried about. He'd created a clear mental picture of the Rose manse. Home to a painter of pistachio shells and an interviewer of plants, it would be a tiny cottage, a trailer, maybe. Whatever it was, his meticulously taught Southern manners would carry him through the weekend. Even if he had to share a bathroom. "Are you afraid the sheets won't be clean, or something like that?" he hazarded.

She gave him an odd, sidelong glance. "Of course not."

"There won't be enough towels?"

"There will be a plethora of towels."

That took care of linens. "Is Sonia inclined to serve unusual food?" he asked.

"Sonia is not inclined to serve any food at all," said Cleo.

Even that was all right with Bryce. He'd packed some health bars that were reputed to have taken heftier men than he to the top of Mount Everest. He wouldn't die of starvation over a weekend.

"Don't worry," he repeated. "Let's just relax and have a good time."

The day was sunny and cool, and along the Merritt Parkway the trees were laying a carpet of yellow-and-scarlet leaves. Next year he'd be around to see bare branches against a wintry sky, to watch for the first ice on the road. A balloon of excitement began to expand inside him at the thought of his future.

"The deal with Whitehall is all firmed up now," he said, feigning nonchalance.

"Julia told me," Cleo answered. Her face, which had looked anxious, suddenly lit up. "I'm awfully excited for you. I bet you're floating on clouds. It's such a good company, and you'll get to see Nopro onto the pharmacy shelves. I know just how you must feel." She smiled at him. "Your dream has come true."

The sun coming through the window sent a shaft of warmth through his chest. "It does feel good," he admitted, amazed at her complete understanding. "Of course, it's going to be a lot of work, too, leaving the lab in shape to be managed by somebody else and moving here." He glanced at her and observed that a little of the spark had gone from her eyes.

"Is Francine excited about it?" she said.

He wasn't sure how she knew about her, but he decided to be matter-of-fact about the reality of Francine. "No," he said.

"She doesn't want to move?"

"No."

"I'm sure she'll change her mind," Cleo said, and he could hear the anxiety return to her voice, "after she gets used to the— Take this exit," she shouted suddenly, a split second too late for him to take it conservatively. His heart had stopped pounding, although he couldn't vouch for the heart rate of the driver who had been to his right at that particular moment, when she said, "Take a left here." He wheeled, tires screeching, into a tree-shaded lane. "And a right," Cleo said a mile or so later. This time he was prepared. "Left here. No, next left."

He was wondering if he should tell Cleo that Francine was even less excited about her "baby project" when Cleo directed him into the driveway of a large, elegant house. Was this turning into a Sabrina story? Cleo was daughter to the butler who even now stood on the graceful brick stoop polishing the brass door knocker?

He got his answer when the massive front doors flew open, tossing the butler into one of the rhododendrons that flanked the entrance. As he flailed wildly in the bush, trying to extricate himself, a couple burst through the doorway crying, "Cleo! Baby! You're home!"

The woman, her voluptuous body clad in a voluminous silk dressing gown, focused on Bryce and came to a breathless halt. Her hair was kohl-black; her eyes, bright and snapping, matched. "You are Bryce Hampton," she said. "I am Sonia Rose." She held out a hand, long, white and regal, then changed her mind and kissed him quickly on both cheeks. "Welcome to our home."

"Really, Rifferton, your uniform is not up to standard today," Thornton Rose told the butler, frowning, as the man bowed their little group into a massive foyer.

"No, sir," Rifferton murmured, nursing a scratch on his cheek with a spotless handkerchief while attempting to free a twig from his hair. "I'll attend to my appearance at once, sir, if I may."

"By all means," said Thornton. "Everything's under control here." Cleo's father was a trim, elegant man wearing a black velvet smoking jacket and a silk ascot. His sandy brown hair was thinning, and his brown eyes were lively. After giving Cleo a generous hug, he turned to Bryce with outstretched hands. "My boy," he said, too warmly for Bryce's comfort, "we are so pleased to meet you. Cleo has told us so little about you. You must have a drink. What will it be?"

Something about the enormous marble-floored entrance, from which a broad, curving staircase soared upward, made Bryce feel oddly helpless. And Cleo—Cleo of the boundless energy and sparkle—stood beside him looking like a half-cooked squid noodle in her somber attire, limp and lifeless.

For reasons he couldn't understand, Bryce felt a deep, insistent desire to put his arms around her. He forestalled this impulse by looking at his watch. Somewhere in the world it must be five o'clock. "A drink sounds good, sir," he said formally. "What are you having?"

"Thornton makes peerless Manhattans," said Sonia. "I believe he has a pitcher at the ready."

"A Manhattan, please," Bryce said, who'd been hoping for red wine at the most and utterly despised Scotch and fruit in the same glass.

"Our friends call mine Serial Killers," said Thornton, his eyes twinkling.

"I can probably handle one," Bryce said. He'd been taught to rise to any occasion, and this was an occasion that warranted rising to.

"One Killer coming up," Thornton said, vanishing through a door beneath the staircase.

"Bryce," Sonia purred, "we're so glad that you're thinking of giving us a grandchild, and Thornton's parents are beside themselves at the prospect of a great-grandchild. It's a shame they couldn't be here this weekend, but Natasha has an audition in Los Angeles."

"Natasha?" said Bryce. "Is that Cleo's grandmother?"

"No, she's Grampa's star chicken," Cleo said swiftly. "She dances. What are you writing now, Sonia?" she hurried to ask. There was a desperate sound to her voice.

"Scabiosa, *a Tragic Life,*" Sonia said, her expressive face going long and sorrowful as she clasped her hands over her bosom.

"Beg pardon?" said Bryce, who was still trying to absorb the concept of a dancing chicken. The Funky Chicken? he wondered. Or a bit of classical ballet?

"I am deeply into the story of *Scabiosa,* an old, old plant that has survived such hardship, such threat!" Sonia said passionately. Her dressing gown, an elaborate thing of rose-and-cream silk, parted discreetly as her breasts heaved.

Bryce couldn't stop himself from glancing at Cleo. Her own beautifully rounded breasts were severely subdued beneath the woolly sweater. A smile teased at him in spite of his nervousness. He remembered her asking if his mother had a big bosom. She wanted this baby of hers to have a chance to be less spectacularly endowed. This baby of hers. This baby of theirs.

Bryce shivered suddenly, although the foyer was Indian summer warm and filled with light. It was all coming together in his head. At last he was close to understanding Cleo, her hopes and her fears, why she wanted and needed this baby.

"Let's go to the library," Sonia said, seizing Cleo with one arm and Bryce with another. "This entrance hall is such a cold, formal place. Of course," she added, hurrying her team down a wide hallway lined with paintings Bryce could have sworn he saw in the museum the fateful day he met Cleo, "Thornton's great-great-grandfather built the house, and he was a cold, formal man, at least until he married Great-Great-Grandmother Roxy. Here we are." She ushered them into a wood-paneled room lined with books, rich with Oriental rugs and awash in velvets and paisleys in the vibrant colors of the blooming plants that filled the window seats. "Now take off your shoes and for heaven's sake, relax! You're both so tense. New York does that to people, I've always thought."

Under no circumstances would Bryce take off his shoes. He wanted to be ready to run at a moment's notice. A fanciful Victorian-style display case, its contents softly illuminated, drew his attention, and he moved slowly toward it. Inside, poised on pins above small beveled mirrors, were hundreds of open pistachio shells, each decorated in the minutest detail. As he examined one that was painted to replicate the interior of a yacht, Sonia's throbbing voice spun him around in alarm.

She read from a manuscript displayed on a dictionary stand.

"Painfully, painfully I made a seed, knowing that through my suffering and death a baby *Scabiosa* would rise from the dank earth the following spring.

But in my last throes I observed a bird walking toward me, a tall bird with a stilted gait.''

"How terrifying for her," Cleo said. "I hope the bird didn't…''

"Yes," Sonia said flatly. "It ate the seed. One must write the truth, darling, even when it demands graphic descriptions of violence. However…''

Bryce was just getting into the drama of the bereft *Scabiosa* when Thornton bounded through the door with a small silver tray. "Killers," he announced, tripping over the corner of an Oriental rug, "coming uh-uh-uh-oops!''

The room fell into silence as Thornton observed from the floor, Cleo and Sonia from an upright position, the rivulets of brown fluid dripping down the lapels of the most expensive navy blazer Bryce had ever treated himself to. Sonia moved toward him and plucked a cherry from the folds of his pocket hankie, popping it into her mouth as she viewed the damage.

Cleo suddenly came to life and groaned.

SHE WISHED she could climb into one of the pistachio shells—the vampire's coffin would be her first choice—and close the lid over herself. The visit was already a disaster, and they'd only been there fifteen minutes. Now that Bryce had been clenched by Sonia and drenched by Thornton, now that he'd actually heard a floral potboiler and seen the pistachio shells, he'd never agree to father her child, never.

With a quick, alarmed breath she swept into action. "Just look what you've done, Thornton," she scolded as her father clambered up from the floor. "Give me those cocktail napkins." With a small damask napkin she began to dab ineffectually at Bryce's lapels. "We can save his jacket, but his shirt is soaked, and his tie—oh, Lord, look at his tie.''

Thornton looked. "Nice-looking tie," he complimented Bryce.

"It's ruined, is what it is," Cleo snapped.

"I am sorry, my boy," Thornton said hastily. "I tend to be a bit clumsy."

"And still," Sonia said fondly, "you insist on serving drinks yourself when we have a perfectly coordinated butler for that purpose."

"I've also ruined some excellent drinks," Thornton observed, reaching down to spear pineapple, orange sections and a few more cherries off the rug with a stray toothpick. He rose with his little kebab aloft. "I'll just run back to the kitchen and…"

"I'll do it, darling," said Sonia. "Ring for your valet and ask him to attend to Bryce's clothes."

"I…" said Bryce.

"Couldn't you just…?" Cleo interrupted. As always, she felt overwhelmed by her parents. She loved them and was amused by their eccentricities, and one day, if she could ever get a word in edgewise, she'd tell them so. But what she wanted more than anything in the world was to have a normal, ordinary little girl to have normal, ordinary conversations with and read normal, ordinary stories to in the evenings. They would not be tales of grieving *Scabiosa*.

This was no time to daydream about the future. She had to protect Bryce from further insult or damage. She didn't want him intimidated by Edgar, the valet Sonia had hired for Thornton out of sheer necessity, but it was already too late. Edgar stood in the doorway, tall, thin and supercilious.

"You rang?" he said. Then in a reproachful tone, he continued, "Oh, no, Mr. Thornton, not again."

"Yes, Edgar, again," Cleo answered, tight-lipped. "Can you restore Bryce's blazer, and wash and iron his shirt, and give him one of Thornton's ties?"

"In time for dinner at the country club," Sonia added.

"Bryce is such a gorgeous young man I want everyone to meet him."

"Oh, Sonia, do we have to go out for dinner?" Cleo implored her mother. Had Sonia somehow misunderstood the purpose of the weekend?

"We don't have to, but we are," Sonia said implacably, "so get with it, Edgar."

"I..." said Bryce, but seemed unable to formulate a sentence. Cleo hoped he wasn't having a stroke. Edgar moved fluidly around Bryce, touching a long finger to his lapel, his collar, tsk-tsking. "I'll do my best," he said at last, "but really, Mr. Thornton, Miss Sonia, we must remember to have our guests on weekdays when the cleaners are open. I am not a miracle worker. Come along, sir."

"I..." Cleo heard Bryce say as Edgar whisked him away. Bryce was still walking straight and tall. It wasn't a stroke, but it was a crisis as far as her project was concerned. And time was running out. He would soon start testing Nopro, perhaps on himself.

7

BRYCE PAUSED at the top of the stairs and glanced down at himself before he took the first step. He was wearing a paisley smoking jacket, cashmere and lined in something that was either silk or doing a damn fine impression of it. It was too big for Thornton, so whose was it? Someone whose body lay hidden in the basement, a victim of the dangerously clumsy Roses?

He'd fallen into a French farce with a cast of thousands, and he couldn't think of anything to do but listen for his cues and make up his lines as he went along. He moved down a step. Funny thing was, he was enjoying the sense of hanging on the brink of something. It was like being on vacation.

When had he last taken a vacation? Until he'd begun going out with Francine, he'd been utterly focused on his work. When fate had paired them, he'd known she wasn't the sort of girl to go away with him to Paris or Tuscany. As if he hadn't already figured it out, she'd told him so. Nor was Francine the sort of girl to sit quietly at home while he went away to Alaska or Africa. She'd told him that, too. That left him stuck between staying in Atlanta to enjoy the celibate life or going away by himself, ending his single hope of marriage and children, a warm, happy household to come home to when his brain had exhausted itself.

Bryce took one more step. But why had he assumed that coming home to Francine and their children would make him feel warm and happy?

He pressed a hand across his forehead. It felt cool enough, but he was clearly feverish. Once they were married, Francine would create the same kind of household he'd grown up in, and his father hadn't found anything wrong with his mother's home base. In contrast, he wouldn't dream of coming home to a household like this one, however warm, however welcoming. A vision leaped into his mind, a vision of Cleo waiting for him in a dressing gown that revealed voluptuous breasts when she breathed, when she held out her arms.

Uncomfortably aware of the rush of blood to his groin, Bryce stiffened his backbone and continued down the stairs.

"HE LIKES YOU," Cleo whispered, pressing a fresh drink into his hand. For a brief, badly needed moment she had him to herself while Sonia organized an hors d'oeuvre and Thornton mixed enough Serial Killers to cover future accidents.

"Who?" Bryce said.

"Edgar. He gave you our best guest jacket."

She could tell from the look in Bryce's eyes that this needed some explaining. "You're hardly the first person Thornton's poured a drink on," she explained. "We have a small but tasteful collection of smoking jackets for emergencies. This is by far the nicest one."

"I don't want Edgar to like me," Bryce said, his eyebrows shooting up. "I mean, he's very attractive, but he's not my type and I don't want to lead him on."

Cleo managed a laugh. "Don't worry," she assured him. "Edgar would never make a pass at a guest. It's just that he's the only discriminating person in this whole house. Thornton and Sonia love everybody. The butler lets in door-to-door salesmen, the chauffeur picks up hitchhikers and stray pets and the head gardener feeds the woodchucks instead of driving them away. But Edgar is picky. We have this one awful smoking jacket he offers to men he doesn't approve of.'' She paused, suddenly overwhelmed by anxiety over the fate of her motherhood project. ''Bryce...''

''What?'' he said suspiciously.

She bit her lower lip. ''I really am sorry the visit has gotten off to such a bad start. I promise Edgar will make your clothes better than new, but are you all right? Not too alarmed by us? Will you survive the weekend? Are you...?''

To her surprise, he smiled. There was a deep dimple in his left cheek she was just now noticing. Had he smiled so rarely in her company that she was actually seeing it for the first time? It was utterly charming. ''I'm fine,'' he said softly. ''I'm enjoying the novelty of all this.'' The sweep of his hand took in the flowers, the manuscript and the pistachio nuts. ''It's not like my home.'' His smile deepened. ''But you warned me it wouldn't be.''

''I didn't want you to come,'' she confessed, tilting her head up to him. She was only getting close enough to whisper, but she heard his quick intake of breath, saw his arms jerk as though he were thinking of putting them up to ward off a blow. ''I was afraid that if you met Sonia and Thornton you'd be afraid to avver by abee...''

Her words were garbled inside the mouth that quickly covered hers. She was too shocked to protest, too shocked to do anything but lean into the kiss, relishing the firm fullness of his lower lip, the maddening touch of his tongue against hers. When his arms enclosed her, she realized he hadn't been afraid she was going to wreak accidental havoc to his body; he'd only been deciding whether to give her a hug.

She needed a hug, and it felt so lovely, so sweet to be hugged by Bryce. She'd waited so long for someone who could make her feel like this....

Her eyes opened wide, blinked once in disbelief. She couldn't let Bryce hug her! She certainly couldn't let him kiss her! They had a business deal, and he had Francine.

Kissing wasn't on the agenda, but, *dear God, it felt so good!*

He drew away so slowly that their lips stuck together and finally parted with a tugging of skin. Bryce drew back, stared at her. "For some reason, Cleo," he said in a formal tone, "I occasionally feel a strong need to kiss you."

She struggled to hide the wild elation that was making her light-headed. "Why do you suppose you feel this occasional strong need?" she asked him, hoping her interest sounded scientific.

He frowned. "I don't know. Just now I wanted to reassure you, so I thought a hug might be a good idea, but the kiss..." He drew back to study her face. "It may have something to do with the shape of your mouth," he said finally.

"What is it about the shape of my mouth?" Cleo asked, dying to know.

He tilted his head to one side, still studying her. "There's something sort of inviting about it. It's so full, it makes you think about kissing, that's all," he concluded, sounding impatient. "It's an edible mouth. It reminds me of a pizza or a piece of marzipan, who knows? I don't even mind that it's brown instead of pink. I never imagined myself kissing a brown mouth."

"Do you like chocolate?"

"Sure. Doesn't everybody?"

"Maybe that's it," Cleo suggested. "Chocolate lips were a big Valentine's Day thing when I was a kid."

"Hmm," Bryce said. "Could be."

Sonia swept into the room bearing a tray of tiny new potatoes, halved and topped with sour cream and caviar. Cleo ate two, just in an attempt to recover from Bryce's kiss. Chocolate lips might explain Bryce's reaction, but what about hers? She wanted him to be the father of her baby, not her lover! So why did she wish so desperately that he'd need a chocolate fix again, and soon?

"WE MUST LEAVE by seven-thirty," Sonia announced. "Cleo, you and I should dress. Saturday night is black-tie, remember."

"Black-tie?" Bryce said. "I'm afraid I didn't bring..."

"Not for you, darling," said Sonia, giving him a warm smile. "Thornton won't be wearing a tux, either. But I do so love to dress up, don't I, Cleo?"

"Oh, darn it," Cleo said, snapping her fingers. "I completely forgot. I have your new dress in my hanging bag."

Sonia seemed delighted by this news. "I'll wear it tonight. It will need pressing." She glanced at her watch. "Florence's Lawrence Welk rerun should be over by now, don't you think? If it's not, I'll press it myself."

The two women swirled out of the library, leaving Bryce alone with Thornton. He wondered who Florence was. Another member of the staff, one who couldn't be disturbed during her favorite television show? Why not? She'd fit right in with the rest of this crew. He was the one who was out of place.

"You're sure I won't look out of place in my blazer?" he asked Thornton.

"My great-grandfather founded the country club," said Thornton. "We can wear Mickey Mouse boxer shorts if we want to. How about another Killer?"

"No, thank you, sir. Three's definitely my limit." The study had taken on a tie-dyed pattern behind his eyes, all the vibrant colors running together.

"Cleo's a wonderful girl, isn't she?" said Thornton.

"Yes, she is," Bryce said.

"Smart, too."

"Very smart."

"In fact, there's a bit of Great-Great-Grandfather Rose about her." Thornton frowned. "That doesn't happen often in the family. His characteristics seem to have gotten a bit muddled down through the generations."

"Yes, sir." *More than a bit!*

"For one thing, she insists on working."

"Well, a lot of people..."

"There's no need for her to work. Why can't she just enjoy herself like other young things do?"

"A lot of people enjoy working." He got it all out this time.

Thornton's expression said he couldn't imagine anyone actually enjoying work. "She doesn't do it for money, that's for sure. She's already inherited quite a lot, and I must say the townhouse was a good investment."

"She owns the townhouse?"

"Yes, of course." Now Thornton's expression suggested that it was quite impossible not to own the place you lived in. "And she's always managed money well. Not a wasted penny, even when she was a little girl."

"Remarkable," said Bryce. It seemed that Cleo was a very rich woman.

"She's a looker, too," said Thornton.

"Very attractive," Bryce murmured. What was Thornton getting at?

"Wonder why she doesn't realize it. Ah, Edgar. You have Bryce's clothes?"

Edgar paused in the doorway, making a slight bow. "Yes, indeed. Mr. Hampton, I've laid them out in your room. May I help you dress?"

"No," Bryce said.

"Then I'll show you to your room. Mr. Thornton, run upstairs like a good boy. I'll be along shortly."

"Yes, Edgar," Thornton said obediently.

Bryce plodded up the stairs behind Edgar, thinking about Thornton's last comment about Cleo. "Thanks, Edgar," he said a few minutes later, gazing at a spotless shirt and impeccable navy blazer. "You polished the buttons," he said, noting the gleaming brass.

"No, indeed," said Edgar, bristling. "That is Rifferton's job."

"I'll mention it to Rifferton on my way out," Bryce said.

"Claude will bring the car around in thirty minutes," said Edgar. "We'll see you downstairs then?"

"On the dot," Bryce said, looking forward to a shower to wash away the cobwebs in his brain.

Edgar paused in the doorway. "Miss Cleo is quite a special person, don't you think?"

They're after me, all of them. "She's a very attractive woman," he said.

"When I came to work here, I wondered why she hadn't married," Edgar mused. "Then I saw the pattern begin to unfold."

"The pattern?" Bryce was interested in spite of himself.

"Yes. She'd bring home one young man after another, but…"

"But what?" He held his breath.

"A day with Mrs. Sonia and Mr. Thornton ended every relationship," Edgar said, sighing. "One young man was so eager to escape that he rode a prize horse back to Dartmouth, then had to pay a fortune to return it by hired horse trailer."

"A very immature man," Bryce said abruptly, wondering why he felt so defensive. Sonia and Thornton were weird, sure, but if Cleo was the prize…

"Quite my feelings, sir. But I'm afraid the consistent tendency to flee on the part of a variety of young men has left Miss Cleo with the feeling that she is not, if I may use the term in its broadest sense, a desirable woman."

He showed no signs of moving from the doorway. Bryce began to count the precious minutes he had left to take a hot shower, or a cold one, and while he counted, he observed that Edgar was staring at him fixedly.

"Some man of true character could do her a great service by dissuading her of that notion," Edgar said. "For example, by offering marriage instead of a sperm donation." With that parting shot, he slammed the door behind himself.

It's a madhouse around here. Any man of true character would run like the dickens. Then Bryce made such a rush for the shower that he almost forgot to take his pants off before he flung himself beneath the soothing stream.

"CLEO WILL BE WITH US in a moment," Sonia trilled, darting down the stairs in impossibly high-heeled gold sandals. She looked so great that Bryce started analyzing her dress. It was black. It looked like layers of whatchacallit... chiffon...piled on top of each other, with each layer coming to a point in a different place. He didn't understand women's clothes, but he knew why Cleo had designed this dress for her mother. It showed off her shoulders, still as creamy-white as Cleo's, while minimizing her bosom and the lush curve of her hips. It made her look terrific.

"Mr. Thornton, are you certain this is the jacket you want to wear?" Edgar wore a pained expression as he attacked Thornton's attention-getting green plaid hacking jacket with a clothes brush.

"Of course it's what I want to wear," Thornton said irritably. "Why else would I be wearing it? Ah, here's our girl."

Bryce's eyes went to the top of the stairs. Cleo was wearing black, too, a simple, short dress with spaghetti straps, but the top moved gently with the sway of her breasts, the skirt with the movement of her hips, in a way that was as complex as one of Bryce's mathematical formulas. Watching her long, elegant legs descend the staircase one breathtaking step at a time, he was surprised to feel his pulse race and an alarming sensation attack the lower half of his body.

She was beautiful, exquisitely beautiful. She glittered in the light from the crystal chandelier, her hair shone and her eyes sparkled. A peculiar thought struck him. He began to contrast the Cleo he'd met in the museum with the Cleo he was seeing now. The early Cleo had been clumsy, touchingly so, in every sense of the word. Her dress, while pretty, had hidden her Miss America legs, her vamp's breasts, while the glasses had done their best to squash her spiky lashes and hide her compelling eyes. And he'd liked her even then, had kept her business card, had been unable to stop thinking about her. But this Cleo...no man in his right mind would be able to stop thinking about this Cleo. What had happened to change her so drastically?

She saw him, or saw the unfocused blob he'd appear to be when she wasn't wearing glasses. She paused halfway down the stairs, reached into a small beaded bag and pushed the glasses onto her nose. Whatever it was she saw in his face made her quickly shrug into the white satin jacket she'd been dangling from one finger.

At least she tried to shrug. A crystal button snagged on a spaghetti strap, leaving her imprisoned with one elbow cocked out rakishly above her head.

He rushed to the rescue. "You look fantastic," he whispered, unhitching the button and carefully sliding the jacket sleeve over her arm. His breathing quickened as his hands brushed against her, as his position one step above her revealed the bare, velvety nape of her long, graceful neck, her pink shell ears. The source of the glitter was a diamond in each ear, simple, enormous diamonds, and a narrow, plain bracelet paved with more diamonds circled a slender wrist. Her lips were full and pink, not brown, and her nails glimmered like pink frost. He wanted to grasp those long, slim, capable hands, to plunder those pink, inviting lips.

"And for my next act..." she said, giving him a dry glance.

Everything Thornton and Edgar had said or alluded to about Cleo's self-image threaded through Bryce's brain, and more pieces fell together.

Without further incident the four of them climbed into an enormous, ancient silver Rolls-Royce. Bryce and Sonia faced the glass screen that separated them from a burly, red-faced driver. Thornton and Cleo sat opposite them. It disappointed Bryce to note that Cleo seemed determined not to catch his eye.

Something inside her has given up. The answer, too often, has been no.

A tiny hope bloomed in his heart. He could make her see herself differently, if she gave him time. He owed that much to her, just for adding the weird twist to his life that was close to turning a cookie-cutter kind of guy into an intrepid adventurer.

CLEO LEANED BACK against the car seat and tried not to look at Bryce. What had he been thinking while he watched her come down the stairs?

He'd been waiting for her to trip and roll the rest of the way down. He'd been wondering why Thornton was wearing green plaid for a black-tie occasion. He'd been asking himself how much of the voluptuous, wild and crazy Sonia would show up in baby Anne's personality. He'd been wondering why he'd come here, and if he could get away before his navy blazer had been dealt more blows than even fine fabric and English tailoring could handle.

It was par for the course. The faces of Stefan, Rufus, Kevin and many others made cameo appearances in her mind. If she were pretty enough, desirable enough, one of these men might have been able to overlook her background, which she had to admit was—different. It was so different, in fact, that not a single one of them had tried to marry her for her money.

She couldn't even buy the husband and family she wanted more than anything else in the world!

8

THE ROSE FAMILY KNEW how to make an entrance. Thornton swept them into the dining room of the old, elegant club with a self-assurance that bespoke his founder's roots, not his green plaid jacket. Waiters bowed. Cries of "Sonia! Thornton," and "My goodness, here's Cleo!" followed them as Sonia serpentined her way among the tables, stopping for a kiss here, a word there.

Their table was a special one, offering a magnificent view of the lighted grounds and the golf course. With considerable relief Bryce dropped into a chair, then remembered his manners and leaped up to seat Sonia and Cleo. Sonia, however, wasn't ready to sit down.

"There's Lydia Wilcox," she exclaimed, gesturing toward a dour-looking woman seated a few tables away. "I especially want her to meet you," she murmured to Bryce. "She's been lording it over everyone with stories of her new grandson." She turned. "Lydia, darling," she sang, raising her voice considerably more than was necessary, since at the same time she was whisking Cleo and Bryce toward the woman. "You remember Cleo. She's having a baby soon, and this delightful man—" she gestured grandly toward Bryce "—is the sperm donor. Bryce Hampton, Lydia Wilcox."

Lydia's eyes widened, bugged out of her thin face. "Spuh. Spuh, spuh," she stammered, gazing wildly at Bryce.

"Here, darling, have some water," Sonia said to Lydia.

"You too, Bryce," she added, selecting a water glass at random. "Did something go down the wrong way?"

"Having a baby?" said the woman across from Lydia. "How exciting. When?"

"When, darling?" said Sonia. "Ten months? Eleven?"

Cleo must have realized he was choking to death, because she began to pound his back. "Mother," she said between blows, "you're shocking everyone. Let's not announce the baby until I'm pregnant."

"Pregnant?" said a woman from the table on the other side. "Then this must be your new husband, Cleo. Please do introduce us." Her syrupy voice contrasted sharply with the sour look on her face, which suggested she was just now finding out she hadn't been invited to the society wedding of the year.

Still strangling, Bryce plunged into the conversation. "No, no," he croaked. "We're not married."

"Sonia said donor," roared the woman's husband. "To what? Why aren't you on my list for the Colitis Foundation?"

"Sperm donor, darling." Sonia's voice carried like a bell. A funeral bell.

Behind his back Bryce heard a hiss. "Did she say sperm donor?"

He froze. He knew that voice. It belonged to Herb Hardy, on whom the future of Nopro depended. Slowly he turned, and weakly he smiled. "Herb," he said. "What a surprise." He held out his hand, hoping it wasn't clammy.

"For both of us," Herb Hardy said, focusing a steely gaze on Bryce. "What's all this about?" he said, keeping his voice low. "You assured me that you had nothing going on with Cleo Rose, and now I'm hearing this preposterous…"

"These are our friends the Braithewaites," Julia Hardy interrupted, "our hosts this evening. Nice to see you, Bryce. Excuse me, I must speak to Cleo."

In the relative quiet, now that he was a few tables removed from the hubbub that surrounded Sonia and Cleo, Bryce slid into Julia's chair. Surrounded by the two men and facing a quite normal-looking Mrs. Braithewaite, he felt safe for the first time in hours. "Herb," he said courageously, "do you have a minute?"

"I certainly do," Herb murmured. "Help me understand what's going on here, Hampton. I know you're a scientist with an open mind toward the experiment and all that, but Whitehall is a very conservative company. Did I hear that woman say you were going to be her daughter's sperm donor?" His voice went on the rise. "How can you even think about marrying one woman and...and fertilizing another one! A single one! The developer of Nopro helping a single woman get pregnant!"

Bryce noted with alarm that Herb's voice had risen to the decibel level of Sonia's. Rapidly he examined his priorities. What did he care most about? Nopro? His own reputation? Cleo's reputation? Francine's feelings? Working for Whitehall?

He consulted the air above his head and took a long shot. "Mr. Braithewaite," he said, addressing the Hardys' host, "have you ever noticed that the Roses, while a credit to this fine community, are completely mad?"

After a stunned silence, it was Mrs. Braithewaite who spoke up. "It's not something we talk about," she whispered, "but yes, we have noticed that they are somewhat nonconforming. You know it's true, Chester."

"Cleo's the most sensible one of the bunch," Chester Braithewaite admitted, "and she's a dingbat herself."

Bryce experienced the oddest reaction to Chester's description of Cleo. While the conversation was going exactly as he'd hoped it would, he had an odd inclination to slam his fist into Chester Braithewaite's potbelly. Cleo a dingbat? How dare he describe her that way.

Get a grip, man! Forget Cleo! Save yourself! Save No-pro! Think about poor, innocent Francine!

Maybe I can save all of us.

He swallowed and moved his clenched fists to his knees. "That aside," he said smoothly, "I've been caught up by accident in Cleo's slightly eccentric plan to have a baby without benefit of a husband. I am trying to…" He paused again, looking for the right words. "…to handle it…" Would a hand over his heart help make the point? He decided against it. Too hammy. "…so nobody gets hurt. You understand."

Mrs. Braithewaite's expression said, "What a nice boy!" Chester's said, "I'm working on it." Hardy's was inscrutable. Bryce glanced over at Cleo. Her face was flushed, embarrassed and still utterly beautiful. As though she felt his gaze, she returned it. Their eyes met, caught, clung. In hers he saw despair, and the thought of Cleo defeated once again hit him hard in the gut.

His throat constricted, blood pounded at a vein in his temple. He'd made his decision: Cleo would have the baby she wanted, no matter what.

Now that he knew where this farce was heading, he knew what to say next. "If you can pretend this evening never happened," he said, "I assure you that the next time we meet, I'll have the situation—" he made a broad, sweeping gesture with his hands "—completely under control." He smiled.

"No more nonsense about being a single woman's sperm donor," Herb said, looking him hard in the face.

Damn. He'd hoped Herb wouldn't corner him. Still… He took the plunge. "No. I will not be a single woman's sperm donor," he said firmly. There. He'd said it. Perspiration broke out on his forehead. He wiped his forehead, then wiped his hands on his trousers.

"I suppose," Herb grumbled, "I have to be a little more

flexible. If these Rose people are known nonconformists and you've been caught up in the tide of…"

"Herb." Julia Hardy's voice, coming from just above her husband's head, was commanding. "Let's dance."

Bryce stood, thanked Hardy for his understanding, thanked the Braithewaites for their hospitality and sought out Cleo.

On the dance floor, Sonia and Thornton performed a flamboyant tango. Cleo sat alone at the table, and her eyes were desperate. His heart went out to her. His feet followed. He was quickly by her side.

"I ordered endive salad and duck for you," she said. "I hope that's all right. Oh, Bryce, I'm so sorry. How could I have known the Hardys would be here tonight? Or that Sonia would choose to introduce you as my sperm donor! She didn't mean any harm. She's just a…a loose cannon," she concluded. "You never know what's going through her head, but whatever it is, it comes straight out her mouth. She didn't realize you were interviewing her and Thornton—she thought they were interviewing you, and she was only trying to say she approves you as the father of her grandchild. If I've blown your deal with Whitehall or threatened your relationship with Francine, I'll never forgive myself." She was close to tears.

"Cleo," Bryce said, "dance with me."

It dammed her flow of words. "What?" Her eyes were wide. "Why?"

He'd floored her. She'd expected him to run, not invite her to dance. Until a few seconds ago, it was the last thing he'd expected to hear himself say, having given some serious thought to the cost of replacing his Italian loafers if he danced with Cleo. Now he didn't care about his loafers.

"Because I want to dance with the most beautiful woman in the room," he said, slipping an arm around her waist and grasping her hand, pulling her up with him as he rose.

To his eternal gratitude, the band segued into a slow number.

"You're a kind, polite person, Bryce," Cleo sighed, fitting herself into his rhythm, "and I'll always remember how hard you tried not to embarrass me. I mean, I'm already embarrassed beyond belief, but you didn't add to it by…"

"Shh," Bryce said softly. His hand tightened its grasp, his arm gripped her a little more tightly. "You didn't blow the deal with Whitehall." *And my relationship with Francine is over.*

"I have to ask you one question," said Cleo. Her breath was a puff against his cheek.

Do you love me? I think so. "Ask away," said Bryce. "I'm getting used to your questions."

"What were you doing in Herb and Julia's bed at the Plaza?"

No, he would never be ready for her questions. "I was making an utter fool of myself," he said, and told her the whole embarrassing story, right down to the Brooks Brothers boxer shorts.

She laughed a little, the laugh softening her breasts against his chest, increasing his feeling of closeness to her. "That explains why Julia…" She halted.

"Why Julia…" he prompted her.

"…teased me about that night, said she'd noticed the way we, um, looked at each other. How silly."

"Yes," Bryce murmured, thinking just the opposite.

"I assured her we were only engaged in a business transaction," said Cleo, "but I didn't want to tell her I was trying to talk you into a sperm donation, for heaven's sake, so I told her I was making you a dress."

Bryce felt his face redden as he came to a dead stop in the middle of the dance floor. "Making…me…a…dress?" he hissed violently into her ear.

"For Francine," she whispered back.

He noticed the change in her tone, but was too relieved to hear that Herb and Julia were not adding "transvestite" to his list of dubious personality traits to attach any significance to it.

"Oh," he said softly, "for Francine." He moved her slowly around the floor.

"Blue angora, to match the cap you bought from Delilah."

So that's how she knew. What she didn't know was that his feelings about marrying Francine had changed. But they'd done enough confessing for the evening. Holding Cleo was having the most amazing effect on him, and he wanted to savor it. As he nestled his head to hers, his mouth went dry. Her satin cheek rested against his; her eyelashes tangled with his. He couldn't help imagining bodies tangled in tangled sheets. He shuddered, backing the telltale half of himself away from her to keep her from knowing how deeply she aroused him.

He felt her tighten up; he had a sinking feeling that the only reaction of his she'd picked up on was that he had backed away.

IF ONLY IT WERE REAL. Cleo sank into Bryce's embrace, let his cheek slide against hers, imagined turning her head the slightest bit, just enough to let her mouth make contact with his. Imagined moving her body toward his, fitting herself into him, accepting his maleness and offering him her womanliness.

Doing something so aggressive would only confuse him; he was dancing close because where he came from that was the polite thing to do, and his cheek rested on hers because he'd learned to dance that way in dancing school. She'd said the very idea of their being attracted to each other was silly, and he'd agreed.

Once again, goodbye romance.

Wait a minute! You already knew romance was out of

the question. A sperm sample from the perfect donor—that's all the relationship with Bryce is about. Romance just isn't in my cards.

But I can have a baby, Cleo thought fiercely. *I can have someone of my own to love and cherish.* The thought comforted her so much that she relaxed a little, moved forward into Bryce's embrace, rested her breasts against his chest and wanted to moan with pure pleasure.

She didn't know how to interpret his labored breathing. Thinking she'd probably scared him, she moved the upper half of her body away, which only brought the lower half closer. And through the thin fabric of her dress, she felt the truth about his opinion of her.

It left her breathless, her heart pounding, her thoughts troubled. It made her wonder if she might be wrong about his feelings for Francine. And then he backed away.

Stiffly they circled the floor, but Bryce's mouth moved softly against her ear again. "It's not a chocolate-lips thing," he murmured.

"What?"

"The thing about the Valentine chocolate lips when I was a kid. Tonight your mouth looks like strawberry ice cream, but it's having the same effect on me."

It was the story of her life that the music changed to a samba, and Thornton cut in.

SOMETHING HAD CHANGED between them, and Cleo didn't know what it was. When, at long, long last, they returned to the car, Bryce sat beside her, the two of them facing the glass screen, with Thornton and Sonia across from them.

"You were a big hit, Bryce," Sonia said with satisfaction.

"Thank you," Bryce murmured.

Cleo was surprised to hear amusement in his voice. And he hadn't run. Instead, he had danced with her. Thinking about their moments on the dance floor sent a jolt of electricity through her body, swelling her breasts, hardening her nipples, making her squirm uncomfortably against the leather car seat. Had anyone noticed? Sonia and Thornton dozed lightly across from her, and Bryce...

He'd tensed up. His eyes were wide, gleaming blue. He reached out to grip her hand. "Cleo," he hissed, "what is that thing climbing up the glass?"

Cleo dug in her bag for her glasses and put them on. Just behind Thornton's head, on Claude's side of the glass, a small, hairy paw crept up the glass, slid back down, then crept up again. Two pointed ears appeared in her line of vision, followed by a pair of shining eyes.

"Looks like a kitten," she said, and put her glasses away.

"Why is there a kitten in the car?" Bryce asked her. "Put your glasses back on, for God's sake. There's another one, and another." His eyes had gone from gleaming to glazed.

Normal people didn't understand kittens in the car. Cleo pressed a button on her door handle and spoke. "Claude," she said, "why do we have kittens in the car?"

"Kittens?" Thornton said suddenly, opening his eyes. He spun, gazed directly into the wild, crazy eyes of a black-and-white kitten and emitted a small yelp.

Claude's amplified voice responded. "Cat deserted 'em in the garden shed," he said. "Gardener's afraid they'll run off his chipmunks. I'm just keeping them out of his way for a while."

"So. That explains it," said Thornton, and closed his eyes again.

Her eyes still closed, Sonia said, "Try to find homes for them, Claude. They can't live in the car. It wouldn't be healthy for them to grow up with so little freedom."

"No, ma'am," said Claude.

Cleo noted that Bryce was following the conversation with ominous fascination. Would this be the last straw, the final bit of eccentric behavior that would make him flee the house screaming, motivate him to summon a car service in the middle of the night to take him back to civilization?

"I'll take one," he said.

Cleo froze. "What did you say?"

"I said," Bryce said, turning to her, "that I would take one kitten. No, I'll take two. I'm gone a lot. They'll be company for each other."

"Why?" she challenged him.

"I don't know," said Bryce. He suddenly looked stunned. "I really don't know. It just seems like the right thing to do, get a cat. Two cats," he amended himself.

"You haven't even seen them properly," Cleo protested. "You don't know if they're cute and sweet or wild and mean. You don't know what the mother was like...well, yes you do. She deserted them!"

Bryce yawned, then settled back against the seat as though he'd gotten over being stunned and was starting to feel comfortable with the notion of himself as a cat owner. For once, it was Cleo who felt as though she'd fallen through Alice's looking glass.

"I'll bring them up to be cute and sweet," he said sleepily. "Doesn't matter what the mother was like, or the father. You can't always tell, you know, how a kid's...I mean, a cat's going to turn out by looking at the mother and the father."

He drifted off. He didn't realize he was still holding her hand, no longer gripping it, just holding it loosely and gently. Cleo tentatively lifted one finger to stroke the back of one of his, feeling the soft brush of short, crisp blond hair.

The worst thing that could possibly happen had happened. She had fallen in love, deeply, irrevocably in love with a man who was planning to marry another woman, a man she'd promised never to see or call upon again if he would just be the father of her baby.

He was wrong, of course, about the kittens. It did matter what their parents were like. She was just like her parents, wasn't she? As crazy as Sonia, as creative and klutzy as Thornton, doomed to be an oddity for the rest of her life?

Cleo sighed, relegating her heartbreak to the spot inside her where the other heartbreaks suddenly seemed to have vacated the premises. She would, naturally, take the third kitten.

"OH, BRYCE, SHE'S USING her litter box!"

"I hoped that was what she was using."

Cleo smiled. It was a good thing they had had the distraction of three kittens on the way back to the city. Without them, they might have driven in silence. She had to ask him for an answer, yes or no, and she dreaded the moment. Nor was he helping her out, but then he probably hated to tell her no.

"Here we are," he said, pulling up in front of the townhouse.

"Bryce..."

"Let's get the kittens inside..."

"And the litter box..." Cleo added.

"...before we talk about anything else."

Cleo bit her lip. "I was only going to ask you about your blazer. Are you sure you don't want me to try to get a little more of the egg off the lapel?"

Bryce waved a carefree hand. "It was due for a cleaning anyway," he said. "Thornton's got quite an aim with an egg spoon. Have you ever thought how odd it is that a klutz like him can paint those tiny shells?"

"Well, yes," she admitted. "There's a medical word for it, like when a polio victim grows up to be a superathlete, or a hearing-impaired person becomes a musician. Overcompensation, that's it. But in Thornton's case..." She paused. "Nothing else makes sense at our house. Why should that?"

It was nice to hear him laugh. Her hopes rose a little as they stuffed the three kittens into the kennel the gardener had given them. Bryce picked up the kennel and Cleo's weekend bag, then set them down on the sidewalk.

"I hate to stick you with the heavy stuff," he apologized, "but don't you think I have a better chance of getting the litter box into the house right side up?"

"Definitely," said Cleo, glad to be relieved of the responsibility.

Accordingly burdened, they chose to take the elevator. It was extremely small. Even over the kittens' protests Cleo could hear Bryce breathing, could see the rise and fall of his muscled chest, could watch the splotch of drying egg expand and contract. The door opened and they spilled out. Feeling rattled, Cleo groped for her key, her glasses, and eventually got the apartment door open.

"I'll give you a tour," she said. Acting positive, she added, "You'll want to see how Anne's going to live."

Kittens scampered across tables and sofas as Bryce contemplated Cleo's living room. Her decor was as warm and real as she was. She could have spent whatever she liked, but she'd chosen an eclectic mix of everything from antiques, probably from her family, to things that looked like flea-market finds. A faded old Oriental rug and walls the color of a flowerpot tied it all together. There were plants and fresh flowers everywhere.

"You always surprise me," he said at last. "I expected something...wild." He wandered into the dining room, which was dominated by a long narrow harvest table flanked by soft chairs covered in a dark red check. He thought about his own cold glass table and black-lacquered chairs. "Mmm," was all he said.

As though she felt shy about it, she gave him the merest peek into her bedroom, then opened the next door. "This will be Anne's room," she murmured.

Bryce walked into the room. As he took in the cheerful

wallpaper, the touches of bright primary color, the red-cushioned rocking chair that sat by the window, something funny happened to his heart. It skipped a beat. His chest felt tight; his eyes burned. *Anne's room.* One day there might be a baby in that cradle, a dark-haired little girl with eyes like Cleo's. And Cleo would pick her up, crooning softly to her, take her to the rocker by the window and sing her a song...

Then he would take a turn rocking her.

Cleo says this is a business deal. She said the very idea we might have personal feelings about each other is silly. But I can change her mind. I will change her mind. I just have to figure out how.

HE DOESN'T LIKE IT! Or he likes it, but he's telling himself no baby of his will ever sleep in a cradle with red plaid ruffles around it! Say something, her heart pleaded with his.

"Babies like bright colors," she hazarded. Anything to break the silence.

"Cleo..."

"I know," she said despairingly. "It's time to talk about the issue at hand. So to speak," she added quickly, because she hadn't meant to make a joke of it. "I know what a terrible time you had this weekend, and how strange it all seemed to you, but I promise you, Bryce, Anne will have the most careful, the most loving care."

"Cleo..."

"And I guess you've figured out that I have plenty of money to bring her up right. She'll go to the best schools."

"Yes, I..." He frowned.

It was her last chance. "You know all that and still you're not sure!" Cleo cried. "I wish I could make you understand that we won't ask anything of you, nothing at all! From the beginning you've made your role more important..." She halted when his frown deepened. "Well, of course it's important," she amended herself hastily. "I mean, it's crucial. What I'm trying to say is that you're not crucial afterward. I honestly mean it when I tell you that as soon as I'm sure I'm pregnant, you can vanish into thin air and I won't ever bother you again. You can go on with your life, marry Francine, become the kind of man Whitehall wants you to be.''

A sad, sick feeling struck her as she said the words. It wasn't what she wanted to happen, not at all, but it was what she'd contracted for and she had no right to ask for more. "So you see," she said, hearing her voice falter, "it's silly of you to worry so much about whether it's the right thing to do.''

His frown lines had smoothed out a little. He gazed at her as she spoke, and when she finished, waved a dismissive hand. "There's no need to keep on arguing your case with me, Cleo. I've made my decision. I have decided...''

"Please, Bryce, think it over just a few more days," Cleo pleaded with him. She was frantic with frustration thinking of the time and emotional energy she'd invested in him. She couldn't let him slip away, leaving her to start all over! "I know it's not the way normal people do things...''

"...to do it," said Bryce.

Cleo's eyes were brimming with tears. "In a few years you'll think back on this and tell yourself how silly you were to refuse such a simple, uncomplicated request to... What did you say?''

"I said I'll do it." Bryce gave her a calm, reassuring smile. "I will be the father of your baby." He reached back to pluck a kitten off his shoulder.

STUNNED, CLEO OPENED her mouth, closed it, opened it again. Words spilled from her brain, but her brain had interrupted service to her vocal cords. Sternly she instructed her eccentric nervous system to get back on the job. *Think. Speak. Try hard to say approximately what you're thinking.* "You will?" she squeaked. It wasn't a particularly intelligent response, but it was better than making fish mouths.

"Yes. I've thought it over, and I agree that it would be best for the human race if Anne had a fifty-fifty chance at some left-brain activity." He shook his head. "After this weekend I realize that without an infusion of logic, order and normalcy, Anne will end up interviewing nuts and painting scenes on violets."

"Oh, Bryce, I don't know what to say!" *That's an understatement.* "You've made me so happy!" She clasped her hands together to keep from throwing her arms around him. *I need my chart. I need my thermometer. I have to call my gynecologist and tell her she's about to be my obstetrician. I need to select a sperm bank for Bryce, and a cradle for Anne, and a tasteful announcement that says, "No gifts, please." No, the cradle and the announcement can wait. First things first. First a sperm bank. No, first listen to what Bryce is saying.*

What he was saying temporarily burst her bubble. "On one condition."

"Condition?" Her voice was no more than a whisper. "What's the condition?"

"I want to father this baby in the usual way."

Why was I so worried? All he wants is to father the baby in the usual way. How sweet. Good old Bryce. Just like him to want to make me pregnant in the...

She sat down hard in the rocker that was fortunately just behind her and not resting on a throw rug or anything unstable. "You want to *what?*" she gasped.

"I want to do it the ordinary way." His calm, assured smile had returned.

"You mean you want us to..." She moved an index finger rapidly back and forth between the two of them.

"Yes."

"But Bryce, we can't do that!" She bolted out of the rocker, standing up to face him while it thumped wildly behind her.

"Why not?"

"Because...because...that carries all sorts of emotional connotations! That wasn't part of the deal!"

"It is now," he said implacably.

"But why?" she wailed.

"Because I am not going to one of those sperm banks to, you know..."

"You mean to m..."

"Don't say it! That's exactly what I mean. I'm not going to do that publicly, no matter how much you want Anne to have my genes."

"You don't do it publicly! They give you a private..."

"That is my last and final word on this subject." Bryce folded both arms across his chest and glared at her. "Do it my way or not at all."

"Ah," Cleo breathed, staring at him. She couldn't find a hint of emotion in those gorgeous blue eyes, no emotion but stubbornness, anyway. He meant what he said. If she wanted him to father her baby she would have to...

And if she did, he would know she hadn't kept her end of the deal. He would know she wanted to make love with him, wanted him to love her, wanted him to be a family with her and Anne. She couldn't let him find out. It would be too humiliating when he said, "I'm sorry, Cleo, but I'm leaving. Our business is finished."

And that's exactly what he would say. Bryce was going to marry a girl in a blue angora hat, a girl as normal as he was. It did seem a little out of character for him to insist on having sex with her, Cleo, but he was a scientist, after all, and probably saw it as a scientific necessity.

She, on the other hand, wasn't the least bit scientific. She was pure emotion, and at the moment, all that emotion was focused on him.

Aware that she had returned to making fish mouths, Cleo made a sudden decision. She'd read that women often pretended to enjoy sex more than they actually did. Well, she could put on an act that would convince him she wasn't enjoying it. She might even convince herself in the process. And the added bonus was that she could taste love with Bryce that one glorious time. It would be a memory she could hold to her lonely, aching heart for the rest of her life.

"What about Francine?" she said.

"If Francine can't understand that this is a separate part of my life," Bryce said solemnly, "then she isn't the right woman for me to marry."

From what little she knew about Francine, she had gauged her to be exactly the sort of person Bryce ought to marry. And he knew her better than she did. She thought it over for a few more minutes, gazing uncertainly at him. "Well, okay, then," she said, "if you're sure."

A flicker of something crossed his face before the implacable smile settled in again. "Good. It's decided. When?"

A stab of pure, raw need hit her so hard between the thighs that she sat down again. She crossed her legs and cleared her throat. "I keep a temperature chart. I know how to predict when I'm going to ovulate." She paused. "Is ovulation too personal a thing to discuss with you?"

"We're talking about making a baby together. Nothing is too personal."

"Okay, then," she said uncertainly. "The theory I've decided to test is the one that suggests that you and I should..." She paused again to do the rapid motion with the index finger.

"Right, right," he said impatiently. "When?"

"Forty-eight to thirty-six hours before ovulation. When the moment is right, we have twelve hours."

"When will that be?" he repeated. "Approximately."

She thought. "Well, I'd guess about three weeks from now."

"Three weeks! Thanksgiving?"

Surprised by his vehemence, she gazed up at him. "Yes, somewhere around Thanksgiving. Is that a problem for you?"

YES, DAMN IT, IT'S A PROBLEM for me! A serious, pressing, urgent problem. He'd been hoping she'd say, "Right now would be fine."

Pulling himself together, he said, frowning, "I need to get back to the lab. I was hoping to take care of it, ah, now."

"I wish I could arrange it for your convenience," Cleo said regretfully, "but making sure the baby is a girl complicates things quite a bit. You see, if we, ah, did this at the wrong time, I might get pregnant, but the baby might be Anthony instead of Anne. And as a single parent, I don't feel that I can have a string of babies. I just have this one chance to have the little girl I've always wanted."

What he wanted to do was fold his arms around her and say, "Why does someone as beautiful, as desirable as you think she has just one chance? The world has to be full of men who'd like to have a string of babies with you, and one of those men is right here, right now.''

But he couldn't say that. He had no reason to believe she could find everlasting romance with anybody as dull, as ordinary as he was, even though he'd begun to realize he wasn't as dull and ordinary as he'd thought. A smile teased at the corners of his mouth as he thought about the crazy weekend he'd survived—and had to admit he'd enjoyed.

Still, those old tapes from childhood were playing loud and clear through his head, and he knew he couldn't be happy if he didn't do things in the right order. At this very moment Francine might be deciding to forgive him. Cleo's blasted temperature chart had given him a window for making sure Francine understood that their relationship was over before he tried to convince Cleo that she might like something about him besides his great genes.

The way he was going to convince her was to love her as she'd never been loved before. When he'd finished, she wouldn't think of him as dull and ordinary anymore, and she wouldn't be able to handle the concept of ''just once'' any better than he could.

If he did succeed in convincing her, he ought to take her to meet his parents, and his parents ought to meet Cleo's parents. That prospect cooled his boiling ardor to a simmer, which, on reflection, was a good thing.

''I suppose I should go home, then,'' he said, trying not to gnash his teeth, ''and wait for your call.'' He hesitated. ''The timing's such a hair-trigger thing, I'm going to give you my cell-phone number. You call, I go straight to the airport and grab the first flight to New York.''

''Go first-class,'' said Cleo. ''My treat.''

He'd pay for the ticket himself, but he wasn't going to argue with her. ''Anything special I should do in the meantime?'' he asked her seriously. ''Eat plenty of protein, maybe?'' He already knew the answers, just as he knew a great deal about plotting the sex of a child, but he wanted to have the pleasure of listening to Cleo talk about this wonderful thing that was about to happen.

She blushed. "Wear, um, boxer shorts," she suggested.

"I already do."

"Nothing snug fitting," she hurried on.

"The jeans go to the back of the closet," he promised.

"And…and…a, um, a buildup in the, you know, the count is a good idea."

He didn't know a dark-haired woman could turn as scarlet as Cleo was at the moment. She was asking him not to have sex with anyone else until their mission was accomplished, as though he could tolerate the idea of having sex with someone else while he felt this way about her.

No need for her to worry anyway. His "count" was already up to about a zillion. Sperm might be small, but a zillion of anything could make an impression, and he realized that his baggy Brooks Brothers boxers suddenly felt snug. Trying not to wriggle himself too noticeably into a more comfortable position inside them, he nodded sagely. "You're right, of course." He sighed. "It won't be easy, but I'll make the sacrifice for your cause."

"One last thing."

"Mmm-hmm?" His mind had taken a dangerous drift off into a daydream of relief from snugness.

"I hate to ask, but would you mind having a blood test?"

As much as he'd put her through in the past few minutes, he thought he could hazard a genuine smile, even risk grasping her chin lightly with two fingers to force her to look up at him. "In my business I'm required to have a blood test every month," he said gently. "I can assure you, Cleo, I have the cleanest, purest blood in the history of mankind."

She smiled back. "Type?"

"O positive."

"Normal, normal, normal," she sighed. "I knew you were perfect the day I picked you out."

He wanted her to expand generously on that statement; he wanted to kiss her, wanted to feel her full, delicious breasts crushed against his chest and to wrap those long, long legs around himself.

Instead, he gave her the cell-phone number, collected his two kittens from under the bed and halfway up a living-room curtain and left for the airport. Any other behavior might threaten his "perfect" status. Considering the way he was planning to sneak up on Cleo's blind side, he was as imperfect as a man could possibly be, but there was no need to disillusion her.

"HE LOOKS NICE," Sandi said doubtfully. "I was spying," she admitted, "when he brought you home."

"He is nice," Delilah said. "He bought a hat for his mother."

"A hat for his mother," Macon said. "What a guy!"

"And a hat for his girlfriend," Cleo pointed out.

"My worst hat," Delilah said.

"Doesn't mean he doesn't love her," Cleo worried. She collapsed backward into the lounge chair, snuggled a mohair throw around herself and looked sadly at her barely touched glass of wine. The Millhouse dog, wearing an expression as depressed as hers, tiptoed across the patio to lay his head across her stomach. The black-and-white kitten, its claws embedded in the throw, hissed.

"If he loves her, don't you think it's sort of strange that he's willing to father your baby?" Deke said.

"He explained his feelings to my satisfaction," said Cleo.

"All she's asking for are a few measly sperm," Sandi protested. "It's not like he's being unfaithful. All he has to do is go to a sperm bank and…" She halted when the patio fell into silence, looking from one set of eyes to another. "Is there something I don't know?"

"The plan has changed—just a little," Cleo said delicately.

"Miss Manners wouldn't want you to ask for details," Macon said.

"I don't want to know the details," Sandi said.

"I'm in a little bit deeper than I meant to be," Cleo said so softly that her tenants all leaned toward her.

"You're in love with him," Sandi breathed.

Cleo rallied. "Who said anything about love?" she scoffed. "I admit I find him attractive. Of course, I always found him attractive, or I wouldn't have asked him to be Anne's father, but he refuses to go to a sperm bank. He insists we make this baby in the usual way."

"Which presents a problem for you because you've fallen in love with him," Delilah said flatly.

"Yep," Cleo said, drawing her knees up to her chest.

"How do you know he's not in love with you?" Sandi said. The possibility of romance shone in her eyes.

"Me? Him? Forget it."

"He got through a weekend with your parents," Macon said, who'd been there.

"Macon!" chorused Sandi, Deke and Delilah. The dog barked, perhaps remembering the talking rooster. The baby burped. They'd all been there.

"Yes, he did," Cleo said. "They adored him, and he was everlastingly polite and understanding, even though Sonia had clearly blocked out that he was deciding whether to impregnate me, not whether to marry me, and he either blew off or cemented his relationship with Whitehall Pharmaceuticals at the country club, I couldn't quite figure out which, and he took two stray kittens home to Atlanta, and Edgar liked him, which is saying a lot, and he gave Sonia some excellent plotting suggestions for Scabiosa, *a Tragic Life,* and sent her three dozen red roses and the most elegant thank-you note, and I have this terrible premonition that Thornton is even now painting a pistachio shell into a tiny womb with a sperm sailing into it and a Nopro pill lurking inside the upper half of the shell like a villain waiting to pounce."

"Should you be drinking that wine?" said Deke.

Cleo gave him a frosty glance. "I'm not pregnant yet."

"Do you take your temperature in the morning or at night?" said Sandi.

"Both," said Cleo. "Constantly. Seventeen times a day. Good night, my friends. I have an appointment to go upstairs and breed. Brood," she corrected herself, scooping up her cat. Her exit from the patio was somewhat less queenly than she had hoped it would be. Had the corner of that brick always stuck up like that, or was Manhattan about to have its big earthquake?

"SURE," MACON SAID, "I can do that without going to jail."

"Good," Cleo said, "because I wouldn't be able to visit you much after Anne is born. Start with the *Atlanta Constitution* society pages. Go on to *W* and *Vogue*."

"I've got the picture," Macon said.

"Then find me one, some," said Cleo. "I need information." She perched on Macon's guest chair to sew fine, perfect stitches into Julia's red silk dress.

"Her name is Francine Ingersoll," he announced a half hour later.

"Is there a photograph?" She hung the dress over Macon's Star Trek poster in order to hover over him.

"Um, yes."

"With Bryce. Let me see it." She gazed at the screen. The blob of black-and-white dots at the right was unmistakably Bryce. She knew from the set of his shoulders, the flash of his smile, from the way he looked down so protectively at the blond, tiny-waisted woman at his side.

She was no more than a girl, but she looked back at him with a woman's knowing gaze. She was dressed in ruffles from slim shoulders to hem. They were probably blue. Cleo skipped quickly to the caption: "'Miss Francine Ingersoll with Dr. Bryce Hampton Jr. at the Plantation Ball.' Why'd you have to show me a picture of them together?" she complained.

"Only way to find out her last name. Now that I've got it, I can search under her name instead of his," said Macon.

"Please do," Cleo said glumly.

"'Francine Denman Ingersoll was escorted by Bryce Maynard Hampton Jr.'"

"'Francine Ingersoll and Bryce Hampton Jr. enjoying a slow dance at...'"

"I thought you were searching under her name," Cleo snapped.

"I am."

"Okay. Keep going. I guess."

"'Francine Ingersoll and Bryce Hampton Jr. attended the...'"

"'Rotarians Bryce Hampton and Fred Foxworthy with Francine Ingersoll—'"

Francine was real. Francine and Bryce really were a couple. The problem was a real one. For a few minutes Cleo brooded. "What are the dates on all these pictures and mentions?"

"Last three years, and the latest one's a couple of months ago."

Cleo brooded some more, examining the implications of this information. "See if you can find something more recent."

"Why? Wouldn't you be tickled pink if he'd stopped seeing her?"

Cleo fell silent. "No," she said at last. "I promised him that my project wouldn't affect his relationship with her."

Macon searched. "Last one's still a couple of months ago."

"Curses." Cleo puffed out a breath of air. "Now do a deep search on her. Starting with her birth certificate."

"Here's where it gets semi-illegal," Macon protested.

"I have to know if she's right for him."

"I won't do it," Macon said. "Are you trying to get me out of this apartment? Then say the word. I'll move. No need to send me to jail."

"Don't be silly," Cleo said. "What would I do without you? In fact, do this for me and next month's rent is free."

Macon's hands quivered on the keyboard. "Free rent?"

Cleo had her answer a day later. All the evidence indicated that Francine Ingersoll was the perfect wife for Bryce Maynard Hampton Jr.

"YOUR MAMA AND I," Francine said, "have decided that you're having a little case of prewedding nerves. That's what all this silly stuff is about, wanting to move north, and meeting that crazy woman who wants you to be the father of her baby. And, for heaven's sake, buying a seat on the plane for those two cats." She stared at the kittens, who were systematically turning a copy of *Southern Living* into papier-mâché. "It's just not like you, Bryce, but I'll be here for you, darling, when you're yourself again."

"I used frequent-flyer miles for the cats," Bryce muttered, struggling to control his irritability. For almost three weeks he'd been trying to convince Francine that he was going to take the job with Whitehall Pharmaceuticals. For three weeks he'd said in the politest, kindest way that she needn't worry about going with him because she wasn't invited. And she still didn't get it. Each time she called and asked to see him he said no, but each time she somehow managed to track him down.

On the sunny Saturday morning before Thanksgiving, she'd tracked him down at his mother's house where he was having a go at her stopped-up disposer. Bryce suspected collusion between them. He'd found a quarter in the disposer; his mother would have made do with a penny. All right, if he had to, he'd go over it one more time. He put down the wrench.

"It's not prewedding nerves. We are not in a prewedding mode here. What I'm trying to tell you is how very sorry I am that there won't be a wedding, at least not for you and me. I deeply regret this, truly I do. I hate hurting you."

"And you're not going to, honey," Francine said sweetly. "We just have to wait for this thing to pass. It will, I know, in time. I do wish," she said plaintively, "you would glance at a few china patterns with me while we're waiting."

If he didn't stop grinding his teeth they'd soon be too dull to chew meat. "We don't need to look at china patterns together, Francine, because we are not going to spend our lives eating off the same china. You and some wonderful man who deserves you far more than I do are going to eat off one pattern of china while I am eating off another." He picked up the wrench again, needing something to brandish. "Hell, I may decide to eat off paper plates, but whatever I'm eating off, it will be in a different dining room, in a different city. Therefore, Francine, I have no vested interest in your china selection. You may choose whatever china appeals to you, although it would be thoughtful of you to wait for that wonderful man I referred to earlier, the one who deserves you far more than I, to help you choose."

It was a good thing his cell phone rang. He had a feeling he was about to go over the edge. "Hello," he said abruptly.

"It's time," said a familiar, warm, throaty voice.

The wrench clanged to the tiled floor. "Be there in a jiffy," he said hoarsely.

"Trouble at the lab?" Francine said, picking at an incipient hangnail.

"No," said Bryce, "I'm going to New York."

"But why?" Francine asked, her eyes very wide.

He'd told her everything, about the baby and his ambivalent feelings about Cleo, a hundred times already. Now he looked her squarely in the face. "I am going to New York to fertilize an egg with an X chromosome," he said.

"Oh, Bryce," she said comfortably, "can't you think about anything but work?"

Her silvery voice followed him all the way to his car, where he'd kept a bag packed for the entire three weeks, just the way an expectant father might when the time drew near to take his wife to the hospital. Except that there were a few things in the bag that no expectant mother would be caught dead in.

10

"INTO THE CAR," Delilah yelled. She held the leash of the Millhouse dog and seemed ready to use it to whip the rest of the tenants into submission.

A limousine that resembled Moby Dick waited in front of Number Seven. Cleo did a double take at the sight of it. "What's going on, Delilah? Where are you taking everybody?"

"To the beach house," Delilah said. "Sandi, Deke, get yourselves down here on the double!"

"But why?" Cleo said. Delilah's "cottage" in Easthampton, a spacious house she'd obtained by plying her trade and taking stock tips offered by her grateful clients, was a delightful place to spend the weekend, but it was cold today. The wind coming off Long Island Sound would be fierce, and freezing rain was predicted.

"I don't want you sitting around wondering if we're sitting around wondering. Macon," Delilah shouted, "what are you doing up there?"

"Making backup disks," Macon yelled from the fifth floor. "I can't leave without my work."

"Oh, these people," Delilah muttered. "Sandi, Deke, what's the problem?"

"We can't go. We don't have enough Pampers," Sandi said, materializing at Delilah's shoulder with enough equipment hung over her shoulders to stage a "How to Care for Baby" workshop.

"For heaven's sake, they sell Pampers in the Hamptons," Delilah snapped. "Let's get this show on the road!"

As if by magic, Deke appeared, more heavily burdened than Sandi and carrying the baby to boot. Behind him, Macon struggled with a laptop, a printer, a scanner and a briefcase that undoubtedly held the precious backup disks and one change of underwear and socks.

As one, they directed a last "rescue us" glance at Cleo, then piled into the waiting limousine and sped away. She was alone, waiting for the man who would father her baby, the man she wished could be hers forever, who had the wife-elect of his dreams waiting at home in Atlanta, but who had a scientific interest in improving the Rose family gene pool.

She was in a state. She hadn't been able to find anything to guide her through the uncharted seas she was soon to go bounding, lurching, tumbling across.

Scratch "bounding, lurching, tumbling." Substitute "gliding unemotionally."

There were books to tell you how to welcome the man of your dreams for a night of blissful love, books that told you how to shoo the man away forever. But the freelance writers of the world had not seized on the chance to write books, magazine articles or pamphlets on what to wear, how to look, how to behave, when you'd just summoned your sperm donor to heed the call of your thermometer.

So there was certainly nothing to tell you what to do when you were madly in love with your sperm donor.

When this was over, while little Anne peacefully napped, she'd write the book. By then, she'd be an expert on the subject. In the meantime, a crisis of this order called for extraordinary creativity.

"SORRY ABOUT THE DELAY," Bryce said, hauling the cat kennel through the door to Cleo's apartment. He unlatched the door, and the kittens raced out to consult Cleo's cat about possible damage they could do.

"Don't apologize for the weather," Cleo said. "I'm just glad you landed safely." She gave him a gracious, hostessy smile. "Let's have dinner first, shall we? It's so difficult to do business on an empty stomach. The kittens do seem delighted to see each other again, don't they?"

Bryce blinked. He was still in his disposer-repair ensemble, consisting of a baggy pair of khaki trousers that he'd combined with a black turtleneck sweater and topped with the black leather jacket he'd been storing in the car for the cooler northern weather. Here stood a man who, with his yowling seatmates, had narrowly escaped death from the icy rain and hail that buffeted the plane from Tennessee northward, all for the sake of Cleo's temperature. At last he was on solid ground and eager for a night of love. Instead, she was offering dinner, and none too warmly.

"Dinner," he said uncertainly. "Great."

"Do you prefer Thai or Indian?" Cleo asked.

"I like both," Bryce said.

"Then we'll have both," Cleo said.

Her long, long legs were encased in black leggings, and her fuzzy, cropped sweater was a rusty brown that matched her lips and fingernails. Once upon a time the look would have turned him off; now it was having the opposite effect. Regally she escorted him to the dining table, which was set for two. No wineglasses, no candles. In the center of the table was a high-tech food warmer covered with take-out cartons. It was not a romantic scene.

"Honey, you cooked." It came out drier than he'd intended, because his mouth had gone dry at the very sight of Cleo, even though she'd clearly decided the evening was to be strictly business. Okay, he was prepared for that. He pulled out the chair at the head of the table, gestured Cleo into it and pushed her forward, letting his hands brush the crisp silk of her hair, the softness of her sweater.

"Rice?" Her voice squeaked. So she wasn't quite as calm as she pretended to be.

"Yes, thank you."

"Chicken Tikka Masala?"

"One of my favorites."

"Pad Thai?"

It was going to be an interesting dinner. "Absolutely."

"Nan?" She held out the basket of warm, puffy bread.

"Why stop now?"

"And mint chutney. Let's hold off on the lamb and the Thai beef salad until our plates aren't so full."

"Good idea," he complimented her.

"Do you like green-tea ice cream?"

"Very much."

"Save room for it, then."

Bryce smiled. "Maybe we could have dessert...later."

Her glance shot in his direction, then boomeranged back to her plate. The look he'd seen in her eyes was pure terror. What could she be so afraid of? This whole thing had been her idea.

CLEO WONDERED if prayer would be irreverent. Her senses were so keenly tuned that she'd heard the taxi, heard the door slam, heard Bryce's footsteps on the sidewalk and was already in a state of emotional waste when he rang her buzzer from the entryway below. She had to splash her face with cold water before she opened the door to him, wishing she had time for a cold shower. And all that had happened before she even laid eyes on him.

She couldn't allow herself to feel this way about a man who had already picked out the perfect mate. If she couldn't control her feelings, she'd better do a good job of controlling her reactions to him. It would be humiliating if he discovered she had breached their contract by falling madly in love with him.

So while dinner was culinary chaos, her clothes uninviting and her attitude cool, inside she was a frothing mass of torment. He couldn't possibly have meant to look so sexy. He couldn't know how gracefully his shoulders moved when he shrugged out of his jacket, how his muscles rippled beneath the black turtleneck sweater. Well, she knew, and it wasn't making it any easier for her to stay cool.

"May I serve you some lamb?" Bryce inquired. "Looks like lamb with garlic sauce. And I'm ready for some beef salad. How about you?"

"Um, yes, thanks." She hadn't touched her Pad Thai yet, but what the heck. Anything to postpone the moment Bryce would touch her and she would dissolve into a mass of pure sensation, giving herself completely away. Unfortunately the moment couldn't be postponed forever. In fact, not long at all.

"How are we going to go about this?" she asked him formally.

"In the usual way, I guess."

"All right. We'll take off the minimum number of clothes, and get into bed, and then..."

Bryce put down his fork. "Begin the foreplay," he said, matching her tone. "But I think there should be some kissing before we get into bed, kind of a warm-up."

"I don't see why there needs to be kissing or any other kind of foreplay," Cleo said, sweating. "It won't add anything to the likelihood of getting me pregnant. And one theory suggests that if I, um—" her face felt so hot, she knew she was blushing "—ah, enjoy the act too much, it might actually diminish the possibility of the baby being a girl." She studied his face; he didn't seem to like what he was hearing.

"I've done some reading on that theory," said Bryce. He tore off a ragged piece of nan and heaped mint chutney on it. "But if you expect me to perform—I mean, it's not all that easy to perform on command," he added, looking aggrieved. "The pleasure aspect is pretty important."

"Of course, of course," Cleo said hastily before he could heat her up any further by supplying details. "We'll make it possible for you to…I mean, we'll do just enough that you can…"

"I have to warn you," Bryce said, hanging his head as though he were embarrassed, "that the trip here was really frightening. I'm tired and stressed-out from work. We may have to do a lot of kissing and…whatnot." He looked up. "The success of your project depends on it."

Streetlamps illuminated the rain that poured incessantly down the long windows of the apartment. Suddenly cold, Cleo gulped. Even a moment of foreplay and he'd feel the hardness of her nipples, the wetness that already dampened her thighs, and he'd know. Still, he was right. If he didn't want to make love to her, he wouldn't be able to, and if he couldn't, then no baby Anne, after all the time and trouble Cleo had invested in her conception. "We'll do what we can," she murmured.

"And I'm sure we'll succeed," he said politely. He glanced toward the sofa in the living room beyond. "Look at those guys," he said. The kittens lay in a pile of black and white, tabby gray and calico on a down-filled cushion. "Talk about stressed! They're out for the night," he commented. "Let's get started."

BRYCE HUMMED happily to himself while he slapped take-out cartons into Cleo's refrigerator. He was touched to find the makings of breakfast—cream cheese, smoked salmon, fruit and orange juice to go along with the bag of bagels on the counter. At least she planned to let him spend the night. In a few hours he hoped she would want him to spend the night, would lose that gleam of terror in her eyes.

His smile faded. Things were going fine so far, but the hardest part was ahead of him. He had to convince Cleo that it was up to her to arouse him. Glancing down at the front of his trousers, he reflected that a bulge beneath tight jeans was a heck of a lot easier to hide than the cantilevered effect of his present state inside the baggy khakis and paisley silk boxer shorts that were an aphrodisiac in themselves. He closed his eyes and imagined himself swimming off the coast of Maine, the bite of the icy water, the gradual numbing of his feet, his ankles, his calves, his thighs, his...

"Bryce, what is it?"

His eyes shot open. The coast of Maine had helped, but he was thinking he'd better move his mind even further north. "Cleo," he said, and uncertain as to how to hide his physical condition, he pulled her to him—almost. From several inches above her he gazed down into her startled eyes, then touched her full, inviting mouth with his. The forbidding glaciers of Greenland faded into the background as the warmth of her swelled through him, but of course she couldn't know what he was thinking, what his uncertainty was all about. Her lashes flickered. With an expression of complete understanding, she lifted her hands to the nape of his neck and caressed him lightly, sending shock waves deep into his spinal column, then pulled his mouth down to hers.

He was a goner, Bryce thought morosely as he steeled himself against the siren call of her kiss. Her lips roamed over his, tasting, sampling, nipping, before she pulled him tighter and nudged her tongue into his mouth. He quashed the moan that threatened to rise from his throat, instead tightening his arms around her, almost for support. Their tongues touched, converged, tangled sweetly, and the kiss deepened. Cleo leaned into him; he felt her jolt of surprise as their bodies merged.

The feeling was all too delicious. He was giving himself away. Desperately he imagined himself sliding down a glacier on his stomach, wearing nothing but the silk boxers. Unsatisfied with the result of this vision, he reduced the imaginary temperature from twenty below zero to sixty below. It gave him time to slip his hands down her back, to snuggle them into the fuzzy brown sweater, searching for the fine, sharp bones he knew lay beneath it, relishing the way her back tapered down to her long waist, the way her hips flared.

Her hips were no longer beneath his hands. "I think that's enough kissing, don't you?" Cleo asked.

She sounded breathless and her lips were swollen, her eyes heavy. It gave him hope. She couldn't make his blood boil without heating up her own. "It felt very good," he said, biting his lower lip. "We're not quite there yet, but I think after another kiss or two we can call the kissing part finished."

He recaptured her mouth, explored it, probed it. Her eyelids drifted shut; her body felt weightless against his. Slowly his hands moved down to the hem of the sweater and slipped inside it, pushing it above her waist. Still kissing him, she inhaled sharply when his fingers touched her silk-velvet skin, outlining her waist and sliding up her ribs. When his thumbs slid beneath her bra to brush the swell of her breasts, a soft "Oh!" escaped her lips.

For a moment he slid his mouth to her cheek and spoke softly. "I'm not asking too much, am I? If this is going to work, I'm afraid I'll have to touch you...here..." His fingers edged slowly forward, more deeply into the swell. She moaned. "And here..." His fingertips brushed her nipples. They were shockingly hard in contrast to the softness of her breasts. Blood throbbed through his veins as he imagined kissing them, licking, nibbling at them. His hands slid down her hips to cup her bottom. "And here." He brought her tight against him.

"I know, I know," she whispered, almost in a sob, "but don't you think you've touched me enough for now?"

"Afraid not," he murmured back, his voice rough with

rapidly rising need. "We want to be sure, don't we?"

"Yes," she said, but it sounded like a groan.

IF HE TOUCHED HER BREASTS again, if he slid his hands beneath her buttocks again and squeezed ever so gently, the way he had just done, she would explode with the desire that raged inside her.

"Maybe if we went to my bedroom and turned out the lights," she suggested, barely holding her voice together, "it wouldn't seem so personal."

"What a great idea," he said. "The bedroom, I mean. Not the lights. I can't, um—" he turned embarrassed again "—cooperate if it's too impersonal."

It was suddenly too much for her to handle. She wasn't that naive. When he'd crushed her against himself, she'd gained the impression that he was as ready to "cooperate" as she was. Her tautly stretched nerves snapped. "Well, try," she snapped. "Give it a go."

"You're yelling at me." His eyes, big and night-sky-blue, widened. "I sure can't do my part if you're yelling at me."

"Oh, Bryce, I'm sorry," she said. Instantly contrite, she went to him and folded her arms around him. "It's just that I'm so tense and nervous, and I want so badly for everything to go just right."

He drew back and gazed at her, his expression serious. "Tension is the single greatest impediment to getting pregnant. Surely you know that."

"I thought it was an old wives' tale."

"Uh-uh. It's a documented fact."

She gave him a good, hard look. Something in his voice made her suspicious.

"And lack of trust," he added, his face the perfect image of one unjustly accused. "You trust me, don't you, Cleo? You know I won't hurt you."

She gazed at the blond, blue-eyed, all-American guy

she'd chosen to father her little girl and gave in, sighing deeply. "I know."

"Then let's get you relaxed," he said. He led her to the bedroom, stopping to pick up the small bag he'd brought with him, and once there, he dived into it.

"Get into this," he said, looking shy.

In pure shock, Cleo eyed the garment he was holding out to her. One thing was certain: it hadn't added a lot of weight to his suitcase. It was a short gown, a very short gown, black and as sheer as plastic wrap except for a wide strip of lace around the midriff. Tiny slip straps crossed the shoulders. "Isn't it a two-piece set?" she asked him, her mouth dry.

"Yes." He smiled gently at her and handed over a robe that was just as short. It was trimmed in lace in the places she wouldn't have minded showing, like her wrists, and otherwise even sheerer than the gown.

"I meant, didn't it come with...?"

"Panties?"

As the word left his mouth she felt the wetness between her thighs increase. She wanted to sit down somewhere, anywhere but the bed! "Yes," she whispered.

"No, this is it." He smiled again, the happy smile of a man who has presented a gift he knows the recipient will love.

"It didn't come in tall sizes?" she squeaked.

"One size fits all."

All who were five feet tall or shorter! On her, this ensemble left nothing to the imagination.

"It would help," he said, "if I could watch you put it on." He lay on the bed, his head propped on his elbow, watching her with an expression of great interest.

Cleo stifled her gasp. "Oh, no, I really don't think I can."

"You want this baby, don't you?"

Didn't he sound sort of snappish for a man who had

openly admitted his need for sexual stimulation? But, of course, his condition must be embarrassing to him. The Bryce Hampton she knew would hate feeling so vulnerable. "Yes," she said, softening her voice, "I do want this baby." *And I also want you, darn it.*

"Timing is everything, right? Well, I'm tired from the trip, and I've really been obsessing on work recently, and I shouldn't have eaten so much." He yawned.

"Okay, okay," Cleo said hastily. "I'll put it on."

His eyes followed her every move. First she unhooked her bra, and feeling her breasts fall free, knowing he would soon be touching them again, sent a rush of blood to her most secret place, another place he might want to touch. *Get on with it. Get the damn nightie over your head and try to act like you're dressed!*

In one swift gesture she slid out of the sweater and bra and into the indecently short nightgown. She gritted her teeth, then stepped out of her leggings and socks. "All set," she said cheerfully, hearing her voice crack, feeling her knees buckle.

"Lie down," he said, rolling up from the bed to fling back the coverlet and top sheet.

Cleo took tiny steps toward the bed, flattened herself against the sheet and tugged ineffectually at the nightie, trying to pull it down over herself.

"Turn over."

The voice above her was warm, compelling. She turned over, taking as much of the nightgown with her as she could, tugging again to stretch it over her bottom. *Anne,* she thought, *if only you could know what I went through to have you.*

And then his hands were on her and she couldn't think anymore. Warm and slick with scented oil that must have been in his overnight bag, they kneaded her neck, her shoulders; they skidded down her spine, digging at the vertabrae, not stopping until they'd reached the last, supersensitive one in the cleft between her buttocks. He worked his way back up again, moving out from her spine, playing chords across her back until his fingers curved beneath her to meet the soft skin of her breasts. And then slid down and down, stroking her in the very way she had known would be her undoing. When she thought she couldn't bear anymore, she felt his mouth at her neck, at the middle of her back, at that supersensitive spot and moving back up again.

She was melting, dissolving under those fingers, under that mouth. She wriggled, turning herself over, finding his lips on her throat and sliding, sliding.

When his mouth closed around a peaked, throbbing nipple, she cried out. But his exquisite torture was only beginning. He sucked at it, nibbled at it, licked at it until she wanted to cry with pleasure, then moved on to the other one, reducing her to a half-gallon carton of melting ice cream.

"I feel, ah, fairly relaxed now." Her voice shook. "How about you?"

"Pretty close," he said. "Not quite."

Was she imagining it, or did his voice shake like hers? His mouth felt firm enough as it continued its slide down her breastbone, over her navel, where it paused to lick maddeningly inside, and down, down.

She couldn't stand any more. "Really," she said, trying for a semblance of calmness, "I think this is going too far. I mean, you don't need to..."

It was too late. His tongue had found the secret she'd hidden for these many years, was plundering it as though he'd known the secret for centuries. She couldn't resist any longer. She wanted it; she wanted him. Feeling naked in the gown he had brought to her, every inch of her skin felt him, touched him back, needed him.

Oh, it went so much further than need! She had to have

what he was giving her, demanded the gift, arched her body toward it, bucked against it. And he was always there, always there, always.

Cleo arched her body one last time and screamed.

11

HE HELD HER while her deep, sobbing breaths subsided, brushing light kisses over her forehead, her cheeks, her earlobes. His hand caressed her thigh, never getting very far from her still throbbing center. In fact, Cleo thought hopelessly, the throbbing was picking up rather than diminishing. She felt herself edging his hand toward that secret place, toward more pleasure.

It had to stop! This was no way to do business!

"I am definitely relaxed now," she said. She'd been determined to say it coldly, but somehow her voice didn't even come out room temperature.

"I know." The words were a soft puff of air against her cheek, but he didn't stop touching her, circling, pressing.

She shivered. "You probably blew my chances of having a girl." On reflection, she wished she'd chosen her words more carefully.

"*Au contraire,*" he drawled. "Now that the pleasure part is out of the way, you can test your nonpleasure theory."

She hadn't looked at it that way. "So for the next part of the evening, we can concentrate on you?"

"Well, not entirely..."

She'd feel more comfortable if he didn't look so smug. She'd feel more comfortable if certain parts of her felt more comfortable, less as though they'd like to repeat everything that just happened, over, and over, and over.

Get to the point! "Next," she said severely, "you take off your clothes."

When it came to his own body, he was unusually modest for a man who had just done to her what he had done without reserve, without a hint of shyness or embarrassment. The way he skimmed out of his shirt and trousers with his back toward her, then slid facedown onto the sheets—something about it was incongruous.

Oh, well, Cleo thought as he at last lay waiting for her tender ministrations, *we all have our little neuroses.*

All of us except Bryce. Bryce does not have any neuroses. Fear of a woman who's demanding that he father her child does not qualify as a neurosis. It's a normal reaction.

She straddled him, her own center heating up again on contact with his lightly furred thighs. She stroked his ears, the back of his neck, his broad shoulders, the width of his back with butterfly touches. She felt him wriggle; she heard him groan. As her desire for him grew, so did her suspicion.

"I think that's enough, don't you?" she asked him, keeping her voice soft.

He mumbled something unintelligible. She heard, "trip," and "work" and "tired." But he didn't feel tired beneath her hands. He felt hot and edgy, as hot and edgy as she felt moving against him.

She increased the pressure of her fingers on his spine, remembering what he had done to her and repeating it, running her fingernails across the tight, hard muscles of his buttocks. He jolted upward, catching her by surprise. Before she could stop herself, she was moving hotly against him. He turned to her, fully ready for her as she suspected he had been for some time, but she couldn't resist the demands of her body. He rocked her against him, harder and harder, until the ache in her loins became an uncontrollable surge that flew upward through her entire being, shattering her into a million pieces.

She collapsed against him, feeling his arms surround her, felt him still hot and swollen beneath her, felt herself starting to move against that source of pleasure again, and suddenly, painfully, brought herself to a halt.

He'd been ready for her ages ago. They could have had this whole project over and done with in the kitchen, before she ever put on this enticing little black number, before she submitted her body to his arousing touch. He'd taken off his clothes so modestly in order to hide his arousal from her a little bit longer. Deep inside she had known he was playing her along, but she hadn't spoken up because of all she'd heard about the delicate male ego and how easily it could be deflated.

Deflating was not, at the moment, in her best interests.

So she'd believed him when he said he needed more kissing, more touching, when in fact he'd been playing for time to bring pleasure to her.

But why? She could think of a couple of reasons. That delicate male ego, for one. He'd wanted to prove that he was irresistible. But that wasn't like Bryce. It was more likely that with his logical, scientific way of thinking, he'd decided to prove that she couldn't conceive a baby as logically, as scientifically, as unemotionally as she'd intended to. With any luck he'd never find out that it was her love for him that had sabotaged her.

The other possible reason... No. Surely it wasn't possible that he'd come to care about her, too. She couldn't let it happen! She wasn't right for him; Francine was. She'd promised him that all he had to give her was this one chance to have a baby!

She had to deny herself, reject the thing she wanted most at this moment, just to get their relationship back on a businesslike footing. She gritted her teeth, resisting the way his arms were pulling her closer, closer to the source of even greater pleasure than she'd already experienced, trying not to look at the long, muscular, infinitely desirable body that was hers for the taking. He didn't love her; she had merely distracted him from the cool little blonde who would someday put on her blue angora hat and throw snowballs at him in suburban New Jersey. She had to call a halt to all this unnecessary lovemaking.

Bryce, my darling, this is going to hurt me far more than it's going to hurt you. She glanced at the bedside clock. "Darn it," she said. "Time's up."

"WHAT?" HE WAS HARD and throbbing, the ache for her so intense he thought he would burst. The words "Time's up" didn't make sense. Nothing logical was going on in his left brain, nothing creative in his right. All of his cells were busy in another part of his body.

But when she pushed at him, he got the message and complied with it, easing himself away from her. Collapsed on the bed, he clutched a pillow to the most telltale section of his body and waited for the ax to fall.

"My window for conceiving a baby girl just closed," she said regretfully. "We're at the thirty-six-hour-before-ovulation point. If we have intercourse now, I run the risk of having a boy."

"You won't be taking a risk," he said, reaching for her. "I brought protection, just in case this happened."

"Why would we need protection?" she asked him. "The whole idea was to make me pregnant. This was a business deal, remember?"

Where did he ever get the idea she was illogical? "Of course," he said, wishing for a bridge to leap off. "Just a business deal. Once. But not anymore." He tightened his hold on her. She wanted him. He wanted her. It was time to tell her that his feelings for her had gone way beyond business.

"We need a high sperm count, remember?" she said. She sounded quavery, even desperate. She flung herself away from him, rolled off the bed and almost plunged into a thick white terry-cloth robe, tying the sash into a knot so tight she'd probably have to cut herself loose. "If you're still willing, we'll have to wait another month to conceive Anne. For this particular cycle, the right time has passed.''

"Wait until *Christmas?*" He knew he sounded like a six-year-old who was pretty sure his present was going to be a bike.

"If we're lucky," she said, her voice firming up a little, "we'll have you back home in Atlanta in time for Christmas. With Francine."

He didn't want to have Christmas with Francine. He would not have Christmas with Francine. Cleo knew quite well what he wanted to say to her, but she didn't want to hear it.

"Tell you what I'll do," she said, turning her back to him and busying herself with a hairbrush. "I'll keep your cats for you until the next window of opportunity. They must be getting tired of this jet-set life."

"Thank you," said Bryce. He wanted to hit something. She knew how desperately he wanted her, and he'd been ready to tell her he loved her. Now she had frozen the words on his tongue more effectively than any damn glacier in Greenland. It was clear that she didn't love him. She'd been honest from the start; all she wanted from him was a baby.

"I DON'T KNOW how long I can wait to tell Herb the truth," said Julia. "It's killing my conscience. He's the guy who pays for gorgeous dresses like this."

Cleo observed that Julia took a minute out from her conscience attack to scan the mirrored walls, admiring herself in the slim column of scarlet silk. "It's your fault for figuring out the truth," she muttered.

"I couldn't help it, darling," Julia said kindly. "You're as transparent as my new nightgown. I knew as soon as I heard the sperm-donor story that it was true. And I've never lied to Herb before," she fretted. "Maybe I've fudged about what this or that cost, but not about anything important. Gosh, I do love this petaled hemline. I've never seen anything like it.''

"That's what custom clothes are all about," Cleo said, still muttering. But she sat back on her heels and gazed up at Julia. "I am truly sorry I got you into all this, Julia," she said disconsolately.

"I wouldn't have missed it for the world," Julia exclaimed. "Two marvelous dresses and a real-life drama. In fact, the truth is so tangled I don't know how to explain it to Herb. It was a baby you wanted from Bryce, not a chance to knit a blue angora dress. We find Bryce naked in a hotel bed, but you weren't in it with him because he's going with a girl in Atlanta, not with you. He's just having a baby with you." Julia sighed. "What's bothering me is that he told Herb, you know, that night when we went to dinner at your country club with the Braithewaites—"

How could she ever forget it?

"—that the next time Bryce saw him he'd have everything under control. Herb needn't worry about him being a sperm donor to a single woman. Now, that means Bryce lied, and I can't imagine Bryce lying. I dragged Herb onto the dance floor before Bryce could dig himself in any deeper."

Cleo couldn't imagine Bryce lying, either. She and Bryce had such a strange relationship—a strange nonrelationship, she reminded herself—that he hadn't told her about his conversation with Herb or any of the things people in love told each other...because he wasn't in love with her. Sure, he'd gotten a little carried away that night. What red-blooded man wouldn't? But he didn't love her. *Oh, Lord, no, I'm going to cry again.* She made a dive at Julia's hemline, and froze in the middle of one of the petals.

Bryce was definitely not a liar, and yet he'd told Herb he needn't worry about him embarrassing the company by being a sperm donor to a single woman. So what had he meant?

Did he mean he meant to *marry* her out of some over-developed sense of responsibility? But he couldn't! He didn't love her! He wouldn't be happy with her. The problem was worse than ever. She had to convince him to go on with his plan to marry Francine!

And she had to convince Julia not to destroy Bryce's career. She got her tears under control, stuck in a few pins and said, "Has Herb seen Bryce again?"

"Well, no."

"So it's not a lie yet," said Cleo. "You don't need to tell Herb anything."

"I hadn't thought about it from that angle," Julia mused.

"But now you have," Cleo said firmly. "I'm sure Bryce will be able to explain everything. Just think what Herb might do if you told him." She resumed work on the hem. "Would he cancel the contract to buy Nopro?"

"Oh, no," said Julia. "It's only…"

"He'd change his mind about hiring Bryce?" *And it would be my fault!*

"That's a stronger possibility," Julia admitted.

"Bryce would be very upset," Cleo said. "Of course, it would make things easier for him with Francine." He had to marry Francine. If he didn't, she'd feel guilty for the rest of her life.

"Cleo…"

"Mmm?" Cleo had pins in her mouth again.

"Are you sure he wants to marry this Francine person?"

Cleo took out all the pins. "I'm sure he should," she said firmly, "and I'm determined to see that he does."

"How can you possibly know? All you know about her is from the society pages. How do you know what she's really like?"

"I know enough," Cleo insisted. "She's like Bryce, well brought up and normal, not clumsy and ditsy like me, and he deserves…"

"Cleo," Julia said gently, "do you realize you haven't stuck a single pin in me this entire fitting?

"SO WHEN'S THE WEDDING?" Herb Hardy's voice boomed out.

Bryce flipped the phone in the air, caught it and spoke, trying not to sound breathless. He'd been unusually clumsy lately. Must be tension. "The wedding?"

"To Francine Ingersoll! Just making sure you don't leave us off the invitation list," Hardy said genially. "Getting down to business, how close are you to wrapping things up down there? We're pretty anxious to put Nopro on the market."

Bryce was all too ready to get down to business. "I'm looking at May," he said. Then he'd have to tell Hardy the truth. He hoped like hell it would be that he'd been the sperm donor to a *married* woman, Cleo, his wife.

It made him feel very tired to realize that he still hadn't convinced Francine he wasn't going to marry her. The next day they had yet another frustrating conversation.

"How long is it going to take you to get over this nonsense?" she raged at him.

Forever.

"When can we start talking about the wedding?" she demanded to know. "People are asking! Every time I show up at another function with Boxer I feel them pointing at me, laughing at me."

"Boxer's not a laughing matter," Bryce protested. "He's rich and good-looking."

"I know that," Francine said furiously, "but he's not the man everyone expected me to marry!"

Bryce sighed, trying to find a comfortable position on the wicker chair on Francine's mother's sunporch, the frigid December temperature—sixty degrees—having driven Francine's delicate constitution inside. Thank God he wouldn't have to introduce her to winter in New Jersey.

Now he just had to convince her he wouldn't be spending the winters with her in Atlanta.

Then he had to convince Cleo that they should spend their winters, and springs and summers and falls, together. And he'd thought selling Nopro was hard!

IT WAS UNUSUAL for his family to gather for dinner on any occasion except the major holidays. Getting together for dinner meant that his sister, Rebecca, and her husband, Raiford, would have to drive in from a distant suburb with their two perfect children, Ray Jr. and Becky. It forced Aunt Moira to go out alone at night, which she was not reluctant to inform them she hated doing. It necessitated asking Lucy, the longtime family housekeeper and cook, to stay late; Lucy was no more reluctant than Aunt Moira to state her strong preference against doing this. Nonetheless, here they all were on a week night in December, much too close to Christmas, when they would get together again at the appropriate hour of 2:00 p.m. Bryce thought he was probably responsible for this aberration in their behavior.

"Bryce, darlin'," Rebecca drawled just before dessert, "whenever in the world are you going to break down and give Francine a ring?"

"Yes, honey," his mother chimed in. "We've been waitin' for years!" Her blond hair shone in the light from the chandelier. She'd just come from the beauty shop; it was blonder than it had been this morning, and teased out into a perfect, laminated mushroom.

"Rebecca, Mother, Father, Aunt Moira," Bryce said in his most formal tone, "and Raiford, I've told all of you that Francine and I are not getting married."

"But we know you don't mean it," Rebecca cried. "I know, you told us all about that woman in New York you're interested in, but Bryce, you can't really…"

"She's not 'that woman,'" said Bryce. "Her name is Cleo Rose."

"Whatever," his mother said. She looked at him fondly. "You're just going through a phase."

"I'm thirty-five years old, Mother," Bryce said. "It's not a phase."

"It most certainly is," she exclaimed. "Why, you and Francine are the perfect couple. Her mama and I knew it right off. You're just a little nervous about making such a big commitment."

"I was nervous about making a commitment to Francine," Bryce said stubbornly. "I'm not nervous about making a commitment to Cleo." *I'm past ready to make a commitment to Cleo, if she'll only let me.*

"And that's why you're runnin' off to New York," Aunt Moira chided him.

"Cleo?"

"No!" Aunt Moira snapped. "Your fear of makin' a commitment."

"I'd made a decision to move with Nopro even before I met Cleo," Bryce insisted. "And I repeat, I'm not afraid of making a commitment!" He swept his gaze around the table. "I just don't intend to make one to Francine!"

"How could you do this to me?" his mother wailed. "Francine's mama wants to nominate me for president of the Garden Club. And as a former president, she wields so much power! If she gets mad at me I'll never get to be president. I'll never even get to be program chairman!"

"Is there any possibility I was adopted?" Bryce asked.

A snort came from the head of the table. Bryce shot a glance at his father, who had buried his face in a large damask napkin. Good Lord, the man was laughing! "Father," he said, "I've been honest with Francine. I just don't love her!"

"Then don't marry her," said Bryce Maynard Hampton Sr.

"Maynard!" shrieked Bryce's mother.

"Daddy!" shrieked Rebecca.

"Grandpa!" shrieked Ray Jr. and Becky.

"I knew you should have married into a better family, Sarah Louise," said Aunt Moira, the folds of her chin quivering.

Tucked into the breast pocket inside his jacket, Bryce's cell phone rang.

"Second chance," the caller said cryptically.

"It could explode!" Bryce shouted.

"What?" said Cleo.

"I'll be there as fast as I can make it." He looked at his watch. Damn! Could he get a plane this late? "Trouble at the lab," he lied, marveling at how easily the lie had sprung to his lips. "Bye, folks, it's been great."

He felt bad about leaving his father to the lions. He wished he'd taken time to get to know the man better.

12

"YOU'VE GOT TO BE KIDDING," he told the airline ticketing agent an hour later. "No more planes to LaGuardia tonight? Newark? JFK?"

"Nothing until five in the morning." She gave him an aggrieved look. "People don't like planes flying over them all night. They complain. We listen. Airlines have hearts. Want me to book you on the 5:10?"

"Sounds like my only option," said Bryce, subduing a snarl. It wasn't her fault. It wasn't his fault. It wasn't Cleo's fault. It was her damn temperature's fault! When he was sure he wouldn't yell at her about her temperature, he got out his phone and called Cleo. She sounded depressed even before she heard the news.

"Maybe we just ought to forget about it," she said in a small voice.

Forget about it? Give me a break! "No!" Bryce snapped, because his libido was snapping at him. "I mean, no," he said more gently. "We'll give it a try. If nothing else happens, I'll be there in time." *Just in time, just barely in time.* He chewed on his lower lip, listening to Cleo not saying anything. He couldn't bear it if she told him not to come. He couldn't bear it even if she wouldn't let him do anything but cuddle her. What he wanted, what he really wanted, was…

It shocked him each time he thought about it, and he thought about it all the time. He wanted to tell her he loved her, he wanted to marry her and he wanted them to bring up Anne together. He wanted it even more than he wanted to make love with her, and that was saying something.

"If you're sure," Cleo was saying in that same tired-sounding voice. "But I insist on reimbursing you for these tickets. They're costing you a fortune."

"Frequent-flyer miles," he said. "Don't worry about it."

She went on worrying. "I should have said it right up front. 'All expenses paid.' Wonder why I didn't think of it."

Because, my darling, when you think, your mind whirls in big, warm circles of color and pattern. It does not dwell on details. "Get some sleep, Cleo." He tried to tease her. "This time you've got to be relaxed before I get there."

That didn't work. "How are Nell and Little Dorritt?" he asked next. "Are they having fun with Oliver?" It was true he was interested, had wanted to call her every day to see if the kittens were behaving, or if they'd learned any new tricks, but what he really wanted tonight was to hang on to her voice as long as he could.

She seemed to perk up a little. "Oh, they're fine. Cute as can be, but they're really a handful. Are you sure you aren't having second thoughts about taking them? I mean, you'd been through a pretty tough evening already when the kittens came along. A couple of kittens must have seemed like nothing compared with..."

He might have to have new curtains in the dining room, but he was not having second thoughts about Nell and Little Dorritt. They were good practice for fatherhood. "Positive," he said. "I've missed them."

"Really?"

"Really. And whatever you think you owe me in plane fares, I bet I owe you triple in repairs."

She actually laughed a little. "We'll negotiate when you get here," she said. And then there was the silence again. He knew she was wondering if he'd get there in time, and realizing there certainly wouldn't be time for negotiations.

Utterly frustrated by the circumstances, he finally let her go and pondered his choices: take the train back home and sleep for a few restless hours, then start the process all over again, or spend the night in the airport. He chose the airport.

It was not a comfortable night. With his head on an armrest, his knees over the next armrest and his feet resting on a third, he just managed to stretch out on a bank of seats. He had a book to read and work to do. The book was about a man who was getting a divorce and was forced to give up his little girl. Bryce read a page or two, decided that the man was a wimp who deserved everything that was happening to him, got up and put the book into the closest trash can. Settling back into his makeshift bed, he worked at his laptop computer until the battery ran down.

Deprived of amusements, he closed his eyes and willed himself to sleep. Once he got to sleep, the battle was staying asleep. Thoughts of Cleo, of what he was missing at this very minute, of what he so wanted to tell her, kept waking him up. He had reached his deepest sleep when an amplified voice said, "Passenger Hampton, please come to the desk."

Bryce unfolded, grabbed his bag and ran. The plane was boarding; the plane had boarded; he was the last passenger down the ramp. The flight attendant took one look at his face and upgraded him to first-class.

"YOU HAVE TO DO THIS for me, Macon."

"What are you doing in my room? I have a lease, I pay my rent. According to the housing ordinances of the City of New York, this is my home. Go away." After this cogent statement, Macon buried his head under a pillow and went back to sleep.

How could anyone sleep when her heart was breaking? Cleo lifted the pillow, stuck her mouth right up to his ear and said, "Do as I ask and live rent free for a year."

The words must have hit a spot that wasn't sleeping, because Macon slowly rolled over. "Free rent?" he muttered in a sleep-hoarsened voice.

Cleo imagined the vision of a whole new computer system dancing in his head. "Yes. But you've got to wake up and prepare for the job."

Visions of "the job," however, had a negative effect on him. "Be sensible for once, Cleo. I can't do it. Look at me. I'm not…"

"You're actually a very handsome man, Macon," said Cleo, meaning it. "You've identified with the stereotype of the computer dork, that's all. Straighten your shoulders, take off your glasses, make your eyes look sexy instead of staring…you'll be fine. You'll need different clothes," she added on reflection, thinking of Macon's typical outfit—a pair of ill-fitting dress slacks with a nylon seventies-style shirt in a shade like puce. "You have to be convincing. He's a very smart man."

A smart man. A wonderful man. The perfect man. But not my man.

"I can't see without my glasses," Macon protested, bringing her tortured thoughts back to business.

"That's okay. You wouldn't want to be wearing them anyway if he hits you." She had already reached for his bedside phone and was hearing Sandi's voice, sleepy and alarmed. "What do you mean you need some of Deke's clothes? Who is this, anyway? Cleo? For heaven's sake!"

"Hits me?" said Macon. "Wait a minute. Let's talk about this a little."

A shrill voice came up through the elevator shaft. "What's going on here? Are we being robbed?"

"Delilah! Come on up. We need you," Cleo yelled.

None of them approved of what she intended to do, and by the time she got them organized, none of them liked her very much. In fact, she liked herself even less, but she had to do something dramatic, something final. She had to save

Bryce from making the mistake of his lifetime. She loved him too much to do anything else.

WHEN HE APPEARED at her door, she simply reached out and pulled him inside. For a moment they gazed at each other, wordless.

The lights from a tall, magnificently decorated Christmas tree glittered in her eyes. It was midmorning, but she wore a long gown of thin white cotton. It was pretty, soft and feminine. She was ready for him, as he was ready for her. He even had her Christmas present, had been carrying it around with him in his briefcase, just waiting for her call. It was a ring, set with a diamond of exquisite quality, just like Cleo.

"You made it," she said.

"I did my best," he said.

"You always do."

"Do I?" He wanted tender words from her, words that would pave the way to the words he felt spilling out of him, but he knew there wasn't time.

"Yes, and I'm counting on you to do it again," she said. She should have smiled, but the look she gave him was desperate.

It suited his mood perfectly; he felt desperate to hold her, to have all of her. "I intend to," he said, and pulled her close.

THIS TIME THERE WERE NO GAMES. In her darkened room he seized her and devoured her like a starving man. She responded to him fully, too needy to hide the impact his caresses had on her. They clung and held, revealing everything, the hardness, the wetness, the sense of urgency. Each mouth plundered the other; each body sought the other, both seeking and finding what they wanted, the promise of more to come.

He wanted her. It was all she needed to know. He

couldn't be pretending; his desire was too raw, too spontaneous. She would take this gift from him before she sent him back to his real life, the life he was meant to live.

His heart pounded hard with relief and joy. *She can't be faking it. She does want more than my genes. She wants me, the way I want her. When I can think straight I'll tell her I love her, tell her I have to have her, and Anne, and the kind of happiness we can have together as a family, but I can't think now, or speak, or do anything but touch her, feel her against me.*

Clothing dropped away as they moved in a slow dance to her bed. Once there, they fell upon it, tumbling across each other, seeking skin against skin, his chest crushing her breasts, stomachs sliding hot and wet against each other, legs tangling, mouths frantically seeking more.

There was no remedy for the boiling passion but its ultimate fulfillment. Too heated for the delicate caress, the nudge of a searching tongue, they had to have it all. Panting as he rose from the tangled sheets, he positioned himself above her. He meant to take no more than a second to gaze with love upon her face, to see and be further aroused by her swollen, bruised-looking mouth, her heavy eyes, her dilated nostrils, but as he saw the evidence of her desire for him, he lowered himself to her for one more kiss, one deep, searching, promising kiss.

And then, at last, he eased himself inside her, forcing himself to go slowly, to be gentle. He saw her eyes open wide, felt her wetness, felt her hard thrust against him and felt himself in the very depths of her.

She wanted him with a fierceness that made her slide her hands wildly to his back, first to pull him fully into her and then to rake his skin with her fingernails. She was an inferno, a raging fire in a bottomless pit. Only he could reach the flames to quench them. But his deep thrusts only fanned them higher, higher, until she felt consumed by them, vaporized, no longer a body but a white-hot center. And she was pulling him into that center. His heat rose to match hers. They couldn't burn forever. It had to end.

Doing what he wanted, he was giving her what she wanted. A groan tore from his throat as she pulled at him, demanded him, matched his thrusts with her own. The pressure built, the sense of fullness in his body became too heavy to bear and he sought release with the desperation of a dying man.

He felt her last, frantic thrust, he heard her cry out and at last, blessedly, he let himself go.

SHE HAD WHAT SHE WANTED, but it wasn't enough. Their bodies, slick with perspiration, slipped and slid against each other as he rolled to one side and took her in his arms. She nestled against him, giving herself one last respite from reality, giving her heart time to stop thudding and the shudders that continued to rack her a little time to calm down. They didn't seem to want to calm down. Instead, they forced her to reach out for him again. Tears filled her eyes, tears of relief, but also the tears of a woman who was about to break her own heart.

His hand, caressing her face, found the tears. "Cleo," he said softly, "are you all right?"

"Um, just..."

"I know," he said, and bent to kiss the tears away. With his mouth on her tearstained eyelids, it seemed that her mouth was too close, too accessible to be ignored, and then her breasts...

"What if the first time didn't take?" he said, each word a sharp gasp of breath.

"That's always a possibility." The words ended in a sob.

"We'd better make sure."

"That would probably be the wisest thing to."

It was gentler love this time, slower, the delicious ache of their desire building more slowly and peaking higher, more breathlessly, until their eyes widened with disbelief as they reached the crest together and began a tremulous slide down that seemed to last a lifetime.

They clung together, their breathing harsh, their bodies slick with sweat. He wanted to do nothing more than cling to her forever, but first he had to convince her that he was worth clinging to. "Cleo, I have so much to tell you," he said the moment he felt able to speak.

"I have things to tell you, too," she said, "but could we sleep a little bit first?"

He didn't want to sleep, but she sounded so tired. "Sure," he said, cuddling her in his arms. Exhaustion claimed him. Drained of all feeling except tenderness, he held her lightly, her head under his chin, and felt the world drop away.

HE WOKE UP to bright sunshine, to cats tippy-toeing all over him, murmuring to each other, and Cleo, fully dressed, standing over the bed holding a tray. Even though she looked very pretty in straight black velvet pants and a long shirt that matched, he was disappointed not to find her still in bed beside him. The sight of the tray was less disappointing. He was starving.

"Breakfast?" she asked him.

"What time is it?"

"Does it matter?" She smiled at him.

It struck him forcibly that the smile was a sad one. He'd never felt less sad in his life! As soon as he'd had whatever meal this was, he'd tell her he loved her, he'd offer her an engagement ring, he'd turn that smile around. "Nope," he said. "Just the question of a patterned person who eats breakfast in the morning and lunch at noon."

"It's an omelette. Call it whatever you like," she suggested.

He pulled himself up on the pillows, dragging the covers up to his chest, and she placed the tray across his lap. He looked down at a perfect omelette, oozing cheese and herbs, thick-cut buttered toast, sausages and his salvation—a mug of steaming coffee. "Did you cook this?"

"No, Oliver did. Watch out for cat hair. Of course I cooked it."

He smiled back at her and took a sip of coffee. It was wonderful.

"Cream and sugar?"

"I take it straight. Cleo..."

"Eat first," she said. She wasn't smiling at all anymore. He'd better eat fast.

"What about you?"

"I'm not hungry right now." She watched him eat a piece of toast. "That's beach-plum jelly."

"Did you make it, too?"

"No, that's one of Claude's specialties."

"Claude?"

"The chauffeur. The one who rescued the kittens from the gardener."

"Oh, sure." Nothing odd at all about lying here in bed eating the Rose chauffeur's signature beach-plum jelly. He took a bite of omelette, then another, marveling at how his life had already changed, how much more it would change in the future. He was getting used to the idea that most of what Cleo said required a little clarification, and that whatever he asked her, her answer would be a surprise.

He wriggled contentedly between the sheets. Tomorrow he'd give her breakfast in bed. He'd make her a Dutch baby, a big, puffy pancake you baked in the oven. It would wow her. He wondered where he could find maple syrup in the neighborhood. He wondered how he should inform his family that he wouldn't be home for Christmas. If his father had survived the dinner party, he might be willing to serve as liaison.

"Are you feeling pretty good?" said Cleo.

Bryce turned a loving gaze on her. "I'm feeling more wonderful than I ever thought I could."

"Because if you're up to it," Cleo went on without seeming to react to his words or the look in his eyes, "there's somebody I want you to meet."

He clutched at the covers. "I can't meet anybody. I'm naked."

"Take a quick shower if you want to, get dressed and come to the living room. I'll wait for you there."

She'd turned so cold that his perfect happiness took a slide into deep dread. "What is this, Cleo? What are we talking about here?"

"Just do it," Cleo said. She grabbed the breakfast tray, stared at it, handed his coffee cup back to him and marched out of the room, the cats in hot pursuit of the remains of his breakfast.

It was as though last night had never happened. He was pretty sure she wasn't inviting him to meet the minister she'd engaged to marry them. Feeling sick inside, Bryce hit the shower.

CLEO TREMBLED FROM HEAD to toe when Bryce came into the living room. It would be the last time she'd ever see him, and the memory would be a bittersweet one. Unshaven, his hair still damp, and clad in jeans and a pressed blue chambray shirt, he was everything she'd ever wanted and could never have. In fact, his attitude was one she'd come to expect from the men in her life: wary.

She sat on the sofa, surrounded by kittens. After allowing herself one final look at him, she picked up the phone. "Macon. Dear," she said. "Will you come downstairs?" She hung up the phone and gazed as steadily as she could at Bryce. "Coffee?" she said.

He stared back for a long moment. "Cleo," he said at last.

She took it as his response, but he couldn't have her. "Good. I'll get you another cup right now. And Claude wants you to have a jar of his jelly. I've got it all wrapped up.''

"Sit down!" Bryce snapped before she could struggle out from under the cats.

"Okay," she said, dropping back onto the sofa. "I can get the jelly later, I guess."

"Forget the damned jelly! Who's Macon? Why do I have to meet him? Stop being so damned mysterious and tell me what this is all about."

She'd opened her mouth to say something, anything, to fill the time, when Macon rapped softly on the door, then came right on in as though he owned the place, just as she'd told him to. The kittens gave him a disapproving glance and raced away.

When she saw the remodeled Macon, Cleo gasped as loudly as Bryce did. In Deke's soft tan flannels and cashmere polo shirt, Macon the computer dork could have been a figment of her imagination. She hid the gasp with a cough. "Bryce," she said, holding tightly to her resolve, "this is my fiancé, Macon Trent."

Bryce paled. His eyes widened. "Your what?"

Keep going, keep going. Heart, don't fail me now. "My fiancé." She delivered a deep, stagy sigh. "I'm sorry. I haven't been entirely honest with you."

"Hello, darling," Macon said. His timing was off, but he looked credible. This was going to work. It had to.

"Say it one more time," Bryce growled. "He's your what?"

His timing wasn't all that great, either. Cleo forged on. "I was perfectly honest when I told you I wanted to have a baby, and perfectly honest when I said I wanted a left-brain sperm donor." Through the tears that filled her eyes, she viewed Bryce in alarm. He seemed to be gathering himself up to leap at someone or something. "What I didn't tell you was that I was engaged to a man who couldn't give me that baby."

"I'm infertile," Macon said sadly.

Bryce gave him a look that would have rendered most men impotent. Fortunately, Cleo realized, all Macon could see without his glasses were his next lines looming ahead.

"Yes," Cleo rushed on, "Macon is the man of my dreams, but a terrible thing happened in his youth. He was playing soccer..."

"The junior-high playoffs," Macon said, adding some slow, despondent head-wagging to his sad expression.

"When a misplaced kick caught him in the—well, you can just imagine where."

"It was very painful." Macon grimaced.

"Especially when he learned he could never father a child," Cleo said. The worst was over. She could cry now if she wanted to. Bryce would think she was crying over Macon's lost fertility. "So we decided..."

Bryce suddenly came alive. He charged toward her like a wave crashing onto a Pacific beach, shouting, "So you decided to use me to solve your little problem?"

"Don't yell at me," Cleo cried. The tears were rolling now, and she couldn't stop them.

"And I for one want to tell you how much I appreciate what you've done for us." Macon approached Bryce with outstretched arms.

With an inhuman snarl Bryce veered toward Macon. A vase of flowers stood in his path. He knocked it over, spraying the room with water and blossoms.

"Uh-oh," Macon murmured, tugging blindly at a thorny rose stem that was wreaking havoc with Deke's sweater.

"I can't believe this," Bryce raged on. "I don't believe this." He halted, staring at Macon. "It's a joke, right?"

Hearing his next cue, Macon straightened his shoulders, then placed a sympathetic hand on Bryce's arm, the dripping long-stemmed rose still clinging to his sweater. "It's no joke," he said. "Cleo and I are going to be married."

Bryce shook off Macon's hand and balled up his fists.

"Don't hit me!" Macon said. "I'm wearing my—" It was clear that he was realizing he wasn't, in fact, wearing his glasses "—my pacemaker."

Amazed at Macon's ability to improvise, Cleo shot her gaze back to Bryce, who suddenly drooped all over.

"I wasn't going to hit you," he said in a low, tired voice. "I don't think I was, anyway. I don't know anymore. I don't know what I am, much less what I'm capable of doing." He paused, looking first at Macon, then at Cleo. "Maybe I do believe you," he sighed. "I knew you were crazy. I just didn't know how crazy."

"I'm not crazy," said Cleo, "just...determined." Again she had to hurry on, using what breath she had to get this scene over with. "You'll be fine, Bryce. You'll go home to Francine, and she'll soon realize she loves you more than she loves Atlanta, and you'll realize that you've always loved her, and that your best hope for happiness is with her, and you'll forget that I..."

"Forget that you *used* me?" His voice had gone as hard as steel. The Southern gentleman was nowhere in sight. This was an angry man, maybe the angriest man she'd ever been close to.

"I had to do it," she said. "I just had to do it."

"I'll leave so you can say goodbye to each other," Macon suggested.

"We just said it!" Bryce grated. "What you can do for me," he said with a new and frightening fury, "is locate and contain Nell and Little Dorritt! You got my genes, but damned if you're getting my cats! Oh, yes," he added bitterly, "Please accept my *sincerest* congratulations."

When Bryce had gone, Cleo thanked Macon, told him he'd done wonderfully, took Deke's trousers to the cleaners and bought him a new sweater, cried for three days, then gathered up the shards of her heart and prepared to go on with her life. Anne would never know her mother was anything but the happiest single mother in the world.

13

BRYCE ENDURED THE SILENCE at the other end of the phone as long as he could stand it, then said, "Herb, are you still there?"

"Yeah. Hey, could you go back to the part where Cleo wouldn't marry you, but you weren't going to marry Francine, but Francine still thought you were going to marry her, but she didn't want to move to New Jersey?"

"I'll write it down and fax it to you," said Bryce. This was one of the most difficult conversations of his entire life, and his only hope was to stay calm, say the words and wait for them to sink in.

Cleo had not been right. He was not getting over her, he was not learning to love Francine, in fact, couldn't imagine how he had ever thought of marrying Francine. He'd spent a miserable Christmas with his family and had ushered in the momentous year 2000 alone, unless you counted Nell and Little Dorritt. And the next morning he'd made a list of New Year's resolutions, one of which was to tell Herb Hardy the absolute, unadulterated truth, whatever the consequences.

One of the guys at the lab had given him a stress ball. It fit into the palm of the hand like an ordinary rubber ball, but you could squish it into whatever shape your tension directed it. At the moment, his was shaped like a dumbbell.

"Don't even try to write it down." Herb sighed. "I think I'm getting the idea."

"I'm sorry I didn't level with you earlier," said Bryce.

"If you want to withdraw your job offer, I understand." Squish.

"Do you want to stay in Atlanta and marry Francine?"

"No."

"You sure?"

"Positive."

"You still want to come to Whitehall?"

"Yes."

"And you'd be coming here as a single man?"

"Looks like it."

"I see," Herb said, sounding tired. "Well, Hampton..."

That was a bad sign, "Hampton," not "my boy." Squish, squish, squish.

"When I assured you I wouldn't be a sperm donor to a single woman, I didn't know it would be a lie," Bryce said. "I'd realized I was in love with Cleo, and I thought I could convince her I was worth loving. I was wrong."

"I know, I know," said Herb. "I understand. I think."

"I'd better send the fax," Bryce said.

"No, just get your act together and come on up here!" Herb boomed at him suddenly. "Get to work on Nopro. Take your mind off your problems."

"Sir?"

"You heard me. Nobody needs to know you went through a little crazy period, do they?" He sounded hopeful.

"No, sir." Bryce extricated his fingers from the stress ball, which had gone all sticky from the friction he'd been applying to it.

"You're not about to do anything else crazy, are you?"

"Well," Bryce temporized, "I still haven't given up on Cleo. If I can manage to change her mind about this guy Trent... Well, the upshot of it is that if I can convince her to marry me instead, the wedding may not predate our baby by the customary nine months."

A gritty, scraping sound came from the receiver. Herb must be grinding his teeth. "Nobody needs to know that either, right?" he snarled.

"Right." *Unless Sonia finds a forum for announcing it.* Bryce made a mental note to send Herb a stress ball. "Thank you, Herb," said Bryce. "You've been terrific about all this."

Bryce gazed at the stress ball, which was slowly returning to its spherical shape. He didn't feel great, but he felt better.

THURSDAY MORNING: "Cleo, we need to talk. I..."

Slam, silence, dial tone.

Thursday evening: "Cleo, Bryce. I think you..."

Slam, silence, dial tone.

Friday morning: "Don't hang up! I..."

Slam, silence, dial tone.

Friday evening: "Miss Rhose?" He had a two-fingered grip on the bridge of his nose. "This is the SPCA."

"Yes?" said the beautiful, dear voice.

"We hnear you hnave a khnitten who has been chruelly separated from hnis siblings...."

Slam, silence, dial tone.

As time went by, the stress ball lost its elasticity. Bryce felt the same way, that he just couldn't take any more squishing.

"I WANT TO SEE YOU, Bryce. We need to talk."

Deeply into some calculations on his computer, Bryce covered the telephone mouthpiece long enough to sigh deeply. "We've already said everything there is to say, Francine," he said kindly. *If you would only listen.*

"This is really important," said Francine. Her voice had an unfamiliar lilt to it. "There's something I have to tell you. I want you to hear it from me."

She sure wasn't about to tell him she was pregnant. If she was, the world had better get ready for another Messiah. So what was it this time? She'd found the china of her dreams? Italian linens in the right shade of yellow? Neil Diamond would sing at their wedding?

He sighed again, not bothering to cover the mouthpiece. "My house," he said firmly. He was through with tête-à-têtes in Francine's mother's garden, where Francine's father lurked behind the gazebo with the proverbial shotgun, or the sunroom, where he could hear the click of a weapon being loaded in the nearby library. "Come to my house at seven tonight."

"I'm bringing someone with me."

He went on the alert. Her father, shotgun in hand? Her lawyer? This, at last, was the suit against him, or worse, against Cleo, for alienation of affection? With difficulty he remained calm. "Any guest of yours is welcome in my home," he said formally. "I'll see you at seven."

He wasn't ready to leave the lab at six, but he did. On the way home he stopped at a gourmet deli and bought hors d'oeuvres that covered a range of tastes—stuffed grape leaves, potato samosas, salsa with blue corn chips, a creamy French cheese, marinated olives. Francine had never been spotted eating anything, but her father, or the lawyer, might be soothed by a little something under the belt, and he wanted that little something to be to his mystery visitor's liking.

As for belts, his father kept his liquor cabinet and wine rack well stocked, and since he rarely drank, he was ready for anything.

Anything but the man Francine walked in with.

"Boxer!" he said. "You old so-and-so! How've you been? What's your pleasure?"

"He's never been better," Francine said in a voice of

steel, "and he'll have a Coke." At the sound of her voice the cats gave up trying to pounce on the cheese and fled.

Boxer nodded, looking scared. A nice-looking guy, Boxer was, and his eternally innocent face made him look ten years younger than his age. Maybe it was being independently wealthy that kept him young. Maybe it was not having to work, not having a worry in the world.

But now he was scared. Of what? Bryce wondered as he retrieved a can of Coca-Cola from a storage bin, put ice in a glass and arranged these things on a tray. He added a glass of white wine for Francine, and thinking things over, poured himself a couple of fingers of his best Scotch.

"So," he said heartily, "what brings you here?"

Boxer startled him by suddenly burying his face in his hands. "You've always been a good friend to me, Bryce. I can't stand hurting you like this."

"Like what?" Bryce said, feeling as fine as he was able to feel these days. He lifted his eyebrows questioningly at Francine, who was stroking the back of Boxer's neck and murmuring, "There, there."

"We have something to tell you," Francine said calmly. "Boxer, do calm down. We have to do this, darling." She touched his shoulder, delicately removing a fluff of cat hair.

Darling? Bryce began to understand. His heart pounded, lifted, soared. "Yes, darling! I mean, yes, Boxer, best to get it over with. Have a stuffed grape leaf. Make things easier."

Boxer ate a stuffed grape leaf. While he chewed, Francine spoke up. "I didn't mean to do it, Bryce. I didn't mean to fall in love with Boxer. But you were away so much, and Boxer was always there for me, happy to take me to parties, and, well, on New Year's Eve he kissed me, and it just happened." Tears filled her eyes.

"Most natural thing in the world," Bryce murmured paternally, refilling Boxer's hand with a samosa.

"And we picked the same china," Francine said, her pointy little chin quivering, her blond curls bouncing. "It was a test. I sent him into Tiffany's and said, 'Boxer, honey, you pick out your favorite china pattern, and if it's the same one I picked, we'll know this is forever!' And he did, and it is!" She broke down altogether.

At this point Bryce detected a certain shiftiness in Boxer's expression. He knew exactly what the guy had done. He'd gone straight to a clerk and asked which pattern Francine had chosen. *Good old Boxer! Didn't know you were that smart!*

"Oh, Bryce," Francine wailed. "I realized I needed the kind of attention Boxer can give me, and the kind of diamond Boxer can give me." She thrust out a tiny hand. The fourth finger bore a diamond about the size of Bryce's watch face. "And the most important thing, Bryce," she said, her sweet little voice quavering, "is that Boxer will never leave Atlanta. His whole life is here, like mine."

He wanted to get up and do a little dance around his sterile living room, but he felt he had a role to play. "So," he said, long-faced, "it's decided."

"Yes," Francine burbled.

"These things happen," he said softly. "We owe it to ourselves to find happiness, even when it means—" he paused to chew at his lower lip "—hurting others. I will be fine, Francine." He squared his jaw. "It will take time, but I'll be..."

Boxer came to life. "If you can't handle it, fella," he said passionately, "Frannie and I will understand. We'll wait, we'll deny ourselves, until we know you're all right."

Frannie? "No, no," Bryce said hastily. "In fact, now that the first shock is over, I'm already feeling much, much better. It makes me happy," he added for good measure, "to see you happy."

"But you'll be all alone," Boxer protested.

"I have my work," Bryce intoned.

"He does, Boxer," Francine said, "he does have his work. And," she added with a surprising change in her expression, "he may even have another woman." To Bryce's utter amazement, she winked at him.

"I wish you were right," he said wryly, "but I'm afraid that's over."

"Oh," Francine said. "I'm sorry. I really am."

"You are?"

"I wanted you to be happy, too," she said.

Was this the same Francine who had stuffed him into a blue angora cap and left him wilting in her mother's garden? "I don't understand," he said.

She sighed. "I've grown up a lot over the past few months," she admitted. She darted a glance at Boxer, who would have been looking puzzled if he hadn't gotten back into the grape leaves. "I mean, one of us had to." Her eyes twinkled.

Bryce gazed at his one-time bride-to-be and realized that at last he actually liked her. "Thanks for forgiving me," he said softly. "I never wanted to hurt you."

"Okay, then," said Boxer, who was out of stuffed grape leaves, "If you're sure you'll be okay."

"Time heals all wounds," said Bryce, giving Francine a secret smile. "I do have one last request."

"Anything!" Francine and Boxer chorused.

"Have you already chosen your wedding invitations and announcements and all that stuff?"

"Of course," said Francine.

"May I have one of the announcements as soon as they're printed?"

"Engraved," Francine corrected him.

"Engraved," he conceded. "With a blank envelope?"

"Of course, dear," Francine promised. "For your scrapbook, I guess."

"Sort of," said Bryce.

"Don't you want an invitation?" she asked him.

"That would be awkward, don't you think?"

"For your scrapbook, I meant."

"Oh. Well." He imagined the effect of sending an invitation where he intended to send the announcement—to Cleo. Risky. She'd probably send a gift. "An announcement is enough."

"We're picking them up tomorrow," Francine said. "I'll send one right over to you."

CLEO WAS TURNING Martha Griswold's sloping shoulders into crisp, neat squares with a custom-made pair of shoulder pads when the mail fell heavily through the slot in her door.

"Love this suit," Martha was saying. "I'm taking it to Paris next month. Springtime in Paris," she sighed. "I wish Arnie and I were twenty-one again." She returned to practical matters. "What should I wear under it, taupe? Or black?"

Cleo mouthed a response, but she was distracted by Oliver's latest promise of mischief to come. One of the envelopes, a thick, creamy square, had attracted his attention and he was boxing it back and forth between his paws. "Stop that, Oliver," she scolded him. The next step, she knew, would be the systematic shredding of the missive. She was still trying to tape the return-with-payment portion of her telephone bill back together.

Oliver ignored her. With a hiss he buried a paw full of extended claws into the envelope, and before she could get to him, he had reduced it to long, thin confetti. "Oliver!" she cried. "This is—was—important! I'm supposed to go somewhere, or send a present somewhere, or RSVP to somebody somewhere! Excuse me, Martha," she said. "Oliver is eliminating my social life. Think he's doing it on purpose, just to keep me at home with him?'' She shoved the shreds into the empty shoulder-pad box. She'd put them together later, after she'd turned Martha into Joan Crawford.

Her craving for Chinese food had reached the psychotic level. An hour or so after Vestal had delivered dinner for four and she had more or less decimated it, she remembered the box of shredded paper and spread the pieces out on her coffee table.

In another thirty minutes she'd assembled the words—engraved—that read:

Mr. a d Mrs. Eldr d Ing oll
an unce t e mar ge of their daughter
Fra ci e De m n

She didn't need to know any more. She fled to her bathroom and threw up neatly and efficiently. Then she washed her face, brushed her teeth, swished with mouthwash, returned to her dining room and polished off the last of the Chinese food.

The next day she made a trip to Tiffany's. She ordered a gift to be sent to Bryce and Francine. No card. No return address. Bryce would know who sent it, and Francine didn't need to. Since Francine's address lay at home in strips, she specified the address of Bryce's lab, then sat down with the wedding-announcement consultant.

''A beautiful choice, Miss Rose,'' said the woman. ''The art deco engraving on the stark white stock is so dramatic. How many announcements will you need?''

Cleo gazed at the proposed invitation: ''Mr. and Mrs. Thornton Rose announce the marriage of their daughter, Cleome, to Macon Trent, on...''

''One,'' she said.

''One hundred? One thousand?'' The woman smiled.

"One period," said Cleo.

"But we can't…"

"Sure, you can," Cleo said glumly. "Don't worry, I'll make it up to Tiffany's with Anne's birth announcements." Knowing she was leaving merchandising havoc behind her, she returned to her atelier.

IN HIS OFFICE AT THE LAB, Bryce gazed at the enormous sterling silver bowl that had arrived from Tiffany's that morning. No card, no engraving, no anything except the biggest single piece of silver he'd ever laid eyes on. You could skin-dive in it. At last he decided it must be a welcome-aboard gift from Whitehall Pharmaceuticals. Nobody bought anything that expensive with his own money. Bryce tried it out on his coffee table and decided he'd have to have a special pedestal built for it, later, after the move.

SEVERAL WEEKS LATER, Cleo gazed at the china service for eight that had just been delivered by Tiffany's. She should have realized that Bryce's reaction to receiving a wedding announcement would be just like hers: send a gift. Unlike Francine, she'd send a thank-you note, and then she'd send the china back. Tiffany's was used to broken engagements. Too bad, though—the china was the pattern she'd always planned to have if she ever married. What a funny coincidence, a really funny…

"I'm not crying, Anne," she announced to her stomach. "I'm fine. Just a little tear-duct disorder is all."

"YES, I'M FEELING BETTER, and I'll feel a heck of a lot better when you let me go to the bathroom."

The doctor laughed, warming the probe between her gloved hands. "We want a good picture, don't we?"

"Of course," Cleo admitted. "I want to see how long her eyelashes are."

"That might be asking a bit much."

"I will love you to pieces no matter how long your eye-lashes are," Cleo said fondly to her abdomen, patting the slight swelling there.

She lay on the examination table, ready for her first sono-gram, her first glimpse of her baby. She knew Anne was only eight or nine inches long by now, but that tiny package that was her baby daughter could hear her voice. Cleo had stopped swearing and was trying to use precise grammar and complete sentences. And, of course, had stopped cry-ing. No matter how her heart broke all over again each time she thought of Bryce, she firmly shut the thought away. She would still feel like crying when Anne began growing up, when she'd be able to see Bryce in her. But then she could cry at times when Anne wouldn't hear her.

The doctor began her examination, her eyes fixed on the monitor. Cleo's gaze followed hers. There she was; that blob was baby Anne. Cleo's heart pounded with love for her unborn child.

"I guess we love our kids no matter what," said the doctor.

"I'm going to love Anne no matter what," said Cleo. "She's gorgeous, isn't she?"

No comment? When Anne had to be the best-looking blob she'd ever seen? They ought to teach these doctors to be more sensitive to parental pride!

"Looks good," said the doctor. "Good development." She paused. "Looks like a baby anybody could love—" She paused again. "—no matter what sex it is." There was a cautionary note in her voice that got Cleo's attention, along with the annoying way she described Anne as "it."

Cleo patted her stomach again, apologizing. "Of course she is! But her sex is one thing I don't have to learn from the sonogram," she said smugly. "Anne is a girl."

The doctor probed some more, her face an impersonal

mask. "Cleo," she said at last, "Anne may be a girl, but this baby isn't."

"What?" Cleo shrieked.

BRYCE GOT HOME earlier than usual that May evening. He'd practically been living at the lab. Of course, he was trying to get it in perfect shape for the new director of research he'd hired, but the real reason he stayed was that the lab was marginally warmer, homier and more comfortable than the townhouse.

Except for the cats—he did like coming home to them. They were lurking somewhere in secret, plotting an ambush. He went to the kitchen, made a big fuss about opening a cat-food can and soon had the pleasure of their company. The details of the ambush put to the backs of their minds for another occasion, they swirled around his ankles while he divided the food into their two bowls, stood still for being petted, then ignored him while he added to the supply of dry food in their self-feeder and filled their water bowl.

It helped, having Nell and Little Dorritt around. Cleo had given them their Dickensian names, Oliver for her black-and-white kitten, Nell for the tabby and Little Dorritt for the calico. He wondered if Oliver missed his sisters the way he missed Oliver's mistress. Brooding for a moment, he shook off the thought, as he had so many times in the past few months.

The move to Whitehall Pharmaceuticals, due to take place within the week, couldn't happen soon enough for him. He needed a change. He'd sold the townhouse fully furnished, he'd endured the round of goodbye parties and the lab could practically run on its own. The moving company would appear in a few days to pack the personal possessions he'd chosen to take with him. Organizationally he was on top of it. Personally he felt like a stir-fry in progress.

He had hoped beyond hope that when Cleo got the announcement of Francine's marriage to Boxer—Thomas Boxman Wilhoite III or IV, he could never remember which—she'd give her marriage to Macon Trent a second thought. But the time for that had passed; the announcement had named a date in April. So it was done; Cleo was a bride, probably a pregnant bride. He shut the thought out of his mind; he just couldn't take it.

Moving north would help. He was staying in a furnished Midtown apartment for a month to give him time to find a place in Greenwich Village, not too close, not too far from Cleo's place. He wanted to keep an eye on Anne while she grew up.

Anne. My little girl. Bryce rubbed a hand over his chin, feeling the stubble, feeling old and scruffy. In his mind's eye he saw a dark-haired baby lying in her cradle in the room Cleo had prepared for her. He saw himself tiptoeing in, the bright black eyes catching sight of him, a coo, a smile.

And then Macon Trent came through the door and said, "Touch that child and die!" A sudden salty wetness stung Bryce's eyes. God, he was tired.

The distant ring of a phone startled him. Had to be the cell phone, or every phone in the house would be ringing. The cell phone was in his briefcase, which was in the kitchen where he'd dropped it when he came in.

Let it go. Can't be important.

Better not let it go. It's still not too late for the lab to explode, or the moving company to renege on its promises. Dumping papers and professional journals all over the kitchen floor, he finally clutched the phone to his ear.

"You turkey!" a voice shrilled.

"Cleo? What a coincidence! I was just thinking about you. And Anne. And Macon." His heart was pounding hard enough to make him raise his voice. His head swam. It

finally swam around to realizing she had just described him
as a turkey.

"Forget Anne!" she yelled at him. "There we were with
our three Xs and your one miserable Y, and could you get
a muzzle on that Y? No! It just bullied its way through,
like all you Ys, and…and…"

She'd stopped yelling. She sounded close to tears.

"What are you telling me, Cleo?" Not that he had to
ask. But he had to say something to fill the silence, keep
her on the line.

"That Anne's not a girl! I mean the baby isn't Anne
after all. She's a b-b-boy!" she wailed. "How am I going
to raise a boy? I can't throw a ball. I never learned to drive!
How am I going to teach him to drive? I was already worried about teaching Anne to t-t-tie her shoelaces!"

A boy. His son. Bryce didn't give a damn whether it was
a girl or a boy who looked up at him with Cleo's eyes from
that cradle, who cooed and smiled. He just wanted to be
there—when Macon Trent came through the door and said,
"Touch him and die."

"Can't Macon do it?" he asked, puzzlement joining the
many emotions that assailed him.

"Macon?" said Cleo, sounding as puzzled as he felt.
"Oh, Macon." There was a long silence. "I guess you
don't know. Macon and I annulled our marriage." She
snuffled. "Didn't Tiffany's credit your card for the china I
sent back?"

"Annulled." At the moment he didn't give a damn about
his Visa balance.

"Um. Yes. It seemed the soccer accident did a little more
damage than we thought," she said in a sudden burst of
information.

Bryce spent a few seconds just staring into space, then,
still silent, wandered into the living room. On the mantel,
Little Dorritt had taken umbrage at a stylish arrangement

of dead roadside weeds and was pummeling it to dust. Bryce had always felt the same way about that arrangement. Macon. Soccer accident. *Don't hit me! I'm wearing my pacemaker.* Annulment.

"I just wanted you to know," Cleo said uncertainly, as though the silence worried her.

Everything fell into place. Bryce snatched the cat off the mantel and laughed.

"There's nothing funny about this," Cleo sniffed. "You had a simple job to do and you didn't do it right."

"I'll make it up to you," said Bryce. "I'm on my way." He kicked the cat kennel out of the closet under the stairs and put Little Dorritt into it.

"What do you mean, on your way?"

"I'm on my way to New York to help you bring up our son," said Bryce, elation filling him to the bursting point. "It's the least we can do, me and my aggressive Y chromosome." She'd made up the whole thing about Macon just to get him back together with Francine, to make good on her promises. That little stinker! That stubborn, determined, good-hearted little...

"Oh, that will be really keen," Cleo said sarcastically. "You're going to leave Francine and come here to help me raise little Anthony. That will go over big. *How to Make a Marriage Work,* by Bryce Hampton. When was the wedding anyway?"

"The wedding?" *What wedding?* Oh, *that* wedding. "Didn't you get the announcement I sent?" He spied Nell climbing out of a wastepaper basket, her catnip mouse between her teeth, and grabbed her.

"Of course I got it." Cleo snuffled distantly, as though she were trying to hide the fact that she was snuffling. "Didn't you get my silver bowl?"

"Didn't you read the announcement?" He stroked the cat, felt himself calming down, felt his heart reach out to the only person who could possibly have been generous enough to send that bowl.

"I put it back together down to Francine's name. Then I threw up."

As always with Cleo, there were huge information gaps in the statement she'd just made. *I love you, Cleo. I love every crazy cell in your body.* "So I guess you don't know *who* Francine married, either."

"Don't be cute. Francine married you. Okay, I admit it. That's what made me throw up."

Bryce smiled. He could hardly remember how gloomy he'd felt just a few minutes ago, how sad, how hopeless. Now the sun was shining in his heart. "Do you still have the rest of the pieces?" he asked her. At that moment Nell locked her sharp little white teeth into his thumb and he opened his mouth in a silent scream. Shaking her loose, he shoved her into the kennel with Little Dorritt and went back into the kitchen.

"They're somewhere," said Cleo.

Bryce repacked his briefcase. From the living room the cats plotted their revenge in low, dangerous-sounding rumbles. "Find them. Start piecing." He went to his bedroom and threw a few things into a bag.

He couldn't take the cats on the MARTA line. He'd have to drive to the airport. So he'd abandon the car, so what? He sure wasn't coming back.

He was rapidly backing out of his garage when Cleo resumed their conversation. "Bryce," she said in a curious tone, "whoever is Thomas Boxman Wilhoite IV?"

"Let's make him godfather to our son," said Bryce.

"Oh, Bryce!" At last she laughed, sounding as limp with relief as he felt, sounding—

Sounding like the woman he loved, a woman who loved him, a woman who would marry him and present him almost at once with a baby, his baby. "I've been such a ninny," she said, and the laughter turned to tears. "How can I ever tell you how much I love you?"

"Better do it in person, or I'm going to have a wreck," Bryce said, loving her more with every passing second. "Goodbye, darling—for now."

There was no doubt in his mind that Cleo was going to be the most difficult, the quirkiest pregnant woman in the history of time. He'd be going out for green-tea ice cream at the oddest hours, and enduring the most amazing mood swings, and—

Oh, my gosh, Sonia's going to be my mother-in-law! And...

And he had a plane to catch. This time, if he was too late, he'd charter one.

Epilogue

Five years later

"CAREFUL, BEAU, keep the tray level. Oops! No harm done," Cleo reassured Bryce Maynard Hampton III. "I'll pick up the ones that didn't break and put them back on the tray. Daddy won't mind." Seven months into her second pregnancy, she bent awkwardly to retrieve the salmon-mousse toasts.

"Careful, Mommy, don't squish Anne," Beau said worriedly.

"I'll be careful," said Cleo, patting her tummy, where she knew, thanks to modern technology, that Anne Rose Hampton waited to join the family. "Hurry, now, sweetheart, and get the napkins. Daddy will be home soon, and we want to have our picnic all ready for him."

The patio behind the townhouse was beautiful in the late-summer light. "Too lovely to stay indoors," Cleo murmured, "although indoors is pretty nice, too." When Sandy, Deke, the baby and the dog moved to the suburbs, she and Bryce promoted Delilah up one floor and added her apartment to their own. The result was an elegant home from which Bryce, somewhat regretfully, she thought, ventured out each morning to head research and development at Whitehall Pharmaceuticals in New Jersey.

"Daddy!" Beau yelled as Bryce strode through the shop and onto the patio. He flung his arms around his father.

Cleo, observing from Bryce's rear, noticed that Beau must have had quite a bit of salmon mousse on his hands at some point, because now it was on the jacket of Bryce's dark suit.

The dry cleaner, with whom Cleo was on a first-name basis, sent them a Balducci's gift basket each Christmas.

"Hey, you two," said Bryce, hugging Beau back and giving Cleo one of the flashing smiles that still, after five years, buckled her knees. "How was your day?"

"Just great," said Cleo, smiling back. "Like every day. Yours?"

"Fantastic. But I'm glad to be home." He reached over Beau's head to give her a kiss. Their mouths clung, made promises. The passion that marked their relationship from the beginning, a passion that did not dim with time, stood as proof of Nopro's astounding success. Without Nopro, there could be four miniature klutzes smearing mousse on their father at this very moment.

"Want to see the picture I made today?" Beau's voice rose hollowly from a spot below the kiss.

Cleo and Bryce broke contact. "I came home early just to see your picture," Bryce said seriously. "Bring it out here and show me."

Beau sped into the shop. Apparently he managed the elevator all right, because several alarming crashes could be heard through the open windows of the apartment. Bryce and Cleo shared a glance of mutual understanding. In a minute they would know if the only possession they really cared about had broken mere objects, not himself.

"Here it is," cried Beau, emerging unscathed with a piece of dark blue construction paper. "I made the universe!"

Cleo sighed with relief. In spite of himself, Beau had never fractured anything that was attached to him.

"The universe," Bryce marveled. "Wow." He sank into a garden chair and pulled Beau close to him.

"Yeah," said Beau. "See, here's what happens to the stars and the sun and the moon when we can't see them. They have little garages they go into." He opened doors in the solid blue to show bright yellow stars—complete with faces—pasted to a second piece of blue paper. Beside the stars were objects that resembled gas tanks.

Bryce, superscientist and logical, left-brain dad, contemplated this explanation of the universe. "You know, Beau," he began, then paused. He looked at Cleo. He looked at Beau. He saw the two dark-haired, black-eyed, spiky-lashed people who filled the center of his universe hanging on his next words. "I think you may have figured out why we can't see the stars in the daytime," he said enthusiastically. "What a discovery! They have to gas up every day for the next night, so each one has a little garage. I bet the sun has an automatic garage-door opener. I wonder if they need an air hose to stay the same size night after night."

"Bryce!" Cleo hissed. "For heaven's sake! How is he ever going to learn anything if you don't…?"

Bryce shushed her with a finger over his mouth. "Beau will learn everything he really needs to know," he said, his face softening in a smile, "and along the way, he might even teach us a few things."

Cleo caught his gaze, held it and smiled back. There was no scientific discovery yet that could take the place of love.

MEG LACEY

Make Me Over

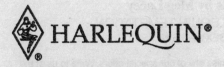

HARLEQUIN®

TORONTO • NEW YORK • LONDON
AMSTERDAM • PARIS • SYDNEY • HAMBURG
STOCKHOLM • ATHENS • TOKYO • MILAN • MADRID
PRAGUE • WARSAW • BUDAPEST • AUCKLAND

Dear Reader,

I love the Smoky Mountains. I wanted to do a book set in a tourist town, and started thinking of what a policeman's life would be like there. Then—what if that policeman had a deputy he'd known all his life and thought of as a friend. And what if this friend asked his help to find her a man. How would they go about it in a small town where everyone knows everyone else's business? Especially when there's a huge tourist attraction like "The Harvest Festival" bringing in lots of new "romantic" possibilities. Then I thought—what if this town also contains some of the most outrageous characters ever to walk around gossiping. Before I knew it, I'd invented Knightsborough, Tennessee, and its inhabitants. All of which gave me the ingredients for a screwball romance. I hope you enjoy this town and its citizens as much as I did—I even plan to visit again, when I get the chance!

Hope to see you there.

Sincerely,

Meg Lacey

Books by Meg Lacey
HARLEQUIN TEMPTATION
734—SEXY AS SIN

For my mother, Ruth, my grandmother, Grace,
and the rest of the Cochran Clan.

1

SHERIFF MACKENZIE COCHRANE had just moved the red queen onto the black king when the phone rang. He jumped. It was the first time it had rung all morning. He considered that a bit odd. He glanced at the clock on the wall. Eleven o'clock. The phone should have been ringing off the hook, especially since it was the height of tourist season and there were only a few weeks until the Harvest Festival.

In the small town of Knightsboro, Tennessee, the phone rang for everything from a suspected break-in to "please get my kitty down from the tree." Why, only yesterday Mac had had a call from a woman who begged him to "talk to my little Bennie, Sheriff, and convince him that if he doesn't eat his vegetables he'll go to jail!" Since the vegetable in question was brussel sprouts and Mac hated brussel sprouts, he'd refused. Secretly he didn't blame the kid for not wanting to eat those nasty little round green things. That wasn't really why he'd refused though. Mac hated people trying to use the police as the bad guy for everything from eating dinner to runaways. Next thing you know he'd be threatening old ladies and arresting poodles.

With some trepidation he picked up the receiver. "Sheriff Cochrane."

"Hi, Mom." He listened for a moment. "No, no I'm not too busy to speak with you." As if his mother had long-distance X-ray eyes, Mac hastily clicked out of the solitaire card program on his computer and pulled up the reports he was supposed to be updating.

Mac leaned back in his chair and put his feet up on the edge of the desk. Getting comfortable, he crossed one booted foot over the other as his mother bent his ear. Molly Cochrane had to wander around the block a bit before she got to the point of her call.

"Uh-huh, now wait a minute, Mom, let's see if I've got this straight." A sound, like a hastily suppressed snicker, pulled his gaze to the doorway of his office. Deputy Nell Phillips stood just inside. "You're telling me you got this information from your cleaning lady—" this time Nell's chuckle was audible, and Mac grinned back as he repeated "—who heard it from Hilda at the farmer's market, who said—" Mac nodded as Nell mimed, *Your Mother?* "—Ted Kilbourne is doing what to her cows?"

Nell attracted Mac's attention as she settled herself more comfortably against the doorjamb. For a second he lost the thread of his mother's conversation as he noticed what a long drink of water Nell was. *Damn woman has legs up to her chin.* Mac pulled his attention back to the phone and listened for another moment. His feet hit the ground at the next bit of information. "They're what? Okay, Mom, I'll take care—yeah, what about Hilda's niece? When? Ma, I wish you'd... yeah, love you, too. Bye." With easy grace he swiveled in his chair, plunked the receiver into its cradle, then stood up.

"What about Ted Kilbourne?" Nell straightened from her casual slouch. "Has his son blown up the chemistry lab again? Seems every time Anna's out of town taking care of her parents, one of the Kilbournes gets inventive."

"Nope. This time the problem's Ted, or maybe his brother, Jed." Mac checked his pockets, looking for his keys. "Seems they're polluting the creek that runs down past Hilda's farm."

"Polluting it with what?"

"Hilda said something about her cows staggering around the pasture. What does that tell ya?" Mac paused, trying to think about the situation seriously, but it was difficult to do when he was looking at a Far Side calendar with an illustration of a bunch of cows playing poker and smoking cigars. A muffled laugh from Nell recalled his attention.

Biting her lips to control her chuckles, Nell said, "You

mean Ted's homemade whiskey is running off his still into the creek?''

Mac's lips twitched. "Sounds like it."

Nell whistled. "That stuff must be hundred proof."

Shaking his head, Mac grinned. "You'd better believe those cows are pie-eyed plastered by now."

When Nell finished laughing, she said, "You never know what the Kilbournes are going to do next, do you?"

"They've got their own standards of behavior. And most of the time, they don't fit in with anyone else's." A jurisdiction as large as Mac's was a mixture of all kinds of people. Some were town born and bred, genteel and used to living by the rules of society, and some, like Ted, still had the hay left in their hair and the independent spirit of the mountain people. It didn't matter who they were, what they did for a living or what they had. Mac was responsible for all of them. Keeping the community safe was his first thought in the morning and his last at night. It wasn't just what he did for a living—it was who he was. His eyes twinkled. *Some days are more challenging than others.*

Nell rubbed her lips with her index finger. "At least they keep things lively."

"They ought to. There's enough of them," Mac agreed. He walked across the room and picked up his hat.

"You're going up there, I take it."

Mac set his hat square on his head and adjusted the brim with a snap. "Yep. Guess it's time to straighten Ted out."

Nell glanced over her shoulder at the lack of activity behind her. "It's a slow day. Mind if I come along?"

Mac walked toward her and took his own look at the squad room. Even though tourists were starting to visit in droves, Nell was right. She usually was, but he didn't like to tell her so. It'd give her a swelled head. Mac had known Nell since they were the size of grasshoppers. Even though they were all grown-up now, sometimes he had to stop himself from playing big brother, or big pain-in-the-neck, depending on the point of view.

"Hey, Doug," Nell said. "You're okay to handle the phones here, aren't you?"

The squad room was nearly empty, and quiet with no printers chattering, no phones ringing, nobody nattering someone else to death. The only noise—and movement—came from Doug throwing a dart at the board on the wall.

The stocky, middle-aged deputy winged another dart toward the center and missed. "Sure. It'll give me time to catch up on my dart throwing before the tournament next Wednesday."

Nell chuckled as Doug's dart bounced off the wall and fell onto the floor. Looking back at Mac, she said, "Behold the strong arm of the law."

Mac shook his head at the pitiful sight. "Bobby Dee and Casey are out on patrol, right?"

"That's right, boss, but it shouldn't be a problem." Doug concentrated on lining up his shot. "They'll be back soon."

"Okay." Mac glanced at Nell. "Maybe you should come along, Slim. I might need a female's touch."

Nell sent him a withering glance as she pivoted on her heel and headed for her desk. "So, now I'm a female? Not a deputy?"

Mac watched her gambol around the room like a growing colt just finding out its legs were meant to race free and wild. She sure covered enough ground when she really started to move, he thought. He waited patiently as Nell shoved her nightstick into her belt loop, then picked up her hat, positioning it perfectly on her short dark hair. When he had her attention again, he murmured in his most provocative tone, "You're a woman, aren't you?"

He watched as she went into a slow burn. Lord, but Nell was fun to tease. She'd always been more fun than his sister, Caitlin. Nell generally gave as good as she got, while Caitlin responded with a cool, controlled, analytical response. Not that Nell wasn't cool and controlled when she needed to be. She was a cop. She just kept her fire banked a notch higher than some.

"I may be, but I'm also an officer of the law, Sheriff."

Nell's hauteur was suddenly so cold that Doug turned to stare at her.

Doug pretended to shiver, before grinning at Mac. "Whew, boss, I think the temperature just dropped thirty degrees in here."

Mac chuckled and walked toward the door. "Come on if you're coming, Nell. Or I'll have to bring Doug. I don't mind taking on Ted Kilbourne, but with his wife gone, there's no way I'm taking on his kids, too."

"Of all the—is that why you think my woman's touch will come in handy? Let me tell you, Mac Cochrane..."

Mac could still hear Nell carrying on behind him as he emerged into the bright sunshine of the October afternoon. He stopped and took a deep gulp of air. He could almost taste the sweetness of the mountain air. Crisp and tangy like a fall apple. He could smell the musky scent of the marigolds crowding to the edges of the big old wooden tubs by either side of the Sheriff's building. Their colors shone beacon bright as the sun hit them. Mac reached into his pocket for his sunglasses and hastily slipped them on.

"You look like a movie poster when you wear those things," Nell grumbled. "Brad Pitt in *The day of the Heroic Cop* or something."

Mac hunched his shoulders. He hated to look like a cliché. Brad Pitt, indeed. He'd always thought the guy a bit too pretty and never could quite see the resemblance. Although women were constantly commenting on it, so it must be so. He knew he was good-looking, but it was something he accepted rather than welcomed. After all, he didn't have anything to do with it—good genes were the culprit. Besides, his looks hadn't stopped his ex-fiancée from practically leaving him at the altar, had they?

"Hit a nerve, did I, Sheriff?"

He glared at Nell, noticing the grin that proved she wasn't awed by him at the moment. "No way, Phillips."

Ignoring Nell's chuckle, Mac strode around the first patrol car in the lot and bent down to unlock the side door, catching sight of himself in the mirror as he did so. *Heroic cop, eh?*

He'd been told over and over again that the aviator style shades lent him a mysterious air, making him inscrutable and dashing. Mac supposed it was good to be a romantic figure. It didn't pay the rent, but it certainly gave him more than his share of women. Too bad he considered all of them only temporary. There was no way he was falling into that love trap again. One woman had already danced on his heart and publicly humiliated him. Only an idiot would leave himself open to another episode, especially in a town the size of Knightsboro. Whatever else he was, he wasn't dumb.

He automatically slid into the driver's side while Nell got into the other side. He started to adjust the seat, then stopped to turn to Nell. "Sorry. Did you want to drive?" As the sheriff he wasn't expected to ask, but he did have manners. His mama had seen to that.

"What, little ol' me, Mr. Sheriff, sir? Ooohhh, I don't think I can handle a powerful ve-*hic*-le like this. I might need to powder my nose and then I'd run right into something while I'm lookin' in the mirror."

Mac laughed. "Just for the sight of you powdering your nose, Slim, it'd almost be worth it." Taking a good look at his deputy folded into the seat next to him, he realized that was true. He couldn't imagine Nell doing something so chocolate-box princessy. That wasn't Nell's way. Nell was one of the most comfortable females he knew, Mac thought, more like one of the boys than a woman. He never had to worry about her. Never had to pull his punches and consider hurting her feminine feelings. Not that he deliberately tried to antagonize anyone. He cared for his people and tried to be a good leader. He preferred to lead by example rather than bullying.

Sending him a quizzical look, Nell said, "What's the matter, is my face on crooked?"

"No more than before." Nell's face looked the same as usual to Mac. She wore very little makeup. She didn't really need it, he thought. Her pixie-cut hair framed smooth skin, tanned to deep honey, as if the warmth of the sun had been captured in her complexion. Her eyes were unique—a slash of brown brow arched over pupils of golden caramel framed by soot-colored lashes. The overall effect was vivid and violently alive in her oval face. Her body was slender with lean, firm muscle tone and she stood tall—about five-eight in her stocking feet. No little bitty woman this, Mac thought. Instead, an amazon who would just as soon pound you as look at you, or so she tried to make everyone believe. Then Nell moved. Casually she stretched an arm back over her head to reach her seat belt. As she did so her chest thrust forward, the outline of a breast firmly pressing against the dark gray of her uniform shirt. The effect was almost startlingly feminine, provocative and stunningly sensual. As was the small noise she made as she fumbled for the strap. Mac almost choked on his swallowed breath.

What the hell! He started to sweat. *Come on, Mac, get a grip. This is Nell.*

He backed up the car as if the cops were after him.

"Mac..."

He could almost imagine his name purring from her lips as she licked his ear, those long, long legs primed for action. Purring—that's a good one. Anxious to escape the direction his thoughts were heading, about Nell Phillips of all people, Mac hit the brakes, then slammed the car into drive and pressed his foot down. The car practically screamed out of the parking lot.

"Mac, what're you doing?"

This is what I get for missing that date last night.

Bracing her hand against the dashboard, Nell darted him a look. "Watch out for Mr. McNulty's Buick. If you hit that your life ain't worth dirt."

"I see it." Mac swerved to avoid the 1950s green Buick parked in front of the produce store. He could have sworn he saw Mr. McNulty's round face peering out of the window at him, too, his mouth open in horror.

Nell fixed him with a stern stare. "Maybe I *should* drive."

Mac fumbled to come up with an excuse for his actions. One besides *I was looking at your body and suddenly fantasizing about what it would be like to take you to bed.* "I...uh...just had the spring adjusted on the gas pedal. I guess I wasn't thinking." To his relief, after one searching glance, Nell let it go.

They drove down Main Street in silence. Recovering from what Mac swore must have been a moment of insanity, he looked around. He noticed Nell doing the same thing. Each of them was actively surveying their environment as cops tended to do, even when they were off duty. And what an environment it was. Mac couldn't have asked for better. The town shone as bright as a freshly shone badge.

Knightsboro was known for its beautifully maintained historical buildings, cozy shops, well-tended landscapes and flowers galore. The jaunty colors of the blooms were overflowing in window boxes, drooping from hanging containers on the gas lampposts and bunched in large wrought iron planters displayed here and there to add to the town's charm. The fresh breeze carried the ripe scent of autumn, mingled with other natural perfumes and topped off by the scent of sticky cinnamon buns from Ada Mae Baker's restaurant. This town was the perfect place to call home. The perfect place to raise a family. The perfect place for a honeymoon. Melinda Jeffries' bed-and-breakfast even had a heart-shaped bed bought from a Niagara Falls hotel that had closed a while back.

Knightsboro was a great town, from the events geared toward visiting tourists, to the charm and quaintness that beckoned people to sample its slow, old-fashioned delights. Both the town and the residents invited—"Y'all come on in and set a spell or stroll through the park or have a piled-to-the-sky ice-cream cone and don't worry about those calories. Y'all can diet tomorrow."

All anyone needed to make Knightsboro complete was someone to share it with.

Mac's brother, Daryn, the supersuave New York City lawyer, dated constantly but didn't have anyone special, either. He sure as hell wished Daryn would get married. Maybe then his mother would stop trying to marry him off and leave him alone. His mother had a terminal case of wedding fever. If she didn't stop trying to set him up with women, he'd go nuts! Mac didn't want to get married, did he? *Nah!* Still, the thought nagged at him. *Maybe I do need someone in my life.*

Mac rolled his neck, trying to rid himself of the tension that seemed to invade him almost without him even being aware of it. *Why the hell am I so dissatisfied with life all of a sudden. I'm aching like I've got the flu and even imagining things about my own deputy, who I've known practically since I was in diapers.* Mac frowned and shifted on his seat as he picked up speed out of town. *This is stupid.* His nerves jumped and his tension increased as Nell crossed her legs, which shifted his attention to the lean limbs covered by the gray cotton of her lightweight uniform. His hand jerked and the car swerved over the center line before he righted it.

"I'm giving up coffee," Mac blurted. "I think I'm drinking too much caffeine."

Nell turned from her contemplation of the forests, which were starting to thicken now that they had left the town and were climbing higher into the mountains. "Caffeine? That's your problem?"

"Must be. I can't think of anything else."

"That's why you're like a bear with a backache?"

"I'm sure of it." He held his hand out. "Look at me. I'm all jangly."

Nell turned, lifting her knee onto her seat to get more comfortable so she could take a better look. She'd never seen anyone less jangly in all of her life. To her, he didn't look nervous—he looked ticked off and ripe for danger. As if something wasn't sitting right in his mind, or his stomach maybe. She wondered what it was. Then she snapped her fingers, saying with a little smirk, "Hey, Mac, I don't think it's coffee. I think you're overtired. Probably the results of that hot date you had last night."

"What hot date?"

"Weren't you supposed to go out with that redheaded tourist you met at Charlie's Place the other night?"

"How'd you know about that redheaded tourist?"

Nell pursed her lips, trying to look as innocent as a Catholic choirboy. "Oh, you know."

"No, I don't know."

Nell grinned. "People talk."

Mac thumped the heel of his hand on the steering wheel. "How come people can't keep their opinions to themselves? They always have to have something to gossip about."

"Only if it's something interesting." As he glared at her, Nell thought, *Ooh, wrong answer.* She'd forgotten how sensitive he could be to loose tongues. Of course, in his situation she would be, too, she thought. Usually he covered it up.

"Who told you about that girl?"

"Nobody told me. I saw you pretending she was a warm piece of cherry pie and you were the ice cream."

With an almost comical expression, Mac asked, "Where'd you come up with that?"

Nell shrugged, then grinned. "I don't know. I guess the entire thing seemed rather gooey to me, that's all."

"Goo-ey." Mac drawled the word, his brow creased in thought. "Nobody's ever called me gooey. Are you trying to tell me my technique needs work?"

"Not at all, Sheriff. I'm sure it appeals to some."

Mac scowled. "I'm sure it does."

His face looked so sulky that Nell didn't know whether to scrub the temper off him or laugh out loud. If he were one of her brothers, she'd tease him until he smiled. Come to think of it, Mac generally had a great sense of humor. But before she could apply herself to putting him in a better mood, she noticed a dilapidated mailbox by a gravel driveway. "Mac. There's the turnoff to the Kilbourne cabin."

Slowing down, Mac turned and carefully negotiated the gravel path. *Driveway* was too grand a word for a lane pitted with deep ruts in more than a few places. Nell hoped they wouldn't break an axle, because that sure wouldn't do Mac's mood any good. He'd probably make her walk back to town!

As they climbed to the top of the hill, Nell noticed the steep drop-off on either side of the driveway. This was a true home for an ancestor of the "hill and holler" people. "This place is practically in the middle of nowhere. Every time I come out here I feel I'm stepping back in time."

"I know what you mean. It's peaceful, though."

As Mac rounded a corner, Nell stared at a log house that stood surrounded by pines. Although the setting was spectacular, it wasn't the type of sophisticated log house that all the back-to-the-country dwellers were building these days. It was an old, lived-in place that looked as if it belonged in a black-and-white film from an earlier era. The basic house was rather shabby—small and blockish with a porch running along the entire length, but to Nell's surprise a newer extra wing jutted off to the right. She jerked her thumb. "Looks like Ted's doing some building." Nell laughed. "The homemade beverage business must be good."

Grinning back, Mac agreed. "At least the cows are buying."

Nell swept a keen eye over the homestead. "Looks kinda deserted."

"Yeah." Mac's tone prompted a nod of agreement from Nell. "That's not good, 'cause then we'll have to go find him." He pulled to a stop as close as he could to the house, but they still had to walk up a path to where the home perched on top of its mountain.

Nell got out of the car and remarked over her shoulder, "If the kids are inside, they'll hear the car." She started up the well-worn track, checking to be certain Mac was following.

"Probably. Better call out, though, so they don't reach for a shotgun."

Nell nodded and called, "Anybody home?" as she rounded a huge rock as creased and pitted as an old prune. The timeless nature of the mountains held true here, Nell thought. For mountain people life had a different reality. Separate from the influence of civilized society, life took on an elemental quality that was more related to nature's whims than man's. She concentrated on the five children who tumbled out the door. Even up here, though, man's nature could still get him into trouble, she thought as she noticed Ted Junior, bringing up the rear.

"Hi, there." Nell smiled and kept walking forward, with Mac close behind. She took a good look at the youngsters from the oldest of about fourteen to one of about seven who was holding the smallest, a squirming toddler in her arms. Nell approached the steps, tactfully stopping at the bottom so she didn't tower over the littlest children.

Junior stepped forward. "Hey there, Deputy. Sheriff."

"Hey, Junior," Nell said. "What's up?"

Junior grinned. "Well, I haven't blown anything up this week, if that's what ya mean."

Mac chuckled. "Glad to hear it."

Junior's sister stepped forward. "It were an accident, Sheriff. Junior was just trying to help Daddy and—poof!"

Nodding, Junior said, "That's right. I was inventing a new formula for—" He exhaled with a whoosh as the oldest girl elbowed him in the ribs.

"Mama said hush up about that or she'd have to give you what-fer."

Mac walked up and sat down on one of the steps, removing his hat. "Hi." He looked straight at the oldest girl and said, "I'll bet you're Jennie. Right?"

Jennie nodded. "Yes, sir."

"Well now, Jennie, I met your mama when she wasn't much older than you. You're just as pretty as she is, too."

Jennie's cheeks turned pink. "Really?"

Nell smiled. Mac's charm, when he decided to use it, was lethal on women of every age. She watched as he made himself seem even more at ease, physically and vocally. His deep voice fell into a more down-home and rhythmical way of talking than was usual. All of this was Mac's way of getting the information without seeming threatening. Nell approved of these tactics. She tried to use them herself.

The third-oldest child, a boy, said eagerly, "Do know my daddy, too?"

"I sure do." Mac looked around for a moment before getting to the point. "Do you know where I can find him?"

Nell watched the kids close ranks, automatically protecting their father. Kilbournes stuck together, Nell thought. She admired that. "Is your Daddy here? Can we see him?"

They all looked at one another for a second. Finally Jennie said, "Not right now."

"Daddy's working," a small voice piped up from the little girl struggling to contain the restless youngest boy.

Nell cocked her head. "Working where?"

"Up yonder."

Before Nell or Mac could say a word, Jennie walked over to the child and took the toddler from her. Jennie said, "Hush, Lily." The little girl subsided with a huff, stalked over to a chair and plunked down.

Junior smiled. "Daddy'll be back soon. We'll tell him you stopped by."

"We're going to stick around and wait a bit," Nell said. For a moment the kids didn't move. Nell searched for something to say to break the silence, but wasn't sure of the best way to disarm the suddenly suspicious children. Mac came up with it.

Smiling, Mac said, "That little guy looks just like Ted. Could I hold him, Jennie?" He held out his arms for the little one and settled more comfortably on the step. "What's his name?"

"Benjie. He's almost two."

Mac nodded, chuckling when Benjie reached for his hat, pulled it off and settled it on his head. "That's a good name. I don't quite remember the rest of your names?"

The younger boy stepped up, "I'm Tyler."

Nell watched Mac make friends with the children, marveling at his easy way with people. No matter who they were or where they were from, he treated people the same—with respect and a light touch of humor when appropriate, of course. Nell envied that. She envied a person who could adapt so well to all situations. He'd even adapted to having his hometown sweetheart throw him over for a man with a better future—according to the sweetheart, at least. How many men could deal with that?

Nell looked at Mac as he played with the little boy and teased the other children. The man looked so perfect he was intimidating, Nell thought, noticing the way his blond hair glowed as the sun peeking through the trees hit it. The way his smile gleamed, his straight strong teeth flashing as Junior said something to him. The way his eyes snapped with life as he glanced over at Lily. A pang went through Nell. She wasn't sure why. What was Mac to her, after all, except an old childhood friend who now happened to be her boss? She caught a whiff of his aftershave—evergreen, or was it juniper? Something strong and masculine, like the man who wore it.

Cindy must have been nuts!

Not that Nell ever did think much of his old girlfriend. To Nell's mind she'd been way too stuck on herself, and she'd treated Mac like her own personal lapdog. Nell had always been surprised he'd put up with it. Unless he was so besotted or used to the situation that he didn't even notice. After all Cindy Gedding was considered "prime" by most of the guys in town, including Nell's brothers. Nell could never figure out how the girl ever did it. How she'd wound all the men around her little finger. If only Nell had one-tenth of the feminine wiles that big-chested blonde had had, she wouldn't be without a man at the moment. *Moment, hell! Man ever. Period.*

Stepping forward, Jennie said, "We have lemonade and cookies. Wouldja like some?" Nell thought no high-society hostess could ever be as welcoming as this young girl. Obviously her mother was teaching her well.

Mac nodded. "That'd be great."

"I'd love some," Nell added, smiling as Jennie organized her sister and brothers into the house to get the refreshments. She glanced at Mac, amazed to see Benjie had fallen asleep in his arms.

Jerking her thumb to the slumbering child, Nell wrinkled her nose and whispered, "How'd you do that?"

Mac grinned. "Luck?"

"I don't think so. Obviously you've got the right technique with kids."

Mac should be a father. He'd be a good one, Nell thought as she watched him remove his hat and smooth Benjie's hair. Stupid Cindy hadn't known a good thing when she'd had it.

"Just with kids?" Mac winked. "What about those smooth ice-cream moves you were commenting on before?"

She rolled her eyes. "All right. You're just full of techniques. Happy now?"

"I've been telling you for years, Slim. Stay here and marvel at the master. You could learn a thing or two."

"Oh, please. You sound like my oldest brother. To listen to him, you'd think his wife had nothing to do with them having their first baby."

Mac winked. "We get to do the real fun stuff."

"What makes you think that part's not fun for women, too?" To Nell's amusement, Mac blushed. She teased, "Well, well, well. Your face is a bit red there, Sheriff. How come?"

Mac shifted around, avoiding her gaze. "Is not."

"Is too."

"Well, damn, Slim." He lowered his voice to a whisper. "It's hard to think about you enjoying sex."

"Why?"

"'Cause I've know you since you were four."

"So?"

"So, it's uncomfortable is all."

Before Nell could say anything else, the kids slammed out of the house, maneuvered past them down the steps and trouped over to a picnic table set under a tree.

"Y'all come on over," Jennie called as she and the other children arranged the pitcher, cups and plate of cookies.

Mac shifted his burden and stood up, smiling as Benjie opened his eyes and started to squirm. "Okay, okay, I'll put you down."

A faint rumble of thunder growled in the distance. Nell glanced at the sky before turning to Mac. "Think we should go looking for Ted?"

"No way. I don't know where that still of his is, and I don't want to know." Mac gestured toward the woods and mountains surrounding them. "But we'd get lost sure as we're standing here. I don't want to be out there with a storm coming up."

Noise from the children captured their attention. They watched as Ted and his brother Jed strolled out of the woods.

At the sight of them, Ted stopped short so abruptly that his brother ran into him.

Finally Ted called, "Hey there, Mac. I'll bet Hilda sent you, right?"

2

"In a roundabout way, Ted," Mac called out, walking toward the two men.

Nell trailed behind him, watching with amusement as the two brothers almost fell over to explain themselves, reminding Nell of puppies. If puppies could be in their late thirties, wear matching blue overalls with plaid shirts, and ball caps.

"It were an accident, Mac."

Jed nodded then grabbed his head. "We had a busted hose."

"Me and Jed's already taken care of the problem."

Nell folded her arms. "You have, huh?"

Mac firmed his mouth, but it was twitching a bit at the corners. "Does that mean you've dismantled that bug-juice maker you've hidden up there in the woods, Ted?"

"Now, Mac, I'm turning over a new leaf. I'm going legit—totally."

"Kind of a shame, though," Jed said. "Those were the happiest cows I ever seen."

"Yep," Ted agreed. "By God, people've been driving up to Hilda's farm as fast as they could to get a jug of that milk."

Nell laughed. She couldn't help it. After a moment, she got control of herself and said, "What did you mean you're going legitimate, Ted?"

"I'm applying for licenses and overhauling my equipment and everything."

"Since when?"

Ted pulled a book out of his back pocket and slapped it for emphasis. "Since me and Jed discovered we got to target our market better."

"Target your market?"

"That's right. Me and Jed are entre...entre—"

"Manures," Jed chimed in. "Entermanures."

"I think you mean entrepreneurs...independent business owners?"

Jed stood straighter and Ted patted his book again. "We got lots of good ideas from this. We gotta put them in action, and the Harvest Festival is coming up, so—"

"Wait a minute." Nell stepped forward. "You're not planning on exposing visitors to your—"

"Of course not, Deputy," Ted reassured her. "Not too many people've got the constitution for my daddy's recipe—"

Jed bowed his head. "God rest his soul."

"—so we have to adapt our product." Ted jerked his thumb toward the table. "Ted, Junior's been working on that in school."

Eyeing Junior, Nell laughed. "That's how he blew up the chemistry lab?"

"Uh-huh." Jed nodded. "We had a miscalculation."

Mac grinned. "Since your recipe tastes like paint thinner and is twice as strong, I'd agree with you. But I'm glad to hear you're changing your ways."

Giving a saintly nod, Ted said, "Oh, we are."

"Good," Mac said, "it'll make my life easier."

Ted nodded, folding his hands solemnly. "That's important to me, Sheriff. But it's a shame in a way. In my daddy and granddaddy's day, it was a lot easier to make a living at the family business. All they had to do was walk down the hill and hand over a jug." Ted indicated the table where his children were sitting. "You want to set yourself down and have some of this lemonade?"

"One quick glass, then we have to go." Mac looked at Nell for her agreement, then joined the kids at the table.

Nell stood at the end of the picnic table and accepted a glass from Jennie. Taking a drink, she said, "This is the best homemade lemonade this side of Ada Mae Baker's restaurant."

Ted nodded proudly. "That's 'cause Ada Mae gave them the recipe."

"You're kidding? She must really like 'em, then, because I've been trying to get that recipe since I was a little squirt."

Chuckling, Mac said, "You can't cook worth a damn, Slim. That's probably why Ada Mae wouldn't give it to you."

"How could you ruin lemonade?"

Mac adjusted his hat. "You'd find a way."

Ted handed her a cookie. "It's time for you to be married and have a passel of kids of your own, isn't it?"

Scowling, Nell commented, "You sound like my mother."

"She's probably right." Jed weaved around the other end of the table, leaning very close to Nell to hand her another glass of lemonade. "Here you go, lovely lady."

At his breath, Nell almost fell over. "Jed, what on earth have you been drinking?"

"I'm the taster for our new product." Jed slurred his words a bit. "We're having a heck of a time getting it right." He peered owlishly at her and attempted to put his arm around her. "Have I ever told you how beautiful you are?"

"Oh, for—" With a quick move, Nell lifted her leg and swept Jed's out from under him. He sat down on the ground with a thump.

The kids started laughing, and shouted, "Way to go, Deputy."

"That's what you get, Uncle Jed."

"Good thing Mom's not here or she'd thump you yourself."

Ted rushed over to pick Jed up. "Jed, what are you doing?"

"Just trying to help."

"Help what?"

"Well, the other day in town, people were saying it's a shame the deputy ain't married yet, so I thought she'd appreciate it if I—"

"Wh-wh-who—" Nell sputtered. She hit her forehead with the heel of her hand. "Oh, great. My mother must be calling everyone in Knightsboro, begging them to find me a man. That's all I need."

"Yep," Jed said. "So I thought I'd help. You're not my type, but—"

"Well, Jed, seeing as how you're married with seven kids of your own, how could I be?"

Jed scratched his head. "Oh. I hadn't thought of that."

Mortified, Nell placed her glass on the table. "I must really need help to find a man if Jed Kilbourne is coming to my rescue," she muttered.

Standing up, Mac came around the table and took her arm, teasing, "I'll gladly offer my assistance, if you'd prefer, Deputy Phillips."

For a moment, Nell stared at Mac. He might be joking, she thought, but she wasn't doing too well on her own at the moment. She licked her lips, studying the amused man standing near her. "You know, I think I'll take you up on that."

Mac recoiled. "Huh?"

"That's a good idea," Ted said, with Jed and the children nodding in agreement. "Mac knows what men like. Don't you, Mac?"

"Well, I guess I do, but…" Mac looked around him like a hunted animal.

"And in return," Nell continued, "I can help you."

"I don't need any—"

"This is good." Ted placed a hand on each of their shoulders. "Don't you worry about a thing." He nodded to his family, who nodded back. "We'll help, too."

The rumble of thunder grew closer. Nell noted the breeze that picked up, stirring the leaves above in a sudden burst of chatter. The air smelled of rain. It also had that unique smell of fall in the mountains—part forest loam and part moisture. It was definitely time to leave. Up here the weather could be soft and gentle as a fawn or mean as an old rattler with a fang-ache.

"We'd better get going, Mac. The storm might hit soon."

Ted gave them a beneficent smile, shooing them in front of him like wayward ducks. "You come back anytime. Always ready to welcome the long arm of the law, not to mention seeing old friends." Ted stood at the edge of the trail.

Jed joined him as they watched the sheriff and his deputy head down the path.

Giving his cheek a thoughtful rub, Ted said, "I'll bet you Deputy Nell will be standing in front of a minister before the month is out."

Jed stuck his hand into his pocket and withdrew his wallet. "And I'll bet you that Sheriff Mac will be the one in front of a minister in the next month."

Ted eyed his brother, then turned back to catch the tail end of Nell as she disappeared down the trail. "You think other people'd be interested in betting on the outcome?"

"Sure," Jed said. "Why not?"

"If we take a percentage, Jed, we can even get some extra cash for our business."

Jed clasped Ted's shoulder. "Now that's thinking like an entremanure."

STOPPING BY A LARGE ROCK on the path down to their patrol car, Nell looked back at the house, which suddenly seemed warmer and friendlier than it had when they'd arrived. To Nell, even the garden looked fuller and more vibrant—the pumpkins rounder, the mums cheerier and the weeds less obvious. A thought flitted through her head—had someone put something in her lemonade? *Oh, don't be dumb!* Shaking her head, she stepped back and stumbled over a protruding log.

Mac grabbed her. "Whoa, there. Don't wanna lose you yet."

"Thanks, Sheriff. Nice to know that old protective instinct of yours keeps coming out."

Mac released her. "It's ingrained, I guess. To serve and protect."

"Speaking of service, let's get it out into the open, okay?"

Mac bunched his shoulders, looking away. "Get what out?"

"I'm going to take you up on your offer, Mac."

"What offer?"

"Helping me find a man."

"Uh…uh…" Mac's jaw dropped as he turned to stare at

her. Frowning, Nell flicked her finger under his chin to close his mouth.

"You'll let in flies. I don't see why you find my request so odd."

Mac regained his wits—sort of. "Because generally you ask my help with finding unruly kids, lost dogs or criminals. Not men."

Shrugging, Nell replied, "That's probably because I've never had a need for your help before."

"Why do you need it now?"

"Because I'm having no luck finding one by myself." She scowled, digging her fingernail into her thigh as she ran her thumb across her pant leg. "And my mother is driving me nuts with her phone calls asking who I'm dating and when she's gonna need to send out wedding invitations. 'Oh, and Nell, I'd like to be a grandmother to your children before I'm too old to lift them—ha, ha, ha. After all, your biological clock is ticking, you know.'" She groaned. "Ticking, hell. According to my mother it's ready to explode! And now she's made my dilemma public information." Nell grabbed her hair. "I can't take any more."

"All mothers do that, Slim."

Nell glanced at him. "Not all mothers have a daughter who is a five-foot-eight cop, a dead shot with a pistol and can throw her date across the room if he tries something she doesn't like."

"Oh." Mac nodded. "Yeah, that could be a problem. It was effective with Jed, though."

Nell chuckled for a moment then looked away, growing serious again. "There are some things I'm not too good at. Take those children back there. You were very good with those kids, Mac."

Mac sent her a wary glance. "Don't get any ideas."

"About what?" Nell jerked her head around to stare at him. "Oh, come on! Are you imagining that I've got you in mind when I say I'm looking for a man?"

"No...I didn't mean..."

"That's good. Because I've known you way too long to

fall for your baby-blue eyes, you know. I've seen you with scabby knees, even seen your scrawny butt when you went skinny-dipping with your brother and mine when we were kids.''

Offended, Mac grabbed her shoulder and gave it a little shake. ''My butt isn't quite as scrawny now.''

Nell chuckled. ''No matter. My point is we've known each other since we were kids. Somehow that kills the romance.''

Mac thought for a moment. ''You could be right.''

''That's why I think you'd be perfect to help me.''

''Well, when you put it like that.''

Nell single-mindedly ticked the next reason off on her finger. ''Then there's your technique. I was really serious, complimenting your technique with children.'' Her mother's hints aside, Nell wanted children. At least she thought she did.

Mac raised a quirky eyebrow. ''According to you, I've got a technique with everyone.''

''You do. I wish I did.'' Nell scuffed the toe of her boot in the hard-packed dirt again. Finally she sighed and looked up. ''Part of the problem is I'm just not very feminine. I know I've got a lot of good qualities, but most of the time men don't stick around long enough to discover them. I think I need some help in...*packaging* myself, I guess you'd say.''

''Sounds as if you've been reading Ted's marketing book.''

''Well, face it, how am I ever going to find a husband if I can't present the merchandise a bit better?''

''I can't believe you're serious.'' Mac tipped his hat back to take a better look at her. ''When did you get this idea? You knew I was just kidding before when I offered—''

''Yeah, but I've been thinking about it for a bit. Since I saw you with that redhead the other night. Talk about the battle of the sexes. Advance, retreat—you two had the moves down pat.''

''You saw me?'' Mac's brows snapped together, obviously trying to remember. ''I didn't see you. What were you doing there?''

''I had a date.''

''A date?''

Like a restless filly, Nell tossed her head, almost losing her hat in the process. "What's so strange about that?"

"From what you've been saying…" Mac stopped, took off his hat, shoved his hand through his hair then jammed it back on his head all in one movement. "Well, Slim, now that you mention it, I guess I don't think of you dating."

"See. You and the rest of the men in Knightsboro." Shaking her head, Nell spoke in a voice she tried to keep extra steady so Mac wouldn't see how hurt she was. She might be asking for his help, but it wasn't the easiest thing she'd ever done. She was just trying to make it seem that way. "I expect it from the rest of the world. I know it sounds dumb, but I wish you thought more of me."

"I think a lot of you."

"Would you think of me as a woman you might want?"

He flushed, suddenly so pink that Nell wondered what on earth she'd said. "Well, would you?" He was quiet so long, Nell folded her arms, shivering as if the coldness that suddenly came into her heart wasn't man-made. "That's what I thought. See. I told you my technique needs a bit of work."

"What do you want me to do?"

"Mac, can you help me make myself more appealing? Sexier?" She hugged herself tighter, afraid of rejection or a big guffaw. In which case she'd have to drop-kick him.

Mac sent her a considering look. "Why? Seems to me I could lose a good deputy here."

"*Why?*" For a moment Nell thought she'd have to surgically remove her eyebrows from the top of her forehead. "Because I need a man, that's why."

"What for?"

She stared at Mac as if he'd just lost every IQ point he'd ever possessed. Her lips twitched as she considered telling him. She might not date a lot, but she still had urges. She was human, after all. Maybe she shouldn't tell him that, though. Inwardly Nell was mortified enough. She couldn't believe she was telling him what she was telling him already! But the more she stared at him, the more her sense of humor came to her rescue. But before she could comment, the light dawned on Mac.

"Oh...oh, yeah. I get it."

"That's why you're such a brilliant sheriff, Sheriff." His face was so red, Nell had to forcibly keep her lips nailed shut so she didn't explode with a belly laugh.

"Slim, I think you're making too much of this. You shouldn't have to make yourself over for anyone. Honest, you're fine just as you are."

Jerking a thumb toward the garden, Nell said, "So's that scarecrow up there, but you'll notice the crows are avoiding him. Why is that? It's 'cause the crows got it figured out. No sex appeal, that's why."

"Nell, trust me. You've got more sex appeal than that scarecrow."

"More than your redhead?"

"Well, as to that, I gotta tell you, I never did make it to that date. I had to cancel it. I spent the night chasin' down a perp who'd broken into the Weathers' house on Summers Lane." Mac rolled his eyes. "The way that kid ran me all over town he must've been a track star. By the time I nailed him and got him into a cell and did the paperwork, it was damn near dawn. I racked out on my living room couch for a while. Then I went into the office."

"So one more disappointed woman bites the dust?"

"Guess so."

Nell laughed at his hangdog look. She turned and started down the path. "It's just as well, Mac. You're always picking women who are wrong for you anyway."

"Says who?"

Nell could almost feel his indignant question breathing down her neck. "Says anyone who really knows you."

"No one's ever said that to me before."

Whirling to face him, she placed her hands on her hips. "Well, duh! Why am I not surprised?"

"What do you mean by that."

"The only people you ask for your opinions are your deputies…and three-quarters of those guys spend their time thinking with their—"

"Hold on. My male deputies are fine, upstanding—"

"So's my German shepherd and his only thought is about trying to make puppies with the little dust-mop dog next door." Mac looked so perplexed for a moment that Nell relented. Obviously his lack of sleep was taking a toll. "All I'm saying is you choose women for the wrong reasons."

Mac grinned, a wicked grin that made Nell yearn to lick it off his lips. She froze. *What the hell is the matter with me? This is Mac, for cryin' out loud. My childhood buddy.*

"Oh, I don't know about that, Slim."

Nell wished she had a fire extinguisher to put out the flame in her cheeks and to hose down the man opposite her. He suddenly looked more dangerous than a fox trying to sweet-talk a chicken. "Okay. Granted the women you choose are appealing for…for…" She scowled as Mac put his fist to his mouth, seeming to strangle. "For more than their personalities."

Now Mac laughed out loud. "Slim. Their personalities have nothing to do with it."

"Even so, you keep choosing women who only want to hang on your arm and stroke your muscles."

"Doesn't sound bad to me."

With a dogged expression, Nell continued, "Or you keep getting involved with those needy types who want a big, strong sheriff to lean on. So, for the long term—"

"There is no long term. It's only dating."

"That's my point. There can be no long term, because every women you choose is wrong for you."

"I don't care." He glared at her. "I thought I had the woman who was right for me. Look what happened."

"Cindy had the brains of a gnat. You're well rid of her."

"Of a gnat?" Mac looked hurt for a moment, then annoyed. "I dated her all through high school and college. I was going to marry her. That doesn't say much for my judgment, does it?" He stormed past her.

Nell followed him, matching him step for step. "Exactly. What do you think I'm talking about?"

Mac hunched his shoulders so high his hat practically covered them. He snarled over his shoulder. "I thought we were talking about your problems, not mine."

"The way I see it, Mac, they're just opposite sides of the same coin." Nell forgot what she was saying, her attention caught instead by the way his buttocks clenched with every stride down the path. She let herself enjoy the sight for a moment. She really had to admit that Mac Cochrane was a yummy man. Broad shoulders, slim hips, lean legs—the body of a well-toned runner instead of a bodybuilder. What a shame they were just friends.

A sharp crack of lightning ripped through the sky. It was followed almost immediately by a drumroll of thunder and a brisk breeze. Mac stopped short, halting so suddenly that Nell ran into him. Another flash followed, then another.

Nell removed her nose from between his shoulder blades. "Damn, Mac. I told you it was going to rain." She'd no more than opened her mouth when the sky opened and the water rolled down in sheets. Within moments they were both drenched. Mac's arm slid around her waist, urging her forward.

"Come on, Slim. We're almost to the car. Let's make a run for it."

He was right. They were closer to the car than the cabin. Together they ran along the path, jumping over the dry branches dislodged by the roaring wind. Nell slid down the remaining slope, only to be caught in Mac's arms. Her own automatically lifted and circled his shoulders. For a moment all reason fled. She forgot about the rain, forgot about the lightning and thunder and thought only of the feel of his body against hers. The clothing pasted to their bodies removed all semblance of restraint, taking her back to the time when nature ruled. She could think only of the way they fit together from chest to thigh. Of the way she could feel his chest beating against her breasts. Of the strength and sinew of his arms as they tightened involuntarily. Nell arched, tempting him to satisfy her ache as their bodies rubbed against each other. The raspy sound of his breathing sliced into her. She started to lift her head, to offer him her lips when she realized what she was doing. She jumped back.

"I...um..."

Mac seemed just as disoriented. "Yeah...uh-huh..."

"We'd better...um, get, um..." She didn't know *what* to say. She'd never been so embarrassed in her entire life. Not even when she was thirteen years old and got her period in history class.

"Get going."

"Yes. Going. Before the back roads, um..."

"Get hard—uh, hard—"

Nell glanced at his face, his expression making it very clear he was not just thinking about the roads. As their eyes met, he flushed. Probably not as much as she, judging by the way her clothes were almost starting to smoke as the rain continued to pelt them.

"Goddammit." Mac whipped around and almost raced behind the car, headed for the driver's side. He waved an arm at the passenger door, and yelled above the storm, "Get in."

Nell was still so shaken by her unexpected desire that she couldn't move. Picking up her feet seemed the most difficult chore she'd ever undertaken.

Mac leaned across the seat, and opened the passenger door. "Will you get in here before you drown?"

At the moment drowning was almost preferable to the embarrassment waiting for her within the confined space of the patrol car. Her mind scattered in twenty directions as she tried to find an alternative. Mac saved her the trouble. Before she could protest, he was out of the car and nudging her toward the open door, practically sweeping her onto the seat like unwanted junk mail. He whipped off her hat and sent it sailing to the rear seat. Then her door slammed closed with an echo that almost outdid the storm.

She could barely see Mac as he came around the car again and slid in the other side. The water streamed down the windows, causing the flashing lightning to take on distorted images. The seat creaked as Mac adjusted it, trying to get comfortable enough to drive. He flipped the switch on the heater; the breeze was cool enough to make her shiver until it started to warm. The radio murmured, its usual squawk muted by static as the storm interfered with communications. Her fingertips still tingled with the feel of sliding over the bottom edge of his hair. She could taste the passion that lingered like overly sweet frosting on a cake. For this moment the patrol car was their own little world. Familiar, yet strange. A world that would either change everything they knew about each other or would be swept under the rug, glossed over as a momentary lapse in behavior. After all, who knew better what surprising actions humans were capable of than a policeman or woman? Confused, Nell sneaked a peek at Mac. Under his hat, his face was carved granite, stony and remote as he started the car. She let out the breath she hadn't known she'd been holding.

A momentary lapse.

Yes, that's right. I'd been talking about getting involved and somehow it had transferred to Mac. Yes, that's it. As Mac threw the car into reverse, Nell reached for her seat belt and snapped it into place as he managed to turn around without getting stuck in the old track. The air between them was so thick she figured she'd need a shovel to dig her way clear. Her woman's intuition told her she'd have to take the first move to bring this situation back to normal. If Mac Cochrane was anything like her brothers, he wouldn't do it. Instead he'd pretend nothing had happened until they got back. Then Mac would ignore it until he felt enough time had passed that he didn't need to comment.

Glancing at the man behind the wheel, she wondered what to say. Suddenly she wondered if her intense physical reaction had been one-sided. Her stomach churned. *What if he'd felt nothing.* There she'd been practically throwing herself at him. Nell thought she was going to throw up. She was reaching for the knob to roll down the window when Mac cleared his throat.

"Nell—"

It startled her so much she swallowed the bitterness at the back of her mouth and coughed instead. Afraid of what he might say, she rushed into speech. "Wow, some storm, eh?"

"Which storm are you talking about?"

His comment was so dry, Nell could have used it for a towel. She sent him a fleeting glance. What did he mean by that? Was he referring to what had happened? *Damn Mac Cochrane.* Why didn't he act the way she expected him to! Like a jerk guy who refused to confront anything that remotely resembled emotions. Well, she sure as hell wasn't going to confront them at the moment. They were too confusing. Annoyed, she jerked her thumb at the window. "The storm that's going to drive us into a ditch any minute."

"The whole thing was unexpected."

That was more like it. "It came up sudden, didn't it?" Nell tried to use her sleeve to wipe off her face, but it was no use.

He plucked at his wet pants, which were outlining every hill and valley of his anatomy. "It sure did."

Nell jerked her gaze away at his comment. His voice was even drier, except there was an undercurrent of confusion, Nell thought. Her eyes dipped to his lap again, remembering how he'd felt against her. She was almost tempted to pursue the subject, but luckily started shaking instead. Her nose started to run and her teeth chattered as she said, "I'm freezing."

Mac flicked the heater on high, then dug into his pocket for his handkerchief. "This is about all I can offer at the moment."

Giving him a grateful smile, Nell took the white hankie, trying to make herself halfway presentable. She started to give it back, then realized she'd also used it to blow her nose. She jammed it into her pocket. "I'll wash this first."

"Thanks. I'd appreciate it."

Nell's lips quirked. "Don't mention it."

"Nell?"

Stiffening at his hesitant tone, she wrapped her arms around her body, trying to prepare herself for whatever he was going to say. "What?"

"Before I, um…"

"You don't have to say anything, Mac."

"Yes, I do. What I was going to say was—"

"I think we should just forget the whole thing."

"I thought you wanted my help, Nell."

"Your help?"

"To find a man. Isn't that what you wanted me to help you with?"

"Yes, but…"

"Well, I'm willing to help."

"Why?" Nell was completely confused, and embarrassed as she thought it through. Obviously he figured she was throwing herself at him and, to avoid it happening again, was offering to find someone else for her.

Mac grinned. "I think you have real possibilities. Matter of fact, you pack quite a punch. Seems to me, for the right man you'd be dynamite."

If her face didn't stop turning red, Nell thought, someone would mistake her for a traffic light. *Possibilities? For the right man?* Mac wasn't the right man, Nell knew that. He was her boss. He was familiar. She'd grown up with him. Just because she would have thrown him on the ground and had her way with him if he'd encouraged her didn't make him the right man for her. It just made him sexy as hell and a good man to practice on. Thinking hard, she nibbled her nail. "So you're agreeing to give up your time to help me make myself more appealing to the opposite sex?"

Seeming uncomfortable, he shifted on his seat. "I don't think it's gonna be all that hard, Nell." He coughed slightly and focused his attention on the road for a long moment. Finally he said, "If you want my help, I want to help. What're friends for?"

Nell glanced at him. Mac looked rather odd. Was he embarrassed or trying not to laugh. She wasn't sure, and didn't want to know. "Okay. Thanks. I'd appreciate it."

"Sure. How do you want to start?"

Nell placed her fingers together in her usual contemplative position. "I think it'd be good if we met at Charlie's Place

Saturday night. It's bound to be packed with tourists and townsfolk. Maybe we'll find a few good candidates." Hoping her smile didn't look forced, she faced him. "*You* usually manage to come up with a date there."

Mac gave her a painful grin. "Good idea. I think I could use the diversion myself."

"Who knows, your redhead might still be in town."

"Maybe we can find you a redhead of your own, Slim."

"Nah, I like dark-haired guys." At least most of the time she did, Nell thought.

"If this is gonna work, Nell, you need to keep an open mind."

"I'll give it a shot."

"Okay. Here's the plan. Meet me at eight, or did you want me to pick you up?"

"Mac, you can't pick me up. Then we'd have to go home together."

His eyes snapped to life. "We would?"

She frowned, positive he was making fun of her. "Not together like that."

"Right. I understand."

Nell was tempted to throw something at him. "Let's make a deal. I keep an open mind and you treat this seriously."

Turning to look at her, Mac nodded. "Okay, Slim. You got a deal. Just one thing, though. If I help you find the man of your dreams—"

"I'll have to help you find the woman of yours?"

"Nope. Definitely not. But what you do have to do is find a way to get *my* mother off *my* back! My loving parent has just promised Hilda that I'd take her niece out when she comes to visit. Have you ever seen Hilda's niece?"

Nell shook her head. "I can't place her."

"Let me put it this way. I'd rather date one of Hilda's drunk cows."

3

SATURDAY NIGHT, eight o'clock sharp, Mac Cochrane strode into Charlie's Place as if he either owned it or was about to arrest everyone in sight. There was a challenge in his step and a danger in the tilt of his chin, which dared anybody around to question what he was doing there. Not that anyone would, of course. He was there often enough. The old mill restaurant, with its bar and dance floor, was one of the most popular places in Knightsboro. At night, people gathered by the wall of picture windows to watch the play of colored lights on the turning waterwheel as it gobbled up the stream only to spit it back out again a few moments later. The stone wall and warm wood tones of the floor set off the mismatched tables and chairs that gave the place charm, instead of looking as if someone had raided an attic and thrown together a bunch of furniture.

The place was jumping, people were everywhere. Laughing, talking, occasionally leaning over to whisper something in a willing ear. It was the usual Saturday night. Mac paused by the entrance to the main room. To his right was the entertainment and dance area, to his left a cavernous bar full of dark woods and soft lights that made you feel like you were going to walk right into an aged barrel of whiskey. He looked around for Nell. She was nowhere in sight. Exhaling, he breathed a deep sigh of relief.

He didn't know what he was getting so uptight about. On the way over here, he'd doubted Nell would show up at Charlie's. He was sure she'd come to her senses and decide not to go through with her request for his help. *A man for Nell, of all things!* It still threw him. Was she really serious? Nell hadn't mentioned it since the day they'd gone to the Kilbournes'. Which was just as well. He'd had the past few days to think about it and a more idiotic situation he'd never encountered. Not even when old Mrs. Minetti had him tracking her cat, Minerva, through the woods to find out where she'd lost her kittens. Not that the cat had ever lost them in the first place, Mac argued. Just because Minerva hadn't wanted Mrs. Minetti to know where they were didn't mean they were lost. It didn't do any good to tell that to Mrs. Minetti. It never did when some of these old-timers could recite chapter and verse of your entire family history, down to how often your diaper had been changed and what you looked like in the bath. Mac got chills just thinking of it.

Sometimes he wondered why he hadn't left and gone to the big city. Then he'd stop and look around at the beauty that surrounded him and find his answer. He'd revel in the silence of a soft summer dawn with only the twitters of the sleepy birds accompanying the sunrise. He'd smell the sweetness of the air, almost able to taste its ripe goodness. Then he'd rub the good Tennessee earth between his fingers and wonder how he could ever leave it. He'd been a bit tempted after his wedding plans had fallen apart. Mac had found it hard to face everyone each day, knowing that his private life was the topic of most people's breakfast conversation.

One thing Mac had noticed, though, about his hometown was that once people left and got all their adventuring out of their system, they tended to come back. Plenty of his classmates had returned. Come to think of it, his brother had even mentioned it casually the last time he'd spoken with him. Not that Mac believed Daryn ever would. In some ways, Mac envied his classmates who'd settled back in Knightsboro with their spouses and families. It was the life he'd thought would be his by now. But maybe it was just as well. For the first time, when he tried to imagine himself with Cindy by his side, the picture blurred. Nell was right. Cindy had looked great, but wasn't the brightest lightbulb in the chandelier. He shuddered to think he might have been married to her when he admitted that.

Checking his watch, Mac leaned his shoulders against the wall. Eight-fifteen. Still no sign of Nell. Should he go to the bar or get something to eat? He'd only had a snack for supper. A nice big steak would just about hit the spot. He shoved away from the wall and started for an empty table when someone shouted his name.

"Mac. Over here."

He looked around. Sitting in a corner of the bar, tucked up comfortably at a small table was his deputy. Not his deputy Nell, but his newest deputy, Bobby Dee Laurance, who seemed to be making best friends with a bottle of beer. More than one bottle from the look of it, Mac thought as he sauntered toward the bar. Well, he was just a kid. Barely twenty-three. Many young people that age could match him. Although as Mac counted the bottles, he hoped his deputy would still be standing later in the evening. *Did I ever do that?* Feeling like Methuselah at the ripe old age of thirty, he approached the table.

"Hey there, Bobby Dee. What're you up to?"

Bobby Dee grinned and saluted him with his bottle. "Not much, Sheriff. Just tossing back a few before I hit the dance floor."

Eyeing the young man's flushed face, Mac said, "Seems to me you're gonna hit the floor faster than you think if you don't slow down."

"Nah, I got a hollow leg."

Mac gave him a skeptical glance. "So did the last guy I arrested."

Bobby Dee laughed and crooked his finger, indicating Mac should come closer. "Problem is, I can't dance. So every time I come here to meet girls, they wanna dance. Why do you think that is?" He frowned for a moment, then took a long pull at his bottle. "So I gotta get loosened up some so all my parts will work together with the music."

Mac laughed. "I've never thought of that solution."

"My mom made me take all these ballroom dancing classes when I was a kid."

"Yeah, mine, too."

Bobby Dee waved toward the dance floor at the other end of the room. "I didn't do nothing like that."

Mac studied the bodies across the room gyrating to a hot beat and had to agree with him. "I hear ya, kid." He waved at the waiter, who brought him a beer of his own without hesitation. "I'll bet you do one heck of a mean waltz though, don't ya?"

With a huge sigh, Bobby Dee shook his head. "I step all over my partner's feet. Truth is, I sucked at dance class."

Bobby Dee's voice was so gloomy that Mac almost choked on his beer. Wiping his mouth, he clasped the morose young man on the shoulder. "Don't worry kid. None of my deputies can dance." He didn't know that, of course, but thought it'd make Bobby Dee feel better. Mac took another long drink. The beer was starting to fill in the emptiness in his stomach. Which meant he'd better get something to eat, and fast.

Nodding at the dance floor, Bobby Dee said, "But it doesn't stop us from trying, does it?"

Mac's gaze followed Bobby Dee's pointing finger. The crowd on the floor had parted—or was it cleared—to reveal a woman in the center of the action. Lowering the bottle from his mouth, he could only stare. *Nell? That's Nell out there?* His eyes almost bugged out of his head as he watched his deputy whipping around. For a woman who could move like a panther when she wanted, she sure didn't bring her stalking skill to the dance floor. His mind flashed back to her sensual stretch to reach her seat belt a few days ago. At least he'd considered it sensual; maybe he was imagining the entire attraction. He'd been in such a damned unsettled mood lately that it could have been him. He pulled his attention back to the dance floor. For a moment more he watched Nell flail around to the music.

"She's missing the beat."

Bobby Dee whistled and agreed, "Yes, sir. I'd say she's missing damn near everything."

Mac agreed with him, almost wincing when Nell's arm nearly sideswiped the man dancing next to her. "Man, that was close."

Laughing, Bobby Dee got to his feet. "Maybe I ought to arrest her before she assaults someone."

Mac slapped his beer bottle on the table. He reached into his pocket and withdrew a notebook and a pen. He flipped it open and made a note to himself. *Work on Nell's dance technique.*

"Wow, Sheriff. Are you going to give her a ticket?"

Grinning, Mac tucked the notebook back into his pocket and headed for the dance floor, saying over his shoulder, "Could be, Bobby Dee. Could be." Leaving his young deputy behind, Mac wound his way around a few tables. Waving at people he knew, he finally reached the wooden floor where Nell was still happily moving to her own rhythm. He bit back a laugh. She might not be the smoothest dancer on the floor, but she was certainly the most energetic. He touched an arm here and there, managing to slink between the closely packed dancers. Tapping Nell on the shoulder, he said, "Hey there, Slim." He ducked to avoid her fist as she swung around to face him.

"I thought you'd chickened out."

"I might have if I'd seen you in action before now." Laughing, he grabbed her wrist and ushered her toward the edge of the crowd. "Let's get you out of here before I have to arrest you as a moving violation."

Protesting all the way, Nell followed him. "Hey, the song's not over yet!"

"Better to retire from the field of battle while you're still on your feet, Deputy." He looked back in time to see a puzzled look on her face. It made him want to smile and groan at the same time. What had he gotten himself into. He pulled her toward the windows on the far side of the room.

Nell waved her hand in the opposite direction. "Mac. I've got us a table right over there by the band. There's this drummer that I think might have some real *potential.*"

Mac pointed at an empty table tucked far into a corner and led her there instead. "I think we'd better go where we can talk without hollering. That way we can decide what we want to do about your problem."

"My problem." Nell rubbed her nose. "I don't like to think of it like that exactly. It sounds as if I have mental instability in my family or something. Or…or…"

"How about lack of rhythm?"

Jerking her hand from his, Nell stopped short to fist her knuckles on her hips in a gunfighter-ready-for-action pose. "What?"

"You're downright dangerous on a dance floor, Slim. I don't remember that for some reason."

"That's because when we were at dances together, you were always too involved with petite beauty queens and airheads."

"Cindy was a cheerleader." Mac knew his provocative comment was like red shorts to a bad-tempered bull, but he couldn't help it, although he was amazed to find himself waving his ex-fiancée. Since he'd seen the *woman* in his cool deputy lose control the other day, he found himself tempted to make it happen again. Nell didn't disappoint him.

Feet firmly planted, head cocked at forty-five degrees and eyes narrowed to golden slits, Nell prepared to annihilate him. "Since your ex-fiancée was also a college beauty queen, plus being a very short woman with huge hair taking up most of the vacant space between her ears, I rest my case."

At the smug look on Nell's face, Mac couldn't contain his laughter even if he'd wanted to, which he didn't. He bent over and slapped his knee, exhaling the mirth he'd been holding inside since he'd first seen Nell Phillips wreaking havoc on the dance floor. When he could finally speak again, the only thing that came out of his mouth was "Ouch." He grabbed his stomach, trying to get himself back together.

With all the dignity she was capable of, Nell looked down her nose at him. "I hope you hurt yourself."

He grinned at his deputy. She didn't look too much like an officer of the law at the moment. Nell was dressed in a scarlet blouse, a pair of dress jeans and tooled leather boots. As a man, Mac approved of the jeans, which were black as night and molded Nell's long form into something as pliable as licorice. He even approved of the scarlet top that set off her golden skin and short dark hair. Of course it might be better if she opened a few buttons instead of having it fastened up to her chin, but he'd get to that. Maybe she could replace her boots with something more feminine—strappy with a bit of a heel. He wasn't sure about why, except there was something vulnerable about the subtle arch of a foot and a well-turned ankle. She could also use some long swingy earrings that would caress her cheeks every time she turned her head. He stared at her for so long that Nell shifted uncomfortably.

"What are you doing?"

Mac stroked his chin and went on doing what he was doing. "Just looking."

Smoothing her palms over her thighs, an action that immediately drew Mac's attention, Nell said, "Why?"

Leisurely, Mac met her gaze. "I'm trying to assess the whole package."

"The whole package being…?"

"You. From head to toe. I'm trying to see you as if I've never seen you before." Lately he'd been thinking he hadn't.

Nell shifted from foot to foot. Awkwardly she jammed her hands into her pockets, then abruptly pulled them out again. "What should I do?"

"We'll get to that. Let's get something to eat first. I'm starving." He pulled out a chair and guided Nell to it. Going around to the other side, he hailed a waitress as he sat down.

The young woman—Sheri, according to her name tag, sauntered over, automatically giving him the once-over before poising her pencil above her pad. With a saucy toss of her head, she said, "Help you?"

Mac winked. "Always." Then he glanced at Nell before smiling back at the waitress and automatically ordering for both of them. "Two of the best steaks on the menu, still mooing—"

"Wait a minute," Nell interrupted. "I'm not all that hungry."

Mac patted her hand. "Don't you worry, little gal. I can afford it." He was trying to treat her as some of his more macho friends might, just to get her used to the wide variety of men out there in the marketplace. After all, Mac reasoned, if Nell wanted to find Mr. Right, she'd have to go through a lot of Mr. Wrongs to get to him. Pulling his gaze from Nell, he smiled at the perky young woman waiting breathlessly to take the rest of his order. "We'll also have baked potatoes and house salads."

"Excuse me." Placing both palms on the table, Nell said, "This little *gal* can't eat a steak that's still talking to me."

"Okay. Make one to the rare side and one to the medium."

Sheri slipped her pad into her pocket. "All righty, then." She leaned forward, allowing Mac a peak at what were very perky breasts that now formed a home for the yellow pencil she was slowly sliding between them. Sheri smiled and said with a breathy tone, "So…"

Oh yeah, Mac thought, his eyes fixated on the pencil. That's a good move, guaranteed to get a man's blood boiling. He hoped Nell was noticing.

"If you're sure that's all."

"It is," Nell snapped. "Run along before I check your ID."

With a startled look, Sheri straightened up and scampered away.

"Nell. What the hell are you doing?"

"Trying to keep you from drooling on the table."

Mac sent her an offended look. "I wasn't drooling. I was noticing how she was noticing me so I could get you to notice how to do it."

Rolling her eyes, Nell said, "Tell me another one."

"I'm serious. You asked what turns guys on." He jerked a thumb toward the disappearing waitress. "Well, that's some of it."

"MacKenzie Cochrane, are you telling me you are actually attracted to something that obvious?"

"No. I'm trying to tell you that many guys are. Remember, we're not talking about me." He sent her a hard look and repeated again. "We're not, right?"

Nell shook her head so violently Mac was afraid it would

come off. "No. Definitely not. You're my boss and an old friend, and might as well be another brother."

"Right. So back to business. Did you notice how she'd opened the neckline of her blouse?"

Nell gave him a strange look. "No. The only thing I noticed was you noticing—academically, of course."

"That's because she wasn't buttoned up like my grand-mother. I couldn't help but notice for a moment." He indi-cated Nell's neckline. "You could easily unbutton a few of those and show a bit of—"

"Well, okay." Her hand lifted to hover above her top but-ton. "How many? One. Two."

Mac watched as she resolutely slipped one flat black button through the buttonhole. Then another. As she hesitated over a third, Mac started to get uncomfortable as he caught his first real glimpse of her creamy skin. He waved her off. "That's enough. You don't want to be *too* obvious."

Nell's lips lifted in a tiny come-hither smile. She blinked, her long lashes sweeping down to rest sensuously on her cheeks for a moment before raising her eyes to consider him. Her eyes burned bright. "You don't?"

"No." *Is it hot in here?* A light sweat broke out on his forehead as Mac glanced away, suddenly aware of tension that hadn't been there before. He had to force his hand into his lap, so tempted was he to slip his fingers inside her serviceable cotton blouse and feel her satin skin. He was positive it would feel like satin from the soft sheen that beckoned him closer, inviting him to touch, to taste to—Mac's hand clenched into a fist. Breathing sharply, he distracted himself for a moment by watching the waterwheel. Then he caught sight of their reflections in the window as Nell relit the candle on their table. The glass showed him a seductive picture of light and darkness as he focused on his blond hair and her dark brown. The flickering candle made their images shimmer, adding a seductive quality to the scene. For a moment he wanted to kick himself for ever agreeing to this idiotic plan in the first place.

"Any other lessons you'd like to pass on, Mac?" Nell purred. "From a male point of view, I mean."

Mac gulped. At the moment the only lesson he'd like to teach would get him slapped into detention. He forced the wild rhythms drumming in his blood into silence. With an effort Mac brought his attention back to the situation. For a second his mind scattered as he met her gaze. His eyes dropped to her lips, full and slightly pouting. He wanted to eat them up. *Eat them up?* Mac's thoughts whirled, then he blurted, "Yes. Nell, when a guy's going to buy you an expensive steak, you smile and take it. Guys love steak. Especially go-get-'em men."

"That was another lesson, you're saying? All that little-gal stuff and the macho act?" She pointed at him. "You're lucky I didn't clunk you. You realize you ordered for me even without asking my opinion."

Mac nodded. "That's right, I did. I know a lot of guys who are just that dense, and trust me, you're going to run into them. So by going along with what they're doing you're playing into that masterful male urge. See what I mean?"

"I should go along even if I hate steak?"

His brows snapped together as he considered her. "You hate steak? Since when? You eat steak sandwiches at the office."

"Hating steak was a hypothetical question."

"Oh. Then yes, even if you hate steak. Now don't get me wrong. I'm not saying that this is my masterful urge. Personally I'd ask you what you'd like to have, and when I do, you'll say, 'Oh what do you suggest.'" Mac folded his arms, feeling smugly superior to the female sitting across the table. "I'll suggest steak. Then we're right back where we started—with a guy buying you a steak."

Nell closed her eyes for a moment. "Mac, there's something wrong with this reasoning. Because what you're really saying is I have to act like a doormat and eat something I don't like so you don't feel like an idiot for presuming I'd like it." Her eyes popped open. "Did I get that right?"

"I'm not saying you have to act like a doormat."

"That's good. Because I stink at being a doormat, and I don't think any woman should want to be one." Her cheeks flushed a rosy red as she warmed to her argument. "If some guy tries to—"

Mac held up his hand, stopping her in mid-rant. "Whoa. Let's calm down, Slim, before you try to throw me across the room. I was just trying to give you a few little tips and pointers. No need to make it into a federal case." Mac didn't blame Nell, though. Something about his advice didn't sound quite right to him, either. But hey, being herself wasn't doing the job for Nell, as she'd already pointed out, so perhaps a bit of deception was in order. That made him feel a bit better.

Nell subsided and chugged her glass of water. "Sorry, I was just...well, you know." Putting it down with a thump, she twisted in her chair to look around the room.

Mac followed her gaze. "How come you were dancing anyway? I thought we were meeting by the entrance."

Nell shrugged. "I got here early and decided to dance."

"Nobody decides to dance by themselves."

"I wasn't by myself exactly." She watched the dancing for a moment then pointed at a man in a shirt and jeans. "I was dancing with that guy over there. That's when I noticed the drummer."

Mac peered across the room. "You were dancing with that little guy in the bright blue shirt? The dude with the cowboy hat?"

"Sort of, but I lost him halfway though."

"He was probably afraid you'd give him a nosebleed."

"If you have something to say about my dancing ability, Mac, I wish you'd come right out and say it. Quit beating around the bush."

"All right. We need to work on your technique." Mac scratched his ear. "How a woman who can move like you can move was moving like you were moving is beyond me."

"What do you mean, who can move like me?"

"Well, damn, Slim. When you want to, you can make a cat look clumsy." A satisfied look settled over Nell's face, reminding Mac that cats ate birds. "We have to translate some of your everyday movement onto the dance floor, that's all."

"You're probably right. I do feel a bit awkward sometimes. You think that's why the drummer was giving me those looks?"

Mac grinned. He would've bet on it, but he didn't want to hurt her feelings. "Is this a local band? Do you know this drummer?"

"No. I've never seen him before."

"Well now, I thought I was supposed to help you. I can't be very effective if you start looking without me, can I?"

Nell gave him an exasperated look. "Geezle-Pete! I was just looking, Mac. I didn't start anything without you."

Letting a smug look creep onto his face, Mac said, "Ah, there you go. You didn't, did you? Know why? Because you obviously *do* need my guidance, that's why. Now if you'd been another type of woman, you would have automatically been on the way to third base by now."

"Since the band is playing until two in the morning, I doubt it."

Mac ignored that. It was too technical and he was on a roll. "Theoretically speaking. Although I have to tell you, I'm not sure that guy is your type."

"Why not?"

"Well, he seems a bit arty for your taste, don't you think?"

"I like long hair and tattoos."

Mac sent her a skeptical look. "Since when?"

Nell grinned. "Since I saw it on him."

After thinking that over for a moment, Mac nodded. "That's fair, I guess. Still I don't think—"

"What happened to that open mind you were supposed to keep, Mac?"

"You're right, you're right. I was thinking you were my straight-arrow deputy instead of a woman."

"See. There you go again." She turned from him and flung her arm over the back of her chair. Her third button gave way so completely that it popped off, but Nell was too busy huffing and puffing to notice. "I am a woman."

Mac noticed. Her blouse gaped open a bit further, exposing more of her skin to his gaze. "You certainly are, Slim. Just keep reminding me every once in a while, will you?" Mac found himself praying he'd see a black lace something that came right out of the *Victoria's Secret* catalogue. No such luck. Standard-issue white cotton. Gotta fix that, he thought.

Sending him a suspicious look, she nodded. "If necessary."

Before either of them could say anything more, the waitress approached with their dinners. Both of them turned their attention to their steaks. As they ate and chatted, Mac pulled out his pad and jotted a few comments.

Nell picked up her bottle of ale and said, "What're you doing?" Mac looked so studious as he bent over his paper. Almost as if he were at a crime scene, Nell thought.

"Just making a few notes on things we might work on, that's all."

"What kind of things."

"Your underwear for one thing."

"My what! What the hell do you think you're doing talking about my underwear?" She whipped her head from right to left, praying no one was paying attention. Luckily most people were gravitating to the other end of the room, and the bar, of course.

Mac waved his pen. "I couldn't help but see it. You popped a button."

"I what?" Nell looked down. Sure enough her blouse was gaping open enough to show the top of her bra. She grabbed the edges together. "Why didn't you say something?"

"I just did."

Nell fussed with her blouse for a moment. "Do you have a safety pin?"

Mac chortled. "Not on me, Deputy. I've got a gun though, if that'll help. You can shoot anybody who tries to look."

"Oh, very funny. I thought the purpose was to get people to look."

Grinning, Mac nodded. "There is that." Then he pokered

up and pointed at her chest. "Nell, this is a golden opportunity, too good to waste."

"What is?" Nell felt a twinge of alarm at the look in his eyes.

"You're ready for action. The main target is in sight and the timing is perfect."

"The main what?"

"Toss your head." Mac pretended to toss his in a way that made Nell wonder if he had a headache. "Get your hair falling around your shoulders in that sexy, tousled look."

"*Hello!* I have short hair. If it falls around my shoulders it'll be because it's falling out."

Mac stared at her for an instant, then laughed. "Right. I was carried away for a minute."

"I'm not sure this association is going to work, now that I think of it."

"Well, Slim. We're about to test it out." Mac stood up and waved.

"What are you doing?"

"Calling the drummer over."

"Do you know him?"

"Nope. But Bobby Dee seems to."

Horrified, Nell looked over her shoulder. Sure enough, Bobby Dee Laurance was laughing and talking to the band's drummer. "Ohmigod."

Mac waved again, watching with satisfaction as Bobby Dee waved back and grabbed hold of his companion. "Get ready, Slim. I think your destiny's approaching."

Nell grabbed her stomach, which was suddenly hurting as if she'd swallowed a whale instead of a juicy strip steak. "I'm not ready."

"Don't worry. I'll help you through the whole thing."

Nell groaned. "That's what I'm afraid of."

4

"HERE HE COMES. Just act natural."

"How can I act natural, my blouse is open to my waist. How natural is that?"

Mac laughed. "You're exaggerating, Slim."

Nell shoved her fingers into her hair, attempting to smooth it but only succeeding in making it stand up like porcupine quills. "Besides, my acting natural is the reason I need your help, remember?"

"Psst," Mac hissed. "Spit on your hand."

Nell frowned. "What the hell for?"

Mac pointed at her then made motions of plastering his hair to his head. Nell followed his directions, thinking all the time that this had to be the dumbest thing she'd ever done in her entire life. If she had had any self-control or confidence at any point, it sure had gone south at the moment. Nell was positive everyone was watching. She could feel curious eyes boring a hole in her spine, to match the eyes boring a hole in her breasts as Mac suddenly shifted his attention to her blouse.

"Hey there, Sheriff. Guess who I found?"

Mac gave her one of his encouraging stares, at least he probably thought it was encouraging. In actuality, it reminded Nell of her mother's gimlet-eyed stare, which she'd felt religiously as a child right after she'd taken a big bowl of chocolate pudding for dessert when she was wearing her Sunday-best dress. The situation was so idiotic that Nell wondered if she was dreaming, or having a nightmare. Since she didn't say anything in response to the statement, Mac jumped in. "A wandering drummer?"

"Nah, he wasn't wandering," Bobby Dee said. "He was just sittin' there."

Nell was gulping air so she wouldn't pass out but, at Bobby Dee's prosaic statement, ended up swallowing a laugh instead. She began coughing so hard she thought her sides would split. Before she could get herself under control she was lifted out of her chair by a pair of strong arms and pulled back against a masculine body. Then the man's arms grasped her around the ribs and proceeded to give her the Heimlich maneuver. For a moment Nell hung there like a piece of overcooked spaghetti. Her gaze dropped to see snake-tattoo-decorated arms pounding her insides. Finally she gasped, "Arghh...I'm going to lose my steak."

Lunging for her, Mac said, "Put her down, dammit. That steak cost twelve bucks."

Nell managed to break the other man's hold enough so that her toes hit the floor. The drummer said, "Sorry, man, I thought she was choking."

Nell gulped a few times to make sure her dinner was going to stay where it belonged. She avoided Mac's eyes but could feel every single eye in the place staring great big holes through her and the rest of her comedy crew. *Great. I come here for a date, and get public ridicule instead.* Lacking the nerve to turn around and look at the man still holding her against his rock-hard chest, Nell delayed for a moment, considering possible options. The only one that seemed appealing was breaking the window and jumping into the water below. Of course, that too had problems. With her luck, the waterwheel would suck her up, she'd get stuck, then go around and around forever, waving between appearances to the diners watching in horror from the windows above. No hope for it. Nell took a deep breath, struggled out of the drummer's arms and turned around.

"Oh!" She stared into the eyes of an eagle wearing an American flag. One of the eagle's eyes was the man's right nipple, but somehow it all seemed to work. "That's...interesting. Very patriotic. Nice touch, the rat caught in its claws."

"That's the government," the drummer said, tossing his long blond hair in a movement that looked much better on him than Mac had demonstrated a few minutes before. He looked down from his considerable height. "Sorry about grabbing you. You okay?"

Okay, Nell, she thought. Now's the time. She batted her eyelashes so hard and fast she was surprised they didn't blow out the candle on the table. "I am now."

The man smiled. "I'm Slick, by the way."

Nell smiled and attempted to give him an admiring look, lashes still fluttering like an out-of-control bird. "You sure are."

"You got something in your eye, Nell?" Bobby Dee Laurance's eyes were wide with concern. He leaned forward to peer at her. "There's kind of a clump there in the corner."

A chortle from behind her sent Nell's glance darting in that direction. Mac's eyes were squinty, the laugh lines radiating out from the corners, cutting so deep they looked like bird tracks. And it appeared he was going to bite right through his trembling lips as he tried to keep his grin under control. She wanted to kill him. Nell's temper boiled over, she glared at Mac, then snapped a look back at her co-worker.

"Thanks for pointing that out, Bobby Dee." She ground her fists on her hips. "I suppose now you're going to tell me I have big black raccoon circles under my eyes from the tears that started when Mr. America decided to crush-me-to-death!"

As her last words reached room-clearing intensity, the resulting silence hung like an atomic cloud. Finally the silence was broken by a huge, loud guffaw of laughter as the drummer bent over and slapped his leather-clad knee.

"Damn, girl. You're a real handful, aren't you?"

Nell tried to calm down, attempting to play the game. She had no choice, Mac had just poked her in the back. "Y—*ou*! should know, Slick. You just had your hands on me."

Slick leaned forward. "Not as much as I'd like, sweet thing."

Was Nell imagining it, or did she feel two hot breaths on

her ear. One from the front, and one from the back. Sliding a look from the corner of her eyes, she glimpsed Mac leaning forward, and so close that she was tempted to ask him to stand in for her while she went to the bathroom. She took a step sideways. "Hold that thought, Slick. I'll be right back. I need to freshen up."

With that, she grasped her shirt in her hands to hold it more tightly closed, checked her pocket for her comb and lipstick and headed for the women's rest room to try to get herself together. Temper and chagrin fought for dominance as Nell shoved her way through the door, hitting it so hard that the door almost annihilated an overly made-up older woman in full country music western regalia, who was stepping toward it.

Nell grabbed for the door. "Oh. I'm sorry."

"That's okay, honey. No harm done." She pursed her lips, which had bleeding lipstick lines, then tapped on her gold front tooth. "That guy must have really pissed you off, honey lamb."

"What guy?"

"You'll never make me believe that you weren't moving through the door that fast if a guy didn't do something stupid!"

"Actually, two—no—three guys did something stupid."

The older woman backed up and leaned against the sink. "Well, don't it just figure." She shook her head and cocked her hip. "No wonder they had to give 'em two heads. One wasn't good enough."

Nell started to laugh. "You think that's why?" *Now why can't my mother see it like this.*

"Had to be. I tell ya, honey, I've been married five times and each time after we broke up I'd wonder why I just didn't buy me a sexy videotape."

Nell stared at the woman, wondering what other words of wisdom might drop from her lips. "How did you manage five men? I'm still trying to find one."

"Well, maybe your standards are too high."

Nell thought of the men waiting outside by the table. "It could be."

"Lower them, honey. It's always a good idea to be smarter than they are. To make them need you so much they give up everything for you, unless what they're giving up is something you want. Then you got to make them give it to you, instead."

Not having to feign her admiration at the woman's insight, Nell whistled. "I worship at your feet."

The woman stared at her for an instant, then giggled. For that moment, Nell could see a lively young girl looking out of the bright eyes still residing in the lady's creased face. No wonder she'd managed to attract five men. "No, you listen to me, honey. You go right on out there and pretend this is the best night of your life. Because if you do that often enough, before you know it, it comes true."

Nell thought about that for a moment, then met the woman's eyes in the mirror. "Okay. I'll give it a shot."

"All right, then. Good luck." The woman patted Nell's shoulder. A brief sound of canned jukebox music and chatting voices drifted through the door as the woman left.

Nell dug her comb from her pocket and turned to her reflection. Dragging the teeth through her short hair, she shaped it into a more defined pixie cut, trying to give herself a sexier look. She massaged the area under her eyes to remove any traces of her black mascara, then located her lipstick and carefully outlined her lips. She met her critical gaze, her bright caramel eyes staring back at her. *What the hell!* She rubbed a bit of lipstick on her high cheekbones to give them some extra color. That done, Nell leaned forward to stare at her image. Just what did people see when they looked at her? Not her physical attributes, those were right there for everyone to discover, but what about who she was? Did anyone look closely enough to see that? To see her as anything besides a cop? Mac could, if he wanted. After all she'd known him practically all her life, which was why she'd instinctively, if impulsively, asked for his help.

Nell tucked her blouse tightly into her jeans, staring at the open neckline. It wasn't that revealing now that she thought about it, but it was close. Three buttons open did not a closed door make, especially if someone was determined to gain entrance. She wondered what it would be like to press her breasts against Slick's chest, then the thought skittered away, replaced by images of the eagle screeching in her ear and using his talons to tear her to ribbons. *Oh, great. Wonderful mental picture. Very inspiring to my love life.* Then she perked up. *So I'll make him wear a shirt.* Although after having seen his chest muscles, she hated to cover them up.

Nell leaned her head against the wall. What on earth was she doing in the bathroom of Charlie's Place talking to herself? She'd arrived with such hopes this evening. She'd felt nervous but alive and ready for anything. She'd fortified herself with a beer then gone looking for a partner and hit the dance floor since Mac hadn't yet arrived. She'd thrown herself into the music, letting it move her in a way she'd not done for a long time. Then Mac took her arm and she was suddenly nervous again. *Nervous of Mac?* That was a good one. He was her boss, but, okay, he was also very sexy. And the damn man did look like Brad Pitt and—damn—she loved Brad Pitt! But he was here to help her find another man. *God knows why I thought this would be a good idea. Maybe I could just stay in here the rest of the night.* That thought was put to rest with the loud thumping that rattled the door.

"Nell—hey, Nell," Mac called. "You okay in there?"

"Go away," Nell called back.

"Come out of there."

"When I'm ready."

His fist hit the door again. "This is the sheriff speaking, huh? Oh, no, nothing wrong, ma'am." Nell laughed as he tried to explain himself to a woman who was obviously trying to get past him. "Uh, yes ma'am. You go right on in. And if you see Nell—"

Nell pushed her way through the door. "That won't be necessary, Sheriff Cochrane. I'm right here."

"What took you so long? Oww—" Mac doubled over as Nell him elbowed him in the stomach.

"That was very rude, Sheriff. Since when is there a time limit? Be glad I wasn't in there with a group of women, or I wouldn't be out till Christmas."

Mac scratched his head, then pushed the front of his hair back. "What was I supposed to think? You raced away. I was worried about you. Besides the more I think about this, the more I don't think this drummer guy is a good choice to practice on. I think if we look around tonight and make some decisions about the type of people who might be suitable, then we'll have done everything we came here to do. What do you think?"

Nell sent Mac a pitying look. "I think that drummer guy is built like an Egyptian god."

"Weren't they the ones with the animal heads?"

Nell pretended to shiver just to see what Mac would do. "He looks like an animal."

Mac growled, "That's because he's got a predator squatting on his chest."

Grinning, Nell said, "That's what I'm going for, except I'm going to be the one doing the squatting." With that, she fixed the image of a black panther in her mind and set her sights on her quarry—the man with the long blond hair, black leather pants, bare chest and tattoos. Nell prowled across the room to the table where Slick and Bobby Dee were still waiting. She could hear Mac behind her, muttering, then hustling after her. But now that she'd decided she might as well go for it, go for it, she would. She circled around the edge of the room, sizing up her best opportunity, the best approach to make sure he knew she was coming and had no choice but to watch, mesmerized. If only she had some music, she might move better. She threw her shoulders back, so her blouse gapped a bit more, and approached Slick.

"Hi," she said, making her voice as throaty as possible. Then she leaned over a startled Bobby Dee, who was sitting at the outside seat, and planted a sensuous kiss right on Slick's sexy lips. Slick seemed no stranger to passion, or to women admiring his stage persona, either—which were probably one and the same—still, Nell was surprised when he reached for her, practically dragging her across Bobby Dee's lap. With that aggressive move, Slick proved himself a bold, sexy male seeming determined to make a meal of her. At least that's the way Nell interpreted it.

Bobby Dee put it somewhat differently. "Wayne, you never would have done this in high school. You were such a geek. No wonder I didn't recognize you at first."

Nell's lips left Slick's. She blinked. "Wayne? Your name is Wayne?"

Slick Wayne blinked back at her. "Yeah. So?"

She was still so close to him that her eyes nearly crossed as she tried to stare at him, noting the slash of red creeping along his cheekbones. "So...I never would have taken you for a Wayne."

"What does that have to do with anything?" He leaned forward to kiss her again.

"I don't know. It just doesn't seem right is all." Nell drew back, sending Bobby Dee an apologetic look for practically lying in his lap like a flopping flounder. Then she stood up, straightening her clothing, which had been disarranged by her little romantic episode.

"I don't use the name Wayne anymore," Slick said with a bit of a desperate tone in his voice as he rose from his seat. "Why don't—"

Nell patted his arm. "Wayne is a perfectly nice name." As she stared at the drummer, she thought, *Thank God, something happened to intervene or I would have been a bigger talk of the town than I already am.* She glanced at Mac, who was standing a bit away from her, pretending to study the crowd. She didn't want to talk to him at the moment, as if he, and only he, were responsible for this situation. As a matter of fact, Nell didn't want to talk to a soul. She wanted to go home and not have to deal with anyone who wore pants and had a potential filled-to-bursting zipper.

"Uh, Slick," Mac said, jerking a thumb. "I think your band's looking for you."

Nell glanced over to the stage in time to see the lead guitarist waving in their direction. "I think you're on, Slick."

"Oh, I'm on, all right," Slick murmured provocatively, seeming to regain his confidence as he walked around the chairs to come closer. "I wanna see you tonight, after this gig. How about it?"

Nell smiled, trying to soften her rejection, "Oh, I'd love to. But I have to get up very early tomorrow, so it might not work. Can I take a rain check?"

Tossing his hair back, Wayne announced in the voice of a man sure of his outcome, "I don't give second chances, babe."

"Oh?" Nell shrugged her shoulders. "Too bad."

After a chagrined look at her, Slick turned and sauntered back to the bandstand.

"Wow," Bobby Dee said, "you sure blew that one, Nell."

"Maybe I wanted to blow that one, Bobby Dee. Did ya ever think of that?"

Bobby Dee stroked his chin. "Nope."

Mac stepped forward. "You got to remember, Bobby Dee, that Nell is a woman of great fortitude. When she makes up her mind to do something, she does it."

"If you say so, boss." Bobby Dee slid him an alarmed look. "An' if that's so, I'd just as soon she didn't make up her mind about anything having to do with me."

Grinning, Mac said, "You've got my word on it."

Nell cocked a hip, grinding one fist against her black jeans. "What does your word have to do with it? We're talking about me."

"Well, you work for me an'…"

"I work for you, period." Nell emphasized her words by flinging her arms wide. "No *and*—"

"*And* I'm helping you out with a little problem at the moment, so I figure that gives me some extra special—"

"No, it doesn't." She would have continued, but Mac's eyes went glossy and transfixed on her chest. "What are you staring at?"

"Uh, Nell, you just popped another button."

"What!" She looked down. Sure enough, now her entire white cotton bra was revealed to all who cared to look.

"You know that open-to-the-waist comment you made before?" Mac snuffled as he attempted to stop his laughter. "Damn if it isn't true."

"Oh…oh, shut up, Mac Cochrane before I—I—" By now Nell couldn't even think straight, so she did the only thing she could do. She folded her arms across her chest and headed for the door.

"Wow, Sheriff," Bobby Dee said as his eyes followed Nell's progress through the room. "I don't know if she wanted to shoot you or cry all over you."

"Probably a little of both, Bobby Dee. A little of both."

The deputy frowned. "I can't imagine Nell crying."

"There's a first time for everything. That's the problem with women. They keep you guessing when they should be getting predictable, like men." Mac grinned over his shoulder as he set off after Nell. "I'll see you later."

"You're going to follow her? *Oh, wow!* That's pretty brave."

"Well, you know me, I'm the big brave sheriff of Knightsboro, Tennessee. No problem too big, or too small." He smiled and adjusted his belt, like a gunfighter off to meet his fortune. "Don't worry, I can handle Nell."

"Yeah, right." Bobby Dee's voice took on a sarcasm that he didn't usually show. "If you don't show up at work on Monday, I'll figure she shot you."

Bobby Dee reached for his beer, which he'd set on the table. He took a long swig. Shaking his head, he peered at his reflection in the window.

"If you ask me, all women are nuts."

"STUPID, STUPID, STUPID. Just when I was getting the hang of it." Nell dug into her back pocket for her car key.

"Getting the hang of what?" Mac was breathing hard as he came up behind her. "Whew, are you training for the Harvest Festival Marathon or something? I've never seen you go anywhere so fast in my life. Except for that time when we were kids and I put the spider down your pants."

"Thank you," Nell said with a sarcastic curl of her lip.

"That was a memory it took me twenty years to forget until now."

Laughing, Mac said, "Sorry." He leaned against her car. "Where're you going, Nell? Night's still young."

Nell slipped him a glance, then turned her key in the lock. "I'm going home to put some clothes on." Nell wondered if she looked or sounded as embarrassed as she felt. It was one thing to be in a professional position where she could put herself into situations that called for unique action, but it was another thing altogether to have your real self out there on display. Nell hadn't thought about that in those terms before. How had Mac coped with his fiancée's rejection a number of years before without showing it, or seeming to show it, anyway.

Mac grinned. "It'd be more fun if you were going home to take some clothes *off.*"

"Give me a break, will you. You convinced me the drummer would be a bad idea, so don't give me grief now."

Mac's brows rose to meet his hairline. "I convinced you? How?"

"When you said this process deserved some thought." Nell looked him straight in the eye. "That was a good suggestion."

"You didn't think so when I made it."

"I did after I heard the man's name was Wayne."

Tilting his head, Mac considered her. "What's the matter with Wayne?"

"I have a second cousin named Wayne, who's gone out of his way to make my life miserable every time I see him, and has since we were three. I look at a guy named Wayne and I see—*Wayne!*"

"Oh." Mac had one of those women-are-incomprehensible looks on his face.

"That's why I put the brakes on."

Mac scratched his head. "Makes some kind of sense, I guess."

"If you were a woman, you'd understand." Nell stared at the man leaning casually against her hood. He didn't seem in any hurry to move, so she moved him. Indicating her blouse, she said, "I have to go now before I catch a cold."

Mac laughed. "Luckily, we men know how to warm up a female."

"Some men, perhaps."

"Yeah, that's the point. Some men are going to be better for you than others."

Nell grimaced. "That's the truth."

Clapping his hands like an overenergetic tour director, Mac said, "I'll tell you what we should do. Let's get together tomorrow afternoon and strategize."

"About what?" At this point, Nell wanted nothing to do with men, period. She was thinking of raising puppies.

"Well, we obviously have a few things to work on, besides your underwear and your dislike of the name Wayne, that is."

Nell started to bristle. Never mind that she had asked Mac for help. When he wanted to do so, he could put up her back faster than most people she knew. "What else do you have in mind?" She bit the syllables out between her teeth.

"Just a few little items I've taken some notes on is all."

Nell yanked her door open. "Okay, whatever! I'll see you tomorrow at one. No, wait, not tomorrow." She didn't want to see anyone tomorrow. She wanted to lick her wounds in silence. Nell didn't know why, though. Thanks to her mother, she was already the talk of the town.

"I'll follow you home."

Stunned, Nell stopped, half in and half out of the driver's seat. "What for?"

"To make sure you get home safe."

"I'm a cop. I know how to get home safely."

Frowning, Mac studied the toes of his boots. "Oh, yeah. That's right."

Nell got back out of the car. "Hey, Mac, don't take this helping thing too seriously, okay? I'm a big girl and I'm perfectly capable of handling myself in any situation."

Mac laughed. "I noticed that tonight. You were smooth as a caramel in there."

"Unmelted, I'll bet?" Nell hunched a shoulder as Mac agreed. "All right, so I need some work on my technique."

"And your attitude."

Hands on hips, she thrust her chin forward. "There's not a goddamn thing wrong with my attitude."

A virtuous look crept over Mac's face, and his voice soothed her like a pack of mentholated cough drops. "Of course there isn't, Nell."

"There isn't." She wanted to stomp on him. "If you ask me—"

"First things first. We'll work on the wardrobe. There's this new place that just opened over in Justin."

Nell stopped mid-cry. "I—what? What kind of place?"

"We can take a run over there after work on Monday."

"Are you talking about a store? What kind of store?"

"It's one of those catalogue stores."

"Sears? Penney's? That's not where I buy my clothes. I'd rather—"

"Nah, this one sells—" he gestured to his body "—frilly little things that really start a man's engine." Mac warmed up to his subject. "I'm telling you, I got a flyer in the mail and my jaw damn near hit the floor. I'll bring it in Monday. It's just this short of being illegal. But damn if I care, when I can look at—"

"Are you talking about a lingerie catalogue? Or are we talking about an adult bookstore, here?"

Mac rubbed a thumb over his jaw. "They do have videos, come to think of it. I saw one that had to do with making men drool."

"Like men need help."

Laughing, Mac said, "We may not need it, but we sure appreciate getting it."

"How come we're starting with my…intimate apparel?"

"We've gotta start somewhere."

Sliding into the seat of her car, Nell said over her shoulder, "How about my dance technique. You made comments about that, too."

"That drummer wasn't interested in your dancing. He was more interested in your underwear and what was under it."

Nell grinned. "Yeah, I know." For a few moments there with Wayne, she'd felt like the most desirable woman in the world. It was a heady feeling.

Mac muttered, "I was tempted to handcuff him."

"Me, too." Nell's grin broadened as Mac snapped her a look. "Until I found out he was named Wayne." Not that that would have stopped her if she'd wanted him so much she couldn't see straight. Up close, lip locked to lip, the chemistry hadn't felt right.

Dragging his notebook from his pocket, Mac made a neat note. "Okay. We're on for Monday night, then?

The man is like a damn bulldog. I must have been nuts when I came up with this idea. Nell rested her forehead on the steering wheel. "I'm not ready for this."

"Sure you are, Nell. Now get some rest tomorrow. Come Monday, we're gonna be busy planning our next few weeks. We've got a lot to do and a short time to do it."

"You make this sound like a major campaign." *Mom was right. I should have done the e-mail dating thing!*

"It is."

Nell started her car, then a thought hit her that made her feel a lot better. "Just remember one thing, Mac. You're the other part of this deal. I'm finding you a woman you can live with."

"I'm not interested in living with a woman. I just want to cancel my date with Hilda's niece and get my mother off my back."

"I'm going to help you with that, too. Now this is what *I* suggest we do." Nell didn't get a chance to go into it as Mac stepped back quickly and slammed her car door. She rolled down her window. "Avoiding it isn't going to help."

"Look, Nell, let's work on one thing at a time."

"There is no way I'm going to be the sole project. We had a deal." Nell pointed at herself, then Mac. "You help me, I help you."

"I didn't mean it, exactly. I was only agreeing because Ted and Jed and the kids were egging us on."

"I don't care. We made a deal in front of witnesses, and if I'm going to become the talk of the town, you are, too."

Mac's lips twisted. "I've already been the talk of the town."

"Well, we'll give them something new to talk about. What do you say?"

"Look, Nell, I don't wanna—"

Wiggling her finger, Nell gave him the age-old taunt. The one that always sent her brothers around the bend. "Don't tell me a big bad sheriff like you is chicken?"

Mac bristled like a porcupine confronting a determined hound. "I'm not chicken."

Nell bobbed her head like a demented hen and completed the job, clucking, "Bawk—bawk—bawk!"

"Knock it off, Deputy."

"Oh, touchy, are we? It's a bit different when the shoe's on the other foot, isn't it, Mac? Tell you what, I'll bet you two weeks of steak dinners that I find you a woman before you find me a man." She watched as Mac thought it over.

"Any kind of steak I want?"

"From ground round to filet mignon."

Mac's eyes narrowed. "You've got a bet."

"Good. See you tomorrow. Oh, and by the way, that store we're going to? I happen to know it's a unisex store. So I figure if I'm gonna' get some sexy lingerie, you are, too."

"No way. I've got all the boxers I want. I don't need anything else."

"Boxers?" Nell chortled, opening her eyes wide. "You're wearing boxers?"

Mac flushed, then jutted his lip in a belligerent fashion. "Yeah. So?"

"I would've figured you for briefs."

"Boxers are what I'm used to."

"Kind of uncomfortable, aren't they?" Nell couldn't help but look at the area in question. "I mean, aren't you sort of flapping in the breeze?"

"I don't flap in the breeze. Where the hell did you come up with that?"

Nell shrugged. "It's what my brother Danny said in high school."

"Danny never kept it in long enough to—" Mac gulped as Nell gave him an interested stare.

"Go on."

"Forget it."

"No, please. I'm dying to know something I can use against my brother. God knows, he's made my life a living hell at times."

Mac cast a glance around the parking lot, obviously looking for rescue. "I think I'd better…"

"Aren't boxers better for the sperm count? I think I read that someplace."

"Drop it, Nell. My sperm count's none of your business."

Nell grinned as she noticed Mac shifting from one foot to another. "You know, this whole underwear thing is looking more promising, now that I think about it. Obviously we both have some changes to make." She lifted her gaze, allowing it to travel from his feet up his long, long legs to his hips. Her grin widened. "I think a pair of those skimpy itty-bitty bikini briefs might do fine."

Mac nodded. "I agree. Men really find those—"

"I meant for you," Nell said gently. "After all, we wouldn't want to squeeze those little sperms if they're not used to it." She couldn't stop her glee from showing through as Mac jerked with surprise.

"For me?" Mac's voice went up three decibels.

Nell sent him a kind smile then started to put her car in gear. "Maybe we can find a G-string with a little cop badge on it, you know, like the strippers wear."

Mac grabbed the window frame of her door. "Maybe we can both get one."

"Well, you told me I need sexy lingerie, remember." She might have known Mac wouldn't take a challenge like that lying down, or standing up either.

Mac's eyes narrowed. "I'll bet you two weeks' pay that you won't have the nerve to wear them."

Eyes gleaming, Nell said, "I'll take that bet, Sheriff." She'd show this guy what Nell Phillips was made of. Her brothers would be proud of her, if she dared tell them.

"See you Monday," Mac stated, the challenge in his voice aimed at bringing her under control. He turned and walked away, leaving Nell to stare at his retreating buttocks.

Yep, Mac in a G-string ought to be an interesting sight. Not that she'd get a chance to see him, of course. Any more than he'd see her. After all, Mac meant nothing to her romantically. He was Mac, for crying out loud—her boss, her childhood friend. Her glance lingered on the clenching and unclenching motion of his firm butt as he strode across the parking lot.

Still, it was something to think about.

5

MAC COCHRANE HUNCHED OVER his desk like a man peering over the plan for the end of the world. He ran a finger around his collar, pulling it away from his too-tight throat as he gulped for breath. He stared down at the model wearing what had to be the most revealing bra, bikini and—*heaven help me*—garter belt he'd ever seen. For some reason his mind kept substituting Nell Phillips in place of the dark-haired woman in the photograph. He could see Nell with those pouty lips begging for a caress, leaning forward with her arms tucked to make her breasts swell toward the camera as if attempting to obliterate the lens, her hip cocked to one side and her long legs slightly apart, giving just a hint of the treasures between. He imagined those sinuous garters snaking down to cup the black stockings, tempting him to run his tongue under the silk where it circled her leg. Of course he wouldn't be able to stop there. He'd have to—

"Sheriff."

Mac Cochrane jumped as if he'd been shot. He automatically grabbed the magazine, whipped it off the desk and stuffed it under his butt, thinking he should have used it to cover up the huge erection he was sporting, instead. He was positive he could feel the beads of sweat rolling off his forehead to drip onto his desk blotter. He attempted to speak, but could only produce gargling noises, so he cleared his throat and tried again.

"Yeah, Doug." Mac tried to pretend that Doug wasn't looking at him as if he'd suddenly escaped from a mental institution. "Something I can do for you?"

"Your mother's here to see you."

"My...*who?*" He squirmed on his seat, the woman's lush breasts burning a brand into his buttocks.

"Your mother." The amused voice came from behind Doug. She waved Doug aside and stepped past him into the doorway.

"My mother!" Mac still couldn't believe it, so he repeated it to make sure it wasn't a mistake.

The small woman standing in the doorway, her faded blond hair glinting in the morning light that slipped through his blinds, grinned at him. "Last time I looked I was."

Now Mac was really nervous. How was he going to stand up and greet her without her eagle eyes spotting the catalogue...and other things. If there was one thing he knew about his mama, she could spot a piece of anything anyone was trying to hide better than an eagle with an empty belly. So he kept his behind firmly planted on the seat, trying to use the position behind his desk to give him some authority. Which was difficult because, at the moment, he felt like a four-year-old with a handful of swiped peanut butter cookies.

"Mama." He tried a smile, wishing his teeth weren't sticking to his lips as he said the familiar childhood word.

"Mac, what's the matter with you? You look—"

"Just the cares and woes of my office, Mama. Don't worry about me."

Molly Cochrane tilted her head and directed a blast of steel-blue gaze in his direction. "I was going to say, you're grinning like a monkey who's attempting to charm me out of my banana."

Automatically Mac stood up, the magazine slipping off the floor to land with a soft thunk that sounded as loud as an explosion. Imagining he'd seen his mother's ears prick up like a spaniel's, he rushed into speech. "Oh, very nice, nice thing to say to your only son."

"You're not my only son."

"Well, I'm the only one in the room. Hell, since Daryn's in New York, I'm the only one in town at the moment."

"I know, darlin'. That's why I want you to settle down

with some lovely woman and have a passel of kids, so I can have grandchildren around my knees.''

"Mama, you don't sit still long enough to have grandchildren around your knees.''

"I would if I had some," Molly said with a sharp look, her Southern drawl taking on a familiar tartness. He'd heard it often growing up. "You know how I love my family, darlin'.''

Unfortunately, Mac did. Generally he appreciated it, but where his love life was concerned, he often wished he'd been hatched from an egg. With a bit of desperation, Mac said, "Mama, there's Daryn and Caitlin to pitch in and make the family bigger. You don't have to put it all on me, you know.''

"Oh, listen to you, MacKenzie Cochrane." His mother chuckled. "You men get the easy part. You get to make the babies, we women get to have them.''

Mac sent a hunted glance toward the door and the room beyond. "Mama, do you realize you're in the middle of my place of work. I have a certain dignity to uphold here.''

"You do?" Molly laughed. "What's gotten into you today? I don't think I've ever heard you worrying about that before.''

"I worry about that all the time." Mac could hardly keep his eyes from twinkling as they met her gaze, but he tried to pretend this was serious business. If there was one thing he wasn't, it was dignified and stuffy.

"Oh, Mac." Molly grinned. "You do not.''

"Do, too. You and Dad raised us to take responsibility, remember. It seems to me that keeping the law's presence pure is the best thing I can do to uphold that.''

Molly Cochrane's eyes narrowed. "What are you up to?''

"What makes you think I'm up to something?''

"There's something not quite sitting right with this conversation." Her glance swept the room. "This wouldn't have anything to do with—''

"With?" Mac could feel himself squirming inside. He imagined the image of the model firmly tattooed on his forehead just waiting for his mother to notice it.

Molly hinted, "This town talks a lot, son."

Flushing, Mac replied, "I know. So?"

"I understand that you and little Nell Phillips made quite an impact on the crowd at Charlie's Saturday night." His mother's voice had slowed to a soft and suggestive under-the-covers drawl.

Mac's fist crashed on his desk. "God dammit to hell and the devil's fiddle if I ever do anything in this town again." He stalked around his desk and began pacing the room. "There I was trying to do a good deed and what do I get for it? Gossip. Innuendo. I bet you think I unbuttoned her blouse, too, don't you?"

"Did you?" Molly asked slyly.

"No, I did not. *Little Nell Phillips* popped those buttons all by herself."

A startled look landed on Molly's face. "Really? I wouldn't have thought Nell had the…the—" Molly waved her hand in the vague direction of her breasts "—the…"

After watching her for a moment, Mac suggested, "Boobs?" He swallowed a chuckle as his mother puffed up to respond.

"I'd never be that crude, young man."

"Oh, sorry."

"Anyway, as I was saying. I never would have thought that of Nell." Molly smiled, regaining her equilibrium. But there was an expression around the eyes that Mac mistrusted. "Now Hilda's niece is another story." *Uh-oh*, Mac thought, *I was right. Here it comes.* "I don't know if you remember Bronwyn, Mac, but that girl is the stuff of dreams. I mean, son, go to bed, put your head down and—"

"We're not talking about big and pillowy, are we? 'Cause if we are, I'm not—"

"Mac." Molly shook her finger at him, much as she had when he'd been nine and used her best sheets to camp in the muddy woods that surrounded his childhood home. "Bronwyn is lovely. I ran into Hilda a few minutes ago and she showed me a recent picture of her. Her skin looks like warm milk."

"I hate warm milk."

Determinedly ignoring him, Molly continued, "Her hair is the color of corn that's ripened on the stalk."

"That brassy kind of corn you feed to the pigs in winter?"

Molly glared at him. "Her eyes are—"

"Blue as a blueberry?"

"Now you're being sarcastic, son. Actually they're kind of a German chocolate-cake brown, but no matter."

Rolling his eyes, Mac said, "Mama, Hilda's niece sounds like a cooking class."

Molly's mouth opened wide to comment, but she gurgled with laughter instead. "You're right. I guess my only point was—"

"To marry me off to the farmer's daughter when I wasn't looking?"

"Now, Mac, I promised Hilda and her niece."

"Well, you'll have to un-promise, Mama, 'cause I'm going to be tied up with Nell for the next few weeks."

Molly's eyes widened until they were as round as doughnuts. "Tied up?"

"I don't think he meant that literally, Mrs. Cochrane." Nell's voice dropped into the room like a life raft on a violent sea. "Mac only meant—"

"Leave it alone, Nell. She knows the truth."

Nell leaned against the doorjamb in her favorite long-drink-of-water pose and stared back at Mac. "The truth…?" she repeated in a careful tone.

"About you and me," he supplied, his body stirring as she slid her hands into her pockets, his ready imagination supplying an image of his hands slipping inside to cup her hips.

"What about you and me?"

"Saturday night. Remember Saturday night?" Mac sure did. It had taken quite a while to quiet his mind, not to mention his body, after he'd left her. Maybe Nell was right. He did need a woman.

Nell's tone became even more cautious. "Which part?"

"The part about your blouse."

Nell gasped. "I can't believe you told your mother about that!"

"I didn't tell my mother. My mother told me." Mac shook his head. "As if I had to tell my mother anything. She knows everything before the ashes have cooled."

Instead of being distressed by his comment, Molly looked pleased. "I do seem to have a pretty good communication network, don't I, son?"

Sending her a sour look, Mac said, "Too good."

"You're just saying that because you were the topic."

"No, I'm saying it because you look so harmless and reasonable that no one would believe you would ever listen to all the gossip this town creates."

"If I didn't keep my ear to the ground, I never would have known half what you and Daryn and Caitlin were up to when you were teenagers. I guess it's stayed a habit."

Nell chuckled. "She's got a point there, Mac."

Molly smiled back at Nell. "And your mother was just the same."

Nell's smile immediately disappeared. "Don't remind me. She's part of the reason I'm in this situation."

"Which situation is that, Nell, dear."

"Nell," Mac commanded, "don't say another word."

Luckily Nell didn't get an opportunity to do so, because Doug's head popped up behind the two women as they stood in the doorway. "Hey, Sheriff, we've got some people out here and Bobby Dee said we might want to get you. You expecting anyone?"

"I'll be right out." Mac grasped at the interruption. He wouldn't have cared if a mob of angry anteaters were tearing up the town. He shot around his desk, on his way to the doorway as if he were a bowling ball hunting for pins. The older and younger women stepped aside before he accidentally knocked them down.

"My, my," Nell murmured as his shoulder brushed hers. "You're a busy man this morning, Sheriff."

"Yep. No rest for the weary." Mac winced. He sounded like the *Farmer's Almanac.* Nell must have thought so, too.

The low, smoky sound of her chuckle got under his skin, reminding him that not long before, he'd been panting and imagining her in lingerie. Not that he'd see her in it, of course. His interest was purely subjective and academic. He was going to develop this woman into a mantrap if it killed him. It probably would because he couldn't explain why his skin prickled as he caught a whiff of her scent, that smooth, tangy smell that reminded him of tart lemon frosted with a vanilla icing.

Mac passed Doug, who was exchanging a word with Molly, then emerged into the short hallway that led to the main room of the sheriff's headquarters. Doug was right. There was quite a crowd standing with Deputy Bobby Dee, including three or four of the town's prominent citizens like Ada Mae Baker, who ran the local sweets shop, and Dub Brannigan, who owned the gas station at the edge of town. The low, determined chatter reminded Mac of a bar on Friday night. No one noticed him for a moment, so he watched, trying to get an idea of what they were up to.

Then Mac cleared his throat in his most authoritative manner.

As he spoke, some of the hum muted and the small crowd shifted to reveal the people occupying center stage—Ted and Jed Kilbourne. A grin trembled on Mac's lips as he stared at the two brothers. They were wearing their usual costume of flannel shirts, overalls and ball caps, but they'd added something new. Jed was carrying a brown leather briefcase, a big old pouch of a thing, probably acquired at the same garage sale as their recent business management books. As important as Jed looked, Ted wasn't left out of this serious business impression. He made his mark in his own way by carrying a huge gray ledger, the type business records were kept in. The book was open and, as Dub Brannigan murmured in his ear, Ted was busily sucking the end of his lead pencil and then marking one of the pages.

Mac tried to gain their full attention. "What can I do for y'all?"

Bobby Dee whirled around, waving at Mac to come over.

"Hey, Sheriff, wait till you hear what T—*oof!*" Bobby Dee gasped as Ada Mae's elbow caught him in the rib. He exhaled, muttering, "Dammit to hell." Bobby Dee felt the full-force glare of Ada Mae's disapproval. "I mean dammit to heck." The stare intensified as Bobby Dee quickly backtracked. "I mean—*heck!* What'd ya do that for?"

"You talk too much, boy." Ada Mae's voice was so dry it almost crackled.

"All I was gonna say is, Mac'd get a laugh outta what—*oof!*" Another elbow got him.

"You ought to use that mouth for something besides talking sometimes, Bobby Dee. You've got the gol'darndest way of blabbing I've ever seen. When folks want you to tell their business, they'll let you know." Then Ada Mae added the finishing touches with a coaxing smile. "Why don't we find a better use for that mouth. You come on down to the shop and I'll give you some of my special Harvest cookies and cider."

Bobby Dee was still kid enough that this shut him up for a moment. Mac smiled at that, then decided it was time to break in, "I hate to interrupt the party—"

"Oh, uh...hey, Sheriff," Jed said with an uncomfortable shuffle. "We didn't know you was here."

Puzzled, Mac said, "This is the sheriff's office. Where else would I be?"

Jed scratched his head, drawling, "Well, sir, we didn't see your patrol car outside or we never—"

Jerking a thumb, Mac said, "It's parked around back."

"Oh," Ted nodded briskly. "That explains it."

Mac frowned as he tried to make sense of the comment. It was too much effort. "What's up?"

Ted looked around, then said, "We, um, we just stopped in to...to...to..." For a moment he sounded like a stuttering motor.

Ada Mae gave Ted a jump start when she broke into his comment. "See about a vendor's license for the Harvest Festival, remember?"

Ted snapped his fingers. "Yeah, that was it."

"A vendor's license?" Stunned at the thought of the Kilbournes possibly peddling rotgut liquor out of a sidewalk cart to tourists at the Harvest Festival, Mac looked around. "What about the rest of you? Are you here in support of this?"

"We, um…" Dub brushed a hand across his forehead. Then he brightened. "Me and Ada Mae just came in to get out of the rain."

Mac glanced toward the bright window, then tilted his head and considered the older man. "You been sampling Ted's moonshine again, Dub? 'Cause last time I had to haul you out of the Dumpster behind Marletta Malvern's house 'cause she thought you were a Peeping Tom."

Dub flushed. "Those days are gone, Sheriff. I've turned over a new leaf."

"He had to," Bobby Dee said with an irrepressible chuckle. "Marletta installed shutters." Another elbow, accompanied by a classic Ada Mae glare, followed. *"Oof."*

With perfect aplomb, Ted stepped forward, patting his gray ledger. "Our bad days are gone, too, Sheriff. We're coming up with a name for our product and we're asking everyone's ideas then taking their bet."

Jed jumped in. "Ted means writin' them down for voting on later."

"Did you say rain, Dub?" Bobby Dee was a bit behind in the conversation, but one item had penetrated and stuck. Shoving a hand through his hair, he stepped to the window to peer through the blinds, wincing as a shaft of sunshine hit him in the eyes. "It's not raining."

Dub's hand floundered about as he indicated the door. "Well, it was. Great big raindrops—"

"That came with the sun." Before Mac could say anything, Ada Mae Baker sent him a challenging stare that looked very familiar. It was the stern "don't you dare sass me back, youngster" look he'd seen her give every kid in town at one time or another.

"Uh-huh…with the sun." No way was Mac Cochrane going to take on Ada Mae Baker if he could help it. The last time he'd tried, she'd reduced him to dust.

"That's right, Sheriff," Jed agreed. "An' we was comin' in to see Doug and y'all anyway."

"About the vendor's license," Ada Mae added.

Ted acknowledged her prodding with a sharp nod. "Yeah, yeah, and the product name." Then he went back to the story he was telling, which was sounding more suspicious than ever to Mac. "And when we seen Dub dart in here—"

"—through the raindrops," Jed added with a solemn nod.

"—we followed him in 'cause we had a bit of business to discuss with him, too, in addition to you." Ted finished with a flourish, obviously glad to come to the end of the story.

All of Mac's suspicions honed in on that statement. He stiffened. "Business? You aren't trying to sell Dub some of that moonshine of yours on the law's property, are you, Ted?"

"Sheriff, no! I told you, we're trying to go legal-like." Ted indicated Jed's briefcase. "Doing it all just like the good book says. We're following all the rules."

"I don't understand. How do you get raindrops with the su—*oof!*" Bobby Dee grabbed his stomach, his other hand perilously close to his gun. "I'll tell you what, Ma'am," he snapped at Ada Mae. "I don't care if you are old enough to be my grandmother. If you give me an elbow one more time, I'm gonna lock you up—Harvest cookies or no Harvest cookies!"

Applause from Molly Cochrane punctuated Bobby Dee's comment. "That a boy, Bobby Dee, you stand up for yourself." From her position right inside the hall, she grinned and stared at the tall, angular woman across the room. "His mother would be proud of him, wouldn't he, Ada Mae?"

Exasperated, Mac said, "Will someone please tell me *straight* why the hell half the town is standing in my waiting room?"

Overlapping comments came from every side. "Bet—*oof.* License...cookies...rain!"

Nell touched his elbow, having just come in behind Molly, murmuring, "I didn't know the sheriff's office could do anything about rain."

A quick grin flitted over Mac's face. "You know our motto, We're Up For Anything."

Nell chuckled, and just then Doug came striding into the room waving a magazine. "Ooh-wee, Sheriff. Is this thing yours? What did they do, come up with a new look for *Sports Illustrated?*"

Horror-struck, Mac stared at the lingerie catalogue Doug was flipping through the air. He couldn't say a word, not even when he felt Nell's stare slipping daggers into his body, from top to bottom.

"Well, of course that isn't Mac's," Molly said, snatching the catalogue from Doug and advancing toward Nell. "It must be Nell's. She's the only one here who'd wear frilly little things like this." Molly sent everyone in the room an arch look. "I hope."

Nell took the catalogue as carefully as if it were a live grenade. Face redder than a tomato, she held it out in front of her, arms extended stiffly. "I...thank you, I think."

"Wow!" Bobby Dee's eyes almost jumped out of his head as he pointed at the back cover of the catalogue. "That is the sexiest underwear I've ever seen. You really wear stuff like that, Nell?"

Nell jerked back to life. "Bobby Dee, if you ever want to see underwear like this, in person on a woman in your lifetime, you'd better get back to work."

Belatedly Mac came to her rescue. Glancing at the clock, he said, "Aren't you supposed to be on patrol, Bobby Dee?"

"Yes, sir." Bobby Dee flushed, reached to the desk to pick up his hat, jammed it on his head and raced across the room to the door, which started a mass exodus. The small crowd surged toward the door like restless movie patrons.

After a speculative glance at Nell, Doug followed them saying, "Hey, Ted, make my twenty a fifty, okay?"

Molly snapped a look from Doug to Nell to Mac to Ted and Jed as they stepped over the threshold of the door. "Ted. Wait for me outside." With that, Molly swept toward the door, then turned in the entrance and said, "I'll let you know when Bronwyn comes into town, Mac."

"You do that."

Molly grinned. "I just love it when you get that uppity tone in your voice, son."

Laughing, Mac said, "Goodbye, Mama."

Nell hadn't said a word, but she suddenly became aware that the catalogue was still in full view of anyone who came into the room. She rolled it up and shoved it in her back pocket. "I might have to kill you," she snarled at Mac, sending him a sideways glance.

"I was only trying to help. You know, get an advance peak at the merchandise before we go to that store after our shift."

"I'm not going to this store with you, Mac Cochrane."

Mac's brows lifted. Imitating Nell from the night before, he bobbed his head like a chicken, calling, "Bawk—bawk—bawk-bawk!"

"All right. Meet me there at six." Nell turned sharply on her heels and marched across the room to her desk.

MAC COCHRANE PULLED UP at the lingerie store thinking he had to be out of his mind to have come up with this idea. He didn't care how many notes he'd made about remaking Nell's image, the sheer fact that he was stepping up to help her choose underwear seemed a bit above and beyond the call of duty. He glanced at the sign. Especially in a place called Fancy Pants 'n Stuff. He cast a furtive look around the parking lot. At six o'clock in October, it wasn't dark enough for him not to be recognized, even in a neighboring town. Of course, since he was still in full sheriff regalia and driving his patrol car, to imagine he was invisible was a bit far-fetched.

He leaned back against the hood of his car as he stared at the display in the window. Unfortunately he had a good imagination and could practically see the mannequins walk, bend and sit. He was red-blooded enough to be affected by the skimpy underwear on the voluptuous figures. It wasn't difficult to stare at the bloodred plunging neckline of the skimpy bra, or the sensuous drape of the black satin nightgown as it flowed over a smooth hip. Just as it wasn't really difficult to imagine it on Nell. He grabbed his notebook and jotted a reminder. Mac believed in being prepared and in planning. To his mind, looking through that catalogue earlier had only been smart. *You look at the options, plan your purchases and then you're in and out of the store like a military campaign.* Nell would probably appreciate his foresight, once she calmed down enough to realize it.

Glancing at his watch, he looked around the parking lot. No sign of Nell. It would be just like her to pretend she'd forgotten, he thought. Then he shook his head. No, it wouldn't. Nell might not like something, but she had the courage to say it aloud. He stared at the models again. What wasn't to like? Men drooled over women wearing this type of thing. He'd be sure to point that out.

He'd soon get the chance, he thought, as Nell squealed to a stop next to his car. He watched as her long legs stretched out of the car. She slowly unfolded herself to her full height. She stood, hands on hips, staring first at him then at the window. With a fierce inhale, she slammed her door then stepped up onto the sidewalk. "So," she said, with a defiant tone, "see anything interesting?"

Mac shrugged. "A few things in the catalogue had possibilities, I thought. And this window is full of stuff a guy would like."

Nell sent him a sly look from under her lashes. "You're a guy. See anything *you* like?"

He stared at Nell for a moment. She was right. He was a guy. More importantly he was here to give her direction on what appealed to men. This was the mission he'd accepted, and by God, he'd see it through. Damn, he should know what appealed to men without getting his shorts in a bunch over the fact that he had to tell her. With that thought, he turned to face the window. He pointed at the red bra and bikini set, then glanced at Nell and jotted a note. "With your coloring, red would be great." He repeated the action, pointing to a black teddy. Trying to keep his voice level, he said, "This is perfect, too. Guys always wonder how they're gonna get it off."

Nell watched and listened to him as he continued dissecting

the display, pretending it wasn't affecting him a bit. Which was a lie. Finally he wound down, glancing at her as she said, "If we don't go inside, people will think we're here to bust the place."

Mac chuckled. "I hadn't thought of that. Maybe we should have changed clothes first." He looked down at his uniform. "Not that you gave me any choice."

"I have something to do later tonight, so I had to come straight from work."

"Okay," Mac said. "Look, I'll go in first, then you come in. That way no one will know we're together."

Sending him an incredulous look, Nell said, "How can they not know? We've been out here talking for ten minutes."

"Oh, yeah. Well, be cool, okay?"

Nell shook her head. "Yeah, sure." If there was one thing Nell didn't seem to be at the moment, it was cool. The pulse in her throat was beating as if her motor were racing into hyperdrive. She tried to delay for a moment by glancing at Mac. "Did your mother tell you to change your underwear every day in case you were in an auto accident?"

Mac blinked. "Yeah. But I never understood what that had to do with anything. Did you?" He was trying to put off going into the store, too, but only because he wasn't sure he could stay as detached as he needed to be. He'd never bought lingerie with a woman before.

Nell gave his response her full attention. "I think it was more a comment on our mothers than on us. You know, if the kid isn't wearing clean undies, then the kid is from a bad, dirty home with a crummy mother."

Arching a brow, Mac asked, "What does it mean if the kid is dirty but the underwear is clean?"

Nell grinned. "Maybe that means the father was in charge of the outside."

"Yep. Could be."

They stood for a moment staring at the window. Neither of them moved until finally Nell said, "Oh for...let's go inside before they think we're perverts or something." Mac's chuckle followed her as she stalked over to the door and yanked it open to step inside. Mac was right behind her.

The first thing Nell became aware of was the wide-eyed look of shock on the face of the young woman standing near the counter. Nell gave her a smile. "Hello."

She bobbed her head, big blond curls bouncing. "Officers, is there some kind of problem?"

"Problem? No, what makes you think there's a problem?"

The clerk gave Nell a nervous twitch of the lips that tried to pass for a smile. "Oh, I guess I'm not used to two police-men—women—*police persons*," she amended, "entering my shop. I'm not doing anything illegal." She bit her lip. "I don't think."

Nell smiled, trying to put the woman at ease. After all, three people on edge was one too many. "Underneath these uniforms, the police are people, too."

Interested now, the saleswoman glanced from one to the other. "Is there anything special I can help you with?"

Mac flipped open his notepad and studied it for a moment. "We need some things that are—" he motioned to Nell's body "—that make a man—" He gestured to his own body. "What I mean to say that, uh, will make a man—"

"Horny?" the saleswoman asked with a sweet stretch of her bright red lips and an innocent expression, belied by the amusement in her eyes.

Nell was so surprised she laughed out loud. Eyes twinkling, she met the saleswoman's mischievous gaze. "Absolutely."

"This is for a police calendar or something, isn't it?"

Taken aback, Mac shook his head. "No, of course not. What makes you think that?"

"Oh, I'm sorry, I assumed…well, never mind." She looked from one to the other. "I can see it's personal."

Mac started to deny that, but the woman paid no attention to him. She closed in on Nell, stepping closer to say, "I have some marvelous new merchandise that I haven't even gotten out onto the floor yet. There's this demi-bra, G-string, garter set and cover-up that will have your guy's tongue on the floor." She winked, then whispered, "Not that it will be on the floor for long, though. I wore this outfit for my boyfriend the other night and, *ooh, honey!*''

"That sounds—" Nell choked "—promising."

The saleswoman pulled what looked like a swatch of black material out of a box.

"What's that?" Mac asked, looking over Nell's shoulder.

The sales woman giggled. "Ammunition, Sheriff." She bundled it into Nell's hands and indicated the dressing rooms at the other end of the store. "Why don't you try it on. You can use those dressing rooms right over there." She pointed toward a door set near the counter, and gestured to Mac. "Or choose our private room so you can model it for your sweetie, if you prefer."

By now Mac had gotten a good look at the swatch of material in Nell's hands. That was the only thing he could focus on, that teensy-tiny bit of solid black satin and a lot of sheer material and lace. "You're suggesting she model that for me? Where's the rest of it?"

The woman smiled. "Of course, she should, if she'd like to. To save any embarrassment we've provided a private room just for that purpose. Pretty innovative, don't you think?" Shaking her finger, the woman allowed a stern expression to take over her face. "We don't allow any funny stuff, though, in case you're thinking there's another reason for the privacy."

Mac shook his head. "Look, we're off duty and I wasn't sugg—"

The saleswoman launched into her lecture. "To our way of thinking, the body is a beautiful thing and what happens between people is beautiful. We see no reason not to allow others to help make decisions about our merchandise."

"I understand your philosophy." Actually Mac didn't understand a damn thing, but he couldn't tell her that. His mind was still stuck on the thought of Nell modeling lingerie.

The woman unlocked the door set discreetly in the wall near the counter, looking back over her shoulder as Nell said, "This is great." Nell fingered the lingerie. "But model? No, no, that's all right. I'm sure I can make this decision by my-self."

Nell's reluctance made all the difference to Mac. Obviously she needed a push. He reversed his opinion. "Hey, Nell, we're here. Might as well go the distance."

"I think I've gone as far as I want to go with you, Mac."

"Nell, this is merely part of the makeover process. The process you asked me to participate in, remember? As far as I'm concerned this is just one more step on the journey. The journey to—" Mac stared at the ceiling trying to find the words "—enlightenment."

Nell sent him a sardonic look. "You sound like Obi-Wan Kenobi in *Star Wars*."

"Well, why not? He was a visionary."

"The problem is the only vision you're going to see is me."

Mac grinned as he looked her over. "Pretty sure of your-self, aren't you?"

Nell tossed her head, allowing the bra to dangle from her fingertips. "I might be."

Eyes immediately directed to the swinging satin, Mac wanted to lick his lips but controlled himself enough to say, "Okay, prove it."

"Prove what?"

His gaze met hers head-on. "That you're a vision who'll keep men up at night."

"That sounds like a challenge."

"If you say so, Slim. Now that I think about it, I'm willing to bet you don't have the guts to try this on and model it for me." He knew exactly which buttons to push. All cops, male or female, responded to challenges the same way—pure ma-cho. It was part of being a cop, whether you wanted it to be or not.

"Says who?"

"Now, Nell, don't take it personally. I understand if you're shy."

"Who are you calling shy?"

Mac tried not to smile. This was the Nell who'd once

jumped off the roof of the porch as a child because he'd told her that girls couldn't do it. "If the sneaker fits..."

Nell turned the handle and yanked the door open. "I'll call you in a minute. Then you can give me your professional opinion."

Mac ducked his head and said with a boyish smile, "Any way I can help."

"Don't push your luck, Cochrane," Nell snapped. Then she stepped into the dressing room.

Mac stood awkwardly by the door, which had practically shut in his face. He could feel the saleswoman staring at him. When he looked at her, she turned away, pretending a great interest in her stock. Mac cleared his throat. "Have you been in business very long? I just saw your catalogue for the first time."

"For about a year. This is the first time we've sent out a catalogue though. We thought it would be fun to send it to men, as well as women, as a trial."

Mac grinned. "It sure got my attention."

The woman grinned back. "It was meant to."

Mac ran out of small talk. He glanced at the door, wondering what on earth was taking Nell so long. There wasn't that much to put on. Just when he was going to pound on the door, Nell said, "You can come in, Mac."

Mac's palms were suddenly damp. He wiped them on his pants and reached for the handle. He stepped into a small suite, the room having a standing three-view mirror in a baroque gold frame, and a small ornate antique love seat with a red brocade cover. A small screen blocked off the corner, the material showing a faint outline of a woman's form behind it. Nell's uniform was thrown over the top of the screen, leaving him no doubt that the woman behind the screen was now dressed in very little. Mac wondered if he'd taken leave of every sense he possessed. He knew his nerves would probably be shot after this little stunt. Whatever had possessed him to come up with this idiotic idea he had no idea. Why hadn't he started with her dance technique, or taught her to cook a halfway decent meal or something? Why start from the inside out? *Because you wanted to, you idiot.*

He tried to ignore that inner voice, but it was hard to do when Nell walked out from behind the screen. Mac was so stunned his knees buckled. Luckily, the love seat was right behind him. He hit it with a thump. That straight-as-a-stick little girl who'd jumped naked into the local water hole with him sure had changed. Slim she might be, but Mac had no idea she was as well built as she was. The brief bra caressed her pert breasts, pushing them up and forward like a pinup's, while the little bikini briefs barely covered what they were meant to hide. The lace kissed the V of her crotch and teased at her thighs, begging him to do the same. He wanted to, Lord, how he wanted to. However he forced himself to ignore her tempting femininity as his eyes were compelled to follow the long line of the garters down her thighs. Unfortunately, Nell had no stockings to attach, but that didn't stop Mac from using every ounce of imagination he possessed. The entire ensemble was frosted with a wrap of sheer material that caught at the throat with a small bow and then divided over her breasts to end at the top of her hips. Light-headed, Mac realized that he hadn't taken a breath since Nell had emerged from behind the screen. He gasped, hoping the sudden gulp of oxygen wouldn't make him pass out. Of course, then Nell might have to give him mouth-to-mouth resuscitation, which had its perks. His eyes collided with Nell's. By her expression, Mac was positive she could see the sheen of desire in his eyes. Before he could say anything, there was a discreet tap on the door.

Nell pulled her gaze from his. Glancing at the door, she called, "Come in."

The saleswoman peeped around the door. "Oh, that looks marvelous on you."

Nell glanced at Mac, who still had not said a word. "You think so?"

Stepping inside, the woman said, "Absolutely. Don't you think so, Sheriff?"

Nodding, Mac tried to open his mouth, but words wouldn't

come. He was afraid if he tried, he'd sound as if he were speaking Swahili. His zipper was so full he was tempted to place his gun over it before it went off on its own. At least that way he'd have an excuse.

Grinning, the saleswoman said, "Yep. I'd say he thinks so. My boyfriend looked exactly the same way last night." She sent Nell an approving glance. "I'd say this outfit is a grade A success."

"Good," Nell said, glancing at Mac.

"And the reason I came in is to tell you we just got in a line of men's items that match this outfit. Isn't that fun?" She pulled her hand from behind her back. "What do you think?"

Nell stared at the dangling G-string jockstrap. Sizing up the potential, Nell looked back at Mac. "I think it's perfect."

Mac found his voice. "Perfect for whom? I'm not buying that."

Nell took the garment from the saleswoman, watched her leave the room then strolled over to Mac. "I agree. You shouldn't buy this without trying it on first."

"Trying it on!" Mac's voice hit a register higher than an altar boy's.

"Of course." To Mac, Nell's smile resembled that of a hungry shark.

"I see no need to…"

Nell tossed him the underwear. "Remember the road to enlightenment."

Mac stared at the material in his hand. At the thought of trying this on in front of Nell, his thoughts scattered. Never mind that she'd just done the same for him. Somehow, to be standing in front of her practically nude was unthinkable. Luckily for him, his beeper went off. Mac seized the pager as if it were a lifeline. He peered at the number. His office. Thank God, maybe it was a crisis. Anything to get him out of here. Waving the pager, Mac met Nell's eyes, attempting to keep his cool. He tossed the jockstrap back to Nell. "Sorry, love to, but gotta go."

Nell placed a hand on her hip. "You can run, Mac, but you can't hide."

Mac headed to the door, looked back over his shoulder and said, "In my opinion, you should buy that outfit, Nell. And talk to the saleswoman about some other things. She seems to know what's what."

"Don't worry, I'll be buying quite a few things here."

Mac waved and stepped from the dressing room, but as he did so, he heard her say, "Including male underwear."

He popped his head back inside to stare at her. "That's—"

"Remember our deal? You help me and I help you."

"I keep telling you I don't really need help, I just want to get my mother off my back."

"Who knows, maybe a change of habit will help you do that. It can't hurt. It might even get you out of the rut you're in."

"I'm not in a rut."

Nell chuckled as her hands swept her cover-up back from her hips so she could place her hands on her waist. "Let me put it this way. You can accept *my* help, or your mother's."

"My mother..." Mac scowled for a moment. Then his sense of humor reasserted itself. "I guess if it's between your choice of a date and Bronwyn, I'd have to give you the benefit of the doubt."

"Tomorrow, at my house after work, we can compare lists."

"What kind of lists?"

"What I'm looking for in a man. What you're looking for in a woman."

Mac stared at the female in front of him. What he was looking for in a woman was standing right in front of him. Which made absolutely no sense. This was Nell, his deputy, his childhood buddy. His sense of unease deepened. Once again he told himself he'd better find a hot, loose woman, and find one fast!

6

NELL WALKED TO HER WINDOW and stared at the parking lot of her apartment complex. Why was she so nervous? Mac had been to her home more times than she could count—as a child, a teenager and now as an adult since she'd moved out of her parents' house years before to live her own life. She caught sight of Mac's car as it approached the driveway. At the moment she felt as if she stood at the precipice, she could either jump or back away to safety. She thought it funny how some moments in life were defined by little happenings. Something unexpected made something unimportant an issue. Without you ever being aware of how it happened. She watched Mac step from the car and give his trademark glance around to check the surroundings, something cops did without even thinking about it. Mac. She'd known the guy forever. Strange how she decided he should be the one to help her identify her future spouse. Or at least help start her in the right direction. He'd always been there for her. Whenever she'd needed him, he'd stepped into the breach.

And here he was again. Good old Mac.

She stared at his long legs as they ate up the sidewalk, at his slim hips, her eyes traveling to his broad shoulders before ending up at his gorgeous masculine face. She stared at him as if she'd never seen him before. In a way she hadn't. She imagined him in the underwear she'd bought for him. Funny, it was almost difficult to do. Something kept standing in her way. Was it her childhood memories? Or her inability to think of him as a sex object. She stared at him again. *Nah—that's not it.* She had absolutely no problem whatsoever seeing Mac

Cochrane as a sex object. She grinned. No woman in her right mind would have a problem with that.

She could feel her body flush as she remembered standing in front of him, in her lingerie, for God's sake! It had taken every ounce of courage to step out from behind that screen. When she did, she hadn't been prepared for his reaction. Nor was she prepared for the reaction his reaction had caused her. She'd had no idea she'd end up wondering, "What if Mac weren't my old childhood friend, and my boss?" Thinking back, she could have sworn she'd seen desire in his eyes, even though he'd taken great pains to hide it. Although enough of his reaction stuck in her mind to make her question their relationship, she'd ultimately dismissed it. Naturally Mac would react that way, Nell thought, any man would when confronted by a half-naked woman. She'd been wearing as much as she'd wear on a beach, cover-up included, but it was different when it was called lingerie and most of the garment was see-through. That put a bit of a spin on the situation.

The doorbell rang. Nell turned from the window. Stomach jumping, she told herself, *Don't be an idiot. You just saw the guy at the station today.* She glanced around her apartment. It was halfway orderly. She even had the table set up with pads of paper and pens, ready for them to work. Still feeling strangely awkward, she crossed the room and pulled open the door.

"Hi."

Bracing his hand on the wood, Mac leaned against the door frame. "Hi back."

Nell wiped her palms on her jeans. They were clammy. She had no idea why. "Do you want to come in?"

Mac grinned. "No, I thought I'd stand out here in the hall."

"Oh, for..." Nell reached out, yanking him through the doorway. "Your sense of humor is going to do you in some day."

"Life's tough, you know."

"It's bound to get tougher."

"Yeah, I know. I have to teach you to dance." Mac pulled a tape out of his pocket and waved it at her.

Nell scowled at him. "I don't think that's funny."

"Me, either. You'll probably step all over me. Or else give me a nosebleed."

"I am not that bad a dancer. I really feel the music."

Mac cocked a brow and tucked the tape back into his pocket. "You do?"

"Yes. I have a love for music."

"Then you should have grabbed the drummer." Mac grinned and raised his hand as Nell moved toward him. "I'm kidding. I'm kidding. I know, his name was Wayne, so it wasn't an option."

"You make me sound very silly. I don't like that."

"Silly? What's silly about blowing off a guy with a name you don't like?"

"It's probably something like blowing off Hilda's niece because Hilda resembles a tree stump and you think her niece is going to be the same."

Two spots of color stained Mac's cheeks. "I didn't say that."

Nell adopted the pose of the righteous. "You didn't have to. It was obvious."

Mac strode into the room. "I think we'd better get to work. I don't have all night."

"Got a hot date?"

Mac frowned. "As a matter of fact, I do."

"With whom? I thought we were going to discuss this. That's our deal, remember. I help you, you help me."

"Well I don't really need your help. I found someone all by myself. Besides, you said you need more help than I do, so you're the priority." Mac shook his head. "I don't need a makeover, just some way to make my mother understand that I'm not salivating to get married."

"Hmm. So how would you characterize this woman tonight? Obviously not marriage material."

Mac tried to keep his expression under control and failed miserably. A chuckle escaped. "Hot, fast and loose. If she comes up to expectations, that is."

"Disgusting," Nell said with a twist of her lips. "You're as bad as my brothers used to be."

"Impossible. I know your brothers too well."

Nell dismissed that. Rubbing her chin, she considered Mac. "So what would you say you like about her, this girl tonight?" As Mac gave her an incredulous look, Nell continued with a game expression. "That's what we are going to discuss, remember?"

Staring back at her, Mac's lips twitched. "I'd have to say it's her stated desire to…"

"To?" Nell prompted.

"To have a good time." Mac enunciated each word so Nell couldn't possibly misunderstand his meaning.

"Mmm-hmm, I take back what I said before. You're really much worse than my brothers."

"Thank you."

Nell gave up and moved to the table. "I'd like to discuss this logically. I've put together a list of my desired types of men. I thought what you could do is teach me the correct response for the personalities. Then I can do the same for you."

Mac stared at her. "You're kidding, right?"

"Absolutely not. I believe in being prepared from this point on. I don't want to chance another disaster like I had the other night." Nell had decided her reputation couldn't survive too many public humiliations.

"Well, this is more like it. It's exactly what I'd expect from you, Slim. The cool, reasonable approach."

"Thank you." Nell was unaccountably pleased to appear as if she was on familiar territory. But who was she kidding? She might appear cool and reasonable on the outside, but at the moment she felt like one big mass of hormones.

Mac pulled out a chair and sat down. Deliberately he folded his hands in front of him and stared at Nell, waiting for her to begin. Nell walked over to join him.

Pulling out a chair to sit down, Nell once again had a few qualms as she met Mac's eyes. He was trying to be solemn and dignified, but she could just see that unholy glint of humor lurking in the back, waiting to erupt. Tell me again why

you started this, Nell asked herself. She could have been sending e-mails to the masses and seeing what was going to happen in the quiet of her own home, instead of holding her
problem up to the public and playing out her matchmaking
dilemma under the noses of the townsfolk. When Mac said
nothing, only looked at her expectantly, Nell gathered up what
was left of her reasoning ability and took control. She flipped
open a notebook, feeling like a reporter on the trail of a sus-
pect. Or a cop. "Very well. Let's begin."

"It's your party," Mac said with a grin that resembled a
demented Doberman.

Nell glared at him. Somehow he wasn't taking this as seriously as he should. The thought hit her that he was nervous,
but she instantly dismissed it. Probably just anxious to get to
his date. She looked down, staring at her notes. "Let's suppose I accept a date with a man who's rather quiet, shy I
suppose you'd say. How should I play that? I mean do I play
the bold hussy and draw him out? Or should I pretend to be
shy myself so he won't feel bad?"

"First of all, Nell, I can't really see you dating someone
who's shy. You don't have anything in common."

"Well, maybe not on the surface, but I'm looking for a
way to relate. The way I figure it, I'm not going to find the
ideal man right off the bat. Isn't that what you told me, that
I'd have to adapt, like the incident with the steak? Remember,
I might not like something, but I'd have to eat it anyway."

"Why would you want to do that?"

"What the hell are you talking about, Mac? You're the one
who told me to do that. That some men are macho and—"

"I never said that."

Feeling as if she'd been poleaxed, Nell stared at him for a
moment before regaining her voice. "You most certainly did."

"I'm sure I would've remembered if I'd said something
like that."

"I was sitting right across from you when you—" *Ouch!*
Nell bit her tongue then shoved her hands into her hair, stirring it up. "You're making me crazy. Do you know that?"

"Good. That's what I'm trying to do," Mac said with a

smug smile. "You should be prepared for problems. The dating road is filled with potholes, and you have to deftly steer around them."

"My God, you sound like a fortune cookie."

"Confucius say—" Mac grinned. "The better to eat you with, my dear."

"Confucius said that?"

"Maybe it was the big bad wolf."

"Ah, now that's a better personality fit. But I think you've got the 'eating' part wrong." Nell gave him a saccharine smile. "Unless you're practicing for your hot date tonight?"

"Could be, Slim. She might be that kind of girl."

"Okay. Let's say I meet that type of guy. What would you suggest? I just lie back and enjoy it?"

Bristling, Mac said, "What kind of way is that to talk?"

"Pretty realistic, I think. You know I'm going to run into a lot of guys who have one thing and one thing only in mind."

"Like Wayne the drummer?"

Nell shuddered, half with distaste and half with remembered lust. "If you just looked at the outside package, the guy was dynamite…all those sculpted muscles, a great butt and that yummy face and silky hair. All draped in black leather. At least some of him was draped in black leather. The rest was draped in skin."

Mac refolded his hands, the knuckles showing a bit white, then shifted on his seat and said, "Let's drop the subject." His face darkened for a moment before he attempted to rearrange it feature by feature into a pleasant, interested expression. "Next personality type."

"We haven't finished this one yet. You didn't give me any hints about the libido-only guy."

"That's simple," Mac said, crossing his arms with a smug expression on his face. "Just pretend they're all named Wayne."

Nell laughed. "That's an idea." Then she sobered and glanced at her pad. "All right, let's get down to business. Obviously, you aren't going to be any help with the shy guy, so…"

"No, no. Let's talk about the shy guy. I personally think you should be pretty aggressive." Mac leaned forward. "After all, the reason a guy is shy is because he lacks the skill to step right up to the bat, to grab the ball, to kick the risky goal, to…"

Nell rubbed a fingertip over her mouth as she stared at Mac, who was just warming up. "How come when a guy wants to make a point, he always does it in sports terminology? Even guys who can't relate to sports use sports terminology. Why is that?"

"You're nuts."

"No, I'm not. You're talking about what? Baseball, football, soccer? What does that have to do with anything?"

"Life's lessons are learned on the fields of play—the teamwork, the reaching for the win. You know that."

"That's what I'm talking about, Mac. I played sports as a kid, but I never looked at them as life's lessons."

Mac sent her an incredulous look. "You should have. You've got five brothers. They made sure you knew about sports."

"I'm not saying I don't understand the terminology. I'm just saying I find it interesting that men always have to step back to sports and athletes to make a point. I don't notice you saying anything about the esprit de corps you find in a ballet company, for instance."

With a revolted snort, Mac said, "And you damn well won't find me saying anything about it, either."

"Yet, dancers are the best athletes in the world. Every muscle is superbly conditioned and their timing is perfect."

"I know that. I'm not uneducated or uncouth. My mama saw to that. I even watch PBS. But if I were to ask a group of guys to work together like the ballet corps in *Swan Lake,* I'd be laughed out of the room."

"You're right, but I'd pay money to see that." Nell chuckled. "Never mind, I got diverted from the real subject. Back to the problem. So what you're saying is, if I find a shy guy I should be aggressive, because he'd really like that because he's too shy to be that way himself, so I should be everything he isn't, then he'd appreciate it. Right?''

Scratching his head, Mac said, "If that sentence had gotten any longer I would have had to come back tomorrow to answer. But I think that's what I was saying."

Nell nodded and looked down at her list. She made a checkmark beside one of the numbers. "That takes care of two types. What about the intellectual ones?"

"Where you gonna find one of those in Knightsboro?"

"Just because I've never personally tried to find one doesn't mean there aren't any here. I'll bet there are many intellectual men in town, not to mention tourists."

"You'd probably have to hang around the library to meet them. I can see it now. There you'll be, peering through the stacks looking for a guy wearing glasses."

"Glasses?" Nell wrinkled her nose. "Oh, intellectual, I get ya."

Mac rubbed his chin. "Of course, my buddy A.J. is intellectual, and he doesn't wear glasses."

"Your brother Daryn doesn't wear them, either, and he's a brain."

"Yeah, he does. Wears 'em to read. The guy's blind as a bat with the fine print. It comes from studying all those law books."

"I don't have to stick to the library. I could also try the bookstore. There's that new one in town with its own little café and everything. I love bookstores."

"You do?"

"Yeah."

Leaning closer, Mac confessed. "I do too."

"No kidding?"

"I love to read. It's one of the ways I relax."

"As long as I've known you, I never knew that." Nell's eyes narrowed. "You are talking about more than the sports pages, aren't you?"

"Why are you so surprised? Because I'm a sheriff?" Thrusting his chin forward, Mac said, "You're treating me like a stereotype—big dumb cop, only good for busting heads and swaggering.''

"I'm sorry, but we're talking about stereotypes—hot woman, jock, etcetera."

"Yeah, but only because it's easier to categorize people you don't know. But you've known me long enough not to do that."

"I didn't mean to hurt your feelings, Mac." She stared at him, noticing the tenderness as well as the strength in his good-looking face. Yes, they'd grown up together, but... "Recently I'm wondering if I've ever known you at all."

Mac returned her look. "I'm beginning to think the same."

For a moment a silence hung heavily, blanketing the room like fog over the mountains. Nell fiddled with her notebook. Finally Mac cleared his throat and said, "Got anything else written down in your book there? Any other types of men. Because if not, I've got some things to go over."

"Let's see." Nell glanced down. "There's the homebody type. The type of guy who appreciates good home cooking and stuff like that."

Mac eyes crinkled. "Good home cooking? And you want to know...?"

Eyes narrowing, Nell snapped, "It may have escaped your notice, but I'm not exactly the little domestic type."

Mac pretended shock. "No?"

"Very funny." Nell chuckled. "Go ahead, make fun. I'll get you back."

"The homebody type of man, huh? I think you'd better hire somebody to do the cooking and you can wear the apron."

Nell felt the heat begin as Mac's gaze touched her body. He said casually, "You'd probably really keep his interest if you just wore the apron. Then he wouldn't care if he had dinner or not."

"That's an approach I wouldn't have thought of."

"That's because you're not a man." Mac winked. "We always approach a problem using both heads. The problem generally is—which one is doing the primary thinking?"

"That is probably the truest thing you've ever said. So it all comes back to the libido-driven guy, does it?"

Mac jerked to his feet. "Not completely."

"You just said that."

"Dammit, Slim. You gotta quit taking me out of context. Now granted, men are generally physically attracted first."

"Okay, no need to go further. I've got it." With a flick of her wrist, Nell closed her notebook. "What else is on your list. Now that we've taken care of the lingerie." Nell snapped her fingers and stood up. "Oh, and speaking of underwear, I've got a surprise for you."

A suspicious look crossed Mac's face like a cloud cover over the sun. "What kind of surprise?"

Nell stood and walked across the room to her bedroom. She disappeared inside for a moment, then reappeared with a bag in her hand. Tossing it to him, she said, "I thought you'd like to try these. It might give you a whole new outlook on the world."

"I don't need a new outlook."

"Sure you do. Everyone does sometimes. If you end up with the wrong women when you're wearing boxer shorts, maybe you'll end up with the right one wearing these." She indicated the bag. "Go on. Open up."

Cautiously Mac stuck his hand into the bag. He jerked it out with a tiny bit of navy-blue material hanging onto his finger like a rattlesnake using Polygrip. "What the hell is this?"

"On the way home, I decided I wasn't the only one getting a makeover. So, I turned around, went back to the lingerie store and bought these. Aren't they cute? Did you see the little cop badge on the front?" Nell grinned. "This way you can say, 'open up—police,' and really get some action!"

Mac turned the material over in his hands. "There is *no* way I'm gonna—"

"Don't be negative. I was told they're very comfortable."

"By whom?"

"The saleswoman."

"What does she know?"

"Her boyfriend wears them."

"That's no recommendation. According to her, her boy-friend's a sex-starved maniac."

Nell chuckled. "Anyway. Next time you go out, wear these."

"I don't have time to change tonight. I'll have to try them another time. Mac shoved the briefs into his jacket pocket and withdrew the cassette tape. He waved it at Nell. "Let's get back to business here."

"You're really going to give me dancing lessons?"

"Sure, what do you think?"

Nell held out her hand for the cassette. "Let me see. I don't recognize this group. Where'd you get this?"

"I forgot to bring tapes, so I just grabbed some from the shelves behind Bobby Dee's desk."

"The confiscated merchandise rack at the station?"

"Yeah. I figure whatever it is, it's got a beat." Mac stripped off his jacket and stretched like a man warming up for a championship bout. "Put it on, okay."

"Okay." Nell walked over to the stereo and inserted the tape, pressing the button. She stood awkwardly for a moment, not sure what to do. Then Mac grabbed her hand and pulled her toward him as the throbbing rhythms rolled forth. "Mac, what kind of music is this?"

"It sounds kind of Latin, doesn't it?" He pulled her closer to him, almost forcibly bending her elbow so he could lead. "Let yourself go, Nell."

The music beat into her brain. For a moment she fell against him, her muscles lax, until she realized what she was doing. Every muscle in her body froze. "The cassette cover must have been wrong. This is a tango, isn't it?"

"A tango?" Mac steered her backward, his body so close that they almost moved as one. "I hope not. I don't know how to tango."

"Then how're you going to teach me?"

Mac stopped and stared down at her. "You've got a point, Slim."

She tried to unpeel herself from him, recognizing that if

she didn't, the way her body was reacting to his nearness, she might get to know him much better than she'd ever anticipated. *It's the music. Not Mac.* She felt the jolt of his blue eyes. *No, not Mac. Of course not.* She licked her lips. "Why don't we try this lesson when you've got the right music."

Mac stepped back, relieved, Nell thought.

"That's probably a good idea." He brightened. "It could have been worse. I could've brought a polka."

Nell chuckled. "That would have been worse all right." For a moment they stood awkwardly while the sensuous rhythms of the tape filled the room. With a deep breath, Nell plunged into the subject that had been consuming her. "I've been thinking, the dart tournament is this weekend. People will be coming in from all over. That might be a good time to...to, uh..."

"To bite the bullet?"

Nodding, Nell attempted to keep some dignity. Not that it was at all possible in this situation. "To look for a man, yes."

"Okay. Tell you what. We can take some of those personality types and set up a situation and then practice your response, if you want."

"I don't know about practicing, maybe we should go straight to on-the-job training."

"You could have a point." Mac clapped his hands, resembling a quarterback calling to break the huddle. "Hey, I can coach from the sidelines. How's that sound?"

"Like a play-by-play approach, you mean?" Saying it aloud made the idea sound like one of the dumbest ones she'd ever heard.

"Yep. You make the moves and I'll make the calls."

"Mac," Nell said, vaguely uneasy. "There's something else. I'm not sure how to handle this. I mean, you told me I should act sexier and dress sexier. Is it your opinion, as a man, that I should get...uh...physical immediately?"

"Physical." Mac frowned. "As in kissing or going to bed?"

"I don't know. That's why I'm asking you."

"What have you done in the past?"

"Well, duh! That's my problem, isn't it? What I've done in the past wasn't working. At least it wasn't working long enough for happily ever after." The music swelled to a heart-stopping crescendo. "Could it be my technique?"

"Maybe I should evaluate your technique."

Nell's mouth widened until she was sure it had swallowed her entire face. "How much of my technique?"

"Just the first part, the kiss that's supposed to lead to other things. That should do it. I can make an assessment from that."

She took a step toward him, blood throbbing in time with the beat. "That would be a logical approach."

"I agree." Nodding his agreement, Mac stepped toward her, also.

The air vibrated as they met in the middle of the room and exchanged glances. With a determination that bordered on fanatical, Nell lifted her hands to his shoulders. Mac's hands grasped her waist. Nell wanted to speak but decided she'd better get this over with. "Just remember, this is research. So there's no reason for either of us to feel funny. It's like the lingerie, right?"

"Research. I agree completely, Slim." His head lowered as she lifted her face.

Her voice quickened in time with her pulse. "The right approach means the right result."

"I've always found that complete and intense preparation wins the day." His lips came closer, so close she could feel his breath on her cheeks.

"Analysis is—"

"Nell," Mac whispered. "Shut up." Then he took her lips and made them his.

At his first touch Nell disappeared into a gauze-covered world, where the only clear image was so unclear it seemed to disappear in the distance. Where the present only contained the white-hot heat of his mouth on hers. The music burned her soul as his lips seared into hers. Her hands moved into his hair, stroking, caressing, feeling every sensation as the strands slipped over her fingertips. His arms wrapped themselves around her waist, pulling her closer until she could memorize every inch of his body as he strained against hers. Nell's lips parted and he used the opportunity to slip his tongue inside to tangle briefly with hers. When he would have withdrawn, Nell pulled him back, aggressively meeting his tongue again with hers, allowing them to tangle and dance, to dip and glide as the music beckoned. Their emotions built as the music raced to its final crescendo, as their bodies strained to release in a tango of their own. However, just as the song was a teasing preparation to passion, so was the kiss. Nell made the first movement—retreating, alarmed by the feelings racing through her. Feelings that could rapidly become out of control if she'd let them. Mac must have felt the same. He loosened his grip and pulled back, inch by inch. Nell wanted him to stay but made no move to keep him there.

The last notes of the music died, leaving only the labored sound of their breathing hanging in the air.

Not certain what to say, Nell concentrated on getting her breathing under control for a moment. Then she realized that though this had been more than she'd bargained for, she must treat this lightly. Not give Mac any indication of how shaken she was by his touch.

Dropping his arms to his sides, Mac let her go completely. "Well…"

"Well?" Nell repeated.

"Well, that's one thing you don't have to worry about."

Her eyes lifted to meet his, surprised to see shock and humor there. "I don't?"

"Nope. I'd say your technique is fine, just fine." Mac passed his hand over his eyes before he continued, "The problem was probably chemistry. If you don't have chemistry, you don't have anything. And it takes two to have chemistry."

"Good, good, thanks for relieving my mind. I hadn't considered that angle. I was just thinking it was me. It's kind of disconcerting to kiss a man and start wondering if you'd left your last load of laundry in the washer instead of shifting it to the dryer."

Mac blinked. "I guess it would be."

"I don't suppose that's ever happened to you?"

Eyes twinkling, Mac said, "Afraid not. But then I'm not big on laundry."

Nell grinned. "No, I don't suppose it has, considering what you said about where a man's thoughts generally come from."

"It's a dirty job, but somebody's got to do it."

Nell laughed. "Right. And speaking of that, what time's your date tonight?"

Glancing at his watch, Mac groaned. "Eight o'clock. I've got to go. Any other lessons will have to keep."

"That's okay." Nell walked over to get Mac's jacket. Turning, she handed it to him as he walked to the door. "You've given me enough to think about for one day."

"Me, too," Mac muttered under his breath as he grabbed his jacket and stepped into the hall. He stopped and turned to face Nell. "The dart tournament? That's still a go?"

"You bet." It couldn't be anything else, Nell thought. Not with thoughts of Mac racing through her mind, confusing her. "I can't wait to try out the new me."

Mac glanced back at her. "You know, Slim, the old you wasn't so bad." With that, he waved and headed for the stairs.

Wrapping her arms around her waist, Nell hugged his words close. *Not so bad. Maybe not, but everything changes.* Nell whispered, "Wait till you see the new me in action."

MAC STOOD IN THE PARKING LOT and stared at Charlie's Place. It was lit up like Christmas and the Fourth of July. This dart tournament was always one of the key events in the weeks before the Harvest Festival. It seemed to start the ball rolling, and it had gotten larger during the years. What had started as a small-town get-together to sell a bit more food and drinks at Charlie's had rapidly become a winning event. Now it even had big money in prizes. From professionals to tourists looking for action and a warm place to get to know others, people came in from all over to try their luck. Mac was one of them, though he wasn't as dedicated as many of the participants. Nell had even been practicing some.

Nell. Damned if he could figure her out. Just when he

thought he had, she shifted shapes on him. She'd gone about her work, cool as glass all week long. Never mentioning by word or action their situation, or the kiss that had almost blown him apart. What had he said about chemistry? Sometimes you had it, and sometimes you didn't. Well, as far as he was concerned, they were so volatile they might explode if shaken. And he'd been shaken from the moment his lips touched hers.

Naturally, after spending a better part of the week thinking about the situation, he'd decided the physical reaction was natural. After all, Mac thought, anyone who's caught up in a romantic situation of some type—and helping Nell appeal to a man applied—develops attachment by association. What had happened between him and Nell was nothing more than familiarity and a concentration on romance.

Tucking his shirt into his jeans, a relieved Mac swaggered toward Charlie's. Snapping his fingers to get the juices pumping, he felt it was a night when he couldn't lose. Unfortunately, he was a bit overconfident. As he walked, Mac grimaced, trying to surreptitiously adjust his jeans without anyone being the wiser. *Well, hell! What possessed me to try wearing these damn briefs tonight of all nights?* He needed to be his most attentive to the game, and to Nell. He didn't need to worry about picking his underwear out of his butt. And that's where it was. That skinny little thong tucked itself between his cheeks like a kite string. *Hell if I know what people find so sexy about that!* As far as Mac was concerned, he might as well take the damn things off. He was stopped only by the knowledge that the one thing standing between the 'real him' and the greedy teeth of his zipper was this little tiny bit of blue material. The thought of being zipped up by the short hairs wasn't appealing at all. So he might as well grin and bear it. He wouldn't let a little situation like this get him down.

He stepped inside the bar's front entrance. Charlie's was really jumping. It looked like a Saturday night, even though it was Friday. People were everywhere, milling around, laughing, applauding and generally enjoying themselves. He sent a quick glance around the room. No sign of Nell yet. He glanced at his watch. Seven-thirty. Cracking his knuckles, Mac decided the night was young, the purse was big and the whole evening was in front of him waiting for the action to begin. Rubbing his hands together, Mac acknowledged that he was a real action junkie. Most cops were, at heart, even if they didn't admit it. There was that pulse-pounding excitement that was always only a trigger's second away, even in a town like Knightsboro. Of course his action didn't always have the intensity of a big city, but then a big-city cop didn't have the chance to escape the everyday pain and rejuvenate in nature. Which was another reason he'd stayed in Knightsboro instead of heading off to brighter lights. Not that he'd find any brighter lights anywhere tonight. A dart tournament might not have the cachet of a tennis tournament, but at least it was one step up from bowling.

He looked around for Nell. Still no sign of her, which probably meant he should be looking for her on the dance floor, like the last time. He walked farther into the main room, stopping by a recessed area that served as a coatroom in cold weather. Propping his shoulder against the wall, Mac peered toward the dancers. Nope, no tall, violently gyrating person assaulting anyone to be seen in sight. A tap on his shoulder had him swinging around.

"How are you doing?"

Any knowledge of the English language fled as he took a good look at Nell. At least he thought it was Nell. He wasn't sure, though. Nell didn't have such big eyes, all shadowy and secretive, all smudged as if she'd just rolled in from a bout of hot, heavy sex. Nell didn't have a mouth so curvy and luscious, so moist and tempting. She didn't have a body that was poured into a tight little black dress with a low sweetheart neckline that set off the high-riding curves of her breasts, or legs that stopped the heart with that flirty little skirt skimming the tops of her thighs. And Nell definitely didn't have a foot that arched high and slim in a pair of high heels with a strap that drew a man's eyes to her trim ankles, then begged him to travel straight and true back up the road until he'd revisited every dip, hollow and curve he'd already lingered over on the way down.

This couldn't be Nell. Or if it was, who the hell had he been looking at for the past few years?

"What's the matter with you, Mac? Is my makeup on crooked?"

Mac took a deep breath. "Nellisthatreallyyou?" It came out as one word. He sounded like a two-year-old on speed. Licking his lips, he tried again, overemphasizing every word and letter. "Nell, is that really you?"

"No, you idiot. I'm an alien who's taken over Nell's body."

"And some body it is," Mac muttered.

"What?"

"Nothing." Mac couldn't stop himself from giving Nell another once-over. "I thought you'd be on the dance floor."

"They're not playing a tango."

Mac chuckled and jerked a thumb at the band, which was, at least, energetic and loud, if not talented. "I don't think that group would know a tango from a tangerine."

Nell sidled a bit closer, walking her fingertips up his chest to twirl in the hair peeking over his opened collar. She licked her lips, instantly drawing Mac's attention.

Mac's eyes widened, his breath quickened, his arms stiffened—and so did the rest of him. His teeny little bikini briefs suddenly got so tight he felt like a grade-school kid getting a wedgie. His voice squeaked out in high C. "Nell! What the hell are you doing?"

She leaned closer, allowing her breasts to touch his chest. Bringing her mouth to his ear, she whispered, "Just applying the lessons from the master." Then she licked his ear.

That was all it took. Mac grabbed her, pulled her so there wasn't room for plastic wrap between them, turned swiftly and pinned her against the wall.

7

STARING INTO HER BIG BROWN EYES, Mac was breathing like a racehorse. He was pressed so tightly against Nell that he practically shared each breath. Her ripe, raspberry lips beckoned—and dammit all, he wasn't a saint. He couldn't help but taste, just once. Mac didn't try to justify it. Sometimes you just have to go with the flow. This was one of those times. His lips touched hers. There was an element of familiarity, but it was overlaid by an exciting strangeness. Nell, but not Nell. Mac, but not Mac. He settled in against her, wishing this moment could go on forever. Or at least until he came to his senses. Shifting his head, he molded his lips to hers, not surprised when her mouth opened to take his deepening kiss. With the electricity charging through him, he would have been more surprised if he had not lit her up like a searchlight. He pressed against her, shuddering when she gave an excited little wiggle as she responded to him. The slight growl in her throat urged him on, until his blood started to boil. Where it would end, Mac didn't know.

"Mmm-hmm."

The clearing of a throat forced Mac to open his eyes. The sight of a face in his peripheral vision leaning in close to him, startled him further. "Ahem, 'scuse me. Sheriff?"

Mac tore his lips from Nell's. "What?" he barked, turning his head to see Ted Kilbourne staring a hole though him.

Ted's face took on an expression that resembled a sixteenth-century martyr facing a religious tribunal. He folded his arms around his business ledger. "Sorry to interrupt, but your mama sent me over."

"She said it was very important," Jed added, peering over

Ted's shoulder. "Or we never would have interfered with you and—*Nell!*" Jed tapped Ted. "Look Ted, it's Nell. Isn't it?"

Ted leaned in a bit closer, examining Nell, who still had not said a word. She didn't seem able to speak, Mac thought. Her eyes were still closed, her face bright red and her breath racing so much that with each rise of her chest she seemed ready to fall out of her dress. Mac would be all too happy to catch her if that happened.

"Well, well, well. It doesn't look like Nell exactly."

"Betcha it is, though."

Ted glanced at Jed, then hugged his ledger, looking off into the distance as if seeking wisdom. "However, do we ever really know someone else? What we generally see, what we generally know and what we generally think we think we know isn't always the same."

"Thanks, Shakespeare," Mac muttered. "Could you back off a bit and take your philosophizing elsewhere."

Ted nodded energetically. "Yes, yes, of course."

"You look like you're very busy here," Jed agreed.

"We're just practicing, that's all," Mac said. "It's Nell's big night."

"It is?" Ted elbowed Jed. "Hear that?"

"Course I did. I'm right on top of you, ain't I?"

Nell finally snapped, "Could all three of you take four giant steps back before I get claustrophobia?"

Mac stepped backward, pulling the two brothers with him. The brothers were blabbering with each step. "Oh, yessir. Sure thing. Wouldn't want to ruin the big night. No sirree, bob. Could be a big night for us, too."

Mac nailed Jed with a glance. "You said my mother's looking for me? What's my mother doing here?"

"I'm sure I don't know, but she's right over there by the dart tournament."

Flipping up his ever-present ball cap to scratch his head, Jed said, "Didn't she say something about Hilda?"

"Hilda?" Mac's antenna went up and he whirled around to look in the direction of the dartboards. "She's not here, is she, Ted?"

"Who, Hilda?"

"No, not Hilda—her niece."

"Which niece is that, Mac? By gum, Hilda's family breeds like a bunch of rabbits. Ain't that right, Jed?"

"Yep. If her cows bred like that, she'd be the richest farmer in the valley."

Mac rolled his eyes. "Providing you didn't poison them first."

"Now, Mac," Ted said with a wounded look, "you know all 'bout that being an accident. We fixed the problem."

Nell came back to life. "Excuse me. You don't need me for this discussion, fascinating though it is. I'm just going to freshen up."

Mac grabbed her arm and pulled her to him, holding on to her like a drowning man with a life preserver. "You're fresh enough."

"Mac, for God's sake, let me go."

"We were very impressed with your practice, Deputy Nell. Seems to me any man would come running the minute you wiggled your little finger. Right, Ted?"

"Absolutely," Ted agreed.

"Thanks," Nell said in a faint voice, accidentally meeting Mac's glance.

"I was impressed," Mac said, his body responding to her look, his juices starting to flow all over again. His mouth watered as he took in the tousled sexuality of the woman pressed against his side. "I was very impressed."

Nell turned so red he thought he'd have to hit the fire alarm. Mac tried to get his still-raging emotions under control, sending a guilty look at Ted and Jed. The two brothers were looking at the floor, scuffing the toes of their big clumpy boots delicately across the wood in an effort to remain noncommittal. Mac watched Nell lick her lips and almost went down for the third time, except for the one part of his body rising to the surface. Damn underwear, he thought, shifting uncomfortably. "Come on, Nell. Let's go see some action." Nodding at Ted and Jed, Mac started to guide her across the room to the bar.

Watching them cross the room, Ted flipped open his ledger and said to his brother, "I'd say, we've already seen some action."

Jed rubbed his finger alongside his nose. "Yep, I'd say you're right. But I got a feeling we're gonna see a lot more."

"Let's see if we can up the ante. There's a lot of people here we haven't even approached yet."

Jed slapped his knee. "By gaw the way we're going, we're gonna be one of them 'Fortune Five' guys before you know it."

Praying everyone in the room was concentrating on something other than them, Mac kept Nell close to his side as they crossed the room. The only problem was, as Mac strolled, Nell tried to hustle, which made their progress a bit uneven.

"Slow down," Mac hissed, yanking on her arm.

"Can't you go faster?" Nell complained, straining to move.

"I don't want to go faster. I might run into somebody I don't want to see."

"Are you talking about Hilda's niece or your hot date from the other night?" Nell slid him a look. "I never asked. How'd that hot date go?"

"What makes you ask that?" Mac tried to avoid answering. Truth was, the date was the pits.

Nell shrugged her shoulders. "Curiosity. That's all."

Setting his jaw, hoping Nell wouldn't inquire further, Mac said, "We didn't have anything in common."

"I thought that was the point," Nell said with a polite expression. "I didn't think you were dating her to talk."

"I wasn't, but still, is it too much to ask for a woman to put two coherent words together."

"Given the type of women you're usually tied up with— probably."

Mac immediately started thinking about tying Nell up and all the interesting possibilities that could bring. Naturally his underwear responded in the usual way, the way it'd been responding since he first caught sight of Nell Phillips this evening. The way he was going, the damn thing would stretch to the size of a grocery sack by the end of the evening. Mac tried to wiggle his butt around to shift the material. Of course, he didn't want Nell to know what he was doing, so he tried to continue walking, but his feet kept getting tangled up.

"What's the matter with you, Mac. You're walking kinda funny."

"That damn underwear you gave me keeps riding up."

Nell's mouth formed a perfect O. "How could it? There's nothing to ride up. There's not that much material."

He glared at her. "There's enough so that it's uncomfortable as hell."

Nell giggled as she looked at Mac. "Maybe Hilda's niece will appreciate it."

"That's not funny." He wiggled a bit more, stopping to pretend to adjust his belt.

Indicating an area in the lounge, Nell said, "Your mother is giving you a mighty strange look."

"No." Mac had to fight the urge to duck behind Nell.

Nell elbowed him. "Remember the cowardly lion? Think to yourself 'what would he do in this situation?'"

Mac cast a desperate look around, after he caught a sight of a tall, broad, smiling young woman standing next to his mom. "I don't think a medal pinned to my chest is going to help."

Nell grinned. "Buck up, big guy. Maybe better times are coming. You said your hot date was a bust."

"I never said that."

"Oh, all right. You indicated it, how's that?"

"All I said was—"

"Your mom's waving you over."

"Run," Mac muttered.

"You can't run away from your own mother."

"I can, too. And if you have any sense you'll do the same. It's every man for himself." The only thing that stopped him from bolting was Nell's tight hold on his arm.

"It doesn't look good for the sheriff to turn tail and run."

"That woman with my mom might be Bronwyn."

Nell sent a glance to the woman standing by Mac's mother. "If it is, she looks very pleasant."

"Oh for—" Lacking Nell's backup, Mac knew he had no choice. He approached his mother, much like a man on the way to the gallows. Plastering a huge smile on his face, Mac said, "Hi, Ma."

Molly Cochrane wasn't fooled. She arched a brow and said, "Hello, son. I have a surprise for you."

Recoiling, Mac would have turned tail, except Nell kept prodding him forward with an insistent finger in his back. He was positive his smile was slipping a bit as he met his mother's amused glance. "S-swell."

"Don't you want to know what it is?"

"What? Not who?"

Molly reached behind her and tugged the young woman forward. "This is Bronwyn, Hilda's niece."

Bronwyn grinned, her blue eyes warming as they met his. Nell was right, she did look friendly, thought Mac. Which was good, since it was obvious that he'd have to have some type of conversation with the woman, or his mother would probably wrestle him to the ground and beat him up. "Hey, how's it going?"

The woman's grin broadened to reveal a slight space between her front teeth. It wasn't unattractive, just a bit unexpected. It gave her a lot of charm, as a matter of fact. She wasn't quite as large as he'd first thought, most of the breadth of her came from an oversize sweatshirt and sweatpants. "Not too bad. And you?"

Clamping Nell to his side, Mac said, "This is Nell." He tried to make it sound as if they were together, but Nell was having none of that.

Extending her hand to grasp Bronwyn's, Nell said, "Hi. I'm Nell Phillips."

"Nell's one of Mac's deputies," Molly Cochrane added.

"Yes, you mentioned he was a policeman." Bronwyn gave him an admiring look. "That's so cool."

Managing to get her arm loose, Nell backed up. "I have to get going. I think the women's round in the dart tournament is getting ready to begin.

Mac made a grab for her. "No, it isn't."

"Sure it is, Mac. Women go first, so you have time to stay and get to know Bronwyn." Nell winked at Molly and strolled over to the crowds surrounding the dartboards.

Mac glanced at his mother. Seeing the determination in her face, he gave up and accepted the inevitable. He indicated that Bronwyn precede him to an empty table and trailed in her wake, attempting to tow his mother along with him.

"Mac, what are you doing? I'm not coming with you. You go and have a good time. She won't be here too long."

"She isn't my type."

"She's a lovely girl. Give her a chance. Besides, your type is generally not the type you should settle down with anyway."

"For cryin' out loud, Mama, I'm not going to settle down with—"

"Tut, tut, tut. MacKenzie, you just quit carrying on like a two-year-old and go have some fun."

"I'm not sure this is my idea of fun."

"I swear, I'm going to be decrepit by the time any of my children decide to settle down. I don't know what I'm going to do with you." She placed her small body behind Mac, positioned her shoulder and gave him a shove in Bronwyn's direction.

Mac grinned. "Pushy little broad, aren't you?"

"You haven't seen the half of it, son."

Mac glanced back at his mother, only to notice her sending a speculative glance in Nell's direction. He intercepted the glance she gave him without realizing he'd be looking. By her expression, it was obvious that Molly had gotten an idea that he had been doing more than saying hello to Nell a few minutes ago. However, if that was so, Mac wondered why his mother wasn't trying to push them together instead. Not that it would do any good. Even if he had overreacted a few moments ago, it was understandable. Nell looked too damn hot for him not to. He'd have had to be dead five years to not respond to the woman who'd come on to him. Even if it was only practice, which is what Mac was sure it was. He'd have to be sure that his mother understood that, too.

"Mac, Bronwyn's waiting. I promised Hilda you'd be nice to her. Don't make a liar of me, please."

Put like that, Mac had no choice. "Yes, ma'am." He smiled at his mother and went over to be sociable. He sat down at the table and proceeded to draw Bronwyn out, all the time keeping half his focus on Nell to see how—and what— she was doing.

NELL WAS DOING QUITE WELL—relatively speaking. The dart tournament was an ideal place to meet people. People of all ages, personalities, physical types, married and single. For a woman prepared to try her wiles, it was better than she could have imagined. She noticed men noticing her, too. For the first time, Nell felt admired and sexy. Mac had confirmed it when she'd first walked in tonight. Nell was very happy he'd been there to practice on before she hit the floor for real. Truth to tell, she'd been very nervous when she'd gotten dressed. As Nell had looked in the mirror before she left home, she felt the dress was too much, the underwear was too little, the makeup was too dark, and the thoughts tortured her. Then when Mac turned and looked at her, she was positive she would be a success. That was the reason she'd started to flirt with him like that. Of course, that was the reason. It wasn't enough to suppose she was sexy and desirable, she needed to confirm it.

Good Lord, had Mac confirmed it. When he'd pressed her against the wall, then plastered himself against her, Nell almost forgot who she was and what she was doing. She'd forgotten she was in the middle of Charlie's Place. With Mac's lips on hers, she'd have been perfectly happy to practice all night! Luckily Ted and Jed Kilbourne had brought her crashing back to earth. From that point on, Nell made an effort to be nonchalant about the episode, even though it had been difficult.

She had to force herself to not look over her shoulder for Mac, wondering if he and Bronwyn were hitting it off. She grinned. Leave it to Molly Cochrane to shake things up a bit. She glanced over her shoulder and met Molly's gaze. Mac's mother had a speculative expression on her face that Nell didn't quite trust. Then someone said her name and she forgot about Molly. Stepping up to the throwing area, Nell took her darts and tightened up to wing the first dart at the target. She let fly and just missed a man standing near the target.

"What are you doing there? Move over. You put me off my shot."

The very tall man, who struck Nell as good-looking and really knew it, sent her a patented smile. "Just admiring the view," he said.

At that moment, Nell decided he was a perfect specimen. Throwing back her shoulders to emphasize her breasts, and lifting her chin, Nell gave the guy her sexiest smile. At least she hoped it was sexy. She felt rather like a monkey grinning so it would be accepted into its tribe. In a way, that was accurate, she thought. Here she was seeking entrance into the tribe of desirable women. Nell grinned at that, watching as the man, too cool to grin back, sent her a studied smile. He stepped aside so she could throw another dart. Nell threw it and just missed the bull's-eye. The man moved up the room, closer to her. She tried another throw and washed out. The man reached her side and slipped his arm around her waist.

"Nice try, babe. Let me buy you a drink, then we can find something else to do."

God, she hated men who called women "babe." *Wait a minute, Nell. That's not fair. Remember the game? How to apply yourself to the right personality?* Mentally she reviewed the personality types she and Mac had discussed. Not that their discussion had been that illuminating, except for the tango, that was. The tango had opened her eyes to feelings she had no idea she possessed. Feelings that made her very uncomfortable as she remembered them. Her attention leaped back to the man in front of her. "What did you have in mind?" Nell purred, watching as the man lapped it up. She nestled closer to his side, a kitten seeking warmth.

The man's good-looking face swooped, almost burying itself in her hair like a bat with no motor control. He sniffed, loud and long. "Oh, babe, you smell good."

Ready to respond with a suitable reply to his come-on, Nell glanced a long way up at him. From this angle, all she could see was his nose. It was like wearing 3-D glasses. His nose seemed a lot larger this close up than it had seemed across the room. His nostrils flared—in a sensual way, she supposed. That's what they always did in the romance novels she'd read. Unfortunately, she had a perfect view of his nose hairs as he inhaled the scent of her...what? Shampoo, perfume, mascara? Who the hell knew what odors were around her. Nell glanced at the crowd. The guy could have been sniffing someone else's perfume. There was sure enough of it in the packed room. Pulling her attention back to the man next to her, still sniffing like a hound on the trail of fresh meat, Nell whispered, "I put it on just in case."

"Just in case what?"

She walked her fingers up his chest. "Just in case I found some man who could appreciate it." The move didn't elicit the same type of physical response from Nell that it had when she'd tried it earlier on Mac, but it sure seemed to start the same kind of fire in the man next to her.

The man snagged her around the waist and drew her out of the main crush of the crowd. "You've found him, babe."

Now a bit alarmed at what she'd started, while being very careful not to show it, Nell pressed her hand on the man's chest. "Not so fast. I don't even know your name."

The man nuzzled her ear. "I'd rather introduce you to the rest of me."

"I'll bet you have one of those names you're ashamed of, huh? Like Wayne or something?" For a moment she almost hoped it was Wayne. She had doubts about the wisdom of this entire thing. There was nothing wrong with remaining single, regardless of her mother's campaign to push her into a joint tax return.

A puzzled look settled on his face. "What's the matter with Wayne?"

Nell pounced. "That's not your name, is it?"

"No, but I don't see anything wrong with it. Unless it's *your* name."

"No. I'm Nell."

"Call me Rick."

"Rick...Rick." Wrapping her tongue around it, Nell tried it out to get the taste of his name on her lips before she sampled the real thing.

"That's right." His gaze plunged into her cleavage. "Oowee, you are some babelicious babe."

Babelicious? Nell bit her lip. *Rick, Rick...thick as a brick!* Damn Mac Cochrane, Nell thought, this is all his fault. Nell wasn't sure how, or even why, but for some reason this Rick didn't measure up to her personal requirements for a lover. *Maybe my standards are too high.* Maybe I should look for someone I can mold into my ideal man. The man with her was easy enough on the eyes at least. Nell looked up at him and cooed, "Want to dance?" She coaxed him in the direction of the dance floor.

"For a chance to really get my hands on you, I'd dance through hell, babe."

Nell's mouth and stomach twitched. *I'm gonna hurl!* Who could listen to a line like that and keep a straight face, Nell wondered. Mac would have been on the floor if he'd heard it.

Mac. Forget about Mac. He's got his own fish to fry tonight.

Nell peeked up from under her lashes at Rick's smug expression. Obviously his cheesy statement had worked successfully in the past. *Maybe it's me. I'll have to try harder.* After all, short of writing a script, nothing would ever go exactly the way she expected. It shouldn't, or it would take all the mystery out of life. For a moment she wondered how Mac was faring with Bronwyn. Talk about unexpected. His mother had given him no warning at all, just sprang the girl on Mac without giving him a chance to back out. Nell really admired those tactics.

"Did you go to sleep down there? Didn't you hear what I said." Rick's voice sounded a bit annoyed.

Nell met his glinting gaze. "Of course I did. I was so overcome at your sacrifice, I couldn't speak."

"Cat got your tongue, huh?"

Letting her eyes wander over his face, Nell decided that, in her entire life, she'd never met someone who was so good-looking and so resembled a block of wood. She kept her thoughts to herself though, saying instead, "You are so witty. Where do you think that expression comes from?"

"What expression?"

"Cat got your tongue."

Rick tried to turn her so he could get both arms around her and move her out to the deck overlooking the river, instead of the dance floor. "Who cares. I don't like cats."

Nell resisted his attempts and sidled in the direction of the dancers, instead. "I don't think it referred to a real cat."

"Come on, babe. Let's not waste time. I like you, you like me. What say we get it on."

Uh-oh. "Oh, Rick…not only witty, but subtle, too."

"Huh?"

Nell turned and hooked her arms around his neck. She had to admit, the guy's superbly hard muscled body made up for the lack of density between his ears. She couldn't help but feel her pulse jump a bit as she leaned against him. Rick was a virile, sexual animal and she would have to be dead not to respond in at least a teensy way. But falling onto one of the chaise lounges to make love on the deck in full view of Knightsboro wasn't in her game plan. She'd already given the local gossips an opportunity to blather earlier when she'd seen Mac, even if they had been tucked away from everyone's sight. She looked up at Rick and licked her lips. "Dancing does things to me." She licked her lips again, letting the tip of her tongue protrude a bit to tempt him. She felt like a complete idiot. What had been coming naturally with Mac now seemed so forced. It didn't seem to bother Rick.

"Gotta tell ya, babe, if I get any more turned on I'm gonna hum."

Playing for time, Nell freed herself from his arms and backed up to the dance floor. Rick followed her. "I'll hum with you." She started to move, in her usual energetic way. To her surprise, Rick was with her every step of the way. He was an excellent dancer, a fact he pointed out to her as he whirled her around. Nell's flirty little skirt was flipping up and whipping around enough that she wondered if she was revealing her undergarments to the world. Not that there was that much to show. Wearing her new lingerie had seemed a good idea at the time, but in actuality, to wear her revealing panties, garter belt and stockings to this event was probably too bold a move. Idiotic more likely, she thought as her skirt flared and he whirled her around. Luckily the music segued into a slow and sensual rhythm, which enabled her skirt to do the same. Rick pulled her toward him, wrapping himself so closely around her that she thought she'd have to ask him to breathe for her.

Tightening his arms even more, Rick said, "Good tune, eh, babe?"

"Yes," she squeaked as the rest of her oxygen rushed out.

His face dipped to nuzzle her ear, his tongue roaming inside until she giggled. That wasn't the response he was looking for, she supposed, but she couldn't help it. He'd tickled. His eyes sharpened as he drew back to look at her. "Sorry," Nell murmured. Obviously the man was not used to not being taken seriously. He renewed his attention, slipping his hands down her back to pull her closer to him as the music urged them to practically make love on the floor. Oh Nell, she thought, if your mother could only see you now. The thought passed through her mind that she might be a bit more comfortable if it had been someone else doing the groping. Then she dismissed the thought. Rick wasn't doing anything more unusual than any of the other couples out on the dance floor. It was silly to be uncomfortable. At least that's what she thought until his head dropped to nuzzle into the neckline of her dress. At the same time his hands descended to slip under her dress and cup her bare buttocks. As the man felt her skin he growled and got a bit bolder.

Nell didn't think, she reacted—instinctively. Her knee came up, catching Rick in his most vulnerable area, her hand curled into a fist and swung upward to connect with his jaw, then when he was off balance, she grabbed his arm, whirled around to tuck a shoulder into his chest, bent and threw him across the dance floor. Rick crashed into a table by the wall, before rolling off to end up on the floor. Everyone on the dance floor gasped, or laughed. The band paused, then continued to play as if nothing had happened. Not quite an everyday occurrence, but not an unusual one in a bar-restaurant that catered to such a variety of people.

"Not quite what we'd practiced, Slim." Mac's voice came from behind her.

Nell couldn't help but laugh. "You don't think?"

"No, but after having caught a glimpse of your luscious legs and half your buns a few minutes ago, I don't blame the guy for wanting a better look."

Blushing, Nell said, "It wasn't the look I was objecting to."

Mac grabbed her shoulder. "What? Did he try something?"

Sending him an amazed glance, Nell said, "Do you think I usually throw men across the room for the fun of it?"

"Good point. Still, it's only natural when you consider the way you look and the way you were acting."

Nell glanced over her shoulder at him. "What's wrong with the way I was acting?"

"Nothing." Mac grinned. "That was the problem."

Nell watched as Rick got to his feet, then turned to glare at her. She didn't blame him for wanting to murder her, but she wasn't sure how to handle it. Taking a tentative step in his direction, she was checked by Mac.

"Not a good move. If that was me over there, I'd give my last buck not to see you again. Much less talk to you."

With a small grin, Nell said, "So much for my on-the-job-training experience."

Ushering her off the dance floor, to stand near the windows, Mac said, "Well, at least we both gave everyone something to talk about tonight. If anyone's even paying attention. And don't forget the reason most people are here is the dart tournament. How'd you do?"

"As you can see, I washed out in the first round."

"Yeah, I wasn't much better. Bobby Dee is doing great though, so the honor of the sheriff's office is upheld."

"Great." Nell looked around, suddenly realizing Mac was alone. "Where's Bronwyn?"

Startled, Mac looked around. "I don't know. I was watching you."

"You were watching me?"

"Yeah. You on a dance floor is cause for alarm, Slim. If I didn't keep my eye on you, you'd probably clip somebody." Mac chuckled. "Which you did anyway."

Nell gave him a halfhearted smile. "Not because of my enthusiastic dancing. It was more a case of stopping wandering hands and mouth."

Mac's face darkened. He looked over at Rick, who was now on his way to the bar. The look promised that he'd take care of him later. For no understandable reason, a thrill of delight raced down Nell's spine. She tried to ignore it, but it was there.

"Anyway," Mac continued, "I saw what was going on, jumped up and—" he got a comical look on his face "—I left Bronwyn sitting there still talking, I guess."

"Not anymore. Look." Nell pointed in the direction of the bar. Bronwyn was chatting and laughing up a blue streak with Bobby Dee. "Something tells me you've lost her to another police officer."

Mac followed her gaze. Grinning, he said, "Looks like it. She's actually a lot of fun, I discovered. Not my type, no matter what my mother thinks, but a good person."

Giving him a sideways glance, Nell said, "I hope no one ever calls me a good person in that tone of voice."

"I meant it. I just don't want my mother to get any more ideas, so I'm being careful."

"You'd think your mother was in your back pocket the way you're talking."

"If there's one thing I know about my mother, she's got a network of spies everywhere. I don't want to give her any hope."

"Well, since she's coming this way, followed by Ted and Jed Kilbourne, maybe we'd better get the hell out of here."

Mac sent a hunted look over his shoulder. "Oh, Lord, what now? Is it too late to run?"

"Not if we slip out onto the deck. That way we can escape through the grounds."

"You're on, Slim." Mac grabbed her hand and dashed toward the French doors at the far end of the room. Giggling like children, they escaped onto the deck.

Stopping to catch her breath, Nell was caught by the sight of the old mill standing solid in the moonlight. She sighed and walked to the railing. "Oh, isn't it a beautiful night, Mac. I love a half-moon. It's so romantic."

"It is? I would have thought a full moon would be more romantic."

"Not to me. I like the mystery of a half moon. Wondering what the other half will reveal. Not quite sure, still looking. I guess that's how I think about romance. What about you?"

"I don't think about romance."

"Oh, that's right. I forgot."

Mac joined her at the railing. "It is a beautiful night, though. I've always loved this old stream, and the woods. When we were little, Daryn and I used to hike around here. We'd have our peanut butter sandwiches and picnic by this old mill. It didn't look the same then. It was pretty run-down and a lot smaller."

"It was an old gin joint or something, wasn't it?"

"They ran a lot of illegal booze out of here, or so my dad and grandpa said."

Nell turned and stretched her arms wide against the rail. "I didn't know that."

Mac glanced at her, then shifted uneasily. His eyes came back to her. "Lord, Slim, I don't blame that guy for making a pass. You look beautiful in that outfit."

"I...thank you." Nell was stunned, and so overcome with a sudden longing that she didn't know what to think.

His hand lifted toward her, then dropped at his side. "Your skin is so white."

"I'm wearing black, it shows off my—"

"I don't think that's it. I think it's you."

"I didn't get much of a tan this summer." Great, Nell thought. Real smooth. She couldn't help it. Suddenly she was more nervous than she'd ever been in her entire life.

"Your eyes are so...I could drown in them."

"What are you doing, Mac? This is me, Nell, your deputy, remember?"

Mac moved closer, leaned down and whispered, "No. My deputy never looked like this ever."

"Well, I hope not. I'd never get any respect." Nell tried to pass it off as a joke, but she could hear the slight tremble in her voice.

Mac smoothed her hair, tucking it behind her ear. "Plenty of proposals, though."

"Most of them like Rick's, I'll bet."

Reaching down, Mac cupped her chin and turned her face to his. "With the right person, you'd welcome them."

"You're right. I probably would." Nell licked her lips, so badly did she want to lean over and press her lips against his. His thumb smoothed her bottom lip, teasing until she opened her mouth. She took a deep breath, shivering, aware of the slight breeze that rose from the water below and rocked the tops of the trees. Or was she shivering because of Mac?

"It's a shame to waste the evening—the moonlight...you."

"Waste not, want not, my granny used to say."

"I want to kiss you, Nell."

"I want you to kiss me, Mac."

He gathered her into his arms and honed in on his target. Nell let herself go, relaxing completely into his embrace, more at home than she had any right to be. His lips pressed gently, then patiently licked at hers until she kissed him back. With a groan, she tried to rein herself back in, frightened by the feelings flooding her, demanding she take more and more, demanding she give more and more. Tearing her lips from his, Nell turned to grasp the railing, looking out into the night. Mac wrapped his arms around her, pulling her back against him, so close she could feel his response to her nearness. She dipped her head and he nuzzled her neck, pressing kisses up to her ear before taking the lobe between his teeth, first nipping then sucking. She didn't laugh this time. The tickle was too exciting, too demanding that she respond. It felt right. A long, low moan forced itself between her lips. This was the way it should have felt with Rick, Nell thought. Pure sexual excitement, animal attraction, no regrets.

Mac's hands moved up to cup her breasts. Nell knew she should stop him. If she didn't she'd be lost. They'd be on the ground making love, unable to call a halt. It was time to be reasonable, Nell told herself. It's the situation, that's all, unknowingly repeating Mac's justification to himself earlier.

Finally she found her voice. It was low, throbbing with need and husky with desire, but it was her voice, Deputy Nell Phillips's voice, doing the speaking. "Mac, this is just practice, right?"

Mac stilled, his hands cupped over her breast, the fingertips resting on the swell of her flesh. Hot breaths jerked in and out of his mouth, then a sigh escaped, blowing across her temple. Finally he murmured, "That's right, Slim. Just practice."

"I guess I'd better get home. I'm on duty tomorrow."

"Yeah, me too."

Neither of them moved, until finally Mac dropped his arms from around her and stepped back. Turning aside, he clasped his hands on the top of the broad railing and said, "Be careful going down the steps, okay? Unless you're going to go back through the restaurant, instead."

"No. I don't want to see anyone again. I'd rather walk around the outside." Embarrassed to look at him, Nell skittered sideways. "I'll see you tomorrow, Sheriff."

"Okay, Deputy."

Nell walked to the steps and had just started down when Mac's voice whispered across to her one last time, "Take care and drive safely, Slim."

She looked back over her shoulder to where he stood, tall and solid in the moonlight. For a moment, the pain of leaving him almost overcame her, but she forced it aside. "You, too,

Mac. Sleep tight.'' She hoped she'd managed to stop her eyes from saying *sleep with me*. Given her choice, she'd take the man home and tie him to her bedposts.

Looking after her, having read the expression in her eyes correctly, Mac had to resist the urge to pluck at his zipper. *Damn tight underwear*. For both their sakes, he'd have to find Nell a man—and fast!

His mother, standing by the window, would have disagreed if she'd known his thoughts, especially after she'd arrived in time to see Mac holding Nell in the moonlight. Smiling, Molly turned around to motion to Ted and Jed, who'd been stopped at one of the tables by some ''clients.'' Ted was busily jotting notations in his ledger, but he looked up when Molly waved.

As they came up behind her, Molly said softly, ''I'll bet you boys a hundred bucks that my son and Nell Phillips reach the altar at the same time.''

''At the same time?'' Jed scratched his head. ''What're the odds on that?''

Thinking hard, Ted tapped his pencil on his ledger then said, ''I'd make it fifty to one. Don't that sound right, Jed?''

''Sounds good to me.''

''That sounds very good to me, too.'' Molly Cochrane glanced out at her son, etched in moonlight, standing still and lonely. She smiled as only a mother can, a ferocious bear protecting her cub. She'd get that boy married if it killed her. But she wouldn't let him know what she was doing. With Mac, diversion was the best approach. Eventually he'd realize what was right for him, or her name wasn't Molly Cochrane.

8

FOR THE NEXT TWO WEEKS, Nell and Mac worked hard to get their relationship back to normal. At least as normal as it could be, Nell thought, for two people who were trying to arrange dates with other people when they both had a yearning for someone else. Not that either of them would admit that, of course. Instead, Nell spent half of her time drawing up lists of the qualities she admired in men, and the rest of her time crossing off those qualities as she compared them to her dates. As far as Mac was concerned, he wouldn't give her the list she'd asked for, so Nell saved him the trouble. She walked into Mac's office, ripped a page from her notebook and plunked the piece of paper onto his desktop.

"This is your list of desired qualities in a woman. I made it up for you."

"What do you mean, you made it up for me? I can make my own list."

"Maybe you can, but you won't. I've been trying to get you to do this for weeks. You keep avoiding me." She hitched a hip onto his desk, tapping her notebook against her thigh. "After my recent dating experiences, I've decided that instead of trying to fit me to the personality, I thought it might work better if I list some of the things I'm looking for in a man. That way it's easier to fit the man to me, instead of vice versa."

"That's fine, but I don't see why you did it for me, too." Mac picked up the paper, peering at it. "A sense of humor? I don't need a comedian."

"The sense of humor is self-defense. The woman is going

to have to put up with you. And you're a pain in the ass sometimes.''

"You're not much better, Slim."

Nell waved her notebook. "I know. That's why a sense of humor is on my list, too." God knows, she'd needed one lately.

"What else we got here?" Mac scowled at the paper. "Independent? I don't want independent. I'd rather have a doormat.''

"You would not. You're just trying to make me angry so I'll stop tormenting you and let you get back to your solitaire game.''

Mac flushed, flashing a guilty glance around, as if the entire squad was standing in the room watching him neglect his work. "Don't you have something to do, Deputy?"

"Yes I do, now that you mention it. I have to find you a date for the Harvest Ball."

"I'm not going. I might have to work."

"No, you don't. If I'm going, you're going."

"Who're you going with?"

Nell said in her haughtiest voice, "I don't know yet. Someone. I'll dig up someone, or you will. Then we'll dig up someone for you, too."

Mac grinned. "I'm not robbing graveyards for a date, Slim.''

"At least they wouldn't talk you to death like your last one.''

"You've got a point. My ears rang for a week."

"So what's on your most-wanted list?" Mac grabbed her notebook. After checking it over for a few moments and comparing it to his own, Mac looked up and said, "We've got the same things on here."

"We do not."

"Yes, we do. It's in a different order, but it's the same."

"Let me see that." She grabbed the notebook, looking from it back to his list. "Well, I'll be dammed. We do."

"That's not right, Slim. We're two different people, you

know. And look at this—sexually interesting? What the hell is that?''

''What I meant was—''

''Mine should say 'hotter-than-a-hellfire furnace' and be done with it.''

''Mac, that's not all you're looking for. You keep saying that, but I know it isn't true.''

''How do you know?''

''Because that night when we...'' The night was engraved in her memory—the feel of his lips, his hard body, his desire. Even now, her nerves jumped with longing.

''I thought we agreed to forget that night. We were both under a lot of pressure that night.''

''I know. We agreed it was the underwear, but—'' Forgetting was easier said than done. By the way Mac was avoiding her eyes, she thought he felt the same. No matter, they had to move beyond this attraction.

''But nothing.'' Mac shook his head. ''For the life of me, I don't know why that lingerie store is still in business. The damn stuff is so uncomfortable you wanna rip it off your body as fast as you can.''

Nell grinned. ''I think that's the point.''

Mac struggled not to grin back. ''Even so...''

''Never mind. Look, this is what I thought we could do. I'll give you my list and you give me yours.''

''But you wrote mine.''

''Mac, do you have to be so literal?'' Nell rolled her eyes and, then not giving him a chance to answer, continued, ''Okay. As I was saying, you give me yours and we'll both go out and try to find people who match the characteristics we have on the paper. How does that sound?''

''It sounds very logical. Which really worries me.''

''This will work. I'm positive of it.'' She tore her list from her notebook, folded it and stuck it in Mac's shirt pocket. It poked up like a handkerchief with ruffled edges. Then Nell took Mac's list and tucked it back into her own pocket. ''We've got the rest of the week to find someone. With all the tourists and people back in town for the festival, this will be a piece of cake.''

"There's too much going on right now to bother with this, Slim. There are too many opportunities for mischief." He ticked them off on his fingers. "We've got the Harvest parade, the craft show, the dance and all the other Harvest activities, then that new research laboratory opening with a big to-do…''

Nell waited for him to wind down before pointing out, "And your mother is still watching your every move like a hawk and throwing women in front of you like leftovers. And my mother is calling and bonging 'tick-tock, I'm your biological clock' every other day. She's worse than the crocodile chasing Captain Hook! I'm telling you I can't take much more. If I don't get lucky here somehow—'' Nell bit her lip. She was so unsettled lately, wanting, wanting—what? She was afraid to inquire too closely into her restlessness. She took a deep, cleansing breath, trying to slow her rapid pulse. She exhaled to center herself, and said, "Maybe a more thoughtful approach is what we need. Like this one. I can even make a form, then we can interview people scientifically.''

Mac gave her an incredulous look. "Scientifically?''

"Attraction owes as much to scientific reasons as it does to emotional ones. It's based on pheromones and—''

"You saw that on one of those TV learning channels, didn't you?''

"I might have. So what?''

"Cable TV followed by a market-research form? This is a real multimedia approach to dating, isn't it?''

"I had no idea that you were so closed-minded and unprogressive as to reject a well-thought-out approach to romance.''

"Who am I to reject science and statistics for good old-fashioned lust?'' Mac teased. "Okay, Slim. I guess it won't hurt. But make it a little form. There's no way I'm gonna run around town with a big old ledger, like the Kilbournes.''

"What are they doing with that book of theirs anyway? Every time I ask someone, they clam up. Even Bobby Dee.

And you know eventually Bobby Dee tells everything he knows.''

"I think they're collecting names for their new beverage. Since they're going legit they need something friendlier than *rot gut-likker*."

Nell whistled. "I'm impressed. That's not a bad idea to find out what type of name the public responds to. A very businesslike approach by the Kilbourne brothers."

"Yep, that garage sale was really good to those two ol' boys."

Grinning, Nell said, "I'd better get back to work. I'm on patrol this afternoon."

Mac patted his pocket. "Keep your eyes peeled, Deputy, who knows what you'll find out there."

"You never know," Nell agreed. Walking out the door, she prayed to find someone soon—for both of them. Or they'd have to take out personal ads.

THAT AFTERNOON, Nell was parked in her patrol car on Route 42, tucked in the middle of a turnaround area, ostensibly alert and waiting for some unwary motorist to drive by her radar detector. In reality she was studying Mac's list and wondering where she'd find the perfect specimen to tempt him when a brilliant candy-apple-red Miata screamed by her. Nell jerked, looking up from the paper. She didn't need the radar gun to tell her this was a citizen in one hell of a hurry. She could tell by the blur of motion the car left behind. Nell tucked the list between her teeth, slammed her car in gear, tromped on the gas pedal, flipped on the siren and took off in pursuit. Idiot driver, she thought. What type of person flies by a cop sitting in plain view, without even hitting the brakes at the last minute? That's damn near un-American!

She answered her own question: someone in a rush to get somewhere, someone too arrogant to think they'd be caught, or someone oblivious to anything other than their primary focus. In other words, a person with tunnel vision—the worst type to have on the road. Nell followed the Miata for a bit before the female driver obviously figured out that the cop car racing behind her car was actually trying to pull *her* over. Stopping close behind her at the side of the road, Nell reached for her hat, then opened the door, sliding from her car. Adjusting her uniform and putting on her "cop's game face," Nell sauntered up to the sports car. She looked alert, but relaxed, which was misleading. Any cop worth his or her badge knew that an innocent-looking car could contain instant death. The problem was being alert without seeming edgy enough to provoke a situation. Nell reached the driver's door and placed her hand on her waist, near her gun and her billy club.

She leaned down just enough to acknowledge the young woman behind the wheel. "Ma'am."

"Oh, not 'ma'am.'" The perky blonde covered her face with her palms briefly before tilting her head to send Nell a whimsical glance. "Whenever someone calls me 'ma'am' I feel as if I need a cane."

Nell blinked, trying to keep from smiling. Actually she agreed. Some kid at the grocery store called her "ma'am" the other day and she almost locked him up. Instead, she went to the drugstore and bought antiwrinkle cream. Nell kept her thoughts under control, however, responding with her blandest expression and voice. "Yes, miss. May I see your license and registration, please."

The woman handed both items over, and said, "You're not going to give me a ticket are you, Officer? I'm late for an appointment. That's why I was speeding. I got lost."

"An appointment?"

"Yes. I'm a photographer. I'm doing visuals for a magazine story on the Harvest Festival they have every year down in Knightsboro. I'm supposed to meet the mayor in ten minutes."

Studying the license, Nell said, "Have you ever been in Knightsboro, Ms. Buchannan?"

"Nope. Looking forward to it though. I haven't photographed vegetables in a long time."

"I think you'll find more than vegetables to take pictures of. Sit tight, please. I need to check your license."

"To make sure I'm not a dangerous escaped prisoner, right?"

Nell grinned. She couldn't help it. The woman had an infectious humor that demanded response. "Something like that." She walked back to the car and activated her computer to run the information on the license. Dallas Buchannan, single female. Nell picked up the list she'd thrown down on the seat when she'd stopped the car. Scanning the itemized personality traits, Nell mentally checked off each one before nodding decisively. Dallas Buchannan was good-looking, had a good sense of humor, seemed intelligent and, most important, she wasn't likely to become a permanent resident. Nell didn't want to examine why that last fact was so important. Now Nell's only problem was, how could she get Mac and Dallas together without throwing her in jail? Nell glanced at the information on her screen and, realizing Dallas had no record and no outstanding warrants, decided she'd give her a warning instead of a ticket.

Emerging from the patrol car, she walked back to the Miata and the woman drumming her fingers on the steering wheel. Handing her the license and registration, Nell said, "Tell you what, Ms. Buchannan. I'm only going to give you a warning. After all, if you're going to make our fair city famous, it's the least I can do." Her voice hardened. "But take it easy. I don't want to see you burning rubber like you did a few minutes ago."

"Yes, okay, uh...?"

"Deputy Nell Phillips. I'm with the Knightsboro Sheriff's Office."

"Oh, that's fortunate. I have to check in at the sheriff's office anyway, to make sure I don't need any permission forms in order to photograph on town property." Dallas smiled. "Now I'll know someone."

Perfect.

"Then you'll be seeing more of me, Ms. Buchannan. I'll probably end up showing you around Knightsboro, or my boss, Sheriff Cochrane will." Now Nell would have to see how she could maneuver them into going to the Harvest Ball together. The more she thought about it, this woman seemed perfect. Good-looking, but not so great looking that she was a bimbo, probably an interesting conversationalist—and *temporary!*

Dallas tucked the license back into her purse. "Great."

"If you'll follow me, I'll see you get to the mayor's office without getting lost."

MAC COCHRANE WAS JUST SITTING down to a cup of coffee and a plate of Harvest cookies at Ada Mae Baker's diner when a hand clasped his shoulder. "Shouldn't you be eating doughnuts instead of cookies, Sheriff?"

"Not during Harvest Festival," Mac said, waving his cookie. "It's the only time Ada Mae bakes these suckers. Couldn't live with myself if I didn't eat some." Mac took another bite and whirled on his stool. As he looked at the man standing behind him, he was so surprised that he started to choke. "A.J.," he said, crumbs spattering with the words. "I'll be—is that you?"

"In flesh and spirit, friend."

Mac leaped to his feet and folded the man in a big bear hug, then stepped back to beat a manly tattoo on the guy's shoulders as A.J. did the same. "What the hell are you doing here sneaking up behind me?"

"I'm here to visit the reservation. I have to consult with the tribal elders."

Mac sat down again, looking at his best friend from his college days. A. J. Radcliffe hadn't changed a lot in eight years or so. He was a remarkably handsome man—pure Cherokee on his mother's side with hair black as a raven, eyes dark as a deep well and snapping with intelligence, skin tanned and drawn taut over high, sharp cheekbones and a firm chin. His body had filled out some since they were in school. Now instead of rawboned arms and legs, firm broad muscles were etched, denoting grace and power. He was the type of man whose ancestors had carved a top-notch civilization as they moved through the forest long ago. "Hell, A.J., it's really good to see you."

A.J. punched Mac's elbow. "You too, Mac."

"How long are ya going to be here?"

A.J. straddled a stool next to Mac. "Through the Harvest Festival, at least."

"The Harvest—" It was as if a flashbulb went off in Mac's head. *The Harvest Ball.* His eyes narrowed as he considered his friend. Mmm-hmm, Mac thought, A.J. could work for Nell. He had all the right qualities, plus he wouldn't be intimidated by her. Very little intimidated A. J. Radcliffe. "You, uh, married or anything yet, A.J.?"

A.J. stared at Mac as if he'd never seen him before. "Don't you think you'd know if I was? You were my roommate for four years. Just because I don't live here and we don't keep in touch on a regular basis doesn't mean you wouldn't be the first to know if I got myself shackled. What's the matter with you?"

Mac had been wondering the same thing for the past few weeks. He felt off, not himself at all. He was testy and restless—and ached. It was his damn deputy's fault. Every time he turned around he was either thinking of her, or staring at her. She was like some nasty disease. It was as if he'd caught the flu and then kept reinfecting himself. Maybe she was right, it was time for logical action. A.J. was one of the most logical men he'd ever known. The guy was perfect for Nell.

A.J. snapped his fingers. "Mac. I know it's been a while since we've seen each other, but you're staring at me as if I've grown two heads. What's up?"

"A.J., how'd you like to go to the Harvest Ball with a friend of mine who needs a date."

"What type of friend? Last time you set me up with a date, you promised it would be the last."

"You'd really like this woman."

"You said that about the last one, and I still have nightmares about her. It took me all year to convince her that she wasn't my soul mate, no matter what her horoscope said."

"Look, I'm in a bind. Just promise me you'll meet her, okay?" Yep, Mac thought, A.J. was perfect for Nell. He could see it now. Two of his best friends getting together, making a life together. A queasy feeling in his stomach almost doubled him over. Suddenly he didn't feel too well.

A.J. examined Mac. "You all right, Mac?"

Mac clenched his teeth. "I think I ate too many Harvest cookies."

A.J. chuckled. "Either that or you're in love."

"Nah. It's the cookies."

"Cherokees have a saying...love comes from the stomach."

His brow knitting with confusion, Mac stared at his friend. "What the hell does that mean?"

A.J. grinned. "Dammed if I know."

THE WEEK PASSED as if it had wings. A.J. followed through and let Mac fix him up with Nell Phillips, and Mac in turn allowed Nell to fix him up with Dallas Buchannan. However, due to their packed schedules, neither of them spent more than a few minutes in the company of their respective dates.

It's just as well, Mac thought, keeping his eyes level as he looked into a mirror to tie his tie. This way his date with Dallas tonight would be filled with surprises. He could have a good time getting to know her and wouldn't be anticipating anything, nor would he be looking for excuses not to like the woman. Which is what he seemed to be doing with every other female. At least he had since he'd started this idiotic matchmaking activity with Nell. And idiotic was just what it was. Why his deputy had suddenly obtained squatter's rights in his mind was something he couldn't explain. He scowled and tugged his tie into a well-ordered knot. He hated ties, always felt as if he were putting his head in a noose every time he wore one. Which probably wasn't far from the truth tonight. What had possessed him to arrange a double date, as if he were a high school student with a nervous stomach? Thank God, he'd drawn the line at riding to the dance in the same car. At least he'd be spared watching the two of them necking in the back seat, if A.J. and Nell hit it off as he expected. He could see it now, he'd be watching in the rearview mirror as A.J. caressed Nell and... For a moment the image was so real he had to blink rapidly to get rid of it. *Idiot! Don't you want them to get along?* He answered his own question. *Not that "along," I don't.* With an impatient jerk to straighten his tie, Mac left for the dance.

The Harvest Ball was in full swing when Mac and Dallas arrived at the entrance of the Grange Hall. The parking lot was packed with cars and the old building was lit up brighter than a town drunk drinking the Kilbourne brothers' moonshine. Yep, Mac thought, the place was hopping! The music and echoes of laughter couldn't be contained by the large rectangular windows spilling slashes of light onto the ground below. Instead the lively sounds announced good times to everyone approaching.

"The entire town must be here," Dallas said.

Mac smiled down at the woman by his side. "Just about. Not too many people want to miss this dance. It's the official start of the Harvest week festivities." Mac waved to a couple entering the building.

Dallas looked at the people, then slid her palms down her sophisticated black dress and said with a bit of apprehension, "I hope I'm not overdressed for this. That woman didn't seem to be wearing party clothes."

"That's the beauty of the Harvest Ball. People come in damn near anything. Sometimes they even come in costume."

"What kind of costumes?" Dallas's journalistic tendencies jumped on this.

"Well, one year I danced with a rutabaga."

"You're kidding."

"Nope." Mac's eyes twinkled as he noted the wariness in Dallas's eyes.

Dallas nibbled on her fingertip for a moment. "What does a rutabaga look like?"

Mac grinned. "Just like a turnip, except its bottom is purple."

"Whose bottom is purple?" asked a voice to Mac's left.

Mac glanced at Nell, noticing that A.J. was standing close behind. His heart leaped at the sight of her in a red silk dress that hugged all the right places. He tried to keep his tone very casual, which was difficult. "Hi there, Slim. I was just telling Dallas that people come to this dance in costume sometimes."

Nodding, Nell grinned. "That's right. One year, Jed Kilbourne came dressed as a little brown jug. People were swarming all over him thinking he'd brought some of his homemade alcohol with him. It almost caused a panic. Remember, Mac?"

Mac laughed. "Yeah, I do. I thought I'd have to arrest everyone on the dance floor." Mac glanced at Nell, noting the easy way she returned his grin. He shared a lot of memories with this woman. His body warmed at the thought.

"Isn't someone going to introduce me?" A.J.'s plaintive voice dropped into the conversation.

Mac gave his friend a blank look. "What? To whom?"

"To the gorgeous blonde you have hanging on your arm."

"Oh, sorry. I thought you might have met Dallas Buchannan already."

"No, but I noticed her in town the other day. I was talking to your mom, and she pointed her out."

"You were talking to my mom?" Something about the way A.J. said that sent clamors of alarm through Mac's body.

"Yeah, I ran into her at Ada Mae's yesterday and we had a very interesting conversation."

Mac's glance stabbed A.J. "About what?" He didn't like the sound of this, but he didn't know why.

"This and that." A.J. extended his hand and took Dallas's, as carefully as if it were made of the finest crystal. "Hi. I'm A. J. Radcliffe. An old friend of Mac's."

Dallas smiled. "And I'm a very new friend of Nell's and Mac's."

A.J.'s smile broadened as he patted Dallas's hand. "And now me."

"Quit petting my date." Mac reached for Dallas's hand and pulled it through his arm before staring at A.J. Damn, if A.J.'s tongue hung out any farther, he'd start to drool. Glancing down at Dallas, Mac realized she also seemed to have trouble catching her breath. This wasn't the plan. A.J. was supposed to be drooling over Nell. He glanced at Nell. "Pet your own date."

"Thanks, Mac, but I don't need your help on this." Flushing, Nell stepped to A.J. and slid her arm though his. "Let's go inside before we hold up traffic." She indicated a group of people moving toward them from the parking lot.

Mac agreed. "Good idea. Everybody in." Opening the door, Mac shooed everyone through it, making sure A.J. and Nell were first so he could keep an eye on them. Suddenly he felt like a kindergarten teacher. With everyone inside, Mac said, "Nell, I reserved a table over by the dance floor. Follow me." Mac wended his way between the packed tables, stopping every now and then to chat with people and to introduce his date, protectively keeping Nell and A.J. in sight as they did the same. After reaching the table, Mac politely helped Dallas into a chair, then plunked down himself before A.J. could get to the seat at her side. It had seemed the thing to do, since A.J. had rounded the corner as if he was going to sit next to Mac's date. Instead, after helping Nell into a seat across from Dallas, A.J. smirked at Mac as he took a seat on Dallas's other side.

What was A.J. doing? Mac wondered. He was supposed to fall for Nell, not get distracted by a blonde. After sending his friend a warning look, Mac tried to relax but found it difficult as he was wound up tighter than an old drum. He had no idea why. He wanted A.J. to tumble for Nell, didn't he?

As a waitress came over to move around the table, taking the drink order, Nell leaned over to whisper, "You're not going to start talking to yourself, are you?"

Mac snapped her a glance. "Huh? No, why?"

"Your brow's all scootched up and your mouth's moving."

He glanced at his date and Nell's, who were talking together, before saying with as much dignity as possible, "I was singing along with the band, under my breath."

Nell laughed. "Oh, is that what you were doing?"

"This song is one of my favorites." Which was a good thing, because the music was so loud it drowned most of the conversation.

"Hey, mine, too," Nell said. "I didn't—"

"Shh," Mac hissed, jerking his head at A.J. He leaned over to whisper in her ear. "Talk to your date. I can vouch for him. He fits every personality trait on your list."

After giving him a strange look, Nell whispered back in a soothing voice, "Don't worry, I'll talk to him. He seems very nice." *Nice* was an understatement. The man was to die for in terms of looks and personality.

"Do it now. Or I'll do it for you. You need to turn on the charm, remember? Be ladylike and appealing. Remember, we talked about it the other day. Now go on."

Nell hunched a shoulder, pulling away from Mac. She felt as if she'd been slapped with a ruler by her fourth-grade teacher. "Oh, all right." After another brief glance at Mac, she turned to A.J. and asked a question that had him smiling and talking for a moment. Although he wasn't trying to be rude, Nell noticed that his gaze kept drifting back to Dallas as she and Mac laughed and talked together.

After a moment of watching A.J., Nell commented softly, "She's interesting, isn't she?"

Looking a bit embarrassed, A.J. snapped his attention back to Nell. "Who?"

"Dallas. I almost gave her a speeding ticket. That's how I met her. As soon as we spoke, I thought she'd be perfect for Mac."

"For Mac?" A.J. couldn't control his surprise.

"Yeah. She's good-looking, has a good sense of humor, is easy with people, interested in the community and—"

A.J. smiled. "I could say the same thing about you, Nell."

"You could?" Nell was stunned.

"Yes." He winked. "That would make you perfect for Mac."

"No, I don't think so. We're just great friends." So why did the thought that she'd like to be more than friends keep running through her mind like a wounded buffalo?

"You've gotta have friends." Tapping his fork on the table for emphasis, A.J. gave her an intense look and asked, "So how come a gorgeous gal like yourself hasn't settled down?"

"Have you been talking to my mother?" Nell demanded.

A.J. seemed taken aback. "No. I don't even know your mother."

"Sorry." Nell grimaced. "Force of habit. The minute someone mentions settling down, I get this knee-jerk reaction."

Laughing, A.J. agreed. "I know what you mean. My grandmother keeps telling me about how when my grandfather was my age, he'd been married a dozen years and had three strong-as-an-oak-tree boys."

"Ah, then you know what it feels like."

"Hell, I'm willing to bet we all know what it feels like." He gestured around the table, then asked Dallas directly, "Dallas, is your mother trying to get you married off?"

Dallas turned from her conversation with Mac. "My mother and I don't speak much. And when we do, I don't give her a chance to mention it."

Mac grinned. "Now why didn't I think of that."

"Because your mother tracks you down everywhere you go." Nell chuckled. "Or it seems like it lately."

"That's exaggerating a bit, Slim."

"You mean that isn't your mother across the room waving at you. She's sitting at the table next to the Kilbourne brothers." Nell turned and wiggled her fingers back at Molly, giggling as A.J. did the same.

"Oh, damn," Mac said. "Now you've done it."

Dallas glanced over and also waved back to Mac's mom. "I think she's adorable. Why don't you invite her over?"

Mac's face turned white. "Absolutely not."

"Why? I'd like to meet her. Everyone I've met in this town has been great for my story. I really enjoyed talking with Ted and Jed yesterday." Dallas stopped short, her eyes darting from Mac to Nell. "I mean, Knightsboro is such an interesting place. Think what your mom could tell me."

Mac turned even whiter, if that was possible. "Great. A chance to air my matrimonial status in hard-core print. What more could I want?"

Nell rested her elbows on the table, leaning forward. "You

see, there's a bit of a problem here, Dallas. Molly Cochrane hears wedding bells with every woman Mac dates."

"Oh? Oh!" It must have sunk in, because Dallas sent an alarmed glance at Mac, then recovered enough to stand, and said, "Excuse me. I have to go to the ladies' room."

Nell jumped up, too. "I'll go with you."

"How come women can't go alone?" Mac asked Nell.

"We're pack animals."

A.J. winked at Mac. "Now there's a chilling thought."

Chuckling, Mac said, "Okay, ladies. While you're gone, we'll hit the buffet line and bring back some food."

"Good idea," Dallas said with a smile. As she moved around the table, Nell noticed Dallas's fingers accidentally brush A.J.'s sleeve. He started to look up, but controlled himself. Dallas seemed a bit disconcerted, though. She hesitated then moved on.

Uh-oh, Nell thought. She'd have to do something about this. Dallas was here for Mac, not A.J., regardless of what both of them seemed to think. Following the small blonde across the room to the rest room, Nell struggled for the right thing to say to introduce the topic.

Molly smiled at Nell but targeted Dallas. "Hello. You're here with my son. I'm his mother, Molly. I wanted to say hello."

Dallas smiled warily. "Hello to you, too." She backed up toward the rest room door.

Molly followed until they stopped at the door marked Princess. Molly gave the door a narrow look. "Who names bathroom doors? Did you ever wonder that?"

"Someone with a terminal case of cuteness?" Nell suggested, biting her lip to contain a grin as Molly uttered an obscenity Nell had no idea the older woman knew.

"Or a man who thought it would appeal to a woman?" Dallas said.

"You could be right, Dallas." Molly nodded. "And since men never notice what's decorating the door, they probably don't mind being 'Princes.'"

"That's how they think of a certain part of their anatomy, anyway," Dallas concluded as she pushed the door open.

Molly clapped her hands. "You're right. Oh, that sense of humor is just perfect for my MacKenzie."

"Overdoing it a bit, aren't you," Nell whispered.

Molly ignored Nell and kept right on talking, figuratively and literally almost backing Dallas into a corner. If Nell didn't know better, she'd think Molly was trying to scare the woman away. All Nell knew was, if she were Dallas, she'd run for her life!

Before leaving the bathroom, Molly said, "Now Dallas, dear. I'm looking forward to seeing much more of you."

"How much more does she want to see," Dallas muttered as they left the rest room. "She was practically in the stall with me."

Nell chuckled. "The family that stays together…"

Dallas sent her a look as she and Nell wandered back to the table. "Hitting the loo together is not my idea of a great relationship-builder. Mac was right on the money, the woman's lethal. I'd sure think twice about looking at that guy now that I met his mother."

Nell frowned. "You have to look at the guy—you're dating him." Nell wondered again what Molly had been up to, as she'd never seen her behave that way before. Oh, she was always trying to push eligible women into Mac's path, but this performance had been something out of the ordinary.

"Nell, one blind date does not dating-the-guy make."

"Technically it isn't a blind date, because you saw each other before tonight."

"It's close enough," Dallas said, shrugging her shoulders. "He's great, really he is, but not my type."

"What are you talking about? He's totally your type. The man is drop-dead gorgeous, friendly, has a great sense of humor and cares about people." Nell was just warming up. "He's interesting and a great conversationalist."

Dallas arched a brow. "So why aren't you climbing all over a hunk like Mac?"

"Huh?" That comment stopped Nell so short she almost swallowed her lip.

"The more I see of you and Mac, the more I think you're perfect for each other."

"Oh, we are not." Nell couldn't think for a moment, all her jumbled emotions got in the way. "We grew up together. Now we work together. We..." First A.J. had suggested it, now Dallas—could they be right?

"The guy hasn't taken his eyes off you since we got out of the rest room."

"You're nuts. He's watching you." Nell peeped in Mac's direction.

"Well," Dallas acknowledged with a truthful expression, "he could be, but I don't think so."

Since they were standing as still as panicked rabbits in the middle of a room full of laughing and chattering people, A.J. and Mac came over to get them. "Hey, you two," Mac said, "did you get your feet stuck in glue or something?"

"Where?" Nell could barely look at A.J., much less Mac. Suddenly the thought of Mac with anyone else was a pain she couldn't tolerate. Which was so stupid, she thought. This was Mac—old friend, Mac. The guy who had knocked her first tooth out, the guy who had cried in her lap like a baby when Cindy left him high and dry practically at the wedding ceremony. *It's just Mac. And I'm not right for Mac. And he's not right for me.* God knows, it was like falling in love with her brother.

"Nell...Nell..." Fingers snapping under her nose recalled her to her surroundings.

"What?" Her irritated tone made Mac take a giant step back.

Mac frowned. "Nothing. Except, the food's waiting."

Nell stared at him, then very deliberately walked around him to take A.J.'s hand. "Come on, I'm starving." She looked over her shoulder, waiting until Mac took the hint and grabbed Dallas's elbow. She didn't dare meet Dallas's gaze, knowing it would mock her for being a coward.

The rest of the evening passed in a blur. They ate,

laughed…at least Dallas and A.J. ate and laughed. Nell had suddenly lost her appetite. Mac must have, too, because as the evening progressed, his brow darkened until it resembled a tornado ready to touch down. Finally the band took a break from rocking rhythms and played a real slow-dancing tune. Nell glanced at Mac. "That sounds familiar."

Mac closed his eyes for a moment and listened. "Homecoming dance, my senior year in high school—my favorite song. I asked the band to play it."

"I didn't know that." Nell said, surprise written all over her face as she stared at Mac. "It's mine, too, so I asked the band to play it."

"No kidding?"

Dallas bobbed up from her seat. "It's not mine, but you can't have everything. Let's go." She grabbed A.J.'s hand and pulled him up and toward the dance floor.

"Hey, wait a minute," Mac protested to A.J. "That's my—"

"You two should dance to your favorite song—together." Dallas threw the words back over her shoulder in case they missed the point.

Mac frowned as he watched A.J. and Dallas head into the crowd. After a moment he said, "Whaddya say?"

Nell scowled as she watched them merge in perfect harmony. "To what?"

"Wanna dance?"

Glancing over, Nell lifted her brows in a haughty manner. "With you?"

"No, with the man in the green pepper costume sitting at the next table."

Folding her arms, Nell said, "You told me I can't dance."

"I know." Mac sighed. "That's probably why it's a good idea to do it together. That way I can ticket you if you get too enthusiastic."

"Damn you, Mac. That's not funny."

Mac touched her with his fingertip. "Then how come there's this tiny little twitch right at the corner of your mouth."

"I probably need a tune-up."

Chuckling, Mac said, "Now if you were my date, that kind of statement could be entirely misconstrued."

"Well, I'm not your date. Your date is..." Nell looked around. "Where is your date?"

Jerking a thumb to the dance floor, Mac said, "Out there somewhere with A.J."

Nell peered at the couples moving across the floor. "I don't think so."

"Sure they are. We just can't see 'em. Come on, we'll find them if we join them."

"I don't know."

"Come on, Nell. I promise not to deck you if you step on my toes."

Nell laughed. "Okay, as long as you promise." She allowed Mac to pull her into the midst of the other dancers, folding her close. She closed her eyes as the music cast its dreamy spell over the audience. Her head dropped forward onto his shoulder. "Mmm. This is nice."

Mac pulled her closer. "Very nice."

A sigh escaped as Nell felt his cheek rubbing softly against her hair. She could stay here all year, she thought, which startled her so much that she immediately stepped on Mac's toe.

"Ouch! Glad to see you're running true to form, Slim."

"It's your fault. You lost the beat and I was adjusting."

"My fault, huh? Just like it's my fault that my date and yours are snuggled up like two bugs in a rug together out here on the dance floor, right?"

"Well, yes. It probably is. If your mother hadn't scared Dallas into thinking she was mailing wedding invitations as soon as she left tonight, Dallas might not have been so eager to dance with A.J."

"My mother did what?"

Nell looked up and, upon seeing the horrified expression covering his face, broke into giggles. "Oh, Mac, I wish you'd been there. You would have loved it. There was your mom practically throwing Dallas up against the wall telling her how wonderful her big, strong son was. And how she could just tell that Dallas was the perfect woman for him.''

Mac groaned. ''I may have to lock that woman up, relative or no relative.''

''Honest, Mac, the look on Dallas's face was absolutely priceless.''

''Speaking of Dallas, do you see her or A.J.?'' Mac whirled Nell around, to search in different directions.

Both of them inspected the couples on the dance floor but came up empty. After a moment, Nell said, ''Maybe they're taking a breather. There are a lot of people in here.''

''Maybe.'' Mac shrugged, pulled Nell tighter and said, ''Let's see if you remember anything from your lessons.''

''You're on,'' Nell said as they gave in to the music. Letting the familiar song transport them to old times and to newly created feelings. Nell didn't want it to end as Mac whirled her around in a breathtaking spin, then bent her back over his arm in a sexy dip that came close to having her hair touch the floor. Breathless, Nell's gaze met his as he slowly raised her up and smiled, his teeth whiter than a new-snow Christmas. Overwhelmed by his male beauty, she stared into Mac's brilliant blue eyes, which were glittering dangerously into hers.

He wants me.

Wasn't that what Nell was seeing in his eyes? *I want him.* Could he see it in hers? She hoped so. Her breathing increased as she prayed he'd pull her closer, to end their favorite song with a new memory. He tightened his arm, tucking her hand against his chest.

''Have I told you how great you look in red, Slim?''

''No.''

''You look great.'' Mac's eyes flamed. ''More than great—beautiful.''

''So do you.'' She risked stroking his shoulder, shuddering at the feel of the fine wool beneath her fingertips. ''I love charcoal suits.'' She nestled closer, thinking she never wanted to leave this spot, his arms. Which of course, made her realize she didn't belong here. This place was reserved for Mac's date, and for the woman Mac eventually found to share his life. Not for his deputy. She told herself not to be stupid, that he was playing a role.

"Those lessons of ours are paying off, Slim. You look very sexy."

Suspicions confirmed. He was just being nice, doing his job as he saw it by trying to make her feel desirable. Good old Mac. You could always count on him.

Slowly, reluctantly, Nell drew back, feeling as if she was leaving a little part of herself behind. She smiled, a tentative one, but a smile nonetheless. "Thanks for the dance."

"You're welcome, Slim." His voice softened.

"And I only stepped on your toes once." Mac didn't grin as she expected. Instead he gave her a solemn stare.

"It must be a miracle."

"Yes. A miracle." Nell forced herself to step back. Trying to buy time to get her composure, she asked, "See Dallas and A.J.?"

Mac didn't have the opportunity to answer however, as Ted and Jed Kilbourne and their wives came rushing up to them. "Sheriff, I just saw your date and—" Ted tipped his hat to Nell "—your date, Deputy, slipping out the side door. Looks to me as if they're up to no good."

Jed joined in. "You want we should go bring them back? Me and Gladdie and Ted and Anna will find 'em wherever they are and drag 'em back here. By the hair, if we have to."

"I knew you couldn't trust them out-of-town hussies, no way, no how," Anna, Ted's wife, said.

Gladdie agreed. "Remember Clyde Glenschmidtt's wife, the one that ran off with the lion tamer when the circus came to town?"

"I'm not sure I—"

"The whole town was talking about her. This is the exact same thing."

"What about her?" Nell could make no connection between lion tamers and Dallas, no matter how hard she tried.

"She was from out of town, too. You've got to watch them type of women, Deputy."

Nell rolled her eyes. "Thanks for the information. We'll just go find—"

"No, we won't. We'll find them later." Mac said. "Or not."

"But Mac—"

"The night is young, Slim." Mac's eyes glittered. "Ted, go ask the band if they can play a tango."

"A tango!" Nell didn't know who was more horrified, she or Ted. With a mock salute, Ted scampered off. Before Nell knew what had hit her, the sexy, throbbing sounds of a Latin rhythm filled the air, somehow managing to cut through the noise level in the place. She gasped as Mac grabbed her around the waist and pulled her so close she couldn't breathe. "Mac? What the hell are you doing?"

"If the town wants to talk, we'll give them something to talk about."

"I don't think this town needs any encouragement to gossip." She could feel the crowd's eyes boring into them.

Mac grinned, a sharp, feral grin that had all of the juices in Nell's body jolting in response. "Mac," she whispered, suddenly aching with longing.

Mac pulled his gaze from hers, looked up briefly and announced, "Clear the floor before someone gets hurt. The deputy and I are gonna dance."

9

THIS TOWN DIDN'T NEED any encouragement to gossip, Mac thought, not with Ted and Jed Kilbourne around. He watched from across the street as they spoke with Ada Mae, just outside her restaurant. Those two men chattered more than a group of squirrels on high-octane nuts. Mac wished Nell was as talkative. She'd seemed to clam up since the Harvest Ball. Not that he'd been especially vocal himself. Lately, when he was with Nell, his tongue seemed swollen to three times its size. Plus, he'd been having funny little feelings in his stomach ever since they danced the tango at the Harvest Ball. He was beginning to wonder if he had an ulcer, or was catching the flu.

"Hey there, Sheriff." Jed was waving madly as Ted tucked his ledger under his arm and turned majestically to greet him. Obviously Ted's newfound business sense was having an impact on him. There was such a natural dignity to the man that if Mac hadn't known better, he'd have sworn Ted Kilbourne was the head of a worldwide corporation. If it weren't for the overalls and ever-present cap, of course.

Mac crossed the street to join the brothers and Ada Mae. "Hey yourself, boys. Ma'am." He tipped his hat at Ada Mae.

Giving him a smile, Ada Mae said, "Did you come back for some of my cookies?"

Mac patted his stomach. "Ada Mae, I'm still trying to work off the last batch."

"You don't need to worry 'bout that, MacKenzie," Ada Mae said in a dry voice. "The ladies will still be chasing your tail even if you put on a pound or two."

Grinning, Mac said, "Thanks for the vote of confidence,

but my uniforms still have to fit. These suckers are expensive.''

"I noticed your friend A.J. doesn't seem worried about things like that."

"What do you mean? He doesn't wear uniforms."

"Maybe not, but he's been in here for quite a few helpings of coffee and sweets. Of course, there might be other reasons for that."

Ted leaned forward, nodding sagely. "Like a certain photographer lady has been in Ada Mae's, too."

Mac wondered why Knightsboro bothered to have a police force. Ada Mae and the Kilbournes, not to mention his mother, had a pretty reliable watchdog system all by themselves. "I haven't run across A.J. for the past two days. I was wondering where—''

Ada Mae shook her finger under his nose. "If I were you, Sheriff, I'd talk to him. He needs it. Why, there's poor little Nell Phillips pining away over that A. J. Radcliffe, and that blond hussy is doing everything she can to make herself the target of his interest."

"Tsk, tsk, tsk." Jed clicked his tongue, as a hangdog expression wandered over his face like a beagle searching for a fire hydrant.

"Yep," Ted agreed. "Maybe you should talk to your friend."

Ada Mae folded her hands across her spare stomach. "It's not right. I think he misunderstood what close buddies you and Nell are and always have been. That's why he's responding to that hussy."

"You really think Nell's pining over A.J.?" Mac gulped, finding this idea hard to accept. There went his suspicions— no, his hopes—that the sparks they'd created when they'd danced the tango might be the real thing. Instead it was A.J., and Nell was too proud to make a fuss after he'd left the dance with Dallas. Mac ground his teeth. *A.J.?*

"Well, of course she is," Ada Mae answered. "Where's your eyes?''

"That's right," Ted and Jed piped up with one shared voice. "Dang, anyone who's seen her lately can see it."

"They can?" Mac frowned, wondering what could be done. He hated to think of Nell unhappy. Is that why she'd been so quiet the past two days? Mac chewed on his lip for a moment. "I'll talk to him. I don't want to see Nell sad, especially not when it was my idea in the first place to date A.J." His friend was going to do right by Nell, or he'd throw him in a cell and lose the key.

Ada Mae patted his shoulder. "You're a good man, Sheriff."

"Yep. That's so," echoed Ted and Jed, heads bobbing. "We've often said so."

"I'd better go find A.J.," Mac said. He turned away, not noticing the look of satisfaction in the eyes of the three people watching him go.

Jed turned to Ada Mae and asked, "Do you think these two people are ever gonna figure out they really belong together?"

"In a way, I hope not." Ted patted his ledger. " Our odds are looking pretty good. We'll be able to afford two booths at the Harvest Festival the way we're going—and get some advertising, too."

Ada Mae smiled. "Now if Molly can get Nell to fall in line with this idea of hers, too, we may see some fireworks."

Ted chuckled. "Or a wedding. Either one's good for business."

NELL WAS LEANING OVER the meat cooler at the Thrifty Market concentrating on chicken parts when Molly Cochrane clasped her on the arm.

Nell jumped and let out a shriek. Automatically reaching for her gun, she whirled around. "What the—Molly!"

Molly stood with her hands over her mouth, staring at the gun. "Good Lord," she exhaled. "I had no idea meat was so important to you."

Nell slammed her gun back into the holster trying to explain. "I was deciding what I wanted to make for dinner and—"

Fascinated, Molly gaped at her, then chuckled. "And?"

"And you startled me," Nell ended lamely.

A saintly expression descended on Molly's face. "Oh, you poor dear, you're concentrating on chicken legs when you should be concentrating on a man. This is criminal. Mac is just the same."

Nell wrinkled her brow, trying to puzzle that one out. "Mac is concentrating on a man?"

"Of course not."

"Chicken legs?" Nell wasn't too swift at the moment. She hadn't had much sleep since the night of the Harvest Ball. Every time she closed her eyes, all she could see was Mac. Mac smiling, laughing, gazing into her eyes as they danced, his hands on her. She still shivered every time she thought of it.

"Dallas. He's thinking of Dallas."

Nell frowned. "Why?"

"Because he was very taken with her, of course. I know my son and I can tell you, this is the first time I've seen him like this."

"Are you sure we're talking about the same Mac?" For the past few days he'd seemed rather distant and quiet, but not heartbroken.

"Nell, you can try to joke, but it doesn't make it better. I thought his heart would break when Dallas left him flat at the Harvest Ball. Remember how I told you she was perfect for him?"

"But he danced with me and—" Nell stopped. Of course he had. A.J. had left her as flat as Dallas had left him, of course he'd danced with her—to save face, both hers and his. She hadn't looked at it like that before. And there she was, imagining she and Mac...

With a gentle pat, Molly asked, "Could you speak with her, dear?"

"With?" Nell attempted to focus on the older woman, but it was hard. All she could think of was Mac.

"Dallas, of course. That's who we're talking about. I want to see my son happy before I die."

Nodding sympathetically while biting back a grin, Nell said, "Yes, I'm sure you do." Since Molly was barely closing in on fifty-five or so and had the energy and constitution of a spry racehorse, Nell found that a bit of an exaggeration.

Molly reached for Nell's hand. "Just as your mother only wants to see you happy."

"I know." As usual, the mention of her mother made her sigh.

"Nell, I need your help."

"Doing what?" Nell withdrew her hand, wryly marveling at the strength in the grip of this woman who could die tomorrow without grandchildren.

"Getting Mac together with Dallas. I'm sure there was some kind of silly misunderstanding."

"Molly, from the very beginning she was flirting with *my* date. Or he was flirting with her. I'm not sure how it started, but I know how it ended."

"Well, perhaps they both thought you and Mac were an item and didn't want to interfere?"

"Why would they think that?"

"You're very close. Anyone who knows you can see that."

"Of course we're close," Nell huffed. "We grew up in each other's pockets and now we work together."

"But don't you see how that closeness could be misconstrued by strangers?"

Nell rubbed her forehead, where the sudden beginnings of a headache were gathering force. "I suppose it could be, but—"

"I'm sure it was pride and self-defense that made Dallas and A.J. turn to each other. Now we have to figure out how to make it right and give them another chance."

"I—"

"You don't want Mac to be unhappy, do you? Not again? Not when he's finally buried all memories of Cindy."

"Of course, I don't."

Molly patted Nell's arm. "I knew I could count on you. I told your mother that we could make this work."

"My mother knows about this?" Nell's jaw dropped to her waist. Great. Now she'd never hear the end of it.

"Yes, I spoke with her last night."

"Why?"

"Because she's been a friend of mine for the past thirty years. I knew she'd understand."

"And I suppose she did?"

Molly's eyes twinkled. "Oh, she understood very well and agreed with me wholeheartedly."

Something in Molly's voice alarmed Nell. The thought of her mother and Mac's plotting was terrifying. She backed up until she ran into the meat counter. Looking down, she grabbed a pack of chicken wings and said, "I have to go. Don't worry, I'll talk to Dallas. Somehow it'll work out."

Molly licked her lips as she watched Nell dash for the front of the store. Yes, it will, Molly thought. She and Nell's mother had agreed on the phone last night that a wedding right around Christmastime would be lovely. They had to be tricky to pull it off though, because their two children were both so mule-contrary that if they knew what was going on, they'd head for high pasture at a full gallop. Now if they could just get Mac and Nell alone together, then nature could take its course. Molly chuckled, hugging her anticipation close, and whispered, "With a little help from a few friends."

THE NEXT EVENING, those few friends had everything well in hand as they set a trap for their two unsuspecting lovers. Between the four of them, Molly, Ada Mae, Ted and Jed, they made the chosen rendezvous area into a cozy little nest fit for romance.

"What time is it?" Molly asked as she arranged the flowers.

"Seven o'clock. Nell should get here soon," Ada Mae answered. "Ted, you made sure that A.J. isn't really coming, right?"

Ted put the final touches to the logs in the fireplace before he answered. "He and Dallas were only too glad to help out, just like they did the night of the dance."

Molly smiled dreamily. "I knew I could count on A.J. Nothing like a bit of confusion and jealousy to kick everything along the direction you want it to go."

Ada Mae put her hands on her hips. "It's sure taken a long time for Mac to discover the perfect woman for him has always been within spittin' distance."

"For a while, I thought I'd be stuck with Cindy for a daughter-in-law. It chilled my bones, Ada Mae."

Nodding, Ada Mae reached to pat her hand. "You know, Molly, that girl, Dallas, was a good sport about all this. Surprised me some as a matter of fact. But she told me she'd never seen two people as right for each other as Mac and Nell. And so clueless!"

Sighing, Molly agreed. "I swear, that son of mine is so thick I'll probably have to go along on the honeymoon."

Ada Mae placed the stainless steel warmers over the food on the table. "Jed's keeping watch, isn't he?"

"Yep," Ted replied, "he's gonna do his famous bird whistle as soon as he sees the deputy. That's our cue to nip out the back."

Molly lit the candles. "Where's the wine?"

"By gum, I brought something extraspecial for them two lovebirds." Ted bustled over to his backpack and removed a tall brown glass wine bottle, which he slipped into the ice bucket on the table.

"Not from your still, Ted," Molly groaned. "I want the two of them alive in the morning."

"Don't you worry none, Molly. This is grade-A, smooth-as-butter-going-down stock. One sip of this and Mac will probably propose.

"Lord, I hope so," Ada Mae said. "I'm getting tired of having to help Molly get her sons married off."

"Listen up, now," Ted said, lighting the fire. "They should be here any minute."

AT SEVEN-THIRTY ON THE NOSE, Nell approached the door of Mercer's Cabin. The charming refurbished log cabin was part of a bed-and-breakfast group of down-home rental properties run by the same people who ran Charlie's Place. Nell had always liked the look of this little log cabin, tucked off in the woods. Every time she saw it, she fantasized about living in the area as a pioneer, with her only resources being the man by her side and the family she'd make to carve out a space in the wilderness. Fanciful thoughts, but ones she hoped someday to satisfy. At least the man-by-her-side part.

Reaching into her pocket, she pulled out a note and reread it. "Can we start over? Please have dinner with me. Meet me tonight at Mercer's Cabin, 7:30 p.m. A.J.'

Nell had hesitated at first, but changed her mind about seeing A.J. again. Especially since Mac seemed so preoccupied with Dallas. He must be, Nell decided, because he kept talking to her about A.J. all day, obviously trying to make sure she gave his best friend another chance. Well, why not? Nell understood compromise—she was a cop, after all. Sometimes you had to settle for second-best, but that didn't mean it wouldn't be right eventually.

Except for the sharp, shrill whistle of a bird, the woods surrounding the cabin were dim and quiet, as if they were waiting for something. She glanced around. All seemed in order. Except she kept getting a little niggle at the back of her spine that suggested eyes were watching from the dark. Nell spun around, scanning the area with her sharp cop eyes. When nothing unusual revealed itself, she told herself, "Chill. It's probably a raccoon hanging out to raid the garbage can."

As she mounted the steps, she smiled at the welcoming warmth of the electric candles glowing in the windows. Candles designed to tell a weary traveler that he was home. Nell hadn't seen A.J.'s car, so she supposed she was the first to arrive. She hoped the door was open, as she hadn't thought to ask for keys at the main lodge. Gingerly she turned the knob and stepped inside, feeling absurdly as if her destiny was waiting to pounce on her. Better that than a burglar.

The rustic atmosphere was perfect for romance, Nell thought. Music played softly in the background, a friendly fire crackled in the fireplace, which was accented by a thick bear rug hugging the hearth. The pillows on the love seat were plumped and comfortable looking, and the cozy dining table was set with two plates covered by warmers, a basket of bread sticks and an ice bucket containing a bottle of wine. To top it off, a vase of red roses was placed in the center of the table, and tall milky-white candles on each side glowed softly. Obviously someone had gone to a lot of trouble to create a romantic atmosphere. There must be more to A.J. than she'd thought. She wondered where he was.

Nell removed her coat, tossing it onto the love seat. Shivering slightly, she adjusted the red silk wrap dress she'd worn to the Harvest Ball. She didn't know what had prompted her to wear it again. A twinge reminded her that Mac had told her she was beautiful when she was wearing it, but she dismissed it. Of course that wasn't why she'd worn it tonight. Maybe she'd needed the courage the color provided, or the satisfaction of the swingy skirt caressing her thighs. Walking to the fire, she extended her hands to feel the heat, hoping it would warm her.

I wonder what Mac's doing right now? She found the question too uncomfortable to contemplate. For a moment she gazed at the fire, studying the crackling flames. If only——then she caught herself. *Don't look for the future, grab what today offers.* That's all there really was. She watched a piece of log shift and drop, setting sparks flying upward. Nell jumped back, only to whirl around at the sound of the door scraping open behind her. Shocked, she stared at the man filling the doorway.

"Mac?"

"Nell!" He was thunderstruck, as well. "What are you doing here?"

"What am I? What are you?"

Stepping inside, Mac carefully closed the door behind him before answering. "I had a note telling me to meet here."

"A note from…?"

"Dallas."

"Me, too." If Nell hadn't known better she would have

sworn her mother was behind all of this. But her mother was in Florida.

Mac shoved his hand through his hair. "Why did Dallas send you a note?"

"Dallas didn't send me a note."

"You just said Dallas sent you a note."

"No, I didn't."

"Dammit, Nell. Do you have to make everything so difficult all the time?"

"Me? What about you?" If this wasn't just like a man, blustering and trying to turn the blame.

"What about me?"

Nell placed her hands on her hips and tossed her head in a defiant gesture. "You've been treating me like a leper for the past two days."

"I have not." Mac echoed her movement, balling his fists on his hips, leaning forward aggressively. "You haven't said a word to me except for 'this coffee tastes like battery acid,' and 'I'm going out on patrol.'"

"You make the worst coffee in the station house." Nell scowled, then said objectively, "Except for Bobby Dee, that is."

Mac started to reply but changed his mind. He shrugged off his coat and turned to walk across the room, tossing it onto the coatrack. He placed his palm against the wall and stood for a moment. Finally he said, "Can we start over?"

The question hung in the air. Nell could almost see the letters. "I don't know," she said, drawing out the words. "Can we?" She'd love to start again and see where a romantic relationship between the two of them could go, but she had a feeling that wasn't what Mac meant.

Turning, Mac gazed at her. "I got a note from Dallas asking to meet here."

"And I got a note from A.J. asking me to meet him here."

"So," Mac said, "where are they?"

"Maybe they got their places mixed up. They don't know Knightsboro very well."

"A.J. does. He's visited me before. Besides, Cherokee land

starts about forty miles from here, so he's familiar with the area anyway.''

Nell folded her arms. "Okay. Then what do you suggest?"

"How about they mixed up the times we were supposed to meet here?"

Nell's gaze swept the table. With a laugh, she said, "What do you think? They've got split shifts set up? Like a bell's going to ring when it's time for the next couple to move in for a bit of romance?"

"All right. You don't need to be sarcastic." Mac held up his hands. "So it was a stupid suggestion."

"It sure was."

"Well, pardon me! I make stupid suggestions when I'm horny as hell and you're standing there in that hot little red silk thing that makes me want to rip it off your body."

Nell's eyes widened as his words thundered around the room. "You want to rip my dress off?" To Nell, Mac had never seemed more appealing than at this moment. He stood there more handsome than a man had a right to be, his blue eyes stormy as he met her gaze. What are you waiting for, she wondered. *Rip away!*

Mac flushed and turned away, walking to the table to inspect the wine. "Sorry. I don't know what made me say that. Of course, I don't want to do that."

Nell's heart dropped to her shoes. So much for high hopes. Ah well, the entire thing was too good to be true. There she was thinking about Mac and he walked in the door. No wonder she was off balance. Obviously he was, too. One of them would have to make this situation easier. As she stared at Mac's stiff back, she figured she was elected. "I'm sure there's a reasonable explanation for all of this."

"I'm sure there is."

Nell walked over to the love seat and sat down. "We could wait for a while, I guess. Until someone shows up."

"Yeah, okay." Mac turned to face her. "I don't have anything else to do tonight. Do you?"

"No," Nell said, sitting down. "Just being here is all I'd planned."

"Me, too."

Mac rubbed the toe of his shoe along the floor before coming up with an inspiration. "Want a drink? We've got wine over here."

"Sure. What type is it."

Mac picked up the bottle and read the label. "Well, I'll be damned."

"What?"

"This label says 'Kilbourne's Klassic.'"

"Kilbourne? As in Ted and Jed?"

Holding the bottle closer, Mac whistled. "This looks like real stuff, I mean like a real product, instead of something they hauled out of the hills."

Nell chuckled. "They said they were trying to go legit. Next thing you know, they'll be singing on the radio."

"I hope it's safe to drink." Mac pulled the cork, poured two glasses and walked over to her. "Let's make a toast."

Nell took her glass, watching him closely, marveling at the way the firelight played over his strong cheekbones and turned his hair to liquid fire. "To what?"

"To your makeover." His glance caressed her for a moment before he touched his glass to hers. "It's spectacular."

Nell glanced away as longing stabbed her in the heart. "It's mostly cosmetic."

Mac sat on the love seat next to her. "No, it isn't. There's something different about you."

I'm in love with you. The thought popped into her mind so suddenly that her hand shook. Mac reached to steady her. Her gaze met his and she was lost. Shaken, she took a big gulp of wine and immediately began coughing. "Lordy...lordy, this...is...strong...stuff." she said between coughs as Mac thumped her on the back.

Finally Mac removed the glass from her hands and set them both aside. "Hold on, Slim. I can't lose you."

"You can't?" Nell could scarcely see him for the tears in her eyes.

"No. I'd never find a deputy like you again."

"A deputy." She coughed a bit more as she struggled to

stand. What had she expected? She reached for her coat. She couldn't stay. She wanted him too much.

"Oh, screw this," Mac said as he yanked her back, tumbling her onto his lap. He smoothed her hair back from her face, staring down at her for a moment before bending to kiss her.

The minute his lips touched hers, Nell was positive she'd been waiting her entire life for this moment. Not that he hadn't kissed her before. But now, with the new awareness of her love for him, it felt different, as if she'd never seen or touched him before.

"Nell," he groaned as his lips moved over hers, seeming to have a mind of their own as they searched for her warmth.

Unable to resist, she opened her mouth, allowing him full access. His tongue slipped nimbly inside to tangle with hers. She wanted to devour him, she thought. But she couldn't tell him, so she let her lips speak for her, hoping he wasn't too dim-witted to understand. If he was, it wasn't obvious as his mouth answered hers, promising everything as it elicited small shivers of response from her. Finally he lifted his lips and moved to press tiny kisses along her jawline toward her ear.

"Mmm, you're delicious." He nuzzled her earlobe and then bit it like a playful puppy. They tussled for a moment. "I could eat you up."

"What are you waiting for," Nell whispered. His lips found hers again, then as if someone had flipped a switch he withdrew, putting her aside to practically leap to his feet and step to the fireplace.

"Mac? Mac? What—" Confused, Nell twisted around to stare up at the man leaning on the mantel, gulping deep breaths, trying to calm himself.

"I'm sorry, Nell. I never should have done that."

"You...shouldn't?" Why the hell not? She'd wanted him to make love with her. What was the matter with that man? Did she need to draw him a diagram?

Shoving a hand through his hair, Mac said, "No. I was out of line. You're waiting here to meet A.J. and I'm waiting to meet Dallas. We can't—"

"Yes..." *We can.* She didn't say it aloud, though. Instead, the disappointment set in, followed by her pride. "Yes. You're right, of course, you're right. Why they could come in the door any minute and we might have—"

He glanced at her, a longing look on his face. "Might have?"

"You know." Nell pulled her gaze from his and adjusted her neckline, which was now gaping open practically to her waist.

Mac could scarcely keep his eyes off her. His eyes practically bugged out as he blurted, "You're wearing the lingerie we bought."

"Correction. *I* bought it. You just went along."

"You wouldn't have bought it if I hadn't bullied you into it."

Nell stood up, trying to put her customary straightforward armor back in place so she could deal with Mac. At the moment she needed every weapon in her arsenal. "You're right. Thank you. I know it was all part of your makeover service."

"That's not the way I'd—"

Nell walked over to the table, trying to put some distance between them. "As a matter of fact, I was thinking I should make a flyer advertising your skill at this sort of thing, Sheriff. I'm sure there are a lot of women out there who would love to have your advice and attention."

"The only person I have ever considered helping is you."

"Why?"

Mac shoved his hand through his hair. "Damned if I know. It's brought me nothing but trouble."

"Well, thank you. Thank you very much."

"You're welcome."

They glared at each other. For a moment the only sound in the cabin was the pop and crackle of the logs in the fireplace. Finally Nell shrugged her shoulders. "Look, Mac. I find this entire helping thing awkward, and I've decided I don't want anything more to do with it."

"Me, either."

"Good. That's settled then. We can go back to the way it was before." *As if!* Nell thought, but it sounded good.

Mac hesitated, then murmured, "Can we?"

The look in his eyes demanded her honesty. They'd been friends too long. She couldn't give him less. She sighed. "We can try, Mac."

A look of deep regret settled on his face, chased by a slight uneasiness. "I'm not sure that's possible."

"Anything's possible if you want it bad enough." And she wanted him. But even as she thought that, another part of her resented him. Why did women always have to be the facilitators? Why couldn't the big ape see that he should walk right over here, sweep her off her feet and make love to her until her legs ached.

"Ummpfft."

Mac made one of those male noises that meant nothing to a female listening, but everything to the man making it. Nell considered it a throwback to Neanderthal days. All he needed was an animal skin and a club. Mac said nothing more for a moment, and Nell wasn't sure what to do next, when her gaze fell on the covered plates on the table.

"Are you hungry?" She grasped the idea of eating, like a lifeline.

"Ummpfft." Mac licked his lips. Probably to jump-start some conversation, Nell thought.

"Pardon me?"

He shoved his hands into his pockets then took them back out just as quickly. "Um…yeah, guess so."

Trying to keep her hands busy, Nell peeked under one of the stainless-steel covers. "We've got spaghetti and meatballs."

"You're kidding?"

"No, why?"

Mac grabbed their wineglasses, bringing them with him as he walked toward the table. "It just seems like a funny menu for a romantic dinner." He handed over her wineglass and sat down at the table.

Nell whipped off the covers and sat down. "It worked for *Lady and the Tramp*."

"No way am I going to shove my snout into a plate like the Tramp just so I can share a strand of spaghetti with you." Mac coughed as he took a big gulp of his drink then dug into his meal.

Nell gave him a provocative little pout as she pushed her spaghetti around on her plate. "Even if it's the only way you'll get a kiss?" What an idiotic comment, Nell thought. What am I doing flirting with this man? Where's my brain?

Mac took another sip of wine then winked. "I've already figured out how to kiss you, Slim. I have to take you by surprise."

They ate in silence for a few minutes, the tension between them getting thicker with every bite. Finally Nell reached for her own glass of wine and took a fortifying sip. She couldn't hold back any longer, this cat-and-mouse game was killing her. She loved him. She wanted him. Even if it meant she'd have to pack up and move later, it'd be worth it. She met his gaze head-on and let him look into her heart. "You don't have to surprise me…unless you want to."

Mac put down his fork. He stared at her for a long moment, his eyes going the cloudy blue of a summer storm, before he whispered, "Nell. At the moment, I'll take you any way I can get you."

"Then stop messing around and take me now, you big idiot!"

Mac chuckled as he pulled her out of her chair and swept her up into his arms. "Remember, you asked for it."

"This is my last lesson, I promise," Nell said as Mac laid her on the bearskin rug.

"I'm not sure who's teaching who," Mac murmured as he followed her down, stretching carefully at her side. "But I'm willing to bet we'll need a lot of practice."

Nell smiled and reached for him. "Practice makes perfect."

Nell felt as if she were on fire. Sliding her arms around his neck, she licked his lips, darting little movements that only whet her appetite for more. She couldn't hold back her feelings any longer. She didn't want him to know she loved him, but if he'd asked her, she would have admitted it without worrying about tomorrow. Tomorrow would take care of itself. For now, there was only Mac, the feel of his lips as they stroked over hers, the heat from his hard hands as he grasped her waist. She sighed, then smiled as his hands continued their path upward. Thrusting her hands into his hair, she pushed his mouth down to her breasts. "Mac, teach me to make love to a man."

"With pleasure." Mac's hands boldly spread the deep V-neck opening of her dress, until he'd unhooked the entire wraparound dress, pushing it aside to reveal her black lingerie to his gaze. "I've been dreaming about this lingerie since you first tried it on." Wonderingly he cupped her breasts, concentrating on her white skin mounded up over the French-cut satin and lace as he followed the curve with his tongue. "Damn, but you're nice."

"Nice?" Nell chuckled breathlessly as he pressed hot kisses onto her skin. "That's all?"

He unhooked her bra, scooped her breasts into his hands and bent to suck first one nipple then the other. After a long moment he raised his head and smiled fiercely. "Nope. You taste good, too. Even better than I thought." He groaned as his passion grew, hard, hot and ready. He started to unbutton his shirt, only to have her push his hands aside and do it for him. She nibbled then kissed every inch of his chest. He gasped as her tongue circled the nub of his nipple. He ground himself against her, seeking her heat.

"Mmm," Nell said, her hands shaping his body, arching her hips to meet his. "You're not as scrawny as you were when you were nine."

Mac chuckled. "Neither are you."

Nell blew on his eyelids. "I'm a woman growed now."

"And you've grown in all the right places," Mac said as he nibbled his way down her hips.

Nell reached for him, kneading his loins with her hand. "So have you."

Grinning, Mac said, "Some places are still growing."

Arching her hips into his, Nell teased, "I'll require further proof."

"I'll be happy to supply it." He circled his hips, then reached to pull her leg over his thigh. Cupping her buttocks he rocked her against him and nibbled her neck until she giggled.

This was the way he'd always wanted love to be—hot and steamy and full of laughter.

Funny that it should be with Nell, he thought. Then he forgot to think as she unzipped his pants and plunged her hand inside to find him. Naturally he had to do the same, jockeying around her flirty little garter belt to slip a finger inside her, deep inside where he found her warm and liquid and hot, oh so hot she almost burned him. For long moments they caressed each other, teasing their passion to the peak, trying to make the feelings last as long as possible. Until finally they were tearing off their clothing, flinging the garments aside so they could concentrate only on each other.

"Mac," Nell whispered as he positioned himself over her. "I want you."

"Nell," Mac whispered back. "Not as much as I want you."

"Prove it."

Mac needed no more invitation. He slid into her, as slowly as possibly, trying to make it last. Then he started to move, rocking forward to send her up and over, once, twice until finally he joined her. At that moment, he was so tied up in Nell, in what he was feeling for Nell that he wouldn't have cared if the entire town had marched in. All he knew was he'd never felt like this before. Never felt the passion, the joy he felt with Nell. As he released into her, it was as if he'd come home. He wanted to tell her, but hesitated, trying to convince himself that he was making too much of it. *This is Nell, the little pain-in-the-ass girl from my childhood.* As his head cleared, he looked down at the woman beneath him. *This is Nell, my deputy, my pupil, my... love.* Naturally, because he suddenly cared so deeply and it confused him so greatly, he was clumsy when he spoke.

"I don't think you need any more lessons from me. You've graduated. You're ready for anybody."

Nell emerged from a golden haze, opening her eyes to look into the dark passion that still lingered in his. But the passion no longer registered. Only his comment did, and it plunged deep. "I've graduated? In other words, slam, bam, thank you ma'am—now go find somebody else?"

Mac blinked. "I didn't mean it like that."

"No. How did you mean it? After all, I practically threw myself at you, didn't I?"

"In a way, but I—"

With an infuriated sound, she pushed him off her and attempted to gather her clothes. She tugged at her bra, which was caught under Mac's thigh, until it finally snapped free and almost hit her in the eye. Awkwardly she attempted to dress. But after a few minutes of squirming around trying to get into her garter belt, she swore loudly and reached for her dress instead. She wrapped the red silk around her, balled the rest of her lingerie into her hand, then stuffed it into her coat pocket.

Mac still lay where she'd left him. And the fact that she wanted to jump him again as he reclined completely nude set her off once more. She was tempted to kick him. Especially as he said, "Nell, what the hell are you doing?" He had that adorable confused look that made her want to kiss his brains out while she was carving him up for fish food.

Embarrassed and hurt, with the love and longing for him still near the surface, Nell exploded. "I'll tell you what I'm not doing, MacKenzie Cochrane. I'm not sticking around so I can be patted on the head and treated like a one-night stand." She slapped at his hand as he reached for her. "I know I *am* a one-night stand, but I don't appreciate being treated that way. I'll admit I practically begged for you to make love to me. I know that you, out of the sheer goodness of your heart, decided to be the big man and finish off my schooling, but as you've said, I've graduated, and now I'm ready for the big time. All I have to do is find someone to do the big time with."

"In a pig's eye you will." Mac jerked up to a sitting position and glared at her. "I didn't mean it like that. I only meant—"

Nell thrust her arms into her coat. "Look, Mac. I want both of us to forget this ever happened. It was a huge mistake. I'm sure if we are rational, we can get over this and continue to work together, maybe even be friends." Looking for her gloves, she yanked her underwear out of her pocket, leaving it to shower onto the floor.

Mac reached for her little French demi-bra, gripping it in his fist. "I don't want to get over this."

"Well, I do!" Nell started to reach for the bra, then gave up as he held it behind him. His laughing eyes invited her to fall on him and wrestle if she wanted to get it back.

"Why get over it? I like you, you like me. We're good together physically—better than good, *great even.* We can hang out together, have fun and this way get both our mothers off our backs." He extended his hand to the side, grabbing her bikini underwear. With a sexy little smile, he let it dangle provocatively from his fingertip. "It's a perfect solution, Slim. I don't have to go out looking for someone, and you don't, either."

Nell snatched her panties from him and shoved them into her pocket. "You mean every time we get really horny we'll just jump each other's bones?"

Mac leaned back and grinned, letting his beginning erection speak for itself. "Sounds good to me."

Nell picked up his pants and his shirt and threw them at him. "I'm beginning to think you're as dumb as a doorknob. No wonder your mother's trying to marry you off. You're never going to manage it on your own."

"I don't want to marry anybody, dammit!"

"Well, I do," Nell yelled.

"Who?" Mac yelled right back, jerking to his feet like an out-of-control marionette.

"Never mind who." Nell whirled around, grabbed her shoes and raced to the door.

"Nell, wait a minute." He hopped around, trying to put his

pants on. "Let's talk about this. Do I know him? Is it me?" He stumbled, righted himself, yanked up his pants and raced after her. "It's not me, is it?"

Nell stopped on the porch, in the act of slipping on a shoe. "Why would it be you?"

"Because, I'm—" He shrugged and attempted a smile. "I thought maybe you'd consider me now that A.J. is out of the running. He didn't show up after all, so—"

"Hear me loud and clear, Sheriff. I wouldn't marry you if you held a gun to my head, slapped me into cuffs and locked me in a cell."

That stung. What was wrong with him anyway? "Back at ya. Plenty of other women would."

"Then maybe you'd better call them up. You can offer to teach them the fine art of making themselves over for a man. After all, look at all the practice you got with me."

"Tonight wasn't only practice, no matter what you think, Nell." He tried to explain, but she hunched her shoulders and stepped off the porch.

"Hey, Slim, come back here. I'm trying to talk to you."

As he watched her stalk off, turning onto the path that led back to the lodge, that's when it hit him. He was in love with Nell Phillips.

Mac slammed his palm against the porch pillar. "Now what the hell am I going to do about that?"

10

OVER THE NEXT TWO DAYS the town exploded with tourists. They arrived en masse to view the Harvest Festival parade and browse the craft show and other festivities that were part of the Harvest Festival in Knightsboro, Tennessee. For the first time in years Mac welcomed the chaos, which generally made a lot of extra work for the sheriff's department. It took his mind off Nell, at least while he was working. No, strike that, he thought, staring out the window at the woman in question. Instead of focusing on the deputy laying down the law to two teenagers on the sidewalk outside the station, all he could see was the willowy form that he'd held trembling against him a few nights before. A woman whose needs and passion were fully exposed.

Mac sighed and pulled his gaze away. Well, maybe he could keep his mind off her if he wasn't looking straight at her. At night was another story. He closed his eyes and he saw Nell—the tip of her tongue as she'd licked at a bit of spaghetti sauce on her full bottom lip; her eyes dark with passion and as fathomless as the deepest depths of the sea; her skin flushed pink and smooth as she'd writhed against the fur rug at Mercer's Cabin; her expression as she'd climaxed— Mac groaned. *Damn woman!* She'd invaded him like a new virus. And he was afraid it was terminal.

"Sheriff? You got a stomachache, or just a hangover?"

He opened his eyes to see Bobby Dee peering at him, standing so close that his nose resembled Idaho.

"Hell, Bobby Dee." Mac jumped back. "Don't sneak up on a person like that."

"He didn't sneak, Mac," Doug said with a grin. "You ever

known Bobby Dee to sneak? He sounds like an elephant on crutches most of the time.''

"Still…'' Irritated, Mac waved his hand. "What do you want?''

"I don't want anything, Sheriff. I was concerned, that's all.'' Bobby Dee's eyes opened wide, revealing his hurt feelings before he continued with a massive attempt at dignity. "You were standing here, grimacing and groaning something awful. I was going to offer you some of that pink stomach stuff.''

Doug snorted. "I don't think that's gonna help. I think our sheriff's got something bigger on his mind.''

Mac glared at his deputies. Had he been that obvious? What did they know? "I have. It's called the Harvest Festival. Remember the hordes of people who've been descending on us for the past few days? That's enough to give anyone indigestion, isn't it?''

Bobby Dee lifted his hat and scratched his head. "I don't remember it bothering you before like this.''

"How the hell would you know, Bobby Dee? You've only been here for a year and you're still so damn wet behind the ears that you don't know what kind of problems this festival can be.'' Mac jerked a thumb at the door. "So I suggest you get your butt out of here. Hit the streets and do your goddammed job.''

"Yes sir.'' Bobby Dee Laurence snapped to attention, practically throwing a salute. He turned on his heel and marched to the door, where he immediately ruined his respectful behavior by saying, "I'm off to save mankind. If I don't return I've probably been attacked by a demented tourist.''

Doug laughed. "Better demented than drunk on Kilbourne's Klassic.''

Bobby Dee popped his head back inside. "Ain't that the truth. I had my first taste the other night. I thought my head was coming off the next day.''

Mac grinned, a bit reluctantly. "Oh, get the hell out of here, Bobby Dee.'' He remembered his own taste of Ted Kilbourne's newly named brew. Unfortunately he also remembered the end result, which brought him full circle to Nell sprawled on the bear rug. He couldn't win. His head started to pound as he walked away from the window.

"You okay, Mac?"

"Yeah. Never better." He hoped he'd been halfway believable. "I'm gonna be in my office." Trying to figure out how to get that stubborn woman to listen to him so he could explain his feelings.

Doug watched him go, then picked up the phone. "Ted?" he whispered. "Hey, this is Doug, over in the sheriff's office. I want to put another fifty on Mac making it to the altar first."

NELL PHILLIPS WATCHED the two teenagers she'd just stopped stroll away, pretending they weren't intimidated by her warning. She felt like intimidating someone—preferably someone six foot two, with blond hair, blue eyes and wearing a sheriff's uniform. Why the hell she had to fall in love with Mac Cochrane she had no idea. There were a gazillion guys out there somewhere. So why Mac? Why was he the only one who could turn her blood to lava and her mind to volcanic ashes? And why now? Why had he never affected her before? He'd always been heart-stoppingly handsome, funny, easy to talk to, so why was it so different?

A hand touched her arm. "Hey there, Nell."

Nell turned to discover A. J. Radcliffe standing by her side. Her mouth opened and closed before she finally got it into working order. "You rat!"

A.J. grinned. "I see you're on to us, huh?"

Before she could wind up into full spring, Nell spun to a stop. "What do you mean, on to you?"

Hair gleaming raven-black in the sun, A.J. smiled. "I mean, you and Mac."

She invited him to continue. "Me and Mac?"

"The cabin? The other night?" Slightly disconcerted, A.J. gazed at her. "Didn't you go?"

"Yeah, I went. And where were you?"

"Having dinner with Dallas."

Nell folded her arms. ''When you were supposed to be having dinner with me.''

''Well, not really. It was all a setup.''

''Why? What did I ever do to you?''

''Huh? Nothing. I did it for my best friend. So he could be happy.'' A.J. spread his arms wide, trying to explain. ''Hell, his mother, Ada Mae, Ted and Jed set it up. They told me both of you were being stubborn, so if Dallas and I could just grease the wheels a bit…''

''You did that all right,'' Nell said, curling her lip. ''The wheels are racing downhill with no way of stopping except to crash.''

''Look, I just happened to pass through town and I ran into Mac and he started talking to me about a date. Then I ran into his mother and…ah, hell. I'm sorry, Nell. I guess I made a mistake. I never meant to hurt you or Mac.''

''Uh-huh,'' Nell murmured, pulling her gaze from A.J.'s.

''Mac used to talk about you at school and, when I saw you together, I thought—'' He raked his fingers through his hair. ''Obviously, I thought wrong.''

Nell felt a sad little smile surface then quickly forced it to disappear. ''No. You thought right from my point of view. Just not from his.''

''There's no chance there's a misunderstanding? When something means a lot to him, he isn't good at communicating.''

''He communicated pretty well this time. I just didn't like what I was hearing.'' Even though she liked the way she was ''hearing'' it.

''Nell, if there's anything I can do—''

''No, you've done enough. Both you and Dallas. She was in on this, too, right?''

A.J. stared at his boots. ''Yeah. The gang got to her same as me.''

''Figures.'' Starting to turn away, Nell said, ''I'm surprised my mom wasn't involved.'' Wait, hadn't Molly said she'd spoken with her mother recently?

"Oh, I think she was. Molly said she'd placed a pretty high bet with Ted and Jed."

Nell whirled around. "What type of bet?"

"About who'd get to the alta—" Suddenly A.J. clammed up.

"To the *what?*"

"Nothing." A.J. shoved his hands into his pocket, rocking back and forth on the balls of his feet. "Just betting on the best name for the Kilbournes' new product. Tasted it yet? The stuff's got a hell of a kick."

Nell scowled as she remembered where she'd tasted it. "I've had the pleasure." And what pleasure it was, she thought, praying she wasn't going to start blushing.

"I think 'Kilbourne's Klassic' is winning, 'cause Ted and Jed were talking about the, uh…contest…yes, the contest, the other day."

She nailed A.J. with her cold-eyed cop stare. "You're lying so big I could use you for a six-lane highway."

"No."

"The bet involves me and Mac, doesn't it?"

"Uh…"

"Who'd be married first? Is that it?"

A.J. looked around, hoping for help. Regardless of the groups of people on the street, no one came to his rescue. Finally he said, "You got it."

"What a mean thing to do."

"It wasn't meant to be mean, Nell. It was done because people care about both of you."

"Oh, give me a break! I'm a damn laughingstock in my own town. I'll never be able to hold up my head again."

He reached for her arm. "It's not that bad."

She slapped him away. "How would you know? Does Mac know about this? Did you tell him, too?"

"Hell, no. And I didn't mean to tell you, it just slipped out."

"Son of a—! Look, do us both a favor and get out of town. Take that blond photographer friend of yours, too. Because the next time I see either one of you, I might have to shoot

you.'' Nell spun on her heel and headed for the sheriff's office
to tell Mac. If she had to suffer being a laughingstock, then,
by God, he was gonna suffer, too!

Slamming her way into the station, Nell ignored Doug's
startled look as she demanded, "Seen Mac?"

Doug jerked a thumb over his shoulder. "Back there."

Nell covered the front room in two steps, then strode down
the hall into Mac's office and kicked the door shut behind
her.

"What the hell?" Mac looked up from his paperwork, half
rising at her entrance only to drop back into his seat as recognized her. "What's up? Town on fire?"

"No," Nell snarled, leaning on the desk. "I am."

Mac eased back in his chair, giving her a long steady look.
"I am, too."

Startled, Nell straightened. "What?" Her hormones went
into overdrive as the expression in his eyes slammed into her
gut.

Clearing his throat, Mac said, "Nothing. What's the problem?"

"You're the problem. You and me."

"Yeah, I know," Mac mumbled.

"You know? How long have you known?" She'd kill him
for keeping this from her. She glanced at him, her heart aching
at the sight of him. Not able to stay still, she had to pace
before she wrapped her hands around his neck—or her body
around his.

"I discovered it the other night."

"I just found out a few minutes ago from your good friend,
A.J." *When?* the other night, Nell wondered. Before or after
their dinner?

"Found out what from A.J.?"

"About the bet."

"What bet?"

Nell stalked around Mac's desk and plunked down on the
edge. "You just told me you knew about the bet."

A slash of red stained Mac's cheekbones as his eyes darted

this way and that. "I thought you were talking about something else."

"Like what?"

"Just something I accidentally discovered." Mac rubbed his chin. "Tell me about this bet? What's the problem? Illegal gambling?"

"Ooh, there's a thought," Nell said. "I wonder if we can get them on that."

"Who?"

"The Kilbournes."

Mac rocked back, balancing his chair on the two back legs. "What are they up to now? I thought they were content with poisoning half the people in the county."

"Nope. Now they're in the marriage business."

"Huh." Mac's chair thumped back onto the ground. "Let me guess. They're into white slavery?"

"Not unless they've got your mother, my mother and Ada Mae mixed up in it, too."

Eyes narrowing, Mac muttered, "I don't like the sound of this."

"They've got the entire town placing bets on who's getting to the altar first, you or me."

"Ah! So that's what Ted's ledger is all about."

"That's right."

"Who's winning?"

"How should I know? That's not the point. The point is— we're the town joke!" Mac's eyes were dancing, which infuriated Nell. Why wasn't he taking this as seriously as she? "What are we gonna do?"

"It'll blow over. It always does."

Nell jumped to her feet, moving closer to Mac as he twisted in his chair to face her. "That's all you've got to say? That's it?"

"What do you want me to say?"

"How about, we're going to string them up from the nearest lamppost."

"The lampposts are decorated with Harvest Festival banners. It wouldn't look good."

Nell poked her index finger into his chest. "Damn you, Mac. This is serious."

Grabbing her hand, he said, "Well, I do have one idea."

"What's that?" Nell said eagerly.

"How 'bout we get to the altar at the same time. Then nobody wins but us."

"Oh, fine idea. We grab somebody off the street and rush over to the justice of the peace so we foil the game." Nell tried to tug her hand from his, but he held on tight. "Real smart."

"We wouldn't have to grab somebody off the street."

"I don't notice anybody lined up to propose, do you?"

Mac shifted, an uncomfortable look shadowing his face, then he plunged into speech so rapid that it got tangled up. "Nellwillyouplease—"

"If you're going to tell me to please shut up, I'm not going to do it. I'm mad as hell about this and—"

"You're so damn—I know how to shut you up." Mac jerked on her hand, pulling her off balance. Nell tumbled into his lap, her momentum overbalancing them, knocking them backward onto the floor. Clasping his arms around her, he rolled them out of the chair until they were pressed together, chest to chest, hip to hip on the ground. Mac's leg was wrapped around one of the chair legs, but that didn't stop him. His lips fastened on to hers as if he was starving.

Nell slanted her lips on his and kissed him back, deeply, longingly, placing a lifetime of emotion and wanting into her kiss. *Why Mac?* Why not, her body answered, even as her mind accepted this was the only man she'd ever love. She wondered how to tell him, then questioned why she was so afraid of confessing.

As their lips spoke for them, the world faded away. There was no sound beyond the rasp of their breathing, no textures beyond the crisp feeling of their uniforms beneath their fingertips as they stroked each other, no images except for the whirling lights exploding behind her eyes as he deepened the kiss, tangling his tongue with hers to probe her passion. For a frantic moment, there was only need. A need that demanded completion. A need so intense that neither could let go.

Groaning, Mac shifted, lifting Nell to straddle him. That broke the spell.

Nell tried to fight her way back from the sensual fog that blanketed her. "Mac. Mac, for heaven's sake. We're in the office."

"I don't care. I want you." He attempted to pull her forward.

For a moment, Nell cooperated. "I want you, too." She kissed him again, then broke it off with a rough movement, wiggling as she attempted to sit up. "What's that noise?"

Mac grabbed her hips, his hard hands pressing her fiercely against his loins. "Do that again."

"Mac, listen. It sounds as if all hell's breaking loose out there."

Mac blinked, then rubbed his hands over his face as if he'd just awakened from a hundred-year sleep. "What noise?"

"Can't you hear somebody yelling? It's coming from the front room." Nell attempted to scramble up, her legs still twisted with Mac's as he tried to do the same. Nell got as far as leaning her elbows on the desk, trying to rise, when Bobby Dee burst in the door.

"Sheriff!" He'd flung the door open so far that it crashed against the wall. The sound banged around the office as Bobby Dee pulled up short at the sight of her. "Uh…hey, Nell. Seen Mac?"

"Well. He's…"

Mac crawled out from behind the desk, his pant leg still caught in the chair, which dragged along behind him like a skeleton. He kicked it free, swore at the ripping sound, then rose to face Bobby Dee, who was still standing, as if stuffed, in the doorway. "What's going on?"

Bobby Dee exhaled, his long breath sounding like a whistle as he looked from one to the other. "That's what I'd like to know."

Nell rushed to explain, sort of. "The sheriff and I…uh, his

chair broke and he, uh, fell backward, then I fell down and our feet got...then—''

"Forget that, Slim.'' Mac ground his fists onto his hips as he stared down his young deputy. "What sent you in here like hellhounds were chewing on your ankles?''

"Sheriff, I just saw Hilda's cows headed toward the craft show. They damn near ran me over.''

Jaw dropping, Nell snapped a look at Mac, then back to Bobby Dee. "You saw Hilda's cows going to the craft show?''

Bobby Dee's chin jutted forward. "Yeah.''

Nell grinned. "Were they buying anything special?''

"Yeah.'' Mac laughed. "Like those pictures that say 'Eat Chicken.'''

"Very funny,'' Bobby Dee said with a sulky look on his face. "They aren't there to shop—they're drunk. I swear those cows are lit up better than an old bachelor on Saturday night.''

Mac came around the edge of his desk. "What the hell are you talking about, Bobby Dee? How do you know they're drunk?''

"'Cause they're staggering around and heading toward the front gate. The Ladies' Aid Society is having a fit.''

Unbelieving, Nell shook her head. "How could they be drunk? Didn't Ted swear he'd fixed his still so it wouldn't overflow into the creek again?''

"He gave us his word.'' Mac nodded in agreement. "And once he gives his word that's usually it.''

"Then something must have gone wrong, because they're down there, Sheriff. And they're plastered.''

Nell put on her most innocent expression. "Bobby Dee, are you sure you aren't the one who's been drinking. Hilda's farm is quite far from the location of the craft show. How'd they get there?''

"Beats me,'' Bobby Dee responded, "but Hilda's husband swears he's gonna get the Kilbournes and teach them what-for!''

Mac shoved his hand through his hair. "Aw, damn. That doesn't sound good.''

"Hey, Sheriff," Doug said, appearing in the doorway jus' over Bobby Dee's shoulder. "We just got a report in. We go' a riot starting. There's a big old group of black-and-whit' cows attacking the scarecrow displays down at the amphithe-ater."

"Attacking?"

"See, I told ya." Bobby Dee nodded. "Boozy bovines. Don't know what they'll do."

"And," Doug continued, "there are a lot of drunk tourists running around with weapons chasing the cows."

"What kind of weapons?"

"The person on the phone didn't say. Just said it looks like a Stephen King novel and we'd better hurry."

Mac snapped into action. "Okay, get Casey back in here. and call in our reserves. We might need 'em if this gets out of control. And Bobby Dee, let's break out the riot gear."

"Yes, sir." Both Doug and Bobby Dee scurried off in different directions with Mac close behind.

"Mac," Nell called. "Should I break out the guns?"

Mac paused in the hallway. "For drunk cows and tourists? Hell, I hate to—"

"We don't know what the caller meant by weapons, Mac. You know how these things can get out of hand when people have been partying."

Mac gave her a brief smile before racing down the hall. "Not to mention the cows."

Nell opened his desk drawer, got the key to the spare guns and proceeded to empty the cabinet that stood in one corner of Mac's office. Five minutes later she hurried into the front room of the station house, where she found Mac and the others shrugging into their bullet-proof vests.

"Where's mine?" she asked Doug, who pointed at his desk. Nell immediately put hers on and began checking the ammunition in her gun.

Mac looked over and saw her. "What the hell do you think you're doing?"

"Gearing up. Like you told us."

"Not you."

"Why not me?"

"Because...well, because..."

Nell frowned impatiently. "Because..."

He grabbed her arm and hustled her away from the others. "You're not going."

"What do you mean, I'm not going? Why not?"

"It could be dangerous."

"What?" She hunched a shoulder. "Oh for—life is dangerous."

"No, I mean you could be in danger and I don't want that to happen."

"From what? The cow who jumped over the moon? Get real. It's more likely one of our deputies will shoot me." Nell attempted to walk away, but Mac hauled her back.

"You're a woman."

Jerking her elbow away, Nell said firmly, "I'm a cop, Mac. Not a woman."

"The hell you aren't." Mac practically spit the words out. "More than that, you're my woman and I'm not going to let you go."

Nell tossed her head in a haughty manner. "*Your* woman. Suddenly I'm chattel, I belong to you? Since when?"

"Since before when we—"

"No, you don't. Don't lay that on me. Sex has nothing to do with the way I do my job and you know it."

Mac ignored that, searching desperately for an explanation. "Besides, I need somebody to man the radio back here, Slim."

"Look, I'm a trained professional. Plus I'm a crack shot if you need it."

"I know, but you're also great at keeping it together in an emergency. There's still the rest of the town filled with tourists to look after. I need you here." Mac didn't give her a chance to say anything else as he turned on his heel and beat a rapid retreat for the door.

Stunned, Nell watched him go. *A woman. Now I'm a woman?* He'd never treated her like a woman on the job before. Now since they'd made love, she was suddenly incapable of doing her job? Nell sank into a chair. What should she do now? Mac had always been a fair employer. They'd always had a strong working relationship. *My job's a great part of who I am. If I don't have that, what do I have?* The town was laughing at her, Mac was undermining her professionally because of a herd of cows, and she was so head over heels in love with him that she had no hope of ever recovering. Now what?

I'll have to quit.

The solution jumped into her mind, bringing on a pain that was almost physical. She reached for a pen and paper to write her resignation before she changed her mind.

MAC COCHRANE STOOD OUTSIDE the gate of the fairgrounds known as the Knightsboro Amphitheater and watched as a bunch of tipsy cows and tourists were rounded up by his deputies. Only half of his mind was on his job though. The other half was with Nell. He'd acted like an idiot. Of all the things he should have said, "you can't go because you're a woman" was at the bottom of the list. He should have said, "I love you till I can't see straight and I don't want you to get hurt, so you have to stay here." Not that that would have been any better, he thought. Nell might accept the I-love-you part, but the rest would go over like vegetables with carnivores.

That brought his attention back to the cows and the smattering of tipsy tourists who were enjoying the show. Mac pointed at a group of teenage boys, who looked as loaded as the animals. They staggered around and waved beer bottles. The boys were jeering and attempting to throw a rope over the cattle. "Bobby Dee, arrest those kids before Hilda's husband turns them over his knee and blisters their butts. We'll let their parents do it for him."

"Yes, sir."

Mac watched his deputies bring the situation, which had been badly exaggerated, under control, and he made his decision. "Doug, take over here. I'm going back to the station."

"But Sheriff, what if—"

"Doug, if you're gonna tell me that you, Bobby Dee, Casey

nd those other three guys can't handle some drunk cows, owdy teenagers and a few pie-eyed citizens then I'm gonna ave to find myself some new deputies.''

Doug snapped a salute. "Don't worry about a thing here, Mac. We'll keep you apprised of the situation."

"Thank you." Mac jogged to his car, got in, turned the ngine over and switched on the siren. He prayed he'd get ack to the station before Nell decided to do something stupid. He wasn't sure what, but God knows, if ever a woman was apable of coming up with something, it was Nell. Tires quealing, he pulled into the parking lot and raced toward the loor. He skidded to a stop inside, practically right in front of Nell's desk.

She gave him a cool glance. "Forget something?"

"My best deputy." He tried an ingratiating grin but had a eeling he looked like a dog with gas pains. "Luckily, I didn't eed her. The whole thing was blown out of proportion."

"What? No wild-eyed, snorting bossy-cows for the big bad heriff to catch?"

"The cows were there all right, and drunk...not because of the Kilbournes though. It had nothing to do with them. Some high school boys out for a lark snatched them from Hilda's farm, gave them a boatload of beer and brought them down in a pickup truck. Their parents are gonna be hearing from us."

"Ah. That's it? So, no real chance to be a hero, eh?"

"You're really ticked off, aren't you?"

"No. What gives you that idea?"

"My bones are freezing up from the blast of Arctic air from your luscious lips." Obviously humor wasn't going to work, judging by the look she gave him.

"Clever." She thrust a piece of paper at him. "Let's see how clever you are after you read this."

Mac glanced down, reading the first few sentences to look up in alarm. "You can't resign."

Nell rose from her desk. "Watch me."

"Nell, wait a minute. I don't want to lose you."

"You should have thought of that earlier, like before you decided I couldn't do my job because I'm a woman."

"That's not what that was about and you know it."

Nell shrugged, turned on her heel and walked out of the office toward the equipment room. Mac followed her down the hallway located by the temporary lockup cells. He stepped inside the room.

"I won't accept this idiotic resignation. You aren't acting very professionally here."

"Oh," Nell said over her shoulder as she removed her vest and her gun, "and you are?" She placed her keys on a table.

That's when Mac made a swift decision, probably the fastest one he'd ever made in his entire life. He'd have to tell her the truth. He'd have to throw himself on his knees and beg her to love him. He'd have to apologize and offer his backside for her to walk on. Then pray she'd let him make it up to her so he could make love to her for the rest of his life. He stared at her as she put all the symbols of her office on the table next to her keys, including her badge. Without a word, he grabbed her hand and pulled her out of the room, automatically locking the door, leaving his keys hanging in the lock. Then he maneuvered her down the hallway until he reached an empty holding cell. He swung her inside.

"You're not going anywhere until you hear what I have to say."

Nell eyed the bars, then gave him a disdainful look. "You have to talk to me in a cell?"

Mac stood by the door, which he'd pushed almost closed behind him. "I don't want you thinking you can go anywhere until you hear me out."

Nell folded her arms and widened her stance to face him down. "All right, shoot."

"This is hard for me, Nell." Nimbly Nell started to sidestep him and head for the door, but stopped as he held up his hands. "Okay, okay. You may have noticed I've been acting like an idiot."

"Oh? When was that?"

Mac flushed. "And I want to tell you why."

"I'm all ears."

"No. I think you're all mouth, Slim. But I'm in love with you anyway."

"What?"

"I said, I love you. That's why I acted like such an idiot. I've never been in love like this before and I don't know how to act. Never mind wanting to ask someone to marry me—of course, there was Cindy, but that didn't count because she asked me." He gazed at her, knowing his heart was in his eyes. "But with you it matters."

"Say it again."

"Again?" Mac blanched, hoping he wasn't going to pass out. "All of that?"

"No, just the part about loving me and marrying me."

Mac could only gaze into her eyes, which seemed huge and wet with tears. "I love you. Will you marry me?"

"Oh...oh my God!" Nell leaped at him, knocking him backward against the door. The door clicked shut. "Of course. Of course, I will." She locked her arms around his neck and moved toward him so fast they cracked noses.

Mac rubbed his nose. "Ouch."

"Oh, shut up, Mac." She pulled his head down to hers.

"Aim better the next time, sharpshooter."

"Like this?" Her mouth fastened on his, drawing a fierce response in return.

"Yes," Mac gasped as they surfaced for air. "Exactly like that."

"I love you, I love you, I love you," Nell babbled, dropping little kisses all over his face. "Let's go home so we can discuss it in more detail."

"You're on." Mac reached behind him to open the door. Nothing happened. He turned to look at it, then reached into his pocket for his keys. Nothing. "Have you seen my keys?" He patted the rest of his pockets.

"Did you leave them in the door?"

Examining the lock, he said, "No, they're not here. Aw, wait a minute, I did leave them in the door. The door to the equipment room." He held out his hand. "Give me yours, okay?"

"I don't have any. I've resigned, remember?"

Mac chuckled. "I'll be damned."

"What do you suggest we do now?"

"Well, you can unresign."

"Okay. Then what?"

Mac bent to kiss her again, a long, satisfying kiss that sent his blood pumping at hyperspeed. "We've got some time. Let's talk about it some more."

"I've finally got you right where I want you."

Mac nuzzled her neck, nipping her ear. "Where's that?"

"Locked up tight."

Smiling, Mac looked around the small cell before picking her up and walking over to a cot. "I'm sorry it's not a more romantic setting."

Nell reached for him as he placed her on the gray blanket. "So we'll improvise."

Mac followed her down and started to do that very thing, taking his time so he could taste and touch her sweetness, when chaos erupted. The hallway door swung open and a small horde of teenagers and adults swept inside, yipping, hollering and singing western songs at the top of their lungs. Mac's deputies were yelling right over them.

"All right, you people, settle down," Bobby Dee warned, "or I'll put you in the dungeon with the rats."

Astonished, Mac and Nell watched as the group, followed by Mac's crack deputies, had a bit of a scuffle in the hallway.

"Hey, kid, if you don't stop whacking me with that rope," Doug snarled, "I'm gonna tie you up with it. Now cool it and get on down the hall."

"Oh my God," Nell said, trying to adjust her shirt. "They arrested everybody?"

"Except the cows."

"Hey, next time you legal-age adults get thirsty—" From the back of the group, Ted Kilbourne's voice rose above the noise "—try Kilbourne's Klassic. It's good for what ails ya."

"We've got some flyers right here, with coupons off the

first purchase,'' Jed Kilbourne chimed in, waving a sheaf of paper over his head.

Nell gaped at Mac. "The Kilbournes are advertising now?"

Mac chuckled. "I think they saw a crowd of people and just seized the opportunity to promote their product. After all, riots mean thirsty people—all that yelling."

Nell grinned. "Just like they seized the opportunity when I asked you to help make me over."

"You've got to admit, that bet was a good way to make money."

Her grin broadened. "Once an entremanure, always an entremanure, you mean?"

Mac laughed, and they sat up as the crowd swarmed closer. "You know, Mac. Something tells me this Harvest Festival is going to go down in history."

Mac gave her a big smacking kiss and said with a grin, "I've always wanted to be a local legend."

Nell pulled him back down on top of her, whispering against his lips. "I'm gonna see that you get your wish."

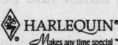